# *Widow's Blush*

Katie —
Happy reading!

Michelle Bennington

# Widow's Blush

## A Widows & Shadows Mystery

## Michelle Bennington

Author Photo Credit: Michelle Bennington

First edition

ISBN: 978-1-68512-457-1

Cover art by Level Best Designs

This book was professionally typeset on Reedsy.
Find out more at reedsy.com

*To my dad, Don Smith. My first hero and storyteller. You gave your all and more than you ever imagined.*

# Chapter One

May 1803

Dead. Ravenna Gordon, Lady Birchfield stood in the center of her drawing room, a fist pressed to her stomach, staring at the lifeless body of Charles Thorne, Lord Hawkestone, England's Foreign Secretary. The discovery left her breathless.

Worse, if this moment could in fact be any worse, a few members of the women's club, *Les Roses Noires*, were due to arrive any moment. They had formed a charitable committee to raise funds for and oversee the development of the Spitalfields House for Penitent Prostitutes—commonly known as the Penitent House. Only two days returned to London from her nine months' mourning in the country, and all was mayhem.

Ravenna knelt beside Lord Hawkestone and felt for a pulse. Nothing. Threads of silver wove through his dark hair, his brown eyes, now yellowed and glassy, were so different from the warm gleam she'd once known. When they were friends. Now she saw only accusation. Just as she'd seen the last time she'd spoken to him—how they'd sparked with hate. She'd dared to hope he'd forgiven her after a distance of time. Instead, his dark eyes smoldered and he turned his back on her, silent, giving her the cut direct in front of everyone at the theater. Sending whispers and rumors through the crowd.

That was a year ago. It had chilled her then. But now, the heat of shame spread over her chest, up her throat, and into her face. Tears blurred her vision. She was certain he hadn't yet forgiven her, even after five years of rebuking silence for her betrayals. How much had changed in those five years. For a moment, she felt separated from herself and wondered who this new creature was who stood in widow's weeds, overlooking a dead body, in a grand home in a part of London that had once been entirely foreign to her.

"Poor Hawkestone. What happened to you?"

He appeared almost unrecognizable to her, decades older with purple lips and a gaunt, haggard frame. She lifted his hand. Frail and bony. The gold ring slid toward the knuckle and spun around. Little white crescent moons marked his bluish nails. She placed his hand, already cooling, on his stomach. So different from the warm hand she'd held five years ago when she'd pleaded for the forgiveness she didn't deserve. She'd stolen government secrets from him in aid of the Franco-Irish rebellion. She'd been but twenty-five, and he'd been thirty-two, both in the zenith of their youth and vitality, though she was rapidly closing in on spinsterhood. They'd become fast friends and lost each other as quickly. And it was all her fault.

"Why were you here? After all this time?" Hope that he'd come to finally forgive her flickered briefly before dying out. She'd never know the purpose of his visit now.

Since that dreadful night of their split, she'd tried to convince herself she'd done the right thing, but a sense of disquiet pervaded. Deep in her spirit, in her heart, she'd always known she needed his forgiveness. Any opportunity of being reconciled to him was now lost forever. At that realization, and with the mad rush of both bitter and sweet memories, she broke into sobs.

The clock in the foyer chimed three, jerking her from her grief. She pulled her handkerchief from the bodice of her black muslin dress and dabbed her face. There was no time to parse through the past, the betrayals, and the memories now. She'd have to think about all of that later. The committee would be here any moment, and since she was not the sort of pretty crier hailed by the great poets, she was assuredly a frightful mess.

But what to do with Hawkestone? She couldn't leave him here. Besides, his wife deserved to know that she, too, was now a widow. She pressed her wadded handkerchief, scented with a hint of roses, under her nose. *Poor Lady Violette.*

Ravenna looked up at the life-size portrait of her late husband, Philip, hanging above the white marble fireplace. She searched his face as if he might have an answer for her. He sat in his red parliament robes at a table loaded with books and papers—his face serious, philosophical, wisdom emanating from his hazel eyes. What would he have done in this situation? He'd been a deeply calming, protective influence in their short, five-year marriage. He was learned, wise, and patient. But he'd died nine months ago, setting her adrift in the expanse of her grief. Typically, mourning lasted a year, but she couldn't imagine giving up her weeds so soon. She waited for an answer from Philip to drip from the heavens into her mind. Nothing presented itself.

"Dash it," she hissed. "I'm sorry, Hawkestone. I promise I'll say a proper and respectful goodbye to you later." She kissed her fingers and pressed them to his cooling forehead. She shivered and pushed herself to her feet. Drawing up the hem of her dress, she clamped down tight on her feelings and ran on tiptoes to the bell pull in the corner to summon Mr. Banks, the butler.

When the knob turned, she pulled open the door and, forgoing all propriety, yanked Mr. Banks inside, shutting and locking the door behind them. "Mr. Banks. I need your help." She pointed to Hawkestone's lifeless form.

Mr. Banks was a sturdy man with thick gray hair and a haunted look in his gray eyes that resulted from his experiences as a veteran in the American Rebellion. He'd supported her from the day she married Philip and entered his ancestral home, Birchfield Manor—a sentiment few of the servants had shared at the time, considering themselves above serving a former actress—and an Irish woman at that. But since Philip's death, Banks had been her most stalwart ally, consoling her through her days and deepest grief. Together, they'd eventually brought the rest of the staff around.

Unruffled, his bushy gray brows lifted. "That is a quandary, milady."

"Yes, but what am I to *do*, Banks?" She clasped her hands tightly, her nails digging into her flesh.

He offered a fatherly squeeze to her shoulder. "Never fear. It'll be well, ma'am. I know a merchant of sorts who specializes in discretion. He'll have a cart we can use to transport Lord Hawkestone to his home."

"A merchant of sorts? What does he sell?"

"Truth be told, he smuggled coffee, tea, rum, and whisky to the colonies during the war."

"And you trust him?"

"I've trusted him with my life before, ma'am."

"Very well."

Banks rang for a footman and provided instructions for locating the merchant and his cart.

She looked at him, helpless as a child in apron strings. "What about the coroner? Or a constable?"

"Considering your station and his, may I recommend that perhaps it's best if Lady Hawkestone called them."

He wasn't wrong. Most commoners and aristocrats alike held a distrust of constables, Bow Street Runners, or coroners. They were sometimes worse than dealing with criminals. Further, she didn't need any attention brought to her house that might feed the rumor mill. "The servants. Won't they gossip?"

"Not if they value their position in this house." He lifted his chin and looked down his large nose. "Though there's little I can do about the servants at Hawkestone House. Unfortunately."

She toyed with one of the long black curls framing her face, curling it around her finger. Her insides flipped like the tumblers she'd seen at the circus last spring. "I should take him myself."

"Milady—"

She held up a hand. "I won't be persuaded. It's the least I can do."

He snapped his thin lips shut and bowed. "If you insist, ma'am. I'll send footmen with you."

"Please bring me a sheet. We'll wrap him up."

He started toward the door.

"And Banks..." She checked her face in the mirror. "Let's do keep this from the servants as much as possible." Servant gossip was the bane of every aristocrat's existence, and it seemed nothing could be hidden from them for long. Everyone in the *ton* had known Ravenna and Hawkestone had fallen out, but they had not known *why*. The prevailing assumption was a lover's spat, an untruth Ravenna did not discourage as it was much less scandalous than treason.

Now, if it got around that he'd visited her and promptly died in her drawing room, that would open a Pandora's Box of questions she didn't want asked or answered. She knew in her heart, however, it was a losing battle. It was only a matter of time before the gossip mill began to churn.

When Banks opened the door, he froze. "Uh, ma'am...Lady Adair—"

Relief flooded her. Catherine. Her greatest friend and confidante. "Please, send her in."

He stepped aside to allow Catherine's entrance and closed the door.

Lady Catherine Adair was a petite, flaxen-haired woman who bore no evidence of her middling years. She wore a height-of-fashion silvery blue dress with matching pelisse and bonnet sporting a large white plume that bobbed as she spoke. "What's a-foot here? The scullery maid, of all people, let me in—" She stopped and stared, putting her tiny-gloved hand over her rouged lips. "Darling, what have you fallen into this time?"

Another knock sounded upon the front door, and soon a cacophony of female voices filled the foyer.

"Oh, no. The ladies are here for the meeting!" Ravenna put her hand to her forehead. "What am I going to do?" She motioned to Hawkestone's body.

Charlotte Hart, Ravenna's lady's maid, and companion, ran into the drawing room, clutching a bundled sheet to her chest, careful to shut and lock the door behind her. Hart was a sparrow—her hair and clothes the color of sparrow's wings, her mannerisms quick and precise. She carried herself erect, daintily, like any well-bred woman trained in a mode of comportment far above her current station.

Ravenna joined Catherine and Hart on the floor, where they spread the sheet beside Hawkestone. She paused, contemplating her old friend. A band of tightness stretched across her chest. She'd give anything to go back and correct her horrible decisions, stop her betrayal, and save their friendship. She shook off the rush of sadness. Leave it. There was a duty to perform and a wife waiting for him at home, expecting him to return alive. This ugly task must be completed.

Catherine squeezed Hawkestone's hand. "I'm sorry it's come to this, my old friend." She stared into his face. A faint smile brushed over her lips as if remembering happier times.

Hart's top lip pouted over the bottom like a rabbit, and her brown eyes shone clear and intelligent. A faint scar, peeking from under her lace fichu, necklaced her throat. With a hint of Scottish in her voice, she said, "Should we say a prayer?"

Ravenna, scattered mentally and emotionally, couldn't recall more than the first lines of Genesis. *In the beginning, God created the heavens and the earth.* And that was hardly helpful for this occasion. "I can't think of any." She blinked at Catherine, who smirked with amusement.

"Given my situation," Catherine said, "I'm hardly fit to offer any prayers to recommend a man's soul to Heaven."

Hart studied Hawkestone. "Shall I say Psalm twenty-three over him? I know most of it."

A dull throb bloomed above Ravenna's eyes. "No, thank you. That won't be necessary." Ravenna patted Hart's knee. "He will receive proper rites and burial at his home."

Catherine put a hand to Hawkestone's shoulder. "We should finish our unhappy task."

Ravenna and Hart nodded. They all wedged their tiny hands under Hawkestone and, with much struggle, rolled him onto the sheet.

"He's heavy as a horse." Hart panted, pushing against him. "He looks awfully frail, but it's like his whole body is filled with cast iron."

Ravenna grunted against Hawkestone's weight. "Catherine, I need a favor." She hated to be thinking about something as frivolous as a meeting just now, but she had a house full of women who had come to discuss the charity project for reforming London's prostitutes.

"Anything, dear."

"Will you host the Penitent House meeting in my stead?"

They pulled the ends of the sheet over Hawkestone's face and feet and tucked the edges of the sheet around him.

"I'll do my best."

Ravenna caught the scent of lilies, sage, and bergamot. Her stomach jolted, and pressure rose in her cheeks behind her nose. She couldn't tolerate the scent of lilies since her husband, Philip, had died. She stood and swiped her skirts into place. "You know Lady Braxton will do most of the talking. All you need to do is be a good hostess, keep them entertained, and apprise me of what's discussed."

"Easy enough." She smiled coquettishly, "I have quite a talent for hostessing. What shall I tell them about your absence?"

"Tell them I have a headache. Any lie will do, really." Ravenna pushed her curls into place and offered a hand to Catherine and Hart to help them stand.

"Ah, yes. The glorious headache that gets us fine ladies out of any undesirable meeting." Catherine stood, chuckling.

Hart planted her hands on her hips. "Ma'am, this looks like a body. How are you going to keep the servants from knowing?"

"Blast it." Ravenna rubbed her forehead. Hart was right, of course. Every chambermaid and footman in the house would be peering from the curtains and whispering about the body-shaped sheet being carried to the cart. She toyed with a curl, looked down at the floor, the body, and beneath the body… "The rug! Hurry. Move the furniture away," Ravenna directed.

The three women worked quickly to shift the furniture and drag Hawkestone to the center of the rug, which was at least twelve feet squared. They rolled him up in the carpet. The job complete, they straightened, panting.

Ravenna fanned herself with her handkerchief, which did little to generate a cooling breeze. "Catherine, please go see to the committee ladies. Hart, get our things and call for the carriage. We're taking Hawkestone home to his wife."

# Chapter Two

Hawkestone House was a home of grand white stone and a façade full of tall windows on the west side of St. James Square.

Ravenna and Hart descended from their carriage and paused beside the merchant's cart. Ravenna looked up into the man's face framed by a broad-brimmed straw hat.He had insisted on remaining nameless and Ravenna accepted it.

"Please wait here. Someone will come collect him directly. I should deliver the news to his wife first."

Ravenna instructed Hart to wait in the foyer then followed the butler into the formal parlor to the left of the foyer. It was pristine, with pale yellow walls trimmed in ornate white molding. A grand mirror hung over the white marble fireplace which was flanked by plush gold-and-white-striped sofa and chairs. At the far end of the room hung a life-sized portrait of Hawkestone when he was full of youthful vigor. She sat with her back to it.

Lady Hawkestone entered the room. She was statuesque, lean, and well-proportioned in a white muslin dress with a demi-train and with honey gold ringlets crowning her head. She and Ravenna exchanged a curtsey in greeting. "Good afternoon, Lady Birchfield. I hope you haven't been waiting long."

Ravenna didn't know Lady Hawkestone well, as their paths rarely crossed. But Lady Violette's reputation as a bright, intelligent, accomplished woman preceded her wherever she went.

Lady Hawkestone sat on the edge of a chair, her smile reminding Ravenna of a dewy meadow filled with sunshine and white daisies. "Shall I ring for refreshment?"

"No, please. Don't trouble yourself. I won't stay long."

"To what do I owe this pleasure?"

Sadness like a stone sunk heavy and deep into Ravenna's gut. She didn't want to carry out this sad duty. She sat on the edge of the sofa and turned to face her hostess. She wrung her gloved hands. "I fear my visit today is an unhappy one."

Lady Violette tipped her head, her smile fading. "I'm sorry. How may I help?"

Ravenna looked into the clear amber eyes full of questioning and apprehension. There was no easy way to do this. It was best to make the cut quickly. "Your husband is dead."

Lady Violette flinched as though she'd been slapped. Then as the meaning of the words landed, her cheeks flushed, and tears filled her eyes. "Pardon?" She breathed. "Are you....how....I..."

Ravenna pressed on. "I'm terribly sorry. He'd come to visit me. I don't know why. By the time I'd joined him downstairs, he'd already passed."

Lady Violette exhaled as silent tears slid down her cheeks. "That can't...I-I-I..." She brushed the tears with shaking hands.

The stone rose from her stomach to lodge at the base of Ravenna's throat. She tried to swallow it down as she dropped to her knees in front of Lady Violette and grabbed her hands in hers. "I'm so sorry. I've brought him back to you. He's outside in my carriage."

Lady Violette folded over against Ravenna, who embraced her and rocked her gently, whispering consolations while she wept.

After some time, Lady Violette sat up, sniffling and shuddering. She pulled a handkerchief from her bodice and blew her nose. "Forgive me. I barely know you."

"Nonsense. I understand what it is to lose a husband."

Lady Violette's eyes trailed over Ravenna's widow's weeds. She whispered. "That's right. I'm a widow now, too." Her bottom lip quivered. She blinked, her thick lashes dewy with tears. "What am I going to do?"

Ravenna returned to the sofa. "I've found it's best to take each day as it comes. It gets easier with time. Or so it's said."

"Is that true?"

Ravenna offered a weak smile. "Easier isn't quite the proper word. Perhaps it's best to say one becomes accustomed to a new life."

Lady Violette nodded and whispered. "I'll ring for the footmen to bring him in."

Ravenna, Hart, and Lady Violette stood somber sentinel as footmen carried Hawkestone's body inside.

Struggling to control her emotions, Lady Violette directed the footmen in a quiet, shaky voice. "Please, take my husband to the library to be prepared. It was his favorite room. We'll need to contact an undertaker and an upholsterer. Use Miller & Hatchett. They're the best." Lady Violette leaned on Ravenna and pressed a balled handkerchief to her chest. "How shall I endure it?"

"It seems impossible in the moment," Ravenna said. "But you will endure."

Lady Violette straightened. "Please give me a moment with my husband." She crossed the foyer to the library, staggering a little, pausing at the door.

Ravenna bit her bottom lip. She knew all too well that weakness in the knees, the cold stone of grief in the gut. She dabbed her own eyes, reliving her own husband's death, feeling afresh the first shock of sorrow and the whirling desolation of mourning. Hart squeezed her hand.

Lady Violette stepped inside the library and closed the door.

A yawn of pain and emptiness opened inside Ravenna. For all of her and Philip's differences, she had loved and admired him. Now, she missed him and yearned for him daily. Even if to argue. Her eyes filled with tears, and she wiped them again. She pulled a sharp inhale. *Forget your own pain. Time to rally. Be strong for Lady Violette.*

Lady Violette emerged from the library, her nose red and face blotchy. "Lady Birchfield, will you please sit with me a while longer?"

"Yes, of course," Ravenna said. She turned to Hart. "Only a few moments longer."

Lady Violette turned to her butler. "Mr. Jameson, please send tea to the parlor and show Miss Hart to the kitchen for her refreshment." Lady Violette turned to the parlor as Jameson took a few steps toward the hall.

A maid scurried by. Something about her, an air, her demeanor, caught Ravenna's attention. Of average height and curvaceous build, she carried herself with confidence and a voluptuous sway to the hips. Her square chin and sharp upturned nose rendered her as neither pretty, nor ugly, yet interesting to look upon. Her straight brows shelved her downcast eyes. From under her mob-cap peeked a burnt-gold chignon decorated with a trio of black silk roses—an odd hair ornament for a servant—it bore a great resemblance to *Les Roses Noires* club symbol. But servants weren't allowed in the club, and she'd never seen this woman before.

Ravenna grabbed Hart's arm and whispered into her ear. "Do you recognize that woman?"

Hart shook her head.

"See her hair ornament?"

Hart's gaze followed the maid.

"See if you can discover anything about that woman while you're in the kitchen."

Hart nodded and followed Jameson down the hall.

Upon entering the parlor, Ravenna sat on the corner of the sofa closest to Lady Violette, who stared at the floor, her gaze distant like a little girl lost and hopeless of finding home. Ravenna sat quietly, giving Lady Violette time and space to come to terms with her new situation. The clock on the mantle ticked loudly, each tick winding Ravenna's nerves tighter. Ravenna wondered how Catherine was managing Lady Braxton and the meeting. The Penitent House had, after all, been Ravenna's idea, and Lady Braxton would no doubt loudly remind everyone of that fact.

Lady Violette broke the silence. "He'd been ill for some time, but I didn't expect..." Her voice trailed off. "I suppose we were still hoping for a recovery."

"May I ask what ailed him?"

"We're unsure. He began to have stomach complaints, violent cramps, and all the usual symptoms that accompany a sick stomach." She gave Ravenna a pointed look.

Ravenna understood she meant vomiting and diarrhea. "I see."

"At first, we thought he'd eaten some bad fish, but the illness continued until he could no longer retain any food. He lost an enormous amount of weight. We consulted a surgeon, but he was equally baffled. He bled and cupped and did all the usual things, but Charles never improved. He lingered like this for months."

A maid marched in with a tea service and set it on the table between them. Ravenna reached for the teapot and poured two cups of tea. "Sugar?"

"No, thank you."

Lady Violette captured the teacup in both hands, like holding a bird.

"Hawkestone's illness sounds similar to my own husband's, though Philip's end came quickly." Ravenna sipped her tea, the warm liquid relaxing the knot of emotion in her throat. "He passed within a couple of weeks. My surgeon suggested it was an influenza."

"Perhaps. Our surgeon thought it might be Irish fever."

"Typhus?" Ravenna frowned. "That doesn't make sense."

"No, it doesn't. What do these resurrectionists really know?" Lady Violette sipped her tea. "We did everything in our power. Used every poultice, plaster, and potion the surgeon concocted to no avail." Lady Violette closed her eyes and shook her head. "I'm so sorry Charles died in your house." She reached over and squeezed Ravenna's arm. "He should've been in bed. I begged him to stay home, but he insisted on going out. He claimed he had a business meeting. I had no idea he was going to visit you."

"Please don't apologize to me. I'm sorry I couldn't help him." She shuddered, recalling Hawkestone's glassy eyes and bloody froth in the corners of his mouth.

Lady Violette set her cup on the table between them and turned in her seat to face Ravenna. "Perhaps I've no right to pry, but *why* did he visit you?" She clasped and unclasped her hands in her lap. "Please understand, I'm not ignorant of your past with my husband. I'm aware he loved you first. That he had proposed to you. I harbor no illusions, and I hold no ill will."

"I don't know. He died before I came down to speak to him." Ravenna wanted to believe that perhaps he'd come to forgive her, to make amends.

"But…" Confusion flitted over Lady Violette's countenance. She seemed to be rolling questions around in her mind. "Do you think it had anything to do with his murder?"

# Chapter Three

Shock rattled Ravenna. Her teacup clattered against her saucer. *Murder?* Ravenna gaped. "Pardon?"

"When the surgeon couldn't adequately explain his illness, Charles came to believe he was being murdered. Poisoned, in fact."

Images of Hawkestone flashed across her mind: purple lips, grayish skin, thin frame, bloody froth on his lips. Though they were signs of a severely ill man, they could as easily be signs of poisoning. A flurry of questions crowded Ravenna's mind. She wasn't sure which to ask first. One popped out of her mouth. "Do you believe him?"

"At first, I thought he was delirious with fever. However…" Her brow wrinkled as she stared at the life-sized portrait of Hawkestone hanging at the end of the room.

"Why would anyone want to poison Hawkestone?"

"I can't be sure. He told me recently that he suspected a political motive. He—" She froze, and a realization dawned on her face.

"What's the matter?" Ravenna followed her gaze to the portrait of Hawkestone. It had been painted in his healthier days when he and Ravenna were still friends. She recalled watching a portion of his sitting. She and their friends had sat behind the painter making faces at Hawkestone until he broke into laughter. This continued until the painter kicked them out of the room so he could work with his subject. The memory drew a wan smile from Ravenna. In the picture, he wore a fox-hunting kit, surrounded by a hound and horse, a rifle cradled in his elbow, cocksure, with fire in his dark eyes. She returned her attention to Lady Violette. "But who would want to kill him?"

Lady Violette touched her coral necklace. She paused, flushing, staring into her tea. The corners of her mouth screwed downward. "I don't like to think of it."

"Of course."

"No. I mean…" Lady Violette shook her head, her honey-gold tendrils shifting. "It's so humiliating." After taking a deep breath, she continued. "I don't think it's political at all. I think his killer is Julia Pence. My husband's latest mistress."

Ravenna flinched. She covered her lips to keep from her lower jaw dropping to her lap. "Oh dear," she whispered.

"I'm sure you've heard the rumors? Everyone has."

"No. I've been away at Birchfield Manor until recently." Why hadn't Catherine told her this bit of gossip? Catherine told her everything.

"Yes. Of course." She twisted and untwisted a corner of her handkerchief. "There've been several girls. I believe Julia Pence was the most recent. But there are many marriages in much the same condition as mine. As long as he maintained discretion, I tolerated his dalliances. After all, he was otherwise a good husband. There are many wives who can't boast as much."

"How long had they been together?"

Lady Violette sniffed. "Does it matter?" She sighed and stood, moving to a window behind the sofa. She stared out the window, the sunlight silhouetting her lean form in her white muslin dress. "My husband always had a penchant for theater girls. What do you suppose the attraction is? Why does a man of breeding and taste cast off a woman of his station in order to keep company with an inferior woman?" She turned to look at Ravenna. "You were once a woman of the theater. Perhaps you can provide some insight?"

Ravenna flushed to again be reminded of her past and that she would never be allowed to forget it, that she would always be an outsider. She turned to talk over the back of the sofa. "I'm sure I can't account for it. Perhaps it's forbidden fruit. People often want what they shouldn't have."

"Yes. That sounds logical, I think." Lady Violette nodded, toying with the tassel on the curtain tie. "Do you think it's a lack of *amour propre*, self-respect? Or is it a desire to escape the responsibility that weighs on a man of quality?"

"Those explanations are as good as any. It could be that a proper wife and home reminds such a man of the weight of his debts and obligations."

"Yes. I suppose a wife is an obligation."

"Not that such behavior should be excused. A true gentleman honors his responsibilities."

Lady Violette leaned against the casement, gazing again out the window. Sun poured in, gilding her frame as she closed her eyes for a moment. Then she sighed, opened her eyes and returned to her seat. "My greatest regret is that I couldn't be a mother." She lifted her teacup. "One can tolerate anything in a husband if there's a child to love." She sipped her tea, blinking rapidly.

"I fear you've been very unhappy."

Lady Violette's demeanor brightened. "On the contrary. I was quite happy. Most of the time. Able to do as I pleased, as long as I performed my official duties as a hostess and my social obligations as his wife at various functions. I wasn't truly unhappy until this last girl."

"Oh? What do you mean?"

A dark cloud passed over her features. "The wench didn't understand discretion. She caused terrible, humiliating scenes both here at the house and in public. The last one occurred a few weeks ago..." Her jaw tensed, and her nostrils flared.

"Don't tell me if it's too painful."

Lady Violette withdrew into herself. She stared at the ivory Turkish rug under their feet. "It was awful. At the theater. She'd learned Charles was there, and she came running into the lobby where we stood chatting with friends and acquaintances." She stroked the saucer's edge with her thumbs. "She shrieked at him. I couldn't decipher what she was saying at first. Something about how he was a coward and had betrayed her. She was hysterical and crying. She shoved and slapped him. Everyone stared at us, whispering and laughing. I thought I'd die of humiliation." Her bottom lip quivered, and her eyes brimmed with tears. "Then I understood, for she said it, screamed it, plain as the day...." She paused, dabbing her eyes.

Ravenna leaned over to put a comforting hand on Lady Violette's arm.

Through gritted teeth, Lady Violette added, "The strumpet said, 'I'm carrying your bastard child.' It echoed throughout the hall." Pink flooded her face.

Ravenna sucked in a breath. "Heavens!"

Lady Violette balled her handkerchief in her delicate fist, knuckles white. "I've never been so utterly humiliated. The tryst was one matter, but for her to proclaim the pregnancy in front of everyone, especially when I've struggled so long to have children. It was..." She huffed, the tips of her curls shuddering with her barely suppressed rage. The cup clattered against the saucer. "It was deplorable! Unforgivable!"

Ravenna didn't think a woman as genteel as Lady Violette was capable of expressing such anger. Ravenna narrowed her eyes. For a woman of propriety like Lady Hawkestone, it would be horrific, tortuous, to be so publicly humiliated while having her own barrenness underscored and proclaimed. But would it be enough to drive her to murder her husband? She didn't like suspecting Lady Violette, but the truth was that she barely knew the woman, and most people, including genteel people, were capable of murder if they reached an unbearable threshold. Had Lady Violette reached hers? And she had the easiest access to him. Ravenna sipped her cooling tea. Men—and women—had killed for less.

Lady Violette again stared into the distance, tightening her fist around the handkerchief. "I need to prove that Julia Pence killed my husband. I'm certain it was her. She was furious with him." She looked at Ravenna, her eyes intense with anger and determination. "It must be done discreetly. I don't want my embarrassment and shame bandied about. Whom can I turn to for help?"

Ravenna didn't want to offer her assistance. After her foray into espionage six years ago, she vowed she'd never do something like that again. It had been too terrifying, too dangerous. Though she respected and liked Lady Violette, she was really only an acquaintance. Ravenna was particular about whom she considered a friend. Yet perhaps this presented an opportunity to earn Hawkestone's forgiveness—albeit posthumously. She could finally forgive herself for betraying him by getting justice for him. It would be the closure she'd so desperately needed for almost a decade. But it was a frightening prospect. "Perhaps Bow Street..." Upon uttering the words, she immediately hated her cowardice.

Lady Violette gasped, a hand flying to her chest. "Never. I'd never trust the most intimate and humiliating details of my life and marriage to those people! Most of them are nothing more than ruffians and brutes."

"Perhaps we know someone—"

"No." Lady Violette bit her thumbnail, thinking. Then her face brightened. She looked at Ravenna. "*You*. You would be perfect. You were once an actress..."

Ravenna shook her head. "No, wait—"

"Yes. It *must* be you. You were once an actress, and now you're a lady. You can easily travel in both worlds, and *because* you're a woman, a widow, and titled, no one will ever suspect you of anything. You must still know people in the theater. You can easily prove that slattern Julia Pence killed my Charles. Then she can be carted off to Newgate, where she'll spend the rest of her life rotting to bits."

"I don't think ..."

Her eyes growing wide, filling with desperation, Lady Violette grasped Ravenna's hand, her nails digging into the flesh. "I'm begging you. *Begging*, Ravenna. Casting aside all my humiliation, all my pride, all propriety. Will you help prove that woman killed my husband?"

"I will." Ravenna said the words before she could stop them. She regretted it instantly.

# Chapter Four

Lady Violette passed into the library to see her husband while Ravenna waited for Hart and for the carriage. Ravenna paced, playing over her meeting with Lady Violette and Violette, annoyed with herself. She toyed with a curl. Was she mad to take this upon herself? And what sort of delusion played upon the woman's mind to make her think that Ravenna was at all equipped to ferret out such information? Only a few people knew of Ravenna's past as a spy: Catherine, her own husband, and Hawkestone. Two of those people were dead.

And though Hawkestone had been furious with her when he caught her, he had assured her of his discretion. "Though you don't deserve it," he'd said, his hand at her throat. "Only because it's more important to protect my own reputation than sully yours." He'd been afraid of looking like a fool or a traitor himself. She touched her throat. Another man might've killed her.

Hart appeared, and they stepped outside. The wind had picked up, and deep gray clouds pushed in from the west. Before getting into the carriage, Ravenna pulled her footmen aside. She pressed a quid into each of their palms. "This is for your discretion about today's events. If I find that you can maintain your secrecy, I'll ensure your pay is raised. Do you understand?"

The footmen pocketed the money and bowed. "Yes. Ma'am. Of course," said the broad-shouldered man.

"It's absolutely critical," she warned. And with a flair for the dramatic, she added, "Anyone who cannot remain quiet will suffer." Let them make what they would of that.

The men exchanged concerned glances and nodded. The leaner man opened the carriage door. "You can be assured, milady."

Ravenna and Hart climbed into the carriage. Ravenna sat back with a heavy sigh.

"Is Lady Hawkestone holding up well?" Hart asked.

"As well as can be expected." She pulled her black kid gloves tighter. "Were you able to discover anything about the maid?"

"Very little. Her name is Mary Smith."

The carriage pulled into traffic.

Ravenna scoffed. "Quite a common name." The carriage swayed and jostled over the stones.

Hart lifted a brow. "A perfect name if one wanted to hide."

"Indeed. Do you think that's likely?"

"Difficult to determine with any certainty, though it's common enough among the servant class. Too many times, one hears of cases where servants commit petty theft in one house, leave, change a name, get a job in another house only to be discovered too late. I can say that she's new to the house and keeps to herself. I spoke with the cook, a chambermaid, the scullery, and a footman, who all kept me company over my tea in the kitchen. They know little about her, though the scullery was impressed that Mary could read and write. Caught her doing it more than once."

Ravenna arched a thin black brow. "Interesting. That is *not* common among servants. Does her position require such skill?"

"No. She's a chambermaid."

Pensive, Ravenna looked out the window. People, carriages, and muck flooded the streets. London's population had increased tenfold in recent years, causing a constant crush of humans, animals, and various vehicles.

Hart said, "Do you suspect her of some wrongdoing?"

"I don't know yet. There's something about her. She doesn't quite fit in with the other servants, does she?"

"She does not."

Upon returning to Gordon House, Hart ran upstairs to finish her sewing while Ravenna retired to the library for a drink.

Catherine was in the library, curled on a sofa in front of the fire. She'd kicked off her slippers and sipped a glass of sherry while reading *Evelina.*

"I wasn't expecting you to still be here." Ravenna removed her black pelisse and bonnet, dropping them in a nearby chair.

Catherine closed her book and sat up, a twinkle in her eye. "How else was I going to find out what happened here today?"

"There isn't much to tell." Ravenna poured a glass of port—a drink that would shock most women as being too masculine—and sunk into the wingback chair across from her friend. "Hawkestone came to visit after four years' silence between us. Before I'd come downstairs to see him, he'd died in my drawing room." Propping her feet on a footstool, and crossing her ankles, Ravenna drained half the glass, her limp body drawing life from the sweet, robust wine.

"How odd." Catherine frowned. "What did he die of? He looked quite ill."

"He did, but I can't imagine what might have caused his death."

"And how's Lady Violette?"

"Distraught, of course. And captivated by a horrible notion that Hawkestone was murdered."

Catherine gasped, throwing herself to the end of the sofa nearest Ravenna and leaning on the arm. "You aren't serious?"

"I am."

Catherine curled her stocking feet up under her, covering them with her skirt. "Do you think she's hysterical?" Rain began to peck at the window.

"No, in fact, I believe she's quite rational." The wine oozed into her veins unfurling into her mind, bringing ease and comfort. "As it turns out, Hawkestone kept a woman. An actress."

"Oh, yes. I'd heard about that. Terrible scandal."

"Which reminds me." Ravenna tilted her head. "Why didn't you tell me that?"

Catherine winced, tracing circles in the velvet sofa arm. "I'm sorry. Given your history with Hawkestone and your row with him, I didn't think you'd want to hear anything about his sordid *affaires de coeurs*. Especially since you'd been a widow only a few months...." She trailed off into a pout.

"At any rate, Lady Violette believes Hawkestone's scorned mistress poisoned him."

"Over the baby?"

"You knew about that, too?"

"Of course. I heard about it the next day. I had just left to go to the Devonshires. But I understand the girl was hysterical and caused a frightful scene. Poor Lady Violette. She'd wanted children for so long. What's she going to do about it? Is she going to report the crime to Bow Street?"

Ravenna licked her lips, trepidation fluttering under the wave of port. "Not exactly. She doesn't trust them and thinks it would be too difficult for them to get information. Rather, she wants me to investigate."

"Surely, you didn't agree to that?" Catherine sat up, the firelight catching her diamond earrings.

"I did. What else could I do? She begged me. She's so sensitive to humiliation, she doesn't want an outsider involved. I couldn't say no." She looked down into her glass. "Besides, it might give me an opportunity to redeem my past transgressions against Hawkestone."

Catherine searched Ravenna's face. "You're referring to the incident in ninety-eight?"

She meant the spying Ravenna had conducted on behalf of the Franco-Irish collusion against the English, where they had attempted to invade English shores via Ireland. The Irish Unity hadn't left her with much of a choice. They'd threatened to make her watch as they tortured and killed her entire family—what was left of them after the English massacres—before giving her the same treatment.

"It might be dangerous. I love an adventure as much as anyone, but, darling, think of it. If someone were willing to kill a man as powerful as Hawkestone, they'd think nothing of killing you."

"I've been thinking." She turned in her seat to face Catherine, curling her legs in the seat. "Lady Violette had also mentioned that Hawkestone believed he was being targeted by a political rival. However, she hadn't believed him because she thought he was mad with fever. So, what if Lady Violette is wrong about Hawkestone's lover? What if this isn't a crime of passion at all but a political enemy?"

"That's possible. Maybe more likely."

"Of course, I plan to find this Julia Pence and speak with her soon. Tomorrow, if I can manage it. But I must look at all possibilities."

"Maybe he was mad. I've seen people with pox driven to insanity."

"Granted. But, what if Hawkestone made an enemy who wanted him dead?"

Catherine frowned. "Then you must *not* get involved. You should contact a constable or a magistrate immediately."

"But if it is politically motivated, a constable or a magistrate might be influenced by the killer or might be connected to the killer. And if it is politically motivated, someone else might be in danger. You see, I don't know whom I can trust."

Catherine pulled at her bottom lip. "Yes, I see your dilemma." She dropped her hand. "What proof does Lady Violette have that he was murdered?"

"Nothing substantial, but you saw his condition. He was quite ill. He might've been poisoned. And if other people are possibly in danger—"

"You're mad," Catherine scoffed and drank her sherry.

"Perhaps." Ravenna leveled a steady gaze at Catherine. "I'm well aware this might be dangerous. But this isn't solely about Lady Violette. It's also about setting my soul right, getting forgiveness. And possibly saving other lives."

"I don't like it." Catherine's pale brows knit over her nose. "But I understand. If I can help at all, you'll tell me."

"I will. Thank you." Ravenna didn't like it either, but she might never get another opportunity for absolution.

The fire spat and cracked, drawing Ravenna's gaze. "You can't tell a soul what I've told you."

"No, never." Like all great confidantes, Catherine had her own lurid past and therefore understood the power of keeping secrets. Anyone with a dark secret could find a loyal friend in her. This aspect made her at once one of the most charming, dangerous, and powerful of the society doyennes. And her ability to keep those secrets ensured she'd be trusted with more.

Ravenna downed the last of her wine, unfolded from the chair, and poured another drink. "Another sherry?"

"Please," Catherine joined her at the occasional table, holding out her glass. The rain now pounded against the window panes as if it demanded to be let in, and the wind whipped wildly through the tree limbs.

Returning the stopper to the decanter and ready for lighter topics, Ravenna asked, "How was the meeting?"

"Lady Braxton was quite displeased by your absence and behaved as obnoxiously as possible."

Ravenna laughed. "She wasn't too hard on you, I hope." They returned to their seats.

"Nothing I couldn't manage. But she…" Catherine looked down her nose and, in her best imitation of Lady Braxton's imperious demeanor and bold voice. "*Insists* that you visit her at Braxton House at your earliest convenience. For I'm most put out with Lady Birchfield. After all, this was her idea."

They laughed.

Ravenna confirmed her earlier intuition. "I knew she would remind everyone that The Penitent House charity was my idea. I am sorry I missed the meeting." Ravenna rolled her eyes. "I'm not looking forward to visiting Braxton House. Though I daresay, however domineering she may be, she has been a godsend for *Les Roses Noires*."

"Yes. She raises so much money because everyone is terrified she will haunt them like a banshee if they tell her no."

Their laughter trickled into a comfortable silence that expanded between the friends as they sipped their drinks and stared into the fire.

Catherine gasped and slapped the sofa arm. "With all the madness, I almost forgot to tell you." In one motion, she moved to the edge of her seat, put her drink aside, and turned to face Ravenna. "Are you coming to my soirée tomorrow night?"

Ravenna smiled sleepily from under her wine haze. Only Catherine could think of a soirée at a time like this. "I think it's too soon to be out much in society. I only came back to London to work on the committee, resume my fencing lessons, and perhaps find my sister and niece."

"Have you heard anything from either of them?"

"Not in these four years, at least. Philip had been trying to help me locate them, but they seem to have disappeared. That's part of why I started the Penitent House charity. I'd heard my sister had fallen into desperate straits, and I hoped she'd catch wind of the charity and show up there. London is such an enormous city, though, I'm not sure I'll ever find them."

"You will. I have my people looking too. But, back to my current mission. It's a private soirée at my house. You must come. If you can entertain charity meetings and fencing lessons, you can come to my home with a few friends. There, I've decided for you. After all…" She leaned on the sofa arm with a mischievous gleam in her eyes. "Lord Braedon is *most* interested in seeing you again. He's spoken of nothing else since he heard you were returning to town."

"And how did he learn of my return?"

Catherine shrugged a shoulder and simpered. "A little bird told him."

"Oh? And would that little bird's name be Catherine?" When Catherine smiled and rolled her eyes to gaze at the ceiling, Ravenna shook her head and chuckled. "I find it most difficult to believe that Braedon would express the slightest interest in me. He could have any woman, much younger and prettier." She cocked a brow. "And probably *has* had many of them, I daresay."

"Braedon has always had a particular regard for you, but there were always… complications."

Ravenna drank deeply from her glass. "Laughable. What complications?" She set her glass aside and relaxed into her chair, propping her feet on the footstool.

"Your marriage, for one."

That touched a nerve. There was something in the word 'complication' that implied she hadn't taken her marriage seriously. She'd loved Philip and had been devoted to him. Granted, their marriage might've begun as a matter of convenience and protection on her part, but there was also passion, respect, and friendship that grew deeper with each passing year.

She glared at Catherine. "My marriage was no mere *complication*."

"Fair enough. I meant no offense." Catherine shrugged, toying with a bracelet. "But you understand my meaning. The other complication has always been the greater one. For Braedon, at least."

"Yes. Lady Dianthe is a complication for anyone she encounters. I wager they're still entangled?"

Catherine tipped her head. "I wouldn't call it an entanglement so much as an *interest*. Fervent on her side and quite waned on his."

Ravenna laughed aloud. "What a savvy politician you are."

A rapscallion smile tugged at the corners of Catherine's mouth. "I rather think Braedon would be a suitable distraction for a young, lonely widow."

"Young?" Ravenna sniffed. "I'm thirty. My days for passionate love affairs and marriage are over. I want only my work, a little travel. Maybe I'll take some art lessons and get a dog. That's all I require."

"Nonsense!" Catherine nearly sprang from her seat. "You are not old. Lady Braxton is nearly twice your age, with men half her age filling her bed."

Squeezing her eyes shut, Ravenna shook her head against the image of Lady Braxton tousling the bedcovers with young men. "I don't care. I'm not Lady Braxton, and Braedon is still far too entangled for my tastes, thank you." She sat up in her chair and reached for her wine.

"Please, Ravenna. You have to take him away from her."

Ravenna snapped her head to gape at her friend. "Catherine. How could you ask such a thing?"

"She's such a horrid creature. She can never make him happy, nor would she be faithful to him. I've tried for years to separate them. I've managed to talk him out of an actual engagement, for now. But rumors abound that they might marry after all. And she hates me so vehemently that it would destroy my friendship with him. Which I cannot allow."

"You know I would never knowingly destroy a couple." She drank her wine. "Besides, I've talked to him dozens of times, and he's never shown any fondness for me beyond friendship. He's an incurable flirt, which can be diverting, but I'd be a fool to ever think he was serious." She motioned toward a plant in the corner. "He'd sooner flirt with that fern if it wore a bit of lace."

Catherine giggled. "Don't be so certain. As his closest confidante, I know a great many things I'm not at liberty to speak of directly..." She inched forward and added conspiratorially, "Therefore, I think you should consider wearing your crimson gown to the soirée. The one with the gold embroidery that favors you so well?"

Ravenna considered the notion. An image of Philip came back to her: looking up from a book, the sunlight haloing him, admiration and desire mingled in his gaze. A deep ache opened in her chest and spread into her gut. No. She lowered her eyes and shook her head. "Absolutely not. I will go to your soirée. In my weeds. And there's an end to it."

When Catherine had left, Ravenna swallowed her tears for Hawkestone with the last of her wine. She lay her head against the back of the chair, closed her eyes, and played through the events of the day. Thinking of Hawkestone reminded her of Philip, which naturally led to thinking of their deaths. She pushed that back.

And then there was Lady Violette. She'd been certain of Julia Pence's involvement. However, Lady Violette herself, in spite of her spotless reputation, was just as likely a culprit as anyone else. It was also probable that Hawkestone's death was natural, and Lady Violette was seeking to strike out at Julia in a fit of jealous pique. Or, the most frightening possibility of all, his death was politically motivated.

She stood and paced in front of the fire. First, she must keep her wits and not jump to wild conclusions. She would need to speak to Julia Pence, get the measure of her. She could be the killer, and then there would be no need to entertain fearful imaginations.

Ravenna pushed against the instinct to write to her stepson, Thomas, to warn him of potential danger since he worked closely with the Foreign Secretaries. However, he wouldn't yet know of Hawkestone's death, and she didn't want to reveal that information. It was best to let that news issue forth naturally through the death announcements in the newspapers and the rumor mill. Otherwise, there would be a great many questions she didn't want to answer.

Rather, she would write and ask to see him tomorrow. That would buy enough time to make it seem plausible that she heard of Hawkestone's death through gossip. Oh, the games the *ton* required people to play. Besides, knowing Thomas, he was probably anywhere but home.

She sat at her writing desk, dashed off a note, and signed it with the nickname he and his brother used for her instead of "mother."

*It's a matter of urgency that I see you at first chance. –Amma*

# Chapter Five

Ravenna rose early to make her visiting rounds to her stepson at Pelham House and to Lady Braxton before trying to find the whereabouts of Julia Pence, which would be a larger task. She paused in the foyer to put on her gloves and give directives to Hart about the dress she wanted to wear to Catherine's soirée that evening when a knock sounded on the front door.

Banks answered the door. "Lady Birchfield is leaving. May I take a card?"

"Who is it?" Ravenna craned her neck, attempting to glimpse the visitor.

"A Mr. Chadwick." His eyes hardened. "A Bow Street Runner."

Mr. Chadwick interjected, peeking in the door. "If I may have a word, I shan't keep you long, milady."

*So soon?* A spark of fear flashed through her. It was not a good thing that a constable was showing up at Gordon House the day after Hawkestone died. She straightened her back and clamped down on the fear, resorting to cool detachment. "Please, show him to the drawing room, Banks."

She rushed across the foyer into the drawing room and took her place by the sofa. A few moments later, Mr. Chadwick entered. Lean and of middling height, he was an older gentleman with a prominent forehead revealed by receding gray hair slicked back with pomade. Sharp intelligence shone from his dark, heavy-lidded eyes.

He bowed. "Thank you for meeting with me, ma'am. Bernham Chadwick at your service."

She motioned to a chair. "Please, have a seat." She sat at an angle to him on the sofa, spreading her black muslin skirt and clutching her folded fan of black Spanish lace. It was a honeymoon gift from Philip. She carried it with her always. In the guard was hidden a thin blade the size of a penknife. She tried not to think of the blade now.

Her knuckles whitened. "How may I help you, Mr. Chadwick?"

He crossed his legs and rested his hands on his leg. He seemed refined and well-bred, quite unlike many of the Runners she'd encountered in her old life. Not that she'd ever been in trouble with one, but they were often in the streets working when she walked to and from her work at the theater.

"I've come to discuss the matter of Lord Hawkestone with you."

Her breath caught instinctively at the mention of Hawkestone's name, and she called upon her old acting days to maintain her composure. "Yes?"

"I'm curious how he came to die here."

Her heart rabbited, throwing itself against its trappings. Lady Violette must've told him. How much had she told him? She wanted to be honest, but she didn't want to incriminate herself and inadvertently reveal her past treason. Something in Chadwick's stoic, observant, and intelligent demeanor made it clear to her that he could see beyond words and wouldn't hesitate to arrest her and lead her directly to her execution. "I'm not certain." She cleared her throat and worked to keep her voice steady. "I was upstairs when he was announced. By the time I came down, he was dead."

"What was the reason for his visit?"

She lifted one shoulder. "I have no idea. The visit was most unexpected."

One brow flinched. "What were you doing when he called?"

"Preparing for a meeting."

"What sort of meeting?"

"A charity meeting for the Spitalfields House for Penitent Prostitutes. It's a charity developed by my women's club."

"Was he a member of the charitable committee or one of its investors?"

"No."

"Hm." He nodded and leaned his head on his hand. His index finger stroked his thin upper lip. He nodded pensively, then paused. He lowered his hand to the chair arm. "How long have you known Lord Hawkestone?"

"We met in May 1797. Not long after I came here from Ireland."

His eyes flashed and locked on her. "You're Irish?"

She sat straighter. "Yes." It was best to be charming, so she chuckled and flashed a coquettish smile. "Surely that's not a crime?"

One corner of his mouth ticked upward, but his eyes sharpened. "Not yet. Fortunately for you." He thought for a moment. "That's five years ago. And when's the last time you spoke with him?"

He was like a wolf circling its prey, closing in tighter and tighter. Her mind raced for an answer that wouldn't incriminate her or pique his curiosity to ask more prying questions. She pulled her face blank, thankful for her training as an actress. "I can't say exactly. It's been a long time."

"Perhaps you could estimate."

She lifted a brow and sat straighter, presenting an implacable front. "I don't recall."

"Very well. How did you meet him?"

"Introduced through a mutual friend." She didn't want to pull Catherine's name into this. Likely Chadwick would discover the connection, at any rate, but she wasn't going to make it easy for him.

Humor flashed across his face. "Ah. Did Lord Hawkestone make a habit of visiting unexpectedly?"

Her back grew rigid and tight, and the muscles under her shoulder blades began to burn. "No."

"You're a widow?"

"As you see." She looked down at her hands. She wished Philip was here. He would intervene. He would know exactly how to manage this man.

"And you live here alone?"

"Yes."

He lifted his chin with a sharp inhale. "Interesting. Why would a married man be visiting a widow who lives alone?" He fixed his sharp eyes on her. His tone was insinuative.

Annoyance prickled her under her skin. "What are you implying?"

"Only that perhaps you had an assignation—"

She gripped her fan in her fists. "How *dare* you accuse me of having an affair with a married man. And while I'm actively mourning my husband, no less."

He remained unruffled. "And yet, he died in *your* home."

Ravenna shot up from her seat. "I thank you for visiting, but I am expected elsewhere at the moment." She stormed to the door and opened it.

"Very well." A faint smile haunted his thin lips as he stood and jerked down his waistcoat. "I thank you for your time. I'll likely visit again. Soon." He bowed and left the room. He stopped in the foyer to don his great coat and gloves. He held his top hat in one hand and paused by the front door. "I've noticed deception is rather like a perfume, Lady Birchfield." He sniffed the air. "I can smell it from here." He clapped his hat on his head and touched its brim by way of farewell, and slipped from the house.

When the door closed behind him, the pressure of fear exploded into a sharp headache in her temples. She ran to the drawing room window and peered through the lace curtain. Mr. Chadwick stepped out onto the flagstones in front of her house, checked his pocket watch, and scanned the street. Then, as if he sensed her gaze, he turned and looked at her. A slow, reptilian grin spread over his lips and touched the brim of his hat again. She ducked away.

There was only one way to protect her secret past as a spy: she had to figure out Hawkestone's killer before Chadwick. If she could stop his investigation in its tracks, giving him no reason to continue, then he'd have no cause to look further into her past with Hawkestone. On her side, only Catherine knew her secret. But she had no way of knowing if Hawkestone had mentioned anything about her betrayal to someone. Likely he didn't say anything to Lady Violette, or she would've brought it up in their meeting yesterday.

She needed to speak with Julia Pence. But there were other matters to attend to first.

# Chapter Six

Thomas's residence, Pelham House on Grosvenor Street, was an unremarkable three-storied row house of buff stone and bow windows that belonged to Thomas's in-laws. Paulson, the butler, a tall, broad man of middling age with a long sharp nose, thinning dark hair, and thin lips, greeted her. "I'm sorry, milady, Lord Birchfield isn't home."

Commonly people of the *ton* would often be home but busy and unavailable to visitors, so she asked, "Are you certain he isn't home? It's a matter of urgency." She wasn't certain it was a matter of urgency, but she thought it might gain an audience with him sooner.

"I understand, milady, but he truly isn't home."

"Where did he go?"

"He only said he had some business to attend to."

Ravenna clutched her folded fan. "Do you know if he received the letter I sent yesterday?"

"Yes, milady. I gave it to him myself."

Her stomach knotted. There was nothing else she could do. "Please..." She pulled a visiting card out of her reticule. "Implore him to respond or return my call."

With a heavy spirit, she went directly to Lady Braxton's to apologize for her absence from The Penitent House meeting. The closer the carriage drew to Braxton House, the heavier she grew. Lady Braxton was a good woman, in her way, but quite overbearing and domineering. And she'd rather be hunting Hawkestone's killer and keeping her past locked up instead of sitting with an abrasive woman who had heart but lacked grace.

The carriage stopped in front of Braxton House, and her footman climbed the stairs to tap the brass knocker on the front door. She held her breath, hoping no one would answer or that the butler would say Lady Braxton wasn't home. Unfortunately, the door opened, and the footman returned to announce in his Yorkshire lilt that Lady Braxton was, in fact, at home. She groaned inwardly and gathered up her skirts to allow the footman to hand her down.

The butler showed Ravenna into the small formal parlor—a vulgar room—decorated in a busy jacquard wallpaper of mauve and burgundy. The walls were of heavy wood, and thick, burgundy velvet drapes hung over the windows. A black marble fireplace stood proudly in the center of one wall. Gold trim and fixtures adorned the room throughout. The room was close and suffocating with a faint, fusty smell of old, wet leaves. Ravenna sat on the edge of a gold-trimmed burgundy sofa, her tightened muscles aching.

Lady Braxton marched into the room. She had emerged from the swamps of common stock and had been fortunate enough to marry up, much like Ravenna herself. If rumor held true, in her youth, Lady Braxton had been, at one time, a favorite model for the famous artist George Romney. Yet, she wasn't conventionally beautiful. She was *too* much—her eyes too round, her lips too thick, her breasts too large, her character too brusque. Quite different from the wispy women artists tended to favor these days.

Lady Braxton didn't even say good morning. "I'm most put out with you. Worse than that, Lady Clerkenwell is put out. You abandoned our *Les Roses Noires* meeting. At your own home, no less, leaving poor Lady Adair to manage in your absence. Bad form. Bad form, indeed."

Lady Braxton had established *Les Roses Noires* as a women's club for the purpose of educating women and dedicated to women's educational and suffrage rights—a noble and much-needed cause. She filled the club with some of the most fashionable—and privileged—women of the *ton*. Ravenna only attended in matters of charity work or compelling lectures.

Lady Braxton's voice boomed as loud as a general's in rallying troops in the back lines of a battalion. "Bad form, indeed. I'm ashamed of you. Lady Clerkenwell is strange and fickle. For whatever reason, she'll negotiate only with you. And, need I remind you the Penitent House charity and the meeting had been your idea?"

Ravenna suppressed an urge to laugh. "I'm sorry. I had an urgent matter to attend to that sprang up most unexpectedly."

"Then why did Lady Adair say you had a headache?"

"That's also my fault. I told her to make my excuses, but I didn't tell her what I was doing."

Lady Braxton narrowed her eyes and pursed her lips. "Most vexing." Lady Braxton waved her hand and planted herself in a nearby chair, her ample legs consuming the entirety of the seat. A brooch consisting of a trio of black roses, the symbol of *Les Roses Noires*, pinned a white lace fichu in place over her vast bosom. "Everyone knows that Hawkestone died at Gordon House yesterday."

Shock rattled her bones. "How do you know about Hawkestone?"

She shrugged and gaped as if Ravenna had three heads. "The servants. The scullery from Hawkestone House was over here this morning borrowing sugar from my cook and told us everything she knew. Perhaps you could enlighten me on the particulars?"

"I'd rather not speak of it." *Blasted gossips.* No doubt the papers would soon catch wind of that bit of news, if they hadn't already, creating a scandal. It wouldn't be long. She sank inwardly.

"Very well." She tapped her fingers on the chair arm. "What I want to know is how will you pry the money out of Lady Clerkenwell's dried-up old claws? We need a kitchen for the Penitent House." The phrasing of her statement didn't escape Ravenna's notice. Lady Braxton had a habit of taking control of projects that hadn't been created by her.

Ravenna sighed under the weight of both Ladies Braxton and Clerkenwell's disappointment. "Yes, I know. I will think of something. Perhaps a gala?"

"Fantastic. Nevertheless, you should call on her today." She snapped her hands together, dropping them into her lap as if that settled the matter.

A footman brought in a tea service and a plate of small cakes. Thank goodness. Ravenna silently blew out her exasperation.

Without asking, Lady Braxton poured the tea, nearly dark as coffee, no sugar or cream, and served a cake to Ravenna. Ravenna politely took one sip of the bitter brew and one bite of the stale ginger cake before setting it aside.

Lady Braxton ran her too-round violet eyes over Ravenna. "I wonder at you, that you're still in your weeds. After all, being a woman of means at your age is the best prospect as a widow." She said it as casually as discussing the weather. Her smile revealed a small gap between her two front teeth.

Ravenna blinked.

"I see I've shocked you quite out of your senses, Lady Birchfield." Her deep laughter shook her generous bosom, which tested the strength of the poor green gingham bodice tasked to hold it. The current Greco-Roman-inspired fashions with their wispy muslins and silks may yet prove too weak to hold Lady Braxton's substantial assets. Hers would be best managed with the stiff armor-like corsets of a medieval woman.

"It's not a fortunate position." Ravenna's voice came out thinner than she preferred as a bloom of grief opened in her chest. Snippets of Philip striding toward her through the open fields of Birchfield, riding his horse and laughing rose in her memory. "I'd much rather have my husband alive and my life the way it was. I wear my weeds to honor the man I loved."

"Oh, a husband may be found anywhere. And things never remain as they were, even if he'd lived."

Ravenna shifted in her seat. There may have been some truth in that statement, but that didn't render it any easier to hear. "Perhaps. Yet, my stepsons and I would prefer Philip alive."

"At any rate, I should think widowhood would suit you. You're still young enough to marry, if you choose, but wealthy enough to remain free. I call that a very happy prospect." She bit into her cake, the crumbs sprinkling the bodice of her dress.

This conversation was a barb in Ravenna's shoe. She tapped her folded fan lightly against her palm. "Since my eldest stepson, Thomas, has claimed his inheritance and title as the new Lord Birchfield, nearly everything is his to dispense with as he pleases. I'm fortunate my late husband provided me with a comfortable living. That's all I require."

"Such dissimulation," Lady Braxton scoffed. "Look at us. Now that we've lived like this…" She swept a hand through the air. "Wouldn't it be much harder to return to our origins?"

Ravenna forced herself to sit a few more minutes under the barrage of Lady Braxton's insensitive and callous remarks and questions and then announced she had an engagement elsewhere.

"Irritating woman," Ravenna muttered to herself as she descended the stairs of Braxton House to climb into her carriage. She returned to Gordon House with barely enough time to prepare for her fencing lesson.

Mr. Norris from Angelo's School was short, lean, and graceful, with bushy brown whiskers and merry hazel eyes. His lithe form moved like a dancer around the floor of the drawing room that had been cleared for their lesson. He held his foil loosely in his hand, his wrist flexible and relaxed. Yet, he moved it with precision and speed.

She received a proper thrashing. Mr. Norris showed no mercy on her for being female—something she both appreciated and resented. In fact, he seemed to delight in setting her down. He wasn't malicious. Rather, the gleam in his eye hinted at admiration and amusement.

After the lesson, sore, stiff, sweaty, and soundly defeated, she set another appointment immediately.

Mr. Norris chuckled. "You've got pluck, milady. And you're improving each time. I'll see you the day after tomorrow, then." He tipped his hat to her and skipped down her stairs, whistling and twirling his walking stick.

However badly he'd defeated her, though, the worst was yet to come. Catherine's soirée loomed a few hours away as the day glided toward its close. She still hadn't had a chance to speak with Thomas or Hawkestone's lover, Julia Pence. Social obligations at the height of the season, even for a widow, never ceased. Yet, if she continued to allow such distractions, she'd have great difficulty finding Hawkestone's killer before Mr. Chadwick. She climbed the stairs to her bedchamber to prepare for the soirée, scolding herself for her failure to accomplish an interview with Julia Pence and commanding herself to do it tomorrow.

# Chapter Seven

The train of Ravenna's black, beaded gown whispered along the checkered marble foyer toward the large drawing room at the back of Adair House. Yes, beads would be frowned on by the more conservative guest, and she would even be regarded as "eccentric" by her more liberal-minded friends, but she didn't care. She loved a beaded gown and the way it sparkled like thousands of little stars in the candlelight. Though the round neckline dipped a little low, it remained respectable, and the long, sheer sleeves with peek-a-boo puffs at the shoulders adequately covered the bruises from her fencing lesson. Her black Spanish lace fan dangled from her wrist, tapping her thigh as she walked. Still stiff from her lesson, she nearly limped into the room.

Since Ravenna had been cloistered from society for the past nine months, she felt like a jutting stone in an otherwise smooth path. The formal drawing room reflected its mistress well—vibrant coral walls trimmed in white and lined with gold-framed portraits and landscapes. The chairs and sofas, blue as robin's eggs, had been pushed against the walls to allow for freer movement and for the card tables to be erected during dinner. Large vases of white lilacs filled the corners, their sweet scent entwined with the citrus, spice, herbal, and floral scents of various perfumes created a pleasant potpourri Ravenna always associated with Adair House.

Ravenna found Catherine standing at the center of a gaggle of friends. Catherine greeted her with a warm smile and a kiss on the cheek while the other ladies, Lady Corliss and Lady Montgomery, whispered behind fans and gloved hands.

Their pointed gazes, mixed with questioning and knowing, were almost impossible to ignore. Something akin to stage fright wafted from the recesses of Ravenna's gut and spread upward and outward through her whole body, like smoke from a thurible. She clenched her jaw, tamping down the feeling and forcing herself to give them a warm greeting.

"I'm so glad you've come." Catherine stepped back, pulling Ravenna's arms wide. "Look, ladies, off with all these wispy white gowns everyone raves after. I think Lady Birchfield may start a fashion for black."

The women tittered and nodded and cooed their agreement, all while flashing cunning glances.

Catherine continued, "This gown renders your widow's blush quite lovely, darling."

"Widow's blush?" Ravenna chuckled. "Whatever do you mean?"

"I heard it somewhere recently. Can't quite recall where, but I remember thinking how fitting the description was because it perfectly describes a woman who's made to look all the paler when wearing her weeds. That paleness is a widow's 'blush.' Where a maiden blushes pink, you blush, so to speak, paler."

Perplexed, Ravenna tipped her head, smiling. "A strange description but apt, I suppose."

Lady Montgomery, wearing an olive-colored bandeau, looked down her hooked nose. "I've heard you've had some excitement at Gordon House recently. Hawkestone, *dead*? In your parlor? I had no idea you and he were...."

Ravenna's spine stiffened, but she forced a grin. "Well, he wasn't dead when he arrived. It was quite unexpected for us both, I think."

"I'm not in the least surprised," Lady Montgomery said to Lady Corliss next to her. "Don't you remember? He had a predilection for actresses."

Ravenna cut her eyes at them. There were many things she wanted to say. Things that would cut these vipers to the core and put this one in her place. Like the rumors about her husband and his supposed membership in the Hellfire Club and some of his horrid exploits within. But she pinched her lips together into a smirk.

"It's in all the papers," Lady Corliss chimed in. The wiry curls, three shades darker blonde than her natural hair, quivered from under her gold-striped turban. "You must've been terrified. Yet, I didn't realize you, and he had...." She glanced at Lady Montgomery. "Reconciled?"

They twittered.

Catherine linked her arm with Ravenna's. "Pardon us, ladies, there is something I would like to speak with Lady Birchfield about."

They turned away, leaving the wretches to whisper among themselves.

"Don't give them a second thought." Catherine waved her hand. "They're so miserable they insist everyone around them must be, too. I would've set them down a few notches if we didn't need their husband's votes for some important matters coming up in Parliament." Catherine, like many society women, worked fiercely behind the scenes to move the wheels of government.

Ravenna selected a pale amber drink from a footman who approached with a tray. "If this is your special champagne punch, I'll have no trouble forgetting my troubles soon enough."

Catherine selected a glass for herself. "I confess there's more brandy in it than usual. So drink much and often. I assure you, thanks to Mr. Banks' merchant friend, tonight's fountain will not run dry."

Ravenna lifted her brow in amused shock. They laughed as Catherine led the way to a pair of chairs near the fire, far removed from the other ladies.

Ravenna leaned into the corner of the leather wingback chair, the green kid leather soft against the bit of bare skin exposed by her dress. "I'll be the last to pick a fight with them as I plan to importune each of their husbands with a large contribution request."

Catherine added, "And, if I smile very prettily tonight, I may come away with some intelligence from the Foxite camp that I can share with Pitt."

They giggled together and sipped their drinks. After a moment, Catherine leaned toward Ravenna and lowered her voice. "In sincerity, how are you since yesterday's terrible affair? I could think of little else since leaving you."

"I'm well, thank you. But every time I closed my eyes to sleep, I saw him lying on my floor, lifeless." A shudder ran over her. "He haunted me all night." She recalled a nightmare where he'd risen from her drawing room floor, though still dead. His hollow, dark eyes stared from a gaunt face with slack purple mouth. He reached for her. She parried with her epee. Yet, his icy fingers gripped her throat. She shuddered and pushed the thought away.

"I'm sorry for it. As you're aware, people are busy as spiders spinning their rumor webs. A few of the ladies have already inquired about why he was at your home and what had happened. I told them he was there asking for Lord Birchfield, having heard he was there. I told them, too, that Hawkestone had died of apoplexy. They seemed to be satisfied with that."

"For now." Ravenna glanced over her shoulder. "It's only a matter of time before the truth is revealed. Which means I must work quickly."

Ravenna drew deep from her glass of fairy magic, both light and strong, rounded out beautifully with a hint of orange liqueur. She delighted in its determined happiness as her muscles and mind unknotted slowly. The heady punch oozed through her body like liquid sunlight. With such magic working in her veins, she could almost forget her worries and cares, along with the regrettable Hawkestone.

Catherine continued, "Have you heard the latest news? Lord Wolfsham has fallen ill, though I understand he's expected to recover. I found out today when I called on Mrs. Fitzhugh. She had the news from her dressmaker, who had it from one of Wolfsham's servants."

How awful. Wolfsham was renowned for his joviality, kindness, and generosity. Everyone liked him. And the few who didn't, no doubt, wondered at their own judgment. "What's the matter with him?"

Catherine shrugged one shoulder, causing her diamonds to pool in her clavicle. "I don't know. I wonder if his affliction is the same as Hawkestone's?" Catherine swirled her glass, tiny bubbles from its contents racing to the surface. She leveled a pointed gaze at Ravenna. "I understand he was one of the men favored to replace Hawkestone."

Ravenna froze. "Wait..." She closed her eyes and pressed her fingertips to the center of her forehead, the veil of champagne punch making it difficult to think clearly. "Wolfsham is favored for the Foreign Secretary position Hawkestone left behind, which is the same position as…" Her breath caught. "Catherine…" She grabbed Catherine's arm. "Philip. Philip died right before Hawkestone, and they both held the same office. Catherine, what if my husband was murdered, too? And now, if Wolfsham is also ill, perhaps Lady Violette is in fact wrong about Julia Pence, and these are politically motivated attacks, after all?"

She squeezed Catherine's hand as the world around her fell inward into a pinpoint of pain that jammed straight into her chest. For nine months, she'd believed that Philip had died of natural causes, but what if he had been murdered? Images of her husband's final days and his symptoms rolled through her mind. So much like Hawkestone: stomach complaints, vomiting, shaking, and grayish skin. But those were symptoms of an influenza, too. She'd never imagined it could be anything else. Tears pooled in her eyes.

Catherine patted her hand. "Oh, dear. Don't overwork your imagination. I'm sure that didn't happen."

"But isn't it possible?" She turned her head and swiped the tears away. She must maintain her composure. She didn't want to break down at Catherine's soirée and ruin it. Ravenna dug her thumbnail into the inside of her wrist to distract her emotion.

Catherine tipped her head, sympathy marking her features. "Darling, anything is *possible*. But it also sounds mad, don't you think? Didn't Philip's surgeon say he had an influenza?"

"Yes. But what if he was wrong? Surgeons are wrong all the time."

"That's true. You could be right." She lifted her hand. "However, don't let flights of fancy wing you away. People fall ill every day. I called on at least five ill friends today and none of them are in the parliament. The simplest explanation is usually the correct one."

"That's true, I suppose." Logically, what Catherine said was true, but trepidation swarmed her body. What if there was more to this and her husband had also been murdered? The thought was almost too much to bear.

The door opened to a small herd of men, their voices a muddle of conversation.

"Rally yourself, darling. Get through this evening first."

Ravenna nodded and gulped the remainder of her drink to still the chatter in her mind.

Catherine and Ravenna peered around their chairs.

"Behold my menagerie, darling," Catherine winked and wrinkled her nose. "They will provide ample distraction."

When Ravenna stood, the champagne punch glittered through her body into her head as they approached the men: Lord Yarford, Catherine's cohabitant lover, their close friend, Lord Braedon, and another man, completely unknown to her who was quite handsome, though young.

As the eldest and most titled, Ravenna took Yarford's extended hand first. He bowed his head over her hand. After a few of the usual pleasantries, Ravenna turned to Lord Braedon. He stepped close, his exotic and alluring sandalwood cologne swept over her, drawing her in.

He wore a perpetual smirk as though he knew all her secrets and was itching to shout them to the room. "Welcome back, Lady Birchfield. Your presence breathes new life into us all."

Tall and broad-shouldered, with dark, wavy hair cropped a la Napoleon, William Finleigh, Earl of Braedon, was an Apollo among men. His black pantaloons hugged his well-formed, muscular legs. His sensuous lips, almost feminine in their fullness, hinted at his reputation for amorous adventure. The light scar across the bridge of his nose and his left brow were intriguing imperfections that only enhanced his allure.

She placed her hand in his. His hand was warm, dry, and rough in the manner of gentleman hands—hands that held horse reins, fencing swords, and guns. His hand also had red cuts and purple bruises across the top. Probably from boxing.

He lifted her hand to his lips. "Your return is like the roses blooming after a bleak winter." Instead of kissing her knuckle he turned her hand to kiss her palm. A scandalously intimate maneuver.

A thrill shot through her. Sucking in her breath, she withdrew her hand, though not as fast or as severely as she should have. The champagne punch was powerful. Her cheeks burned.

"Silver-tongued as ever, I see." Her chuckle sounded high and fragile to her ears. "It's little wonder you've managed to elude so many huntresses each season."

Humor emanated from his frosted blue eyes. "Yet I still manage to take away a sheep or two." He winked.

"Rascal." She laughed, playfully tapping his arm with her closed fan. "I'm certain any hope of your reformation is lost." Shame squirmed in her gut. Only nine months a widow and here she stood flirting with another man. No doubt the champagne punch loosened the grip of her mourning. She dropped the smile from her face.

"Not this evening. Catherine has warned me to be on my best behavior."

*Then perhaps we're all at a loss?* That's what Ravenna wanted to say, but guilt roped the words, pulled them back, and bound them tightly in her mouth. Philip's ghost skittered across the back of her mind. She imagined pain flashing in his hazel eyes if he were alive to see his wife flirting with another man. Shame lit up her cheeks again. She opened her fan and fanned herself vigorously.

Braedon's wolfish eyes gleamed with intelligence and mischief—a look both predatory and thrilling. His attention warmed her like sitting at a fire and drinking tea after a long walk in the snow—both comforting and invigorating.

Thankfully, Catherine interrupted to introduce Lord Edmund Donovan. He was her new *cicisbeo* in title only, relieving Yarford of the duty of carrying Catherine's fan and stole while escorting her to the theater or parties. But Lord Donovan would never gain entrée into her bed in the fashion of a true *cicisbeo*.

Ravenna curtsied as he bowed. His dark gray-green eyes sparked with certainty, spirit, and pride—much like a fine, young stallion. His eyes reminded her of the waters of Fethard-on-Sea on a misty morning: powerful, deep, and mysterious. He hadn't cropped his tousled hair, the color of sun-kissed wheat, but had attempted to tame it into a short ponytail.

Such a hairstyle might be an indication of his politics. For many men, the close-cropped hair signaled their revolutionary politics, their admiration of Napoleon. Therefore, Lord Donovan could well be indicating his anti-Napoleonic, anti-revolutionary stance. Interesting. His smile broke like the sun from behind clouds.

He kissed her hand. "I'm delighted to meet you, Lady Birchfield. I briefly knew your husband. He was a magnificent statesman and will be greatly missed." Only sincerity, no pity, shone in his countenance.

"Thank you."

He continued, "I went to school with Lord Thomas and I believe he's likely to follow in his father's footsteps. He could even be prime minister someday."

"A great compliment, indeed, Lord Donovan." She smiled up at him.

The dinner bell rang and Braedon planted himself between her and Lord Donovan, offering his arm. "Shall we dine, my dear?"

Lord Corliss, a white-whiskered man standing nearby cleared his throat. "I'll say this, any old goat would be a better prime minister than that demmed Tory, Hillingham." Then he clapped Braedon on the back. "Though I don't suppose you can agree to that, can you, Braedon?" He winked. "Not if you want to keep in his daughter's good graces, that is." Then he bellowed laughter at his own joke.

"Sir, in my experience, daughters are more inclined to offer their good graces to any man the father most vehemently opposes."

# Chapter Eight

After dinner, guests flocked to the card tables in the drawing room like pigeons to a statue. Full of pheasant, lamb, fish, vegetables, baked custard, and wine. Ravenna settled with Catherine, Braedon, and Lord Corliss, at a table closest to the fireplace aglow with a low-burning fire.

Braedon sat to Ravenna's left, angled to face her, crossing one leg over the other, resting his hands on his knee. A large ruby glinted in the ring on his pinky finger. "How lucky that I won a seat beside you. Perhaps the cards will also be in my favor this evening."

"I think you ask too much of Lady Fortune, Lord Braedon." Ravenna chuckled, scanning the sideboard for wine.

"Then I must be happy with my lot." Braedon glanced in the direction of her gaze. "Allow me." He winked at her and moved to the sideboard.

Catherine shuffled and dealt out the cards, her diamonds winking with each movement.

"Braedon, I'm glad you're here this evening. I owe you a sound thrashing in Faro since you beat me and took all my money last week."

Braedon placed a glass of wine in front of Ravenna. He bowed over her shoulder, his lips close to her ear. "Your wine, milady. Ever at *your* service."

The tendrils of hair moved by his breath tickled her neck. Little goose pimples formed over her skin. He stood too close, and the room grew increasingly warmer. She snapped her cards closed. "I hope you're not trying to peek at my cards. Do sit down, or I'll think you're cheating."

Laughing, he sat and took up his cards, spreading them in his large, strong hands to study them. He turned to Catherine. "And you, my poppet, would be better off not playing me in Faro. I'll take your money again."

Catherine giggled. "Horrid man."

Ravenna caught a bit of the conversation from a nearby table. "A plague must be upon us. I'm certain of it," Lady Corliss said. "Two men of our circle dead and another so soon taken ill."

Lord Montgomery, a middle-aged man with a paunch, added, "A plague? I'd think that if there were a plague, then a great many men in our circle and their families would be ill."

Listening intently, Ravenna looked between them, considering what they were saying. *Interesting.* The gentleman had a point. Hawkestone had died not long after her own husband, and now Wolfsham, a nominee, was ill. It would seem the "plague" had a specific taste for foreign secretaries.

As if reading her mind, Lord Montgomery said, "I think something more insidious is among us, and none of this is coincidence."

The ladies in the room gasped, and the room fell into harried whispers.

"Ravenna?" Catherine prompted. "Are you going to play a card?"

Ravenna snapped to attention. "So sorry." She tossed a card in the pile.

"Oh, Ravenna," Catherine grumbled. "That was badly done."

"I don't think so," Braedon captured the pile of cards. "Her play aided me greatly."

"Sorry, Catherine. I was…distracted." She looked at the pile and at her hand as her head throbbed. "What are trumps again?"

"Hearts." Annoyance tinted Catherine's voice. She loved cards and made little room for bad playing.

Ravenna threw down a two of hearts.

Lord Corliss captured the pile with a four of hearts. "Montgomery, I believe you're either too deep in your cups or teasing the sensibilities of the ladies. Why would someone want our foreign secretaries dead?"

Montgomery surveyed his cards. "Because we are quite close to war with France." He tossed a card. "Again." He leaned back and looked at Lord Corliss. "Therefore, it's quite likely any number of folks would want to upset our balance. To start, the Americans, the Irish. The French, of course.

Spain."

Lady Corliss looked down her nose at her cards. "Why must we be at war with France again?"

Lord Donovan sipped his wine. "First, no one has declared war—"

"Yet." Braedon pulled a card from his hand, tossing it on the table.

Lord Donovan shot a hard glance at Braedon. "Let's not terrify the ladies tonight, Braedon."

Braedon scanned the room. "I think our English ladies have a stronger constitution than we give them credit for. They deserve the truth. War is imminent."

Ravenna glanced between Donovan and Braedon. "Is that true? Another war?" Too often, she'd seen English troops raid her village and press men into service, though many were so deeply impoverished, they joined willingly just to have food and some little money for their families. Too often, she'd seen groups of men marched away to never return. Yet, it was foolish to think human hearts could ever stop their lust and greed and live peacefully with others. The leaders of nations seemed the most incapable.

Lord Donovan's face reddened, and a vein appeared down the center of his forehead. His sea=green eyes grew stormy. Stretching his neck side to side as though his cravat were too tight, he cleared his throat and continued in a slow, measured way. "Napoleon is breaching the Treaty of Amiens, so we may be forced to declare."

Braedon tsked. "Let's tell Lady Birchfield the truth, Donovan. We made up all that nonsense about the Cape Colony being under French attack in order to justify our military preparations there."

Other card players stalled their play and watched the exchange as though following the volley of the ball in a game of real tennis.

Braedon continued. "We lied and claimed the French had moved against us first. Therefore, Boney is now *en garde* and advances against us. Which means *we* were the first to breach the treaty."

Lord Donovan's cheeks flushed, and knots formed in his jaw. He tapped the corner of a card against the table. "You shouldn't share confidential information."

Braedon laughed.

"You sound like a French sympathizer Braedon," said Montgomery.

"I sympathize only with the truth, sir. Which becomes more elusive each day."

"It's my understanding," Catherine said, studying her cards. "Aside from that unseemly business in the Cape, we violated the treaty because we wouldn't leave Malta. Is that not so?" She switched the positions of cards in her hand.

Lord Donovan narrowed his eyes. "How would you know such things?"

A sly smile tugged the corner of Catherine's mouth. "Darling, I'm privy to a great many things I shouldn't know."

Braedon added, "Yet, she protects those secrets like a dragon guarding her gold."

Catherine chuckled and simpered at Braedon, who reached over to tug one of her frosty curls. It bounced softly into place as she giggled at him.

Lord Donovan turned in his seat to face Catherine's profile. "You're right, in part, Lady Adair. We share the guilt. However, Malta voted for us to remain as protectors. Even they recognize England's presence in Malta is preferable to the French."

Ravenna's stomach twisted into knots. "War is the worst path to follow. Our national finances have been in dire straits for years. We've only begun to recover. Even if our motives were pure, we can't possibly afford another war with France."

"We can't afford not to." Lord Donovan rearranged the cards in his hand. "We must form an alliance. Our best hope is Russia. With their forces and funds, we might be able to frighten Napoleon into peace talks."

"Which, I wager, would be preferable with the instability caused in our own government by the deaths of the foreign secretaries." Ravenna studied her cards.

Braedon scoffed, downed the remainder of his wine, and rose to pour another glass at the sideboard. "Donovan, you're daft to think we might frighten a man bold enough to thumb his nose at the Pope and go to war with Rome. Peace is a fool's game. With our own government divided, how can we bring peace to the whole of Europe? Peace is the elusive butterfly, always flitting inches beyond our grasp."

Lady Corliss interjected, "What a bleak view. I must believe most people are good and peace-seeking."

A flash of condescension passed through his eyes. He bowed his head, and placed his hand over his heart. "One good as you, milady, will always struggle to imagine human evils."

Lord Donovan flushed, and the vein between his brows grew larger. "Aiming for peace is never a foolish task. We must have hope." He poked the tabletop for emphasis.

Braedon filled his glass. "Coddle your hope if it helps you sleep at night. We humans are perpetual hopers. But tell me, who will you get to fight your wars? Shall you continue going through the nation killing men at home because they don't want to be killed on foreign soil? Or pressing them into service against their will?"

Yarford said, "You're referring to Easton?"

"I am."

"What happened in Easton?" Ravenna asked.

Catherine plucked a card from her hand and tossed it on the pile. "Members of our navy killed three people as they attempted to press men into service."

Ravenna recalled the brutish English military that ravaged her own village, and hate swelled in her heart. She muttered. "I can well believe it." An image of Philip floated to her mind and pushed back the hatred. She didn't hate all Englishmen, but she struggled mightily to look upon Englishmen in their red uniforms.

"I don't know why you would mention that Braedon," Donovan said, staring at his cards.

Unruffled, Braedon leaned against the sideboard, swirling the wine in his glass. "Because men are tired of war and women are tired of losing their men to war. But governments never tire of war. How else are we to get men to fight if we don't force them?"

In one quick motion, Lord Donovan threw down his cards and jumped up from his seat. His voice strained with emotion. "How dare you, sir! Napoleon is bent on ruling us all. We must oppose him to protect our country, our traditions, and our honor. Everything we hold dear. Would you suggest we submit to French rule?"

"Sir, I'm certain those pressed men would defend hearth and home on home soil. But where's the honor in forcing men to fight in foreign lands and then killing them if they refuse?"

Lord Donovan, flush with anger, continued. "You've offended the honor of every man who works for the glory and protection of England."

Ravenna interjected, "Which will be all for naught if our foreign secretaries continue to die and our government is thrown out of balance and unable to negotiate with Napoleon or understand how to maneuver against French invasion."

Catherine stood, "Ladies and gentlemen, I believe it's time to put the political talk to rest. Let's enjoy each other's company with a little wine and cards and leave Napoleon in the capable hands of our parliament."

Braedon bowed. "My apologies, dear madam. I know how you cherish your gaming."

Donovan bowed, too. "My apologies, Lady Catherine."

"Now," Catherine beamed and clapped her hands together. "Shall we play?"

The rest of the evening passed smoothly and relatively inexpensively since Ravenna lost only twenty pounds compared to Catherine's hundred into Braedon's hands.

Arriving at Gordon House in the wee hours of the morning, Ravenna entered a quiet home. A low fire burned in her room. She lit a candle on the table by her bed, where a letter greeted her. After undressing, she sat on the bed and took up the letter. It was addressed to her with no return address and sealed with blank, green wax. The writing was unfamiliar, pointy, and sharp like knives.

Odd. She opened the letter to find only a blank page. There were no words. Not even a drop of ink. On its face, this single page seemed innocuous. Yet, someone had taken the trouble to address the page to her. Someone wouldn't go through all the trouble of addressing and posting a letter without including a message unless…her heart vaulted against her chest. The message was the paper itself. The message being that someone unknown to her knew her and where she lived. Her skin prickled, and icy terror trickled down her spine. The Irish Unity. They'd found her.

# Chapter Nine

Most of the night, Ravenna listened to every noise in the house, fearful The Unity was coming to collect their vengeance for her betrayal. She'd spent the first year of her marriage always looking over her shoulder, even after Hawkestone had sent troops to quash the rebellion. Because, in order to make amends with Hawkestone over stealing secrets, and save her treasonous hide from execution, she betrayed what she knew about the Franco-Irish plans to stage an invasion of England from Ireland's shores.

Thorns and razors of fear and guilt entwined over her heart, from which she'd never find freedom. She'd married an Englishman. Though anti-loyalist, and rebellious to the English Crown, they were still her people. But she'd loved Philip, heels over head, and being married to him had given her comfort, security, and provided her with a sense of safety. Under the wing of his political power, she'd allowed herself to believe herself protected from The Unity. Yet, like a nest of scorpions, the Unity always remained in the darkest corners of her mind—quiet, but ever present, waiting to strike. Now she was a widow, no longer under Philip's protection, and vulnerable to their attacks.

After a night of fitful sleep, Ravenna rose early to prepare for a visit to Hawkestone's lover, Julia Pence, to ask a few questions of her.

Hart brought her breakfast of tea and currant scones. "Mornin', milady."

"Good morning, Hart. Have you read the papers yet this morning?" Ravenna wrapped herself in a dressing gown. "Have they mentioned Hawkestone?"

"They have. I brought you the papers, assuming you'd want to see them. Most are saying he committed suicide." Hart poured the tea.

"Suicide?" Ravenna grabbed up a newspaper. "Such egregious lies! Such slander! Lady Violette will be in fits. Do you know what this will mean for her?"

"I do, and I'm sorry for it." Hart opened the curtains to let in the dull morning light. "I hope things will be set right soon. I'll get your clothes." She left the room.

Ravenna flopped into a chair at the table by the window, reading the lies in the news article, praying silently that her name wouldn't be mentioned. She sipped her tea and nibbled on her scone.

The morning papers were rife with stories of Hawkestone's death. Though they hadn't mentioned he'd died in Ravenna's parlor, two of the three papers claimed he'd committed suicide, while one intimated something more nefarious lurked. The writer mentioned that Bow Street was involved in discovering the truth. Once the other papers picked that up, it would fly through London, and the murderer, knowing he was being hunted, might flee. It was imperative that she discovered Hawkestone's murderer—and before Mr. Chadwick.

After breakfast, she poured cool water into the washstand bowl, removed her clothes, quickly washed, and splashed rose water on her skin while recent events rolled through her mind. Though she was certain the recent deaths were politically motivated, she needed to exclude Julia beyond doubt. After all, it was possible she'd made the rounds among the society men. She wouldn't have been the first chorus girl to do so. She also needed to figure out who'd sent that letter to her. Though she suspected the letter came from The Unity, she remained hopeful that it wasn't or that someone had seen who'd delivered it.

Hart entered with Ravenna's clothes, humming Barbara Allen. "Ready to dress, milady?"

"Yes." Ravenna slipped into her petticoat. "I received a letter last night. Did you happen to see who delivered it?"

"I didn't. Why?"

Ravenna stepped away, drew the letter from her bedside table, and handed it to Hart.

She sat on a stool to roll her black stockings over her legs and tie the blue garters—a spot of secret color which made her happy.

Hart opened the letter, frowning. "There's nothing here." She flipped the paper. "Except your address. How strange. Who do you think sent it?"

"I think it's The Unity."

Hart's clear brown eyes flinted and locked with Ravenna's. "I see. It's meant to inform you they're aware of your location." She set the letter aside and helped lower a black muslin dress over Ravenna's head.

"Exactly my thoughts."

"Perhaps Banks can tell you who delivered the letter?" Hart's fingers flew over the buttons on the back of the dress.

Ravenna sat at her vanity so Hart could work her hair magic. "I'll ask him before I leave."

They talked of the soirée and the lies about Hawkestone in the news while Hart wound Ravenna's black locks into braids and ringlets and pinned the mass into a style reminiscent of the ancient Greeks and Romans.

When Hart had finished, Ravenna glanced at her in the mirror. "Thank you, Hart. Please have a hackney ordered. I don't want anyone to recognize my carriage when I pay a visit to an acquaintance of Lord Hawkestone."

Hart's eyes flashed with knowing as she gathered up the cast-off clothes and stepped from the room.

While she waited for the hackney to be announced, Ravenna finished dressing. She sat at her writing desk to dash off a letter to the Penitent House vicar to inform him that she was going to propose the two-deep chaff mattresses to Lady Braxton, who wanted the cheaper straw mattresses.

When the hackney was announced, Ravenna grabbed her black kid gloves, reticule, and fan, rushed downstairs with her letter to the vicar, and handed it to Banks. "Please post this letter for me." She slid her hands into the gloves. "And, bye the bye, Banks, did you see who delivered the letter here last night while I was at Lady Adair's?"

"Unfortunately, no. The scullery brought it to me. When I asked her who left it, she claimed she didn't see anyone, that it had been left in the kitchen door."

Unsettled, Ravenna slipped the strings of her reticule and fan over her hand. "Thank you, Banks." She paused, considering how to warn him about The Unity without alarming him—especially since she wasn't certain of their involvement. "I need the staff to be aware of strangers lingering around our house and report them to us immediately."

He squinted. "Should we be concerned about something, ma'am?"

She bit her bottom lip. "I can't be certain. So, I'd like us all to be careful."

"I'll inform the staff, ma'am." He opened the door for her.

Ravenna descended the steps to the street and stepped through the gate. A footman stood at the ready to hand her into the hackney.

A familiar male voice called out to her.

*Braedon.* Her breath caught. "Lord Braedon, what a surprise." Handsome was too weak a word to describe him. Beautiful didn't quite suit, either. Sublime. That was a proper word to describe his taut, statuesque form in buff pantaloons and an olive coat beneath his black great coat and beaver skin top hat.

He squinted against the sun. "A pleasant one, I hope?"

"Of course." She smiled up at him, a warmth much like the sun spreading through her.

He nodded at the vehicle. "A hackney? Has your carriage broken an axle? Or..." He lowered his voice. "Are you en route to an assignation?" His frosted blue eyes lit with amusement.

"You would think that. My carriage is intact, thank you. I simply need..." She glanced at her footman and whispered, "Anonymity."

"I was right. It *is* an assignation."

"Heavens, Braedon, you have a lurid, and decidedly narrow, imagination. I am engaged in no such thing. I have *business* of a personal nature."

"Wonderful. Then you won't mind if I go with you." Ignoring rules of etiquette, he jumped up into the hackney before she could stop him. "Where are we going?"

She stomped her foot and pointed at the ground with her closed fan.

"Leave the carriage at once." She glanced at her footman. "Or I'll have Cruthers remove you."

The footman blanched and took a step back.

Braedon tipped his head and smiled at him. "I think Cruthers won't mind."

A deep blush crossed the footman's pox-scarred face as he stared at his boots.

He patted the seat beside him and reached out his hand to her. "Darling, you're creating a scene. Best come along." He scooted toward the door and extended his hand to help her inside.

Ravenna balled her fists. "Driver, take me to the Drury Theater." Ignoring Braedon's extended hand, she accepted Cruther's assistance into the carriage, muttering to herself, "Odious man." She planted herself in the furthest corner from Braedon. "I suppose you're delighted with yourself."

"I am. I do enjoy the theater. However, there aren't any shows this time of day, so why are we going there?"

The carriage lurched forward. "*We* aren't going anywhere. *I'm* going."

"That doesn't seem true, given that I'm sitting right here."

"You know what I mean." She stared out the window, picking at the tip of her gloved finger. Shop windows and row houses rolled by. Drivers cursed as they jockeyed for position. Vendors' voices competed as they hawked their wares.

"Ah, I've vexed you. Terribly sorry, my little raven. But I do love a good mystery, and I'm eager to discover why a widow would want to visit the theater alone in a hackney in broad daylight. Let's see. She claims it's not an assignation. I'll accept that. So, it must be…" He thought for a moment. "Perhaps she misses her acting days and longs to take the stage again. Are you hoping to get a part in a play? Will you do a farce? A tragedy?"

She laced her fingers together and planted them in her lap. "Oh, do be quiet, Braedon. It's beyond the pale that you inserted yourself most inconveniently into my affairs."

"You might need my assistance."

Her annoyance warred with her attraction to him. "I assure you, I do not."

"What if some blackguard decided to take advantage of you? I think your

59

footman Cruthers will prove ineffective whereas I can protect you."

She thought of the little blade hiding in the guard of her black lace fan. "I'm not concerned."

He chuckled, "I think I shall enjoy our little adventure. I look forward to getting at the heart of your mystery."

The Drury Theater loomed, a white stone building smudged with soot. Ravenna and Braedon bypassed the stone-arched entries and Doric columns, turning the corner to the backstage entry in the alley.

A long, lean actor in a thin muslin shirt and Shakespearean balloon pants lounged near the door, speaking intimately with another actor similarly dressed. Their white, bony chests peeked through the loose necks of their shirts. They stood shoulder to shoulder and eyed her like a pair of cats as she climbed the stairs.

"Pardon me," she said to the one with a freckled face. "I'm looking for Miss Julia Pence. Do you know her?"

He looked between her and Braedon and flashed a snaggle-toothed smile. "Maybe I do, maybe I don't."

Braedon pulled a small velvet pouch out of an inner pocket. He opened it. "I wager these will help you recall." He held up a couple of shillings.

The man snatched the coins. His hands were red and chapped with dirty fingernails. "She's one of the chorus. Dark hair, wild in the eyes."

"And a mouth like a rabbit," his friend with the large Adam's apple added, sticking his top lip out over the bottom.

The two men sniggered, nudging each other.

Thanking them, Ravenna and Braedon entered the building. Standing just inside the door, she blinked to adjust her eyes to the dim backstage area. Stagehands clustered around the ropes and pulleys, looking and pointing up in technical discussion.

Actors had a hierarchy, easily discerned by the nearness of the dressing rooms to the stage. The lowest of all, the chorus girls and pantomimes, shared the room closest to the alley door. Ravenna peeked inside. Empty. The pianoforte and violins whining in the distance indicated the cast must be on stage rehearsing. The next room brimmed with secondary actors chatting, smoking, drinking, and toying with vocal scales or reciting lines. The scent of cigars and colognes competed with the chalk powder and burnt cork used for makeup and the linseed oil used in set paint.

Closest to the stage were the principal actress's room, with a solitary woman and her assistant working on a costume, and the empty room of the principal actor. From the stage, piano and violin notes frolicked for the dancers in rehearsal. Carpenters shouted and hammered out an offbeat staccato rhythm as they built scene displays.

This was the mad spectacle of the theater the audience never witnessed, the pulse and lifeblood, and the aspect, quite frankly, Ravenna had enjoyed most in her acting days. For a brief moment, a longing to return to the stage tickled at her ribs and feet. Braedon followed at her elbow, hands clasped behind his back. He gazed at the scene with fascination, as if examining the curiosities at the Exeter Exchange.

Ravenna hovered near the velvet curtain, searching the chorus dancers for Julia Pence, but she didn't recognize anyone who matched the description the men outside had given her.

When the rehearsal ended, and the chorus girls trailed off the stage in a cacophony of chatter and laughter, Ravenna tapped one on the shoulder as she passed. "Pardon me."

The blonde girl jumped back. "Who are you?" She glanced nervously between Ravenna and Braedon, ready to flee.

"I'm looking for Julia Pence. Is she here?"

The girl relaxed, scratching her leg. "No'm. She ain't." Her bones jutted under her pale skin.

"Where may I find her?"

When she shrugged, the neck of her dress slipped off her shoulder. She tugged it back into place. "Not sure. Ain't seen her in days." She waved Ravenna closer. "I think the director found out about her being in the family way, and he dismissed her from the chorus."

"Do you know that for certain?"

"No, but that girl there"—she motioned with her sharp chin to a girl laughing with a group in the corner—"showed up not long ago, and I ain't seen Julia since. A shame, too, because that girl lollops around the stage like a drunken monkey." She snorted. "She ain't got none of Julia's grace."

"Where does Julia live? I must speak with her."

The girl, like any savvy street urchin, eyed Ravenna and Braedon, scrutinizing their clothes, their manner of bearing, and speech—all markers of wealth and station. She placed her hands on the small of her back, shifted her weight to one hip, and tipped her head. "Why would the likes of you want to know where Julia lives?" Her eyes glittered with malicious delight. "She steal your silver spoons or something?"

The truth was none of this chit's business, and Ravenna had dealt with too many scheming girls like this one in her time in the theater. "I'm her sister. We've come to carry her home," she lied.

The girl pursed her lips in disbelief. "She never said nothing about a sister to me."

"Have you told all the details of your life to any of these girls?"

The girl considered for a moment. "No."

Taking a lesson from Braedon, Ravenna dug around in her reticule, pulled out a shilling, and held it up. "This is yours if you tell me where I can find Julia."

"She's in a little alley off Tavistock Street, in a white flat at the end of the alley. She rents from Mrs. Lope. It's the one with green shutters."

She handed the girl the shilling. The girl skittered off, her short dress and ribbons flouncing with her skipping steps.

"Surely, you're not going to Mrs. Lope's."

"I am. I need to speak to Julia Pence." She smiled up at him, suppressing laughter. "We can take the coach if you're afraid to walk."

# Chapter Ten

They left the carriage sitting on Tavistock Street near the mouth of the dead-end alley. It was a dark slum packed with the most hopeless of humanity. The air reeked of excrement, smoke, and rotten food.

Ravenna stepped over a homeless drunk passed out in his own urine and vomit. Sallow and sodden men and women with gaunt faces and purple bags under their eyes stumbled out of a gaming hell full of gin, commonly referred to as the blue demon for the havoc it wreaked on lives and families.

"Are you sure you want to do this?" Braedon positioned himself slightly in front of her. "This is no place for a lady."

"I must."

Grabbing Braedon's sleeve to steady herself, she made the widest arc possible around a man urinating against a smoke-blackened wall, only to find herself face to face with a half-clothed woman beckoning Braedon. Dirty children crouched in doorways scratching flea bites with dirtier fingernails. Starving dogs and cats rooted through the rubbish in the street for a scrap of food. She'd heard the Mint out near London Bridge was worse than this, though she couldn't imagine how.

Guarded, Braedon scrutinized their environs. Tension emanated from him. "I'm glad I came with you. I'd hate to think of you wandering this treacherous slum alone. This is lunacy."

She clutched her fan tighter and chuckled nervously, "I confess, I'm glad, too."

He glanced over his shoulder at her, a surprise sparking in his eye before fading to platonic warmth.

As they neared the end of the alley, Ravenna spotted the white flat with green shutters.

She knocked on the door of the ramshackle structure, ignoring the leers and jests of the drunks and prostitutes nearby. Children and babies screamed and cried within.

A woman shouted from inside. "Get the bloody door, you vermin." She heard a thud, and then the door rattled and creaked open.

"Who are you?" The child could not be more than seven years old. Dirt, old cuts, and bruises marred her face.

Ravenna smiled down at the child. "I'm looking for Miss Julia Pence. Is she here?"

The child shrugged, indicating she didn't know.

"Who is it?" The woman's voice called from inside.

The child shouted over her shoulder. "Some lady and a gent."

A meaty woman came grunting to the door. She had a pinched rodent face, dark beady eyes, and a thin, pointed nose. Gray-streaked black curls frizzed from under her mobcap. Her rouged face pulled into a smile, revealing yellowed, gnarled teeth. Her ponderous breasts nearly fell out of her bodice.

"Hello, are you Mrs. Lope?"

"Yeah." She raked her bloodshot eyes over Ravenna and Braedon, lingering over him. "I suppose you're looking for a room?" She leered, her breath reeking of gin.

"No," Ravenna said, blushing at the insinuation. "I'm looking for Julia Pence. Is she here?"

Mrs. Lope scratched her breast. "Nope. Ain't seen that little wasp in days."

Ravenna peeked over Mrs. Lope's shoulder into the house. In the dim light provided by the one small window and open door, she counted two other women and at least seven children, ranging from adolescents to babes, all stuffed into one room. The Spartan accommodations consisted of a small bed, a rickety table, a small cabinet, and a dead fireplace with only a few twigs and newspapers for burning on the hearth.

Mrs. Lope continued, "She's probably lying about with some new gent since her precious lord died."

"You heard of his death?" Ravenna was surprised.

"Oh, yeah. She came in drunk and crying, then broke a chair against my wall. Which she ain't paid for yet."

A child screamed in the background.

Mrs. Lope added, "Then she packed up her things, which weren't much, and ran out. Ain't seen her since."

If true, this description painted Julia as an erratic and disordered woman. It was unusual for a penniless and pregnant woman to give up her lodgings and cast herself on the street. She mustn't be in her right mind. "Did she ever talk to you about the man she was—"

"Tupping?"

"Gently, Mrs. Lope," Braedon warned.

Mrs. Lope guffawed, her breasts jiggling like gelatin.

Unruffled, Ravenna asked, "At any rate, did she ever talk of him?"

She used a pinky nail to pick something out of her teeth. "Some. Might be she loved him, but he was married to a fine lady and all, so he wouldn't love the likes of Julia." She snorted a laugh.

Ravenna bristled. She'd been "the likes of Julia" at one time. Granted, she hadn't been as poor as Julia because she had an aunt who gave her a place to stay. And she'd had the great fortune of being cast in plays rather than being an anonymous chorus line dancer. She shuddered to think how close she'd been to living the life of a Mrs. Lope. She pushed the thought away. "I heard she caused a scene at the theater one night in front of him and his wife. Do you know anything about that?"

She pursed her lips and thought. "Not too long ago, she came home drunk and crying. Going on and on about loving some gent and thinking he'd be idiot enough to marry her as she was in the family way. I called her a stupid fool."

"Do you think she was upset enough to hurt someone?"

She shrugged. "Might be. She's wild, that one."

"Did she ever say anything to that end?"

Mrs. Lope rubbed her nose vigorously with the back of her hand. "Well, folks who want to kill other folks don't exactly go around talking about it, do they?" She heaved a sigh of exasperation, signaling her desire to be done with this nonsense.

Clearly, Ravenna wouldn't get any further with Mrs. Lope. "If she comes back, will you tell her that Lady Birchfield, a friend of her gent, is looking for her? She can find me at Gordon House in Curzon Street. Or, if you happen to hear of her whereabouts, or remember any important information, will you send word to me?"

Mrs. Lope snorted. "Yeah."

Ravenna pulled a calling card and three shillings from her reticule and handed them to Mrs. Lope, hoping, but doubting, that some of the money might make it to the children within the hovel.

Mrs. Lope smelled the calling card. "Cor, it even smells rich." She looked down her nose at Ravenna. "I need to get me a fancy man, too." She raked her eyes over Braedon. "I reckon you'll do, milor'." She broke into a wheezing cackle.

The muscles in Braedon's jaw tightened, and he turned his back on her, his eyes scanning the street.

Ravenna ignored Mrs. Lope's attempts to draw out Braedon. "You'll get a guinea more if you find Julia and bring her to me."

Ravenna and Braedon turned away and had already passed several homes when they heard Mrs. Lope shout, "Wait!"

They turned. She waved at them and waddled toward them, carrying her considerable bulk over puddles and muck. She panted. "I almost forgot. The last time I saw her, when she was all in a rage, I remember her screaming, 'I wish we were all dead. Her. Me. Him. The whole stinking lot of us.'"

Ravenna and Braedon exchanged a concerned glance.

"What if she threw herself in the Thames and ain't alive no more? How'm I to get my guinea then?"

"If you can prove Julia is dead, I'll still pay you."

Ravenna and Braedon resumed picking their way through the filth toward the carriage.

Ravenna shouted up to the driver. "Please take us to Hawkestone House in St. James' Square."

Braedon waited until they were settled into the carriage before speaking. "What an interesting afternoon. I'm glad I joined you instead of going to my club to argue politics and poetry. But I do wonder, my little raven, why *you'd* be interested in a chorus girl from the slums? Is it a work of charity?"

"Yes," Ravenna lied, looking out the window and wishing he'd be quiet so she could think straight. Logic dictated that Julia Pence was a viable suspect in Hawkestone's murder. She'd certainly had motive. Both Lady Hawkestone and Mrs. Lope's stories agreed that Julia had been hysterical about being abandoned in her pregnancy. Further, based on Mrs. Lope's information, Julia had wished them all dead. And poison was commonly considered a woman's weapon. It was possible that Hawkestone's death, Philip's death, and Wolfsham's illness were all coincidence.

Braedon interrupted her reverie. "I think there's more to this story. Perhaps she's connected to Birchfield, the elder? No, the younger." He paused, thinking. His eyes grew wide. "Or Hawkestone."

She lifted a brow, shooting him a side glance, but refused to answer.

He looked askance. "I bet this is somehow related to him. Hawkestone loved theater girls. But you knew that, didn't you?" His eyes glittered impishly.

She stared out the window, refusing to answer.

"Very well. Keep your secrets, my little raven. I'm particularly good at ferreting out what I want to know. I'm a patient man."

Ravenna and Braedon descended from the carriage in front of Hawkestone House as Mr. Chadwick left the house and stepped through the gate. He stopped, only the light in his eyes betraying his surprise. He touched the rim of his hat. "Good afternoon, Lady Birchfield."

Ravenna surveyed him coolly as she fought to suppress the snarl edging her lip when she greeted him. "Mr. Chadwick."

"Interesting that you and I should meet here at Hawkestone House."

Her spine grew rigid. "Is it a crime to visit a friend in mourning?" She held out her hands. "If so, shackle me and carry me off to Newgate."

"That won't be necessary." A faint smile played on his lips. "Yet." He touched the brim of his hat again. He spared a sharp glance for Braedon, then walked away, whistling.

Braedon watched him leave. "Who was that? And why should you be arrested?"

Ravenna sighed and pushed through the gate to the front door. Perhaps she should tell Braedon what's going on. He might be able to offer some insight. Or perhaps he'd heard something at one of his gentlemen's clubs or at a cockfight that would help discover who killed Hawkestone. The footman tapped the brass knocker against the door. She needed to think about it more.

Braedon said, "You won't tell me?"

"Shh. This is not the place or time." She cut her eyes at the footman's back. "I need only a moment with Lady Hawkestone, then we'll leave."

The wind had picked up, and dark clouds rolled overhead. The air smelled of impending rain. The door opened, stopping Braedon from speaking, and entered the foyer. Before Ravenna could tell Braedon she needed a private conversation with Lady Violette, the lady herself exited the drawing room in a black dress and immediately invited them in.

"Welcome, Lady Birchfield, Lord Braedon. It's very good to see you." Her nose was red, and her eyes puffy. "Please, do come in. I'll ring for tea."

Ravenna lifted a hand. "No, please don't trouble yourself. We won't stay long."

Lady Violette led them to the formal drawing room and shut the door. She strode to a chair by the cold fireplace as Braedon and Ravenna occupied the sofa. "This day has been a waking nightmare. Have you seen the horrible slanders in the papers this morning?" She swept her arms through the air. "Suicide?" Her voice rose an octave, indicating a near-frenzied state. "It's too much to be born. Do you understand what that means?"

"I do," Ravenna picked at the finger of her glove.

"Burying him upside down at a crossroads?" Lady Violette's voice broke. "With a stake in his heart? The Crown taking his money and estates? Would they dare? Where would I go? What would I do? Would I be cast to the streets to make my own way?" Her wide eyes flashed with hysteria, and her curls shook with her anger and fear. She perched on the edge of a chair, wringing her lace handkerchief.

"I'm certain Hawkestone would never have killed himself. I'll contact the papers myself, if you'd like." Braedon added. "I'll have them retract that horrible story."

"If you think it'd help? But what shall I do about his burial? Is he to have such a dishonorable end?" Dark bags hung heavy under her bloodshot eyes.

"You needn't worry about that." Braedon's signet ring winked from his pinky. "Who's handling his affairs?"

"His brother-in-law, Lord Derbish. He says he should be buried in Westminster Abbey according to his office, but with these reports…"

"And so he shall," Braedon said calmly. "I'll see to it myself."

"You are very good, sir." She dabbed her eyes and wiped her nose.

"Think nothing of it." He demurred. "It would be my honor to assist you."

Ravenna blinked, surprised. Braedon exhibiting modesty? She never thought she'd see the day.

"You're too kind, Lord Braedon." Lady Violette inhaled a shaky breath, and her shoulders seemed to relax away from her ears. "I suppose you met that dreadful Mr. Chadwick just now? He's a beast. Can you believe he came here and threatened to arrest me?"

"Whatever for?" Ravenna leaned on the sofa arm.

"He thinks you or I killed Hawkestone. He even insinuated that we worked together to kill him."

"Indeed?" Braedon said, both surprise and humor in his voice. "How interesting."

Ravenna flushed, clutching her fan. She cut her eyes at him. "It is *not* interesting in the least."

"How could he possibly think that either of us would do such a hideous thing?" Fresh tears flooded Lady Violette's eyes. "The gall!" She balled her handkerchief in a tight fist.

"What did he say?" Ravenna said.

She looked up at the ceiling, gathering her thoughts. "He asked me humiliating questions about my relationship with my husband, which I refused to answer. And he asked me about my husband's relationship with you and wanted to know why he was at your house." She shuddered with buttoned-up rage, her red nostrils flaring. "Of course, I told him you were only friends."

Braedon asked Lady Violette, "Why would he think that you killed him?"

"Oh," she dabbed at her nose. "Something about the surgeon who performed the autopsy thinks he was poisoned. He thinks I killed him out of jealousy over his affairs."

"How did he find out about Hawkestone's, uh, activities?" Ravenna asked. "I don't know."

Braedon said, "With all due respect, Lady Hawkestone, it was common knowledge. It would've been rather easy for this Chadwick fellow to find out that information."

Lady Violette shook her head and looked down at her hands as she ran the handkerchief through her fingers. "So humiliating. I won't be able to show my face in public for years."

"Nonsense," Ravenna reached over to her arm. "You have nothing to fear or to be ashamed of."

"It gets worse," Lady Violette turned in her seat to face Ravenna. "I'm being asked to appear in front of the coroner and the magistrate, as if I'm some common criminal." She lay her hand over her heart. "They aim to prove I killed my own husband."

"Oh, heavens…" Ravenna glanced at Braedon. "Can they do that?"

He shrugged a shoulder, wincing. "I fear they can. It's an investigation."

"Is there nothing to be done? If I go before the magistrate, the papers will go wild with outlandish stories. My reputation will be ruined forever."

Braedon scooted forward in his seat. "Perhaps I may be of some service. Would you talk to the magistrate and coroner if I could convince them to come here and keep this private without the reporters?"

"Is there not a way to avoid the interview entirely?"

"I shouldn't attempt it. Doing so may give the appearance of guilt."

70

She pressed her fingertips to her temples and closed her eyes. She sat still for a moment, then sighed. "Very well." She looked at Ravenna pointedly. "We must make haste."

Ravenna caught her meaning. "I understand." She rushed ahead. "If I may have a private word with you?"

Both women looked at Braedon. "Of course." He stood and bowed. "Lady Birchfield, I'll wait in the foyer for you."

When he had exited the room, Ravenna said, "I have only a moment to tell you that I attempted to speak with Julia Pence on your behalf today, but haven't yet been able to locate her. I'm hoping she will receive the word that I'm looking for her. Also, Lord Wolfsham has now fallen ill."

"Oh, dear. When? How long?"

"I heard it last night at Lady Adair's soirée. I don't know how long. But it's enough to make me suspect that Hawkestone's death may be politically motivated. I think my own husband may have been caught up in all this, too."

"I'm so sorry, dear."

"This Mr. Chadwick sniffing around has certainly inspired me to get to the bottom of this as soon as possible. I have my reasons for him *not* solving this matter. If there's any way at all that you can delay his work, that would be most helpful to me."

"I don't want to lie to him."

"Of course. I wouldn't want you to do that—"

"I'll try to avoid him as much as possible until you get some answers."

"I couldn't ask for more."

# Chapter Eleven

Ravenna and Braedon returned to the carriage. As soon as the door closed, Braedon frowned at her and crossed his arms over his chest. "I have questions."

A stone dropped into her stomach, and she eyed him like a cornered animal. She didn't want to answer questions. However, if she didn't answer his questions, he might go nosing around and uncover more information. It might be best to placate him.

"Chadwick seemed to think you were complicit in something. Why?"

"Because Hawkestone died in my parlor."

"And he thinks you might've had a hand in it?"

She lifted a shoulder. "It would seem so." She adjusted her bonnet.

"Why?" His sharp wolf eyes narrowed.

Irritation scratched at her chest. "I don't know," she snipped and looked out the window to watch a gent and lady pass by in a springy phaeton. She could feel his eyes stare.

He added, "I'm also curious...when Lady Violette asked you to make haste, what did she mean?"

The carriage rocked gently. She touched her eyebrow and drew in a deep breath to soothe her sparking nerves. "I'm not at liberty to share that information." She gazed at him steadily.

He paused, puzzled. "I imagine your haste concerns the visit we paid to that slum today."

A tense bubble of silence expanded between them. She dared to glance at him. He was staring at her as if he could pick apart the threads of her mind.

"You're attempting to find his murderer aren't you?"

Like a fox trapped in a hole surrounded by hounds, there was no out. "You can tell no one."

"Why are you interfering in this?"

"I'm not interfering. Lady Violette asked me to help."

"Why you?"

Thank heavens the carriage rolled to a stop. She jumped at the door, but Braedon grabbed her by her skirt and pulled her back. She stumbled and fell backward against his solid body. His cologne, spicy and sweet, reached for her, and she fought the temptation to relax against him.

She elbowed him in the rib. "Let go of me, you vile...*rascal.*"

He laughed and released her. She shifted to sit on the seat beside him and slapped his arms with her folded fan. "How *dare* you manhandle me?"

Still laughing, he grabbed her wrists and held her. "Stop it." When Ravenna stilled, he asked, "Why does Lady Violette want you to investigate her husband's murder?"

The time for placating him was finished. Panting, overheated, ready to claw his eyes out, she hissed, "This is none of *your* concern."

She opened the door on the red-faced and baffled footman, who pretended he hadn't heard or seen anything.

Braedon scooted toward her, taking her hand. "I can help you."

Jerking her hand from his and ignoring the footman's offer of assistance, she jumped to the ground, and spun. "I don't require your help, and I don't want it." She ran toward the house.

He called after her, "I'll let you know if I secure that meeting."

Ravenna rushed to change into her fencing kit and met her instructor, Mr. Norris, in the ballroom. Still seething at Braedon's interference, she lunged and cut the air wildly to attack her opponent. Mr. Norris deftly avoided her and parried her every advance.

"If this were a real battle, you'd be dead now. Do focus, milady," Mr. Norris sliced his foil through the air, causing it to whistle. *"En garde."* He planted his stance—left arm up, sword arm leveled at her. His linen shirt bloused around his thin frame. He shouted, *"Allez,"* and lunged at her.

Over and over, he parried and whacked her arm with his foil when her attention wandered. "That is nothing to the pain of being run through, milady. Do focus."

Rain began battering the windows, blurring the exterior world. Focus eluded her. Braedon knew of her involvement in the investigation, and he was going to keep pressing for answers. Chadwick, the coroner, and the magistrate loomed on the horizon like a storm cloud. They'd question Lady Violette, then they'd come for Ravenna. She'd tried to speak to Julia, but she was absent, and a girl like Julia could disappear forever among the million faces on the streets of London. Now, she could only wait for the girl to appear, unless there was someone else she could speak with. But whom?

"Ha!" Mr. Norris shouted as he delivered a whack to her upper arm.

She sucked in her breath. This was proving to be a painful lesson. Rubbing the tender spot above her elbow where another bruise would soon bloom, she circled back to claim her stance. A sense of duty pressed on her. Who else would want to kill Hawkestone? Aside from his wife or mistress, the obvious choice would be a political rival. Lord Wolfsham was in line to be nominated, but he was ill. And he was such a good man, she could never believe he'd murder a political rival. She still hadn't met with her stepson, Thomas. He hadn't responded to her note. Perhaps she should visit Pelham House again. Maybe he could provide some information about Hawkestone's enemies.

When the lesson drew to a close, she removed her mask. Her hair stuck to the sweat on her forehead. Her skin stung in various places where Mr. Norris had corrected her with his foil. She sighed, angry with herself for making the same stupid mistakes over and over. Frustrated, she whipped her foil through the air, then dumped the blade and the mask into a nearby chair. "I apologize, Mr. Norris. I tried, but concentration eluded me."

His brown whiskers hid his lips, but the smile flourished in his blue eyes. "Obviously, milady. That's why I bested you at every turn. There are good days and bad. Next time will be better. Win or lose, it all begins and ends here." He tapped his temple.

"Yes. I'll remember that for our next lesson." She forced a weak smile. "I'll see you out."

She stood at the door watching him pass through the gate. The rain had stopped as quickly as it'd come. Water dripped from the leaves and rooftops and trickled from the gutters. Carriages and horses splashed through the puddles in the streets. A figure stood across the road, hands in his pockets and hat pulled low. The collar of the great coat hid his face. He was watching her house. She was certain of it. A chill prickled her skin. Who was he? One of Mr. Chadwick's men? One of the Unity? She didn't like either choice. Ravenna jumped back, closed, and locked the door. She ran to the drawing room and peeked through the curtains. The man walked away, but her chill continued.

She rubbed her arms, tossed back a dram of port, then dove into practicing various fencing maneuvers until sweat dampened her back and trickled from her hairline near her ears. A knock sounded at the front door, but she paid little heed until Banks announced Lord Braedon.

She stared at Banks, slowly gathering the meaning of his words. Braedon was paying a visit to her? The man nettled her like a fly at a picnic.

Banks looked her over. "Perhaps I should tell him you're out, milady."

She glanced at the clock. She needed to prepare for dinner at any rate. She nearly asked Banks to send Braedon away, then drew back. Perhaps he'd come to tell her that he'd managed to secure the promises he'd made to Lady Violette. Her curiosity overcame her. "No, send him in. Please." As Banks left the room, Ravenna turned, unbuttoned her jacket, and flapped the sides to cool herself. She threw open the casement and stood at the window, letting the cool air wash over her. Her chignon had fallen from the activity, so she unpinned it and ran her fingers through her hair to loosen it.

"Lady Birchfield." Braedon's mellow tenor stroked her name.

She dropped her hair and turned.

He placed his hand on his heart and bowed. "Few things in life have the power to render me so thoroughly astonished and charmed, but you have managed it."

75

A warm spot emerged in the center of Ravenna's ribs just beneath her breasts, and it crept upward toward her cheeks. His enduring gaze made her all too aware that the breeches she wore exposed every line of her figure. Most female fencers wore skirts, but she enjoyed wearing pantaloons. She averted her gaze and turned to the sideboard for a drink. "Would you like some wine?"

"Please. Whatever you're drinking." He picked up the fencing foil and examined it, running his finger down the fine blade. "You'll pardon my surprise. Usually the women I call on are at their pianoforte."

She chuckled. "Yes, I imagine a woman doing anything more daring than embroidering a pillow tasks your imagination." She poured two glasses of port. "However, I believe you're attempting to provoke me."

"Not at all." He laughed aloud. "I confess, I prefer the company of an unconventional woman, provided she isn't also tedious or stupid." He gathered a couple of nearby accent chairs, arranging them by the window that opened over the gardens, a stretch of ground, a stone wall, and the stables.

Ravenna chuckled, handing him a glass of port as she sat in one of the chairs, stretching out her legs and crossing them at the ankles. "To what do I owe the pleasure of this visit?" A breeze swept across the room, billowing the curtains and cooling her sweaty face. The sky remained gray, but less ominous.

He sipped his wine and drew back, surprised. "Port?"

"I prefer it."

His lips shifted into a sly smile. "Delightful." He gazed at her with a blend of amusement and desire. "How did you become interested in fencing? It's not exactly a feminine pursuit."

"True. I thought it might be useful in the event I needed to protect myself."

"A pistol would serve you better and requires less skill."

"I like the activity of fencing. It's like dancing."

"A dangerous dance for a lady. What sort of enemies could a lady such as yourself have to compel you toward the martial arts?"

She thought of the man who'd been watching her house, and another chill trickled over her. "One never knows when an enemy will appear. It's best to be prepared."

"Do you make the sort of enemies that need killing?" The amusement fell into gravity. She averted her gaze to the gardens and drank her wine. A bristling silence filled the room. His cologne was heady, warm, enticing. And thoroughly distracting. Though a large part of her was still annoyed with Braedon for inserting himself into her investigation, a smaller but louder part hoped he would say, "Yes, Ravenna, you. You are on my mind," or some such romantic thing one read in novels. She laughed inwardly at herself. It would be foolish to allow such romantic notions to cloud her better judgment. And, her guilt reminded her, she was still a widow and owed her devotion to Philip. Besides, Braedon was not the best sort of man for her—even if she were inclined to—

He interrupted her thoughts. "I've come from Boodle's, where I met a magistrate by the name of Sir Malcolm Laycroft. He happens to be the magistrate for this area."

She froze, eyes wide, her mind flooding with an incomprehensible tangle of thoughts and questions.

"I mentioned to him Lady Hawkestone's unfortunate position, and he agreed that he, the coroner, and the jury would be willing to meet her at Hawkestone House to save her the embarrassment of a public interrogation."

The private meeting would be infinitely better for Lady Violette. "That was done so quickly. Thank you."

"I've also spoken with a couple of reporters who will retract their reports about Hawkestone and publish corrections to the story, claiming they were misled."

Ravenna arched an eyebrow. "You've been very busy. How ever did you manage such things?"

He gazed out the window. "I suppose I can be quite convincing when I choose to be." He sipped his port.

"Lady Violette will be glad that you've ensured her privacy."

He nodded and seemed to be choosing his next words carefully. "I'm pleased to have been of assistance, but I was thinking only of you, however.

You seem to be under some strain." He leaned on his chair arm, closing some of the space between them. "There is something serious going on, and I wish you would tell me."

She shook her head and looked out the window at the gardens, "I can't." Besides, she didn't even know where to begin if she did want to tell him everything—which she didn't. She didn't want to tell him anything that might cause him to ask more questions, to pry into her past. Her primary concern now was figuring out if she still had time to complete her investigation. It would depend on when the magistrate wanted to call the inquest. "Has the inquest date and time been determined?"

"Not yet. They still need to find jurists and decide upon an agreeable date and time."

"That will probably take a few days."

"At least."

She could discover much in that time. But that gave Mr. Chadwick a few days, too. Her stomach knotted. Lady Violette's last words haunted her, *Make haste.* She didn't have long. "Would you please keep me apprised of the date and time?"

"Certainly." He smoothed his hand over his knee. "There's something else. I think you realize our nation is in a dire situation and, if Wolfsham dies of his illness, it could present a danger to us all."

"How so?"

The ruby in his pinky ring flashed. "Hillingham is losing ground. Since Pitt's resignation a couple of years ago, Fox has returned and works diligently upon winning Hillingham. Fox continues to defend Napoleon and means to convince us that France poses no real threat. He's building a strong following, especially among the House of Commons. Worse, there are still many Pittites who oppose him and a growing number of men are joining Grenville in opposition to both Fox and Hillingham. None of this bodes well, given Hillingham's disastrous affair in the Cape Colony. He made an egregious error in lying about the French invading our territory only to justify our own preemptive military actions. Napoleon is no fool."

"Yes, that was badly done."

His blue eyes intensified. "Imagine how dreadful it would be for us all if the Foxites came to power."

She thought for a moment, running her thumb over the sharp edges of the crystal wine glass. "Fox is mad to think Napoleon's intentions toward us are honorable. Clearly, Napoleon means to destroy anyone who stands in his way of grabbing up power."

"Which is why the death of two foreign secretaries in such a short time only further destabilizes the balance of power in our government. It's weakened any ground that's been gained by your late husband or Hawkestone." He locked his beautiful wolf eyes with hers. "Hillingham's position has weakened greatly since they've died. And with Wolfsham ill…"

He didn't need to finish the statement. It was all in his looks. Wolfsham was the favorite nominee for the appointment. If he died, then all would be thrown into flux again. With the in-fighting between the Grenville, Pitt, and Fox camps, England's throat would be exposed to Napoleon's sword without a strong foreign secretary.

"Indeed. The Foxites are pushing for Nochdale, who would likely advance Fox's platform to work in favor of Napoleon, if for nothing else but to go against the Tories."

Her ears perked at the mention of Nochdale's name. "So Lord Nochdale and Wolfsham are in line for nomination?"

"As is your stepson."

Her eyes widened. "Pardon?"

"I see he hasn't told you."

"No." She sat up in her chair. "I've been trying to see him, but he's always away from home and hasn't responded to my calling card. When did this come about?"

"Apparently too recently for it to have run completely through the rumor mill."

Bile rose in her throat. *Thomas may now be in danger, too.*

Braedon continued. "My point is that Fox has openly stated he aims to stand against anything the Tories attempt. But with Birchfield…" He swirled the wine in his glass. "He's been an under-secretary for Hawkestone and a clerk for his father, Lord Philip. He has excellent diplomatic skills and is well-liked among all factions. Nochdale isn't. And, best of all, he has his father's mind and talents. Birchfield is the most logical and sound choice."

He wasn't wrong. "But he's only twenty-six. Isn't he much too young for such a position?"

"He is young, but those things hardly matter when one is liked by the majority. Look at Pitt, the Younger. Prime Minister at age twenty-four, which is a far more significant position than a foreign secretary."

"Granted. Yet, I don't understand why you're talking to me about what is ultimately Thomas's decision."

"Because, the last I heard, he doesn't want the position."

Relief washed through her. That was a good thing. If these recent deaths were political in nature, he might remain safe. She tried to dampen her excitement. "Why?"

"He seems to think he couldn't do as well as his father. I think he merely needs convincing that it's precisely *because* of his father he should step into the role. He'd enjoy the support of his father's friends."

She stared out the window at the horizon. A strong breeze blew through, carrying the scent of grass and flowers from the garden. Thomas had always been his own man. She'd married his father when Thomas was already a grown man at age twenty-one. Though their relationship had been friendly, she would never be even a mother figure to him. As she was only twenty-five herself when she married, much closer to Thomas' age than Philip's. He likely considered her to be simply the woman to keep his father company. He'd even invented the endearment "Amma" to keep her in her place. She cared about him, but it was difficult to feel close to him. She'd developed a closer bond with his younger brother, Harrison, who'd been six years younger and had opened himself to her affections.

She snapped from her reverie. "I don't understand why you're telling *me* all this. Why don't you speak to Thomas himself?"

"I'd like you to speak to him about accepting the nomination if it's offered."

She smiled slyly. "I thought you could be very persuasive when you chose to be."

"If I speak with him, I fear he would see me as having an agenda to draw him into a faction. I'd rather my plea appear neutral."

"*Appear* neutral," she chuckled. "While you attempt to use me as a puppet to fulfill whatever agenda you've invented?"

"I assure you, my only desire is to thwart Fox and strengthen our foreign office as quickly as possible. I prefer we avoid war, but if we must fight, we had best present the strongest possible front. But Birchfield might suspect deeper political motives on my part and decline the nomination to outflank me."

"Sounds like trying to avoid a tiger only to stumble into a nest of vipers."

Chuckling, he swirled his wine. "Something like that."

It was a tough decision. She wanted to keep Thomas safe, but he would be a good candidate. He had his father's wisdom and steady nature and had no doubt learned a lot from Philip and Hawkestone about the office. Women often worked behind the scenes of the political stage, so Braedon's request wasn't unusual.

"I'll try, but he's not even responding to my letters at the moment, so I make no promises. And I should remind you that Thomas is his own man, makes his own choices."

"I'd expect nothing more. Now…" He finished his wine and stood. "I wonder, dearest Ravenna, if you would join me for a ride in the park?"

She hadn't given him permission to use her name, but the tenderness in his gaze and the resulting fire it caused in her gut quashed any desire to quibble. She rather liked it when he said her name. She was more concerned about being seen with him in public, only nine months a widow. But the day had turned warm and fine, and a drive through the park would be refreshing. Her shoulders tightened. "I don't think it's wise. I'm still in my weeds, and…"

"So don't wear them. Wear a different dress." Her mouth dropped open to his loud laughter. "I'm teasing you, goose."

Ravenna pinched her lips together and cut her eyes at him.

"Besides, you're a widow now. You're one of the freest women in the kingdom. No father or husband to answer to. You can do almost anything you please with little regard for what society says."

"Not entirely without regard." She crossed her arms over her chest. "But I think it wouldn't be proper since you're engaged."

He frowned. "I am not engaged."

"But—"

He clasped his hands behind his back. "My little raven, we're losing daylight. Do you want to go for a ride or not?"

If she were being honest, she did want to go for a ride with Braedon, of all men, in spite of his reputation. However, she hadn't been out riding once since her return to London and she hungered for a change of scenery. Also, while they were out, it might also be a good opportunity to accomplish something on her agenda. "I'll go on one condition. I need to pay a call to Pelham House first."

# Chapter Twelve

With Hart's help, it took Ravenna little time to wipe the sweat from her skin, splash on some rose water, don a gauzy black promenade dress and silk pelisse with lace trim, and dash out of the house to meet Braedon, where he stood beside a curricle. How surprising. Fast men like him typically drove an equally fast high-perch phaeton. She smiled at her own miscalculation. Perhaps he wasn't the flashy Corinthian he was reputed to be.

They sat behind a pair of prancing white Percherons that whisked them toward Pelham House in Grosvenor Square. The mellow afternoon sun danced in the rain-slicked trees that waved in the balmy spring wind. This was the sort of day memorialized by poets, if one ignored the stench of excrement, the drunkards, slatterns, and cursing drivers and focused only on the bright skies and budding trees.

When they stopped at Pelham House, Ravenna discovered, once again, Thomas was away from home. Ravenna left her calling card, frustrated that Thomas hadn't even been home yet and was seemingly ignoring her.

She returned to the curricle in a fret.

"Is all well?" Braedon asked.

"I don't understand why Thomas isn't answering my calling cards. He seems to never be home."

Braedon snapped the ribbons, setting the horses in motion. Soon, they were weaving between drivers toward Hyde Park. She held her bonnet, its black ribbons fluttering behind her.

He said, "He likely hasn't been home at all. No doubt many people on both sides of the parliament are courting his favor, trying to draw him to their side. I'm sure he's been caught up in a whirlwind of parties, balls, cards, dinners, and gentlemen's clubs."

"But if he's never home, how am I to—" She stopped herself. She'd nearly said "warn him." This gave her pause. Braedon was on the inside with government officials and heard many close and private conversations. Perhaps he had an opinion about the recent deaths. "Do you think it's suspicious that men in the Foreign Office are dying or falling ill?"

"You mean, are they being murdered or assassinated?" He eyed her suspiciously. "What a strange question from a lady. Why should you trouble your mind with thoughts of murder?"

She tightened her grip on her fan. "I think the situation seems odd to me."

"Is this related to your private conversation with Lady Violette and your interaction with that Chadwick fellow?"

"That's irrelevant. I only want to know what you think. Have you heard any rumors of enemies wanting Hawkestone, Wolfsham, or my husband out of their way?"

"Political men always have enemies, my little raven, but murder? That would be undignified, dishonorable, and unthinkable for most men."

"Granted. I suppose my imagination has run away with me."

"Perhaps there are spies…"

At the mention of 'spies,' Ravenna grew warm, a hot flash blooming in her chest and spreading up her neck. She turned her face to stare at a newspaper vendor screaming about a dead lord. She opened her fan and fanned herself. "Do you think such people could infiltrate our country and so easily gain access to our politicians?"

"It's certainly possible. Though, if I were a political assassin, I'd set my cap at the Prime Minister, King George, or Prince Georgie."

"But those men would be harder to access, would they not?"

"They would."

"And if the motive was to upset political balance…." Her voice trailed off, winding into a whirlwind of thoughts. Did that mean a killer roamed among their friends and acquaintances? Or that a stranger lurked in the shadows, hunting them? Or could The Unity be involved somehow? They were certainly no friend of The Crown.

"However...." Braedon interrupted her twist of distress. "That seems a bit outlandish. There are men within the government who work in secret to protect our officials. I think they'd be the first to be alerted and work to neutralize any threat." He entered through Grosvenor Gate and guided the horses to the left toward Hyde Park Corner. "Is this why you seemed reluctant to encourage Thomas to take the foreign secretary position if offered?"

Ravenna studied his profile. Braedon was certainly more insightful than she'd first believed. "Yes. That's part of it. I do fear for him, given the current circumstances."

"While it's not entirely impossible we're faced with a political threat„ I think it's unlikely. People fall ill and die of disease and injury all the time."

She released a clipped chuckle. "That's what Catherine said."

"It speaks to your compassionate heart to worry about him, but I believe it's misplaced on this score." He gazed warmly at her, and he winked.

As they traced the path toward the Serpentine, sunlight flickered in the budding trees and spangled the river. The scent of damp earth wafted from the ground, mingling with Braedon's spicy cologne. Her unease draped like a mantle around her shoulders.

Braedon slowed the horses to an amble. "Perhaps we should speak of lighter subjects. For instance, why are you named Ravenna? It's an unusual name."

"My mama was Italian. She grew up in Ravenna and was terribly homesick. Once she married my father and moved to Ireland, she never again saw her home or family." She dug the sharp corner of her fan guard into her leg to distract her rising emotions. "At any rate, Mamma named me for the place she loved most in the world. Papa always said it suited me because of my black hair and eyes and that I was smart as a raven, like my mother."

"I agree with your father. The name suits you perfectly. My name is nothing more than tradition. I was named after my father, and his father before him, and before him. I'm the fifth William Finleigh, Earl of Braedon."

The corners of his eyes crinkled.

"Yet there is something stable and secure about tradition. Are you anything like your father?"

"No, thank heavens."

"Was he so bad?"

He hemmed and his jaw knotted. "Yes." Then he added, "Though I will say, there is one aspect where he and I are the spit of each other."

She looked at him with interest.

"We both have an affinity for beautiful women." He winked at her again.

"Oh heavens, you're rotten to the core." She laughed, shaking her head. "I bet as a young master, you tormented your nurse and tutor mercilessly."

"Every day, in fact." As they followed along the Serpentine, he regaled her with stories of his childhood: how he sometimes pricked his nurse with a pin during prayers until she boxed his ears and the various pranks he played on his ever-patient tutor and servants.

"I might've called you a brat." She laughed.

He chuckled. "You would've been correct."

"I daresay you haven't grown out of it." She smiled at him teasingly.

His mellow tenor rang out in laughter. "I have. Only barely."

They fell into silence again. Her gaze roamed over the park along the horizon where life was beginning to unfold in the manner of tree buds, birds, and squirrels.

"Do you prefer London to Birchfield? Is that why you returned early from your mourning in the country?" Braedon asked over the rattle of the wheels and jingling of the horses' tack.

"I love Birchfield, but the boredom and loneliness became too oppressive. My stepsons are off enjoying the business of their lives. Thomas has taken up his duties as the new Earl of Birchfield and as husband to his new wife. My youngest stepson, Harrison, is at university. Except for the servants, I spent my days alone and entirely without society. I've no great need to be always at the center of things, but…."

"You craved companionship."

"Craved is a strong word, I think…." Her gaze fell on the river, its water rippling and glinting like a beaded dress in a ballroom's candlelight. She shrugged. "I thought being in London around friends and working on my charity projects would lift my spirits."

He smiled impishly. "You mean you didn't come to snare another husband?"

She gaped. "Certainly not." Marrying so soon after her husband's death, or possibly ever again, was unthinkable. Her primary concern was to stay strong enough to get through the days and nights without crumbling.

"So, I'm safe from the marriage snare for another season?"

She laughed aloud. "Safe from me, at least." Her mouth released the next words before her brain reined them in. "I couldn't possibly marry *you* in any case."

"Oh?" Hurt and interest mingled in his expression. "Would I make such a horrible husband?"

Her face burned with embarrassment at being caught out. "You're well aware of what is said about you." She opened her fan to stem the tide of heat rising in her cheeks. "You're trying to provoke me."

"I don't care what bored prattlers say. I want to know what *you* think of my reputation."

Her shoulders tightened. A kind opinion would encourage his pursuit of her, but an unkind opinion would be a lie. She liked him far more than she cared to admit to herself. "You seem a kind and generous sort of man, I suppose."

He rolled his eyes. "You're attempting to pet and placate me like a spoiled child."

Heat crept through her cheeks at his shrewdness, but she stood her shifting ground. "I am not."

"I want the truth. Without missish concerns for my feelings."

Annoyed, she snapped her fan shut. "Very well. You're the most provoking, vexing, irascible, irritating man I've ever met."

He laughed aloud. "Now *that* is closer to the truth."

Scoffing, she shook her head and looked out across the park.

A deep silence passed between them before he added, "Shall I hope that since you found Birchfield Manor so lonely, you won't return there at the end of the season?"

She shrugged. "I'm not sure. I do love Birchfield Manor. And Thomas is giving me the old rectory on the property. It'll make a nice home once the repairs are completed."

Braedon guided the horses down a narrower, less crowded path through a sentinel of budding trees closer to the water. "I like riding by the water. This spot especially reminds me of the little stream around my home in Nottinghamshire."

"You sound as though you miss it."

"I do. I haven't been there much in the past few years. It's all in the hands of the steward while I'm away."

"Why have you stayed away so long?"

"It's...complicated."

She flashed a knowing side glance. "Would that complication be in the lovely shape of Lord Hillingham's daughter, Dianthe?"

The lines around his eyes deepened. "Ah, you've been chatting with Catherine."

Ravenna chuckled. "Yes, and I don't need to tell you how she feels about Dianthe."

"Not at all." Sadness tinted his laughter. "But her concern is unwarranted. I prefer London because there's more diversion here than at Rushingwood." After a significant pause, he added, "And far fewer ghosts."

Ravenna toyed with the strings of her reticule. "I find the ghosts follow wherever you go."

# Chapter Thirteen

A s Braedon turned the curricle at the end of the lane and headed toward The Ring where the most fashionable enjoyed being seen, they encountered a gig pulled by a haughty brown Arabian.

Inside sat Lady Braxton and a female companion. Lady Braxton waved. "Yoo-hoo!"

"Oh, dem," Braedon muttered. "I fear it's too late to avoid the interaction now."

"She's not so terrible." Ravenna's statement sounded more like a question. "I suppose she can be difficult to like, but she gives much time, dedication, and money to charity."

"I can tolerate her for your sake." He drew the curricle to a stop.

Lady Braxton wore a pink and gold turban with a large white jutting aigrette. A matching mantle trimmed with feathers embraced her shoulders, and the fine feather fronds trembled in the wind. Her companion was a curvy woman with bronze-gold hair. Her face hidden hidden beneath the high ruffled collar of her spencer and and her broad-brimmed straw bonnet.

"Lovely day, isn't it?" Lady Braxton inhaled deeply and released a relaxed sigh.

Lady Braxton wore a trio of black roses pinned to her turban, the symbol of *Les Roses Noires*. Her companion also wore a trio of black roses on her bonnet though Ravenna had never seen the woman at any of the meetings before.

Before Ravenna could speak, Lady Braxton said, "I hope you'll consider coming to the meeting next week, Lady Birchfield. It's Wednesday. We'll have England's premier geologist giving a lecture on his most recent findings. And Braedon, tame your jealousy. This is for women only. You men already enjoy every advantage in education."

"I wouldn't dream of interfering, Lady Braxton. I'm content to let the ladies have their studies." He exchanged an amused glance with Ravenna.

Ravenna said, "I notice your friend is also wearing the roses. I don't think I've had the pleasure of an introduction. I thought I'd met everyone the last time I was there."

The woman seemed unbearably shy, looking downward as she spoke. She held her bonnet against the rising wind in such a way as to block a good view of her face. "I've only recently become a member and was too ill to attend the last meeting." She immediately turned away to look out across the park, thus effectively ending her share in the conversation.

Since she'd been so rudely cut off, Ravenna returned to Lady Braxton. "I cannot promise I'll be at the meeting. I may have something else scheduled for next Wednesday."

Lady Braxton sniffed and pinched her lips as though Ravenna had served her cold, weak tea. Raking her eyes over Braedon, Lady Braxton said to Ravenna, "I have no doubt you'll be busy. With such a handsome escort at your side, why should you have time for meetings? Even a widow needs diversion, I say." She spoke to Braedon. "Though, I'd heard that you and Lady Dianthe were engaged. Is that so?"

Braedon paled. Silent, he stared straight ahead, little knots pulsing in his jaw.

Lady Braxton laughed loudly. "Oh, my! Seems I let your secret slip, Braedon. And all while you were attempting to seduce a vulnerable widow." She winked at Ravenna, as if they shared in the jest. "I think he's lost his sense of humor. That's too bad for you, isn't it?"

Ice coated Braedon's words. "You shouldn't put faith in idle gossip."

"Which is why I'm asking you directly. Are you and Lady Dianthe engaged?"

"That is hardly any of your concern. Frankly, I'd go to the devil before I submit to this line of questioning."

Lady Braxton waved her hand. "You're as choleric as a poet. It doesn't signify if you won't cooperate, sir. I'll ask the lady herself." With a nod, she indicated something behind them. "If I'm not mistaken, that's Lady Dianthe only a few rods back."

Ravenna and Braedon looked over their shoulders.

"I believe that is her." Ravenna studied the lithe form and bright blonde, nearly white hair peeking out from under her sage green bonnet.

"How fortuitous." Lady Braxton flashed a gap-toothed smile.

The color drained completely from Braedon's face. This was growing most uncomfortable.

Ravenna said, "I do beg your pardon, Lady Braxton, but I'm getting a headache. I suppose I've been in the sun too long. Braedon is taking me home."

"Another headache? They bloom around you like roses." Lady Braxton waved a plump, gloved hand. "I don't believe it for a moment. You seem hearty enough to me." She shifted in her seat. "At any rate, I haven't yet mentioned the real reason I stopped you."

Braedon glanced behind them again.

Lady Braxton continued, "I'm wondering if you're going to the Melmotte ball tomorrow night?"

"I'll be there," Ravenna said.

"Good, I'll need your help cornering Lady Nochdale. She promised to host the garden party to raise funds for the Penitent House beds, and I mean to hold her to it."

"I'm sure she doesn't need such coaxing." Ravenna had no intention of making herself obnoxious, not even for charity. "After all, she's made the promise and will honor it." Her skin prickled as though she could sense Lady Dianthe's carriage drawing nearer and Braedon's growing unease.

Lady Braxton stood, waving her handkerchief. "Yoo-hoo, Lady Dianthe. Yoo-hoo!"

Ravenna nudged Braedon's knee with her own. She gave him a pointed look and motioned with her head to move forward.

"With pleasure," he muttered, snapping the ribbons, setting the curricle in motion.

Ravenna waved to Lady Braxton and called out. "Goodbye, Lady Braxton. I'll see you soon."

Lady Braxton shouted, "Wait. Do wait."

Ravenna glanced back to watch a vexed Lady Braxton flop down into her seat.

Braedon drove in furious silence. Once they exited the park, his grip on the ribbons relaxed, his shoulders lowered, and the knots disappeared from his jaw. Though he'd regained his composure, they continued in silence until they rolled to a stop in front of Gordon House. He handed the reins to a footman as he jumped down. His strong fingers gripped around Ravenna's ribcage as he assisted her hop from the vehicle.

Her feet on the stones, she looked up into his face. He held her, his fingers pressed into her ribs, not painfully, but insistently. He seemed to be struggling with something. Perhaps it was about Lady Braxton? Or Dianthe? She slid her hands down his biceps, hard and round as stones. His presence, his touch, and his musky cologne were a potent brew. The horses nickered, and she remembered they were in front of the watchful eyes of the servants and passersby on the street. The ghost of her husband stepped between them, and she eased from Braedon's grip, his fingers gliding from her sides. His gaze didn't waver as he caught her hand.

"I apologize for that scene in the park." His thumb stroked her knuckles through the thin kid leather glove. "If it made you uncomfortable or if..." He paused, his eyes lingering on her face. "Dianthe and I are—"

She removed her hand from his. "Braedon, you and I are friends. You don't owe me an explanation." She meant that, yet disappointment wriggled between her ribs.

His gaze locked with hers. "I do hope, very much, to see you at the ball Thursday night, though there's always a chance I might see you before."

She flashed a coquettish side glance. "I'll let the Fates decide." The air around her stilled. A faint tickle brought all the hairs on her arms and neck to attention. She looked around him, scanning the streets.

"What's the matter?"

Nothing seemed out of the ordinary. Only pedestrians, vendors, carriages. But…she craned her neck side to side. She thought she saw a man on the street staring at them. But once a gap appeared between carriages, he had disappeared.

Braedon touched her arm. "Ravenna? What's the matter?" Alert, he scanned the area.

"Nothing. I-I suppose it was my imagination."

He frowned. "If something is wrong…"

"No, truly. I'm well. I made a mistake. That's all."

Ravenna bid farewell and stepped into the house. She watched Braedon drive away, as she filled with warmth and light-heartedness. Yet, she couldn't let go of the notion that someone had been watching them. She closed the door as a shadow of guilt and disappointment weighed on the infatuation enveloping her. Too many obstacles filled the path leading to Braedon. She should put romantic thoughts of him out of her mind.

Grabbing her mail from the foyer table, climbed the stairs to her chamber where she dressed for dinner, then shuffled through invitations to balls, soirées, the Nochdale picnic, an engagement breakfast, and a couple of dinners. She hesitated over a thick letter from Lady Braxton and decided to wait until later to read it.

After dinner and a few hours of writing letters and responses to invitations, Ravenna settled in Philip's old study on the ground floor to enjoy a glass of port while reading Maria Edgeworth's *Castle Rackrent.* The house was asleep. On the table beside her rested Lady Braxton's unread letter.

She sighed. "If I must…." She rose to pour a fresh glass of port, then resumed her seat in front of the fire and opened the letter. The missive began with an invitation to the next Black Roses meeting, as well as a geology lecture. The letter continued with the question of the beds at the Penitent House: what sort, how many would be required, how much they should cost, and if they could be purchased for a cheaper price. She rattled off a complaint about the vicar who believed the prostitutes should have the two-deep chaff mattresses, while she insisted the women from the streets could well live with the cheaper straw mattresses. Then the letter ended with some gossip about Lady Hillingham.

Ravenna blew out a breath of exasperation. Lady Braxton had it in her head that Lady Hillingham sought to steal all the glory and honor for working on the reformatory and threatened to give her rival a proper "set down" at the next meeting. The letter closed with "Truly Yrs." and her signature, which consisted of a single capital "B," flourished at the top in loops like a vertical eight, crossing through the words above before it descended into the straight spine and double arcs to finish the form; it captured the page and overpowered all the other words. How perfectly the bloated and dramatic script matched its composer.

Ravenna set the letter aside and thought about the upcoming fundraiser for the Penitent House—a picnic at Nochdale House. She'd helped develop the invitee list and ran through their names, wondering who she might charm and gently press for funds. Then an idea hit her. She and Hart would go in the morning to select fabric at the linen drapers to make dolls in the event children came with the women who entered the Penitent House. Perhaps the other women would want to do the same. She'd mention it at the meeting tomorrow.

Something knocked against the window. She snapped her head around and jumped out of her chair. Heart racing, panic rattling her limbs, Ravenna rushed to Philip's desk, where he kept his dueling pistols in a case in the drawer. They were loaded, but they hadn't been shot or cleaned for some time. She whispered a prayer that the gun wouldn't lock up or, worse, blow back on her.

She stared at the window, seeing only the darkness and her faint reflection in the glass. Opening the casement, she called, "Who's there?"

A horse clomped by, its harness jingling, and drunken singing voices echoed against the buildings.

A shadow moved near the corner of her house.

Ravenna climbed out of the casement, her dress slipping over wood and stone. Her slippered feet hit the ground, and she ran on tip-toes toward the shadow. Squinting against the darkness, she fought to make out definite lines and shapes. She moved faster as the shadow climbed the wrought iron fence and jumped to the stones on the other side.

Ravenna dashed forward, running up against the fence.

A couple of watchmen holding lanterns lingered on the corner at the other end of the street. She shouted. "Watch here! Gordon House! Intruder! Help!"

The men rushed toward her, their lanterns held high, as the shadow ran down the fog-laden street, the flaps of his great coat billowing.

As the watchmen closed in on Gordon House, she pointed in the direction of the shadow. "He ran that way."

They paused long enough to ask, "What did he look like?"

"I don't know. I didn't get a look at him."

Their frustration flashed over their faces, but they charged after the man anyway.

She waited anxiously for the watchmen. After what seemed forever, they returned, panting.

The one with the beaked nose said, "Sorry, milady. We couldn't find him. Maybe if we'd had a better description..." His voice trailed off into a shrug.

"I understand," she said. "Thank you for looking."

"Rest easy, ma'am," The lean man with kind eyes and tawny sideburns said. "We'll stay around your house tonight. If he returns, we'll catch him."

# Chapter Fourteen

There were no other disturbances at Gordon House for the rest of the night, which did little to calm Ravenna's nerves or help her sleep. Perhaps a touch of laudanum in a glass of port would help her relax. No. It was best to keep a clear head in case the shadowy figure returned. She lay in the bed with her fan, the dagger drawn from it, and her late husband's pistol under the other pillow.

At some point in the wee hours, though, sleep overcame her, and she woke to the full sun streaming through her windows and her breakfast and clothes waiting for her. Hart had drifted in and out like a ghost.

She stood at the window, nibbling a piece of ham, looking down at the street, thinking. Thomas still hadn't responded to her letter or visits. Nor had Julia Pence. She huffed. Wolfsham was ill, so she couldn't talk to him, though she should probably talk to Lady Wolfsham—to warn her, if nothing else. Next in line was Lord Nochdale. He was politically savvy and power-hungry. Admittedly, she didn't know the man well enough to judge his character. She needed to speak with him. She stuffed the ham in her mouth, washed it down with tea, and rang for Hart to help her dress. She'd visit Nochdale first.

Within minutes, Ravenna wore her weeds and sat at the vanity. "Something simple and quick today, please, Hart."

"Will do, ma'am."

A knock sounded at the bedchamber door, and a maid entered with a curtsey. "Ma'am, there's a Mr. Chadwick downstairs who wishes to see you."

She twisted to look at the maid. "Ask him to wait in the library. I'm nearly finished here."

Hart finished pinning Ravenna's hair into a loose ponytail with ringlets trailing over one shoulder. Ravenna tapped a little rouge on her cheeks and dabbed rose perfume on her wrists and neck.

Ravenna jogged down the stairs, her arms full of her spencer, bonnet, shawl, reticule, and fan. She handed everything to Banks. "I'll need these as soon as I finish with Mr. Chadwick. Please have the carriage brought around."

She entered the library. "Good morning, Mr. Chadwick. You're out much earlier than customary visiting hours."

His hands were locked behind his back, holding his hat. His slicked gray hair revealed a large, furrowed forehead. He bowed his head. "Yes. I've been an early riser since my days in the American colonies. I apologize for imposing on your morning, Lady Birchfield."

She remained standing to give a clear signal the conversation would be brief. "I was on my way out. How may I help you?"

"I wanted to inform you that you're requested to appear before the magistrate at Hawkestone House for the inquiry into Lord Hawkestone's death."

"Why should I be there? I had nothing to do with his death."

"Because he died in your house. You were the last person to see him alive. The magistrate has questions for you. It's simply to see if his death warrants an investigation and to see how we might treat the burial."

Her nerves squirmed. She wanted to help her old friend and his wife, but she didn't want to answer questions to officials who might decide to pry into her own life. Perhaps she could testify with Lady Violette so they might support each other. There was safety in numbers. "I wasn't the last to see him. He died before I came downstairs."

He narrowed his eyes. "Nevertheless, you are required to attend."

The only noise in the room was the mantle clock ticking.

She grew warm and agitated under his steady gaze, but maintained her cool demeanor. "Very well. What when?"

"We will meet tomorrow morning at ten of the clock."

She knew she needed to be there for Violette's sake. Begrudgingly, she said, "I'll be there."

"I recommend you aren't late." He clapped his hat on his head and opened the door. "Good day." He touched the brim of his hat at her and sauntered out of the room.

A chill washed over Ravenna. She needed to find some answers soon, or her own freedom might be at risk. As soon as Chadwick was out of sight, she donned her spencer, bonnet, and gloves and headed directly to Nochdale House.

Lord Nochdale was out on his visiting rounds, but Ravenna learned that he'd be at the Melmotte ball later that evening, so their conversation would be delayed only a few hours. She then called at Lady Wolfsham's House only to discover she was out shopping in preparation for a different ball. So that meeting would have to wait.

Ravenna flopped into the corner of her carriage and growled, kicking the seat across from her. "Devil take it!" Frustrated and angry, she returned home, and dashed off a letter to Lady Wolfsham and another to Thomas requesting a visit from each of them. She then worked on writing letters for the Penitent House, completed a long fencing lesson, and prepared for the Melmotte Ball.

Ravenna entered the Melmotte ball wearing a black ball gown with short puffed sleeves and long black gloves. Black beads covered her dress in a lattice pattern. Her black curls were styled a la Grecque and ornamented with a jet ornament fashioned like laurel leaves.

The Melmotte ball did not disappoint. Attendees crowded the house in a magnificent crush. The house was warm, filled with a heady, fragrant mélange of flowers, varied colognes, and candle wax, which merged with the cigar smoke wafting from the card room.

As Ravenna pushed through the crowd toward Catherine, she noticed a woman in a slightly out-of-fashion dress that fit her voluptuous figure too snugly. Wisps of straight, burned-gold hair framed her square jaw.

Clearly, Square Jaw was out of her milieu. She seemed more acquainted with hauling milk buckets from a barn rather than gliding across ballrooms like the fashionable ladies.

Square Jaw stared at someone. Ravenna followed her gaze to Lady Braxton, who nodded in the direction of another person. Ravenna snapped her head around to see the object of Square Jaw and Lady Braxton's silent communication, but it was too late. The mystery person had disappeared into the crowd.

Catherine grabbed Ravenna's elbow, surprising her; she'd have to think about Square Jaw later. In her gold beaded gown, Catherine glittered and bubbled like champagne punch. She put her arm around Ravenna's waist and said to Lord Donovan, "Look here. Are we not night and day personified? Me in my gold and Lady Birchfield in her black."

Lord Donovan's wheat-colored hair brushed against his shoulder. Combined with his black ball clothes and stoic demeanor, he exuded the air of a poet or a painter. His strong calves rounded out his white silk stockings like half-moons. His were the calves of a dancer, but his serious attitude made her question if he'd ever danced.

An ache to dance yawed inside Ravenna. It had been a year since she'd skipped down a line and twirled, her skirts flying out from her ankles. She had danced in secret when cloistered at Birchfield, and as soon as her mourning was ended, she wanted to dance, and dance, and dance. Even now, the music tugged at her, luring her like a siren. She settled for tapping her finger against her fan to the happy rhythm.

With mock seriousness, Lord Donovan tipped his head to consider Catherine's question. "Indeed, you do. Both...."

A familiar mellow baritone rose behind them. "For my part, I prefer the melancholic shades of night." He pulled one of Ravenna's curls.

Braedon. A happy warmth oozed through her limbs, settling in her chest.

She and Catherine turned to greet him. They gasped and spoke in unison. "What happened to your eye?" Swollen, purpled flesh surrounded his left eye. Ravenna instinctively reached to touch it, but paused mid-air to withdraw her hand.

"Oh, that." He touched the edge of his eye. "I'd nearly forgotten about that gem. Received it at Jackson's this morning."

"You boys play too rough sometimes." Catherine planted her hands on her hips.

"And what's this?" Braedon lightly touched a dark blue bruise on Ravenna's upper arm. Her pulse quickened under his touch. "I wonder who gave you that little gift? Perhaps the ladies play too rough as well?"

She smirked and pulled at her glove to hide the bruise again.

"Yet, for all the novelty and delight of seeing you in fencing kit, nothing delights me more than this ball gown," Braedon said.

Lord Donovan laughed aloud. "Ladies fencing? I've never heard of such a...." His eyes met Ravenna's. He flushed and bowed his head. "My apologies, Lady Birchfield. I meant no disrespect. It's only that I've never seen nor heard of ladies fencing."

Braedon took Ravenna's hand. "Yet who can think of fencing?" He pressed her hand to the side of his face, where the bruise began. "This evening, Lady Birchfield is the gentle night personified, a balm to my thirsty spirit, and my aching eye."

"You go too far." She smiled coyly, pulling her hand away. He was a hunter at heart, relishing the chase over the capture. "Careful, Lord Braedon, you risk being called romantic." No peer wanted to be called romantic. It insinuated they held no love for king, country, or the peerage. They were wild, rebellious, and rumored to be Satanic. Worse, they sympathized with Napoleon.

Braedon laughed.

"Quite a fitting title for you, I think, Braedon," Lord Donovan's lip curled.

Ravenna hid a smile behind her fan while the humor drained from Braedon's eyes, and an iciness settled in.

Catherine linked her arm with Lord Donovan's. "Dearest, let's find you a dance partner. There are many pretty girls here to please you." She guided him away.

"You don't like him, do you?" Ravenna said to Braedon.

"Not particularly. But now we're alone and needn't think of the pup any longer. So..." He sighed, clasping his hands behind his back. "What shall you do with me?"

She shook her head and, fanning herself, looked up at him through her lashes. "I fear I haven't the imagination."

"I do." Chuckling, he leaned closer, his breath near her ear. "Perhaps I could corrupt you with a dance?"

She stepped back. "You cannot." She scanned the crowd. Languid ladies and gentlemen milled the perimeter of the dance floor, where dancers pranced up and down the line.

"It doesn't mean you loved your husband less if you dance."

Anger flashed. "It's only been nine months." She fanned faster to cool her burning face. Her mind flashed to Philip in his last days, and any desire to dance was destroyed.

Something across the room snared Braedon's attention. Ravenna tracked the direction of this gaze to the ballroom entrance. Lady Dianthe Hilling-ham.

He touched her elbow. "Let's get a refreshment, shall we? A lemonade or some champagne punch?"

She pulled her arm away, snapped her fan shut, and crossed her arms over her chest. "It seems you're trying to avoid Lady Dianthe. Or that you don't want her to see you with me, isn't that so?"

"I wanted to avoid a scene then, as I do now."

Piqued and overcome with a perverse desire to make him uncomfortable, she said, "For whom? Whom were you trying to spare the embarrassment?"

"I was trying to spare you from Dianthe."

She scoffed. Shaking her head, she looked away, noticing Lord Donovan near a window speaking with Lord Nochdale.

Nochdale was one of the men being considered for the foreign secretary position, and she hadn't been able to converse with him earlier. If she could speak with him, she might be able to work out if he'd had a hand in—or prior knowledge of—Hawkestone's death or Wolfsham's illness.

Nochdale's wig sat slightly askew, and he dabbed a handkerchief against his purplish lips and pale brow. Just then, Square Jaw passed near him. She wore a trio of black roses in her hair. That was odd. Ravenna had never seen her at any social engagements or at any *Les Roses Noires* meetings. Yet, she seemed familiar.

"What are you looking at?" Braedon asked.

Dianthe completely fled her mind and attention. "That woman there by Nochdale. Do you know her?"

"I've never seen her before."

She bit the inside of her lip, ruminating upon Nochdale. "He seems unwell, don't you think? He looks as though he might faint."

"He is speaking with your young gallant, Donovan. Perhaps the pup is wearing on his digestion." He released a clipped laugh.

"Really, Braedon, the things you imagine." She rolled her eyes. "Lord Donovan is *not* my gallant. I met him only a few days ago."

"I've seen the way he looks at you. He doesn't master himself well."

"Don't be ridiculous. You're simply jealous that he's supplanted you in Catherine's attention."

"I've not been supplanted. If I pressed the issue, Donovan wouldn't get a nod from Catherine. I will always be her first favorite. He does me the great favor of diverting her so I might focus my attention elsewhere." He lifted his brows at her.

She laughed, admittedly flattered. "How you do go on. I won't entertain this a second longer." She spun to walk off, but only managed a step before her gown tightened around her legs. She looked over her shoulder to find Braedon holding her skirt. People near them watched the scene, giggling and whispering.

"Are you mad?" She flushed and tried to pry his fingers from her dress, but he was too strong. She rapped his knuckles with her folded fan. Hard.

He let go and sucked his breath through his teeth, shaking his hand. Then he broke into quiet laughter as he rubbed the reddening skin. "Vixen."

"You deserved it. If one bead is missing off this gown..." She turned around herself, inspecting her gown.

Out of the pressed bodies of ordinary people emerged Lady Dianthe Hillingham. She didn't have a single flaw. Perhaps beneath the hem of her dress, she had cloven hooves. Or a strange rash on her back or a very hairy and warty belly. One could hope. Ravenna's insides coiled tight with something too much like jealousy.

Dianthe's eyes were blue as the twilight sky with tiny pinpoint pupils. She had a strange, almost other-worldly quality, such that she seemed to float through the room like Queen Mab. She pressed against Braedon, linking her arm with his. "Good evening, my dear," she purred. "Do say you'll dance with me."

His jaw tensed. He clearly didn't want to dance. "There must be a dozen men here who'd fight to dance with you."

"You're the only dance partner I require."

Braedon attempted to extricate himself from her grip. "Dianthe, you know Lady Birchfield?"

Dianthe laid her head on Braedon's shoulder. "Mm. Yes." She didn't even acknowledge Ravenna's presence. "Come, dance with me." She pulled on his arm, which failed to move him.

"Stop." Warning filled his voice as he glanced around the room.

"I'm inclined to think you don't love me." Now she turned her cold stare to Ravenna. "I wonder why that is?"

A storm bloomed in his features. He lowered his voice. "Have you *imbibed* this evening?"

She continued to pull at him, her voice growing louder and more petulant. "I want to dance."

"I apologize," he muttered to Ravenna, pressing her hand. "It's best for everyone if I submit, or we'll have a horrific spectacle."

Ravenna shouldn't care what Braedon chose to do or with whom he chose to spend his time. So why did it feel as though thorns twisted in her gut? Besides, while she was in mourning, she couldn't dance with him even if Dianthe were on the moon—which was the perfect spot for her and her all lunacy and cold beauty. "Please. Go dance. You've convinced me that procuring a gallant might be best. Perhaps Lord Donovan can assist. Good evening." It was a petty maneuver, but his flinting eyes proved that her barb had landed where she'd intended. She spun on her heel and left him to contend with Dianthe.

Nochdale was in a deep discussion with Lord Donovan and others. She didn't want to interrupt, nor did she want other people to hear their conversation. She'd try again when she could get him alone. She veered toward the refreshment room to get some punch and enjoy a cooler, less confined space.

The refreshment room, a small informal parlor, glowed with candles. Wallpaper of blue and white stripes covered the walls and plants or flower vases filled each corner. The carpets had been removed, and the furniture pushed against the walls.

People lounged on sofas and chairs or lingered around the refreshment table laden with a large bowl of champagne punch, fruit, biscuits, cheese, nuts, and bread. Ravenna selected a cup of punch and stood by an open window, breathing and delighting in the evening air.

A short, plump woman with a large white feather in her mauve turban flopped onto a nearby sofa. She was quickly joined by another woman in a red gown carrying two cups of punch.

White Feather reached for her cup. "We've just come from the theater. The play was good, but there was no one there worth seeing."

Ravenna sat in the casement, staring out over the street, watching people, carriages, and horses go by with link-boys running ahead with their torches to guide the driver. She hugged herself, sipping the bubbly punch and sniffing the air. It smelled of coal smoke, moss, and brine. A nightingale twittered and rustled in the tree outside, and an ache for Birchfield Manor, and her husband yawned in her gut. She missed Philip...his steady, reassuring presence, his forthrightness. He didn't toy with people's feelings. He understood loyalty. She missed the house, the gardens, and the fresh country air.

She leaned her head against the casement, weighing the options of returning to the ballroom or going home. She'd rather go home, stretch on the sofa in front of the fire with a good book and a glass of mulled wine.

White Feather gasped. "I almost forgot! I have such news."

Ravenna's ears perked, waiting for the gossip to drop.

"Lord Wolfsham is dead."

"Pardon?" Ravenna jumped from her perch and approached the women. "Lord Wolfsham is dead?"

"Yes." White Feather seemed half-affronted that Ravenna had eavesdropped.

"When? How did you hear? Who told you?"

"I had it from Lady Braxton."

"But Lady Braxton has been here."

"She was at the theater for the first act, then said she was expected here at the ball. But I decided to stay for the play because I rather liked it." Her feather bobbed with the movement of her head as she looked between Ravenna and her friends. "It was a farce about..."

Ravenna had all the information she needed. "Excuse me." She dashed off toward the ballroom in search of Lady Braxton. She buzzed by Braedon and Dianthe, who skipped down the line to the end of the room where Lady Braxton stood speaking with friends near the dark fireplace.

Ravenna put her hand on Lady Braxton's arm and whispered in her ear, "I've had dreadful news that I wanted to confirm. Is Wolfsham really dead?"

Lady Braxton's brows shot up and her chin tucked into a roll of flesh. "Yes? What of it?"

Ravenna issued a soft grunt of impatience. "Where did you hear it?"

Lady Braxton shrugged and stared as though it were obvious. "Gossip."

"Who told you?"

"I don't remember. You know how news travels like lightning in our little circles. I probably heard it from someone at the theater or from one of the servants. Why are you so interested in Wolfsham?"

"I'm only curious. I'd found out recently about his illness, but I thought he was expected to recover."

Lady Braxton's face lit up. "I understand. Are you hoping your stepson's way is now clear for the foreign secretary position?"

Embarrassed, Ravenna's face burned, and heat trickled down into her chest. She didn't want these people thinking she was angling for political favor for Thomas. She stepped back and put her hand over her heart. "No.

That's not at all—"

Lady Braxton lifted a finger. "You know, he must still get over Nochdale. And that will be no small task."

"I do beg your pardon. My apologies for interrupting. Good evening." Ravenna spun and walked away.

Braedon stepped out of the dancing line to grab her arm as she passed. "What's the matter?"

Ravenna was half-sprung on punch, upset by the news of Wolfsham's death, and had gotten nowhere in her investigation. She'd intended to speak with Nochdale to try to learn something about who might've had designs on Hawkestone's life, but he'd been engaged all evening. She was failing. Miserably. Mr. Chadwick and the coroner were soon going to question them. Their very freedom could be in danger. Lady Violette had trusted her to help and she was failing. To make matters worse here was Braedon dancing with the woman he preferred while leading Ravenna's heart on a string—and she was a fool for caring about him at all.

Tears pooled in her eyes. This was too much to be borne. Suddenly, all her senses opened up and sharpened. She heard, smelled, felt, tasted, noticed *everything*—down to the scuffing of the feet; the glint of light from every bead on every dress and every glass drop on the chandeliers; the scent of the silver polish; burning wax; human sweat and cologne. The music and laughter grew to an intolerable volume as sounds and faces whirled around her. Every fiber of her being seemed to be on fire. She must leave this place. She needed to be home.

# Chapter Fifteen

Ravenna called for her carriage and waited outside. She yearned for the serenity of Gordon House, and she couldn't get there fast enough.

Wolfsham was the third to die. He hadn't even taken the office yet. Clearly something foul was afoot. Lady Violette thought that Julia Pence had something to do with Hawkestone's death, but that didn't explain Wolfsham or Ravenna's own husband. Perhaps Julia had been involved with multiple men. That wasn't out of the realm of possibility. There were courtesans who made a luxurious living of running through powerful, aristocratic men. If true, that would call into question Wolfsham's faithfulness, as well as Philip's too, and Ravenna couldn't believe her own husband had been unfaithful.

Her mind reached back into her past with Philip, searching for any sign of betrayal, but failed to latch onto anything specific. Before she could prevent it, her breath heaved forth, crested with hot tears. Nameless, powerful emotions whirled with gale force through her: anger, sadness, suspicion.

By the time the carriage rolled to a stop in front of Gordon House, she'd regained her composure, descended to the stones, and stepped through the wrought iron gate toward the front door. An eerie stillness surrounded her in spite of the breeze and the noise from the street. She paused. Her skin prickled, and a familiar uneasiness snaked around her, that unmistakable sensation of being watched.

She turned slowly to assess her environs, easing the blade from her fan and straining to press the fear from her voice. "Who's there?"

A light rustle issued from the shrubbery near the door.

She stopped, staring in the direction of the noise, squinting to make out a shape. *Probably the wind. Or a cat. No need to panic.* She took a deep breath. In the partial moonlight, the shadows were too deep to see anything with clarity. She assumed a fencing stance. "I demand to know who's there. This instant."

A cloaked figure about two inches shorter than herself stepped out of the shadows. "I beg your pardon, milady. I'm Julia Pence. I heard you was looking for me."

Ravenna released her breath and relaxed. "Why the devil are you hiding in my shrubbery at night?" She sheathed her dagger. "I might've hurt you."

"I'm terribly sorry, milady. I thought it might scandalize you to come during the day since I'm a chorus girl and all."

"No need to fear on that count, Miss Pence. I was once an actress myself." Yet, the feeling of being watched had not abated. Ravenna scanned the street around them. She felt exposed. She knew the answer before she asked but wanted to be certain. "Were you here last night by chance?"

"No'm."

Unsettled, she opened the door. "Come in. Quickly."

Julia stepped into the house. "Were you an actress I might've heard of?" She reeked of gin and slurred her words when she spoke.

Ravenna lit a candle. "My name was Ravenna Connelly before I married."

Julia gasped. "Oh, I can't believe it's you! Your Lady Macbeth is unequaled. I snuck into the theater every night to watch you."

Ravenna led Julia into the study.

Julia continued. "I still remember. I hid in the behind stage area to get out of the cold and the rain. You must've been the grandest woman I ever seen. But you seemed much taller on stage than you really are, if you'll forgive me for saying so." Her eyes, fixed wide and unblinking, indicated a potentially unraveled mind. "And I remember deciding from the first night that I wanted to be an actress too. Though it weren't reputable work for a woman, I wanted it more than anything."

Such effusive admiration felt like wearing wet, itchy wool. "There's nothing to admire. I started as an orange girl and was fortunate enough to make a friend who convinced the manager to let me act. I got lucky." Ravenna lit an oil lamp and set it on the small round table between the sofa and a chair. "I'd barely escaped Ireland with my life. I had two options, a theater or a brothel. Please, sit."

Julia sat, lowering her hood. She was a pretty girl with hair nearly as dark as Ravenna's and dark doe eyes. Beneath a pert nose, her upper lip lapped over her bottom, giving her a gentle hare-like appearance. Her round stomach protruded from the opening in her cape. She ran her hand over her belly. When she caught Ravenna staring at her belly, she said indignantly, "That's right, I'm with child." She had a soft voice that dipped in a lilting but harried Welsh accent.

"I've heard as much. Your condition does create a problem. Especially since it will make getting another job difficult and you need money. What will you do?"

She shrugged a shoulder, looking down at the floor. "Don't know. I'll find something. I've been taking in some laundry and sewing to get me by."

"Would you like a drink? Wine? Sherry?"

"La, yes. Either'll do." Julia wrung her hands, looking around the room.

As the sherry gurgled from the bottle into a glass, Ravenna said, "I understand the child is Hawkestone's."

"You've heard."

"Word travels quickly. Especially when you shout it at the theater."

Shame flittered over Julia's features. She lowered her head.

"Don't fret. I'm not one to judge you. We're only a couple of theater girls talking." She smiled. That seemed to soothe the girl, and Ravenna needed Julia to believe she was sympathetic. "I do thank you for coming to see me." Ravenna handed a drink to Julia, who clasped it in both hands like taking up a baby bird.

She sat opposite Julia with an arm stretched across the back of the sofa and sipped her port. "Let's start at the beginning. How did you meet Lord Hawkestone?"

Julia drained the glass, then pressed the back of her hand to her lips as if screwing up her courage. "He liked the theater. He'd even come to watch us chorus girls practice." She looked down at her lap, and a gentle smile brushed her lips. "He used to bring me carnations. Two. A white one and a pink one."

Jealousy feathered Ravenna's ribs. She'd once been the recipient of Hawkestone's white and pink carnations after a show. *Ridiculous,* she chided herself. She'd never wanted him for a lover, but that simple gesture with the flowers had made her feel special, nonetheless.

Julia continued, "We were in love. He always talked about how he wanted to leave his wife and marry me." She lifted her chin and shrugged a shoulder. "Of course, it was impossible, him a lord and me what I am. But he made me believe it. He even rented rooms for me." Her voice shook. "I didn't care that I was a kept woman. It was the most glorious time of my whole life. I wasn't cold, hungry, or in the street like I am now."

Ravenna ran her fingers over the plush green velvet on the sofa. "Did Lady Hawkestone know about your arrangement?"

"I think so. But what if she did?" She shrugged, her eyes filling with contempt. "Hawkestone told me gents like him kept women all the time, and the wives accepted it. As long as we was quiet about it and all."

True, to a point. There were still plenty of spouses, even bound in *un mariage de convenance,* who would expect fidelity. Lady Violette was too proud to share her husband, especially with a chorus girl. It was also quite a different thing to carry on a discreet affair within one's own sphere with a married partner than to entangle with an unmarried lover from the lower classes. There were different expectations. Lady Violette might've been able to live with a dalliance in her own sphere, but for Hawkestone to go among the lower classes was unconscionable.

"When was the last time you saw him?"

Julia looked up, thinking. "At least a month ago." That would be too long ago if she were killing him with poison. Unless the poison she'd used had been so strong that it had weakened his constitution and sent him into a steady decline.

"Where did you see him?"

"At the theater. He was with his wife." She grimaced. Her dark eyes glittered with malice. "He had the nerve to bring her, knowing I'd be there." She set aside her glass.

"Do you know why he did that?"

"To hurt me, I'm sure."

"You had a row?"

"Yes."

"When?"

"Which time?" She scoffed, rolling her eyes. "Near the end, we was always fighting." Julia toyed with the edge of her cloak. "But the last fight happened about a month before the night I faced him at the theater, about March, I suppose."

"Did you fight about the pregnancy?"

Julia nodded, pouting. "He was so angry with me when I told him."

"What'd he say?"

"At first, he didn't believe it was his. He accused me of sleeping with other men. I threw a glass at him, cut him across the forehead for that." Her nostrils flared. "I never slept with another man. He knew I loved him."

"Then what?"

"I finally convinced him, and he came round. He made promises. Promised he'd run away with me because his wife couldn't give him children. Promised we'd go to America and start our family. Told me we'd live like a king and queen in America. I think he said those things to get away from me."

"Why do you say that?"

"Because soon after, he had me kicked out from our lover's nest."

Pity for the girl was buoyed by her outrage at Hawkestone. Ravenna had never seen that side of him before. True, he'd always been a flirt, but she'd never known him to be cruel.

"I never met with him again. When I went to his house, he refused to see me. When I sent letters, he sent them back. I showed up at his gentlemen's club and his office. He pretended not to know me. Except once."

"Tell me about that."

"It was outside one of his clubs. He came out, near dawn. I'd waited for him all night. He was drunk. I'd been drinking too. I only wanted to talk to him. He said he wouldn't be trapped and bedeviled. He said he never wanted to see me again and told me to go jump in the Thames and drown myself, for he nor any man would ever want a fallen woman like me." A sob broke from her, and she pressed the back of her hand to her nose.

"What a horrible thing to say." When had he become so vicious?

Julia swallowed her sobs as she wiped her eyes. She continued with a quavering voice. "I told him I'd leave him be, but I at least wanted him to pay for his child, because I couldn't raise it alone. He claimed he was devoted to his wife. Then a few weeks later, I saw him at the theater with her and I...I went wild." She clutched her knees. "I couldn't bear it. I was so angry with him that I wanted to tell her everything. I wanted him to feel the shame and pain I felt."

"Are you aware he's dead now?"

She nodded and broke into tears. Ravenna handed her a handkerchief. "Yes. I can't believe he's gone." She dabbed her eyes and blew her nose.

"Had he been sick during your time with him?"

Julia pursed her plump rabbit lips, and her gaze drew inward. "It seems he fell sick right before I learned I was with child."

"Do you recall anything about the illness?"

"He was pale, achy, shaking hands, weak digestion." She shrugged with one shoulder and leaned onto the chair arm. She crossed her feet at the ankles. A hole had worn in the sole of her shoes, and her dirt-marked stockings sagged around her ankles. "But I didn't think anything of it. I thought he had a bad cold. I guess that's what killed him in the end?"

Ravenna considered the young woman sitting in front of her. The large dark eyes without artifice, the wan complexion. She seemed genuinely grieved and genuinely ignorant.

"So when he returned to his wife, would you say you were hysterical?"

"Oh, yes. I went to a party at another actor's home...you know how we theater folk do after a show." She sniffled as a smile faltered on her lips. "Got two knees deep in my cups that night, I did. When I got home, Mrs. Lope barked at me about the rent, and I lost control. I threw things, screamed, and slapped one of the other women who tried to hold me down."

Clearly, this girl had a vicious temper. The sort of temper that might drive her to murder in a fit of passion. "Did you ever want Lord Hawkestone dead?"

She froze, unblinking. She answered slowly. "Sometimes. Though I loved him." She held out a hand. "Not at first, mind you." She dropped her hand and played with a fingernail. "But the longer he avoided me and denied me, the more he hurt me. The more I hurt, the angrier I became, and the more the hate grew. It don't take much to twist love to hate, milady."

"That's true."

"I hated him for what he did to me and the baby." She slumped deeper into her cloak. "He was wicked to abandon us. I still hate him for it. I'm glad he's dead. I hope he suffered half of what I've suffered."

Madness had twisted this woman's mind. Ravenna couldn't prove she was the killer—yet. But all her looks and her behavior certainly indicated she could be. However, that wouldn't explain Wolfsham's death. Unless she'd been a mistress to both men.

"Do you know Lord Wolfsham?"

"Who? Never heard of him."

She hated to think of it, but thought it was best to ask, "What about Lord Philip Birchfield? Do you know him?" Ravenna waited for the answer, her gut balled up tight as a fist.

Julia shook her head. "No'm. Never heard of him either."

Relief washed through her. Thank goodness. Ravenna studied her. It seemed that her rage burned hot enough to kill Hawkestone, but she didn't seem to be lying about Wolfsham or Philip. Perhaps more than one killer lurked in their midst.

# Chapter Sixteen

Hawkestone lay in a coffin with white linen spilling over the sides. He wore a navy superfine suit. White paste and powder coated his face, and his cheeks and lips were rouged to give the appearance of health and life. Coins held down his eyelids, and lilies surrounded his coffin, their sickening odor filling the room.

Bile rose in Ravenna's throat. She hated the cloying scent of lilies ever since Philip's death. Their perfume had followed her through the halls and rooms of Birchfield Manor for weeks. The odor now turned her stomach. The cold reality of Hawkestone's death cast her out of herself so that she felt as though she floated above the tragic scene. A once vigorous man still in his prime, hewn down like a harvest of wheat just as her own husband had been. The after-show revelries, the conversations over dinner, the dancing, the laughter, the twinkle of candlelight in his dark eyes, all that was now gone.

A burning coal of emotion rose in her chest, and tears flooded her eyes. She patted his shoulder, cold and hard as stone. She whispered, "I'm doing my best to find your killer and get justice for you. Rest easy, friend." She bit her lip and spun on her heel, dabbing her eyes. "I'm sorry. For everything."

She joined Lady Violette in the dining room to await the coroner, magistrate, and jurymen. And Mr. Chadwick. Her shoulders tightened at the thought of him. Lady Violette sat in front of the sideboard, staring out of the sun-brightened window. Her widow's weeds bleached her skin paler than usual, and her honey-gold hair was spun into intricate braids with the ends tucked into a chignon at the crown of her head. The sideboard laden with fruit, cheese, biscuits, and tea stood at the far end of the room as if they were expecting a visit from friends instead of from officials who might take their freedom and throw them in Newgate to rot. Lady Violette and Ravenna sat with cups of tea nearby.

Violette picked at her thumb cuticle. "Waiting is the worst part, isn't it?"

"Indeed." The smile faltered on Ravenna's lips. She glanced at the door. Her nerves crawled under her skin like thousands of little ants.

"Have you found anything out yet? Have you discovered that Julia Pence is guilty?"

"Her motives and deep-seated anger certainly make her top of the suspects. Yet something's amiss. When I asked her about Wolfsham, she didn't know what I was talking about."

"So? What does that have to do with anything?" Lady Violette brought her teacup to her lips.

"Because it explains Hawkestone's death, but not my husband's, if his is connected, or Wolfsham's death."

"Do you think they're related?"

"I suspect they are."

Male voices sounded in the hall.

Ravenna clapped her hand over Lady Violette's and whispered, "Say nothing of any of this. Keep your answers short. No additional information. Please. Our freedom depends on our discretion."

Lady Violette's eyes widened with fear.

The coroner, the magistrate, twelve jurymen, and Mr. Chadwick filed into the room, removing their hats. In an instant, Lady Violette transformed into a gracious hostess. Her face brightened, and she stood, smiling.

"Welcome, gentlemen." She motioned to the sideboard. "Please, have refreshment if you'd like, and when you're settled, we can begin."

No one was more perceptive or socially and emotionally agile than a good hostess, and Lady Violette was among the best in society.

The men, muttering among themselves, hovered at the sideboard, filled their plates and teacups, and meandered to a seat at the table. The magistrate, coroner, and Mr. Chadwick sat in the three chairs directly opposite Ravenna and Lady Violette, and the other men filled in the remaining seats around the table.

Lady Violette reached for Ravenna's hand under the table. Her bony, cold hand practically crushed Ravenna's in its grip.

Mr. Laycroft, the magistrate, a short, chubby, balding man, peered over his spectacles. "Ladies, good morning." He spoke softly with a hint of a lisp on his tongue. "This is Mr. Peterson, the coroner, and Mr. Chadwick, with whom I believe you're already acquainted."

Silver-haired and serious, the gangly Mr. Peterson nodded and clasped his knotted hands on the table in front of him. Mr. Chadwick sat beside him, relaxed, and crossed one leg over the other as if this were nothing more than a tête-à-tête with friends.

Mr. Laycroft continued. "You know why we're here. We are here to discern the manner and cause of Lord Hawkestone's death. Mr. Chadwick believes the death occurred under mysterious circumstances at…." He paused to look down his nose at his paper. "Lady Birchfield's home, Gordon House." He peered over the rim of his spectacles, glancing between the women. Staring at Ravenna, he said, "I presume you are Lady Birchfield?"

"Yes."

"Tell us what happened that day and how you knew the deceased."

Ravenna explained they were old friends and he'd come for an unexpected visit. He had died by the time she came down. That was the truth, though perhaps a bit shadowed. She certainly wasn't going to offer up more information in spite of the expectant stares of the men.

"What was the purpose of his visit?" Mr. Laycroft asked. Mr. Chadwick narrowed his eyes, leaning forward.

Ravenna licked her lips and squeezed Lady Violette's hand. "I don't know. He'd died before I had the chance to speak with him."

Mr. Chadwick inquired, "Is it not true that you told me it'd been many years since you'd last seen Lord Hawkestone?"

Mr. Laycroft glanced at Chadwick, then leveled his gaze on her. "Is that true?"

"Yes."

"So, after such a long separation, why was he suddenly interested in seeing you?"

"As I said, I don't know."

"But how many years passed between the last time you'd seen him?"

"About four years."

"Why so long? Did you move away?"

"No."

"Then why so long?" Mr. Laycroft pressed.

Ravenna was beginning to dislike the hyper-focused Mr. Laycroft. Her desire to lie for self-preservation warred with her integrity. She didn't want to lie. If she didn't lie, she would not only go to prison for Hawkestone's death, but her treasonous past as a spy might be uncovered as well. However, if she did lie, it might buy her enough freedom to uncover Hawkestone's murderer, and her past would remain buried.

Mr. Laycroft's mouth fell open as if to say *Well, we're waiting.*

She reached way back into her stage days and pulled down the mask of innocence. "We'd had a spat. He was upset that I was going to marry another man." That was mostly a lie. A knife of self-hatred twisted in her gut. He had asked her to marry him at one point, and she'd turned him down, but he'd promised to win her over. Then a couple weeks later, he discovered her espionage and the betrayal that forever severed their friendship. She craved a glass of port.

Mr. Chadwick leaned on the table, locking his cold eyes with hers. "So his visit had nothing to do with your recent tryst?"

Lady Violette, dear, sweet, wonderful Lady Violette practically growled. "How dare you make such an accusation. Lady Birchfield's character and reputation are unassailable."

Ravenna looked down into her tea. *If only that were true.*

Mr. Chadwick backed down a notch. "I beg your pardon, milady. I mean no offense to you or your late husband. However, I passionately believe Lady Birchfield is not being entirely honest. My every instinct tells me she knows more than she lets on."

Lady Violette didn't back down. "You're no gentleman to question the honor of a lady in such a vicious manner. You've all but called her a liar."

Who knew Lady Violette had such pluck? The knife twisted deeper in Ravenna's gut. She appreciated the defense, but it only served to pull her lower. She now owed this woman more than she could ever repay.

"Come, come," Mr. Chadwick said. "I know for certain your husband had dalliances, and I'm sure you knew of it because you don't seem at all surprised by that information."

Ravenna tried shielding Lady Violette. "How unkind. Why are you abusing a grieving widow with such fabrications? What makes you think he had affairs?"

"Because I spoke to one of his paramours last evening at the theater. A Miss Julia Pence."

That information shot like a dart through Ravenna. She strained to hide the shock from her face. Julia hadn't mentioned anything about speaking with Mr. Chadwick. This meant he was making great strides in his investigation. She needed to find Hawkestone's killer soon so she could send this nosey investigator back to Bow Street before he discovered information she'd rather keep secret.

Lady Violette interjected. "My husband had a taste for theater girls. It has been a stain on my marriage and a source of pain. How can you be certain that Julia Pence isn't the killer?"

"She could be. Or perhaps you were so jealous of his affair with a younger woman that—"

Ravenna jumped in. "Disgusting insinuation!"

"Presumptuous." Lady Violette talked over him. "You speak as if it's certain he was murdered. I'm not convinced of it. He'd been ill for some time."

Ravenna blanked her face. She didn't want to signal that Lady Violette was lying about her true beliefs in regard to Hawkestone's death.

Lady Violette continued, "This inquest business is nonsense, and you should all be ashamed of yourselves for interrupting my mourning and disturbing this household. Whatever his faults may have been, he was still a most…." Her voice broke. "Beloved man and husband."

The jurymen cleared their throats, murmured, and glanced around, embarrassed.

Mr. Laycroft said quietly, "I do apologize for our intrusion, milady. But as an official in service to the crown, we must understand the cause of your husband's death. Please explain the nature of his illness."

Lady Violette had effectively guided the conversation away from Mr. Chadwick's suspicion. It was here that the coroner, Mr. Peterson, had the most questions to ask about when Hawkestone's illness had begun and the various symptoms he'd experienced. At the end of the interrogation, Mr. Laycroft and Mr. Peterson whispered to each other for a few moments.

Ravenna bounced her leg. Lady Violette sat straighter and put her hand on Ravenna's knee.

"We'd like to see Lord Hawkestone, please." Mr. Laycroft stood, and the other men followed suit. "Where is he being kept?"

Lady Violette told the footman to show the men to the mourning chamber. The men filed out of the room as Lady Violette stared straight ahead, composed and unmoved. When the door closed, and the women were alone, they let out a unified sigh. They leapt from their chairs and paced the floor.

"I'm so sorry for everything," Ravenna pressed one hand to her forehead, the other on her hip. "Thank you for defending me. I don't deserve it. I-I-I—"

"Shhh." Lady Violette grabbed both of Ravenna's hands in her own. She whispered. "Listen. I don't care about your past with Hawkestone. If there was one. The only thing that matters is discovering my husband's killer as fast as possible. For both our sakes."

It seemed as though a lifetime had passed before the men returned. They murmured as they entered the room. The jurymen stood behind Laycroft, Chadwick, and Peterson.

Mr. Peterson clasped his hands behind his back. He towered over the other men and had a long face with a large, beaked nose. His voice was deep and sonorous. "I've examined the body, and given the information you've provided, it's highly likely your husband was murdered. Poisoned, in fact." Some of the jurymen nodded.

The women exchanged worried glances and clasped hands. Lady Violette's voice shook. "What brings you to that conclusion?"

"First, the symptoms you've described. The tremors, the vomiting and such, the weight loss, the stomach complaints. But then, when I examined him, I noticed the bluish fingernails with little white crescents in the nails and bright red patches on the skin. That's typically, in my experience, a sign of poison."

They leaned against each other, and Lady Violette clutched her black-bordered handkerchief to her chest. "Heavens."

He lifted a knobby hand. "Given his position, and his proximity to the royal family and other high-ranking officials, I believe it's of greatest import to discover what happened and to continue investigating his death as if he were murdered." A few jurymen voiced their agreement among the chatter of their colleagues. "I will need to take his body for autopsy, and then we'll place him in St. James Church for a state viewing. Who is in charge of his affairs?"

"His brother, Richard. He lives in 33 Oxford Street."

Lady Violette and Ravenna exchanged a worried glance.

Mr. Chadwick crossed his arms. "There's something foul afoot." He stepped closer to Ravenna, studying her with his steely eyes. "And I aim to find the man or *woman* responsible for his death. As soon as possible." He turned to Lady Violette. "If you recall, the last time I was here, I inquired after his personal papers."

"Yes," Lady Violette licked her lips and glanced at Ravenna. "I recall."

"Now that we're going forward with the investigation, I'll need access to your husband's personal papers, journals, anything that might reveal a conflict or an adversary."

"I'll get them for you."

She disappeared and within a few moments, returned to the room carrying a bundle of papers. She handed them to Chadwick.

"That's it? He didn't keep journals?"

"Not that I've been able to discover. However, if I find them, I'll send them to you directly."

Ravenna bit down on her tongue and dug her nails into her palms, an old trick she used to employ to keep a straight face on stage. Lady Violette was lying. Hawkestone did keep journals. Ravenna had once snooped through them to gather valuable information for The Unity about English forces, supplies, monies, strategy, and deals being brokered with foreign entities. But maybe he had destroyed them.

He narrowed his eyes. "Interesting. Men in his position typically keep records of their lives."

"Insufferable man," Ravenna whispered, turning away to sit in the window, the warm sun on her back.

Lady Violette remained unperturbed. "Thank you, gentleman, for meeting with us here instead of submitting us to a public spectacle." She opened the door and directed the butler to show the men out, effectively putting an end to the inquiry.

Before stepping from the room, the coroner said he'd be sending a cart later to collect Lord Hawkestone for the autopsy.

Lady Violette shut the door, fire in her eyes. "That man, Chadwick, will get my husband's journals over my dead body."

# Chapter Seventeen

Ravenna rushed home after the inquiry to dress for the Penitent House fundraiser—a picnic at Nochdale House—though it was the last thing she wanted to do. The picnic felt like an enormous waste of time with the need to beat Chadwick to the discovery of Hawkestone's killer. She hoped there would be some means of finding out information at the picnic. She could at least speak with Nochdale to discover if he had any malice toward his opponents.

True to her word, she first sent a footman to take a guinea to Mrs. Lope for sending Julia Pence last night. Then she changed her dress, washed her face in rose water, and applied a tint of rouge on her cheeks and lips.

When a knock sounded on the front door below, Ravenna grabbed her parasol, stole, and fan and descended the stairs to meet Catherine. She froze on the stairs when she saw Braedon standing beside Catherine in the foyer. He was the last man she wanted to see. Provoking, ungentlemanly, rakish cad. Not only because of his behavior at the Melmotte ball, but because he possessed an uncanny ability to whip up her anger with seemingly little effort—and enjoy it.

He looked at Ravenna, admiration, and mischief in his gaze. It helped that his tobacco linen suit did little to emphasize his handsomeness. Dark colors favored him best. Yet, in spite of herself, her insides squirmed like a basket of excited puppies. She pulled her stole around her shoulders as she descended the stairs. Still annoyed with him, cool civility was the best she could manage. She understood why a man might choose a young, beautiful woman like Dianthe over a widow in her thirties, but she didn't have to like it.

"Good morning, Catherine. Braedon, I wasn't expecting you. I didn't realize you shared an interest in the Penitent House."

Catherine said, "Of course, he's one of the primary donors."

Her eyes locked on him, and she paused in the middle of the staircase.

He leaned on the balustrade, gazing up at her. "It seems I've shocked you, my little raven."

"He's insisted on anonymity from the start, dear." Catherine patted his arm and smiled at him. "Isn't he good?"

*Irritating man.* Ravenna straightened her back and completed her descent.

"I'm certain I can rely on your discretion?" Braedon winked at Ravenna. "I wouldn't want the *ton* to discover I do, in fact, have a heart."

"Of course. You're the last thing I'd ever gossip about." She was unable to rein the annoyance in her voice.

He chuckled and pulled gently on one of her curls.

She pulled back and slapped at his hand all to his amusement. "Shall we go?" She gripped her fan.

"When did you leave the ball last night?" Catherine asked as they entered the bright afternoon with brilliant cyan skies. "I looked for you everywhere."

Braedon handed Catherine up into the carriage. "As did I." Braedon extended his hand to assist Ravenna. "You seemed upset. Did you leave early?"

"I did." She cut a hard glance at his hand. "Though I'm certain with Lady Dianthe's company, you hardly missed me at all." She barely touched his hand as he assisted her into the carriage.

Braedon filled the seat across from them. "Ah, but there's the rub. Some diversions one wants to have. Others are distractions one must endure."

A sly smile crossed Catherine's lips, and she lifted a flaxen eyebrow. "Clearly, you two had a more interesting time at the ball than I."

"Hardly." Ravenna picked at an imaginary speck on her dress. "The most interesting thing about the evening was learning of Lord Wolfsham's death." She glanced at them to gauge their reaction, but neither seemed surprised. No doubt, once revealed, the gossip flew like lightning through the ball attendees.

"Is that what upset you?" Braedon asked.

"Yes, of course. It's disturbing news."

"True, but hardly surprising, considering his illness."

Catherine, glowing in her daffodil yellow muslin, tsked. "Poor Wolfsham. He was such a good man, too. So kind and witty. And a fabulous Faro player. Who will be my partner at the Devonshire tables?"

"I could play," Braedon offered.

She scoffed. "Darling, you have no skill for Faro. If you weren't so consistently a poor player, I'd think you did it to provoke me."

Ravenna snipped. "Yes, yes, the card tables will suffer a devastating blow, I'm sure. The material point is that in a matter of nine months, we have lost two foreign secretaries and a nominee: my husband, Hawkestone, and now Wolfsham. Does that not worry either of you?"

Catherine shrugged. "Friendships and respect notwithstanding, I'm not especially concerned about the position itself. They'll find someone before Parliament descends into chaos." Catherine opened her reticule and rummaged through its contents. "I'm in need of a comfit. I found the best ginger comfits at Fortnum and Mason."

Braedon crossed his arms and spoke to Ravenna. "Of course, the next in line would be Nochdale." He frowned. "That is, unless your stepson were to usurp him. He certainly could. He'd have the support."

Ravenna declined Catherine's offer of a comfit and turned to look out the window. *Heaven's stars.* Nochdale and her own stepson, Thomas, would oppose each other for a position that seemed to be the deadliest in the land. If Nochdale were inclined to kill off his opposition, that certainly put Thomas in danger. What was Thomas up to? Why was he not responding to her?

The carriage stopped in front of Nochdale House in Park Lane. It was a cold, uninviting structure of white stone formed in a plain rectangle, entirely without ornament or nuance. Rows of windows and a balcony wrapped the entire exterior of the first floor.

After being shown to the gardens, Ravenna, Braedon, and Catherine followed the pebble path that swirled through the shrubbery and flowers. The sun, just past its apex, burned hot and bright and streamed through Ravenna's parasol, casting lace patterns of shadow and light. The still air allowed the birdsong to ring out, loud and clear across the garden. Soft voices and laughter carried over the hedges and flowers as they neared the picnic. The garden bloomed with women in their white muslin and men in their tan, cream, and tobacco linens.

"I feel like a fly in the cream," Ravenna said as pebbles rolled under the thin soles of her black slippers.

"Curdled cream, more like it, here at Nochdale House," Catherine whispered. "He's such a grasping, greedy thing."

Ravenna opened her fan and waved it to dry the moisture beading around her hairline. Even under her parasol, the sun's heat pressed on her. They exited the path and crossed the span of green to a large white tent. Platters of food alongside china, crystal, and silver anchored the white tablecloths. This was how the elite picnicked.

Ravenna, Catherine, and Braedon passed a group of men composed of Nochdale, Fox, and a few of their cronies. All were dour, soft-jowled men of varying heights and girths. With thinning hair and pasty skin, they looked perpetually tired, sick, and grumpy.

For the sake of politeness alone, Ravenna smiled and nodded, wondering when she might separate Nochdale from his friends in order to question him. She wanted to get a feel for his character. She'd heard rumors of his ruthlessness, but she wanted to see for herself. Especially if he might be contending against her stepson for the foreign secretary position.

"Good afternoon, ladies, Braedon," Nochdale greeted them, dabbing a handkerchief around his lips. Purple bags hung low under his eyes, giving the impression of little hard brown buttons embedded in ruched lilac-tinted velvet. He looked much older than the last time she'd seen him several months ago, but then politics had a way of dramatically aging men.

Braedon and Catherine conversed with Fox while Nochdale turned his attention to Ravenna. He wheezed as he spoke. "Well, now, Wolfsham is dead, and already I'm hearing rumors that young Birchfield is lining up with the opposition to sweep my position from under my feet." The skin didn't crinkle at the corner of his eyes. He coughed into his handkerchief.

Hairs stood on the back of her neck. She smiled, hoping to disarm him. "I wasn't aware my stepson had made a decision to pursue the nomination. However, it's my understanding that the foreign secretary office hasn't yet been appointed to anyone." A refreshing breeze fluttered around them and carried the scent of his cologne back to her. It smelled of lily, sage, and bergamot. The scent seemed familiar. Where had she smelled that before?

His eyes narrowed. "I can't imagine the position going to anyone but myself. It will not do. And I won't be so easily put off from having it."

"I'm not sure what you hope to gain by speaking to me of the matter." Her smile faded. "Young men can be so obstinate."

He nodded. "This is true. Always eager to prove their stuff, aren't they? But you must allow that you're the closest thing to a mother the boy has, so he'll listen to you if you were to ask him to be reasonable and step back."

She laughed. "You flatter me. I have no such influence, and if I did, why on earth would I ever do such a thing?"

"Because I aim to be the next foreign secretary." He leaned closer and hissed, "No matter the cost."

# Chapter Eighteen

Nochdale. She had wondered if he was capable of murdering his rivals, but now her suspicions were becoming solidified. She wasn't completely convinced that Julia wasn't involved, but Nochdale had now shot up to the top of her list—especially since three men around the same political position had died.

She staggered back and linked her arm with Braedon's as Nochdale turned to speak with someone else.

He said, "Are you unwell? What's the matter?"

Nochdale had the greatest motive of all—power. He had so much more to gain from destroying his political rivals, and now her stepson may be in grave danger. But how could she prove it?

She dug her fingers into Braedon's bicep.

"Ravenna?" He said closer to her ear.

She blinked and shook off her reverie. "Sorry. I-I lost my balance. I think the sun is too warm," she lied. "I'd like some lemonade."

"Yes, of course." He guided her toward the tent. "What did Nochdale say to you?"

"Nothing. I-I'm well."

He helped her to a chair under the tent, where the cool shade was a welcome respite from the sun burning through her black clothing. "Rest here. I'll get your lemonade."

She squeezed her folded fan, trying to steady herself as she watched Braedon cross the lawn. Nochdale had to be the one responsible for the deaths. She needed to find a way to prove it before someone else, likely her stepson, was killed. But how? Where to begin? She couldn't confront him directly because that would alert him to her suspicions and could put her in danger. And she needed time. She could tell Mr. Chadwick, except he'd have difficulty getting information directly from Nochdale, so he'd have to take a circuitous route to discover anything. That would throw him off of her and Lady Violette for the moment and buy her some time. The best course in this moment was to be observant during the party, listen, and watch. Her eyes darted over the guests and the servants.

Braedon reached the footman, who stood with a tray of lemonade. Behind the footman, maids trailed and scurried between the house and the garden, replenishing the refreshments and carrying supplies.

In this retinue of maids was a familiar curved figure with a saucy walk. Square Jaw. Her burnished gold hair with a trio of black roses sewn around the blue band on her mob cap captured Ravenna's interest. She looked incredibly similar to the woman Ravenna saw last night at the ball, but that was impossible. Wasn't it? Maids did not attend balls. Perhaps she had a sister who'd had the fortune to marry up.

Braedon returned, handing her the glass before taking the seat beside her. She sipped her drink, hating to admit to herself that she rather enjoyed this attention.

Looking out across the yard, he folded his hands in his lap and leaned toward her, speaking in a low voice. "Clearly something is wrong. Would you care to tell me? Are you in some sort of danger?"

She couldn't drag him into this. Even though Nochdale had rattled her and made her desire assistance, and Braedon had connections that could help her a great deal, like it or not, she had to handle this alone. "Thank you for the lemonade." She took another drink. "That's much better." She forced herself to smile.

"What did Nochdale say to you?"

"Nothing of note."

"I don't believe that for a moment," he muttered.

"He only spoke about Wolfsham. He said nothing of any consequence."

He tilted his head, his eyes blazing. "Is that so? Well, if you won't tell me, perhaps he will. And if he won't readily speak, then I'll force the truth out of him." He stood and started toward Nochdale, his hands balled into fists.

"Braedon, no." Ravenna jumped up to grab him. "Please. I'll tell you." She glanced over her shoulder at the whispering matrons, peering over their fans. She guided him away from the tent and spoke in a low voice as they crossed the plush grass. "He said he would have the foreign secretary position at all costs, and he wanted to know if Birchfield had intentions of accepting the position, were it offered to him."

They stood under a canopy of trees that lined a walk leading to a gazebo.

His wolf eyes narrowed. "That's it?"

"Yes. That's all."

He scrutinized her. "There's something else you're not telling me. Are you in some sort of trouble?"

She glanced out across the lawn. Lord Donovan strode toward them. His sandy blond hair gleamed in the sun like a halo. "Oh, look. Lord Donovan is here."

"Thank the stars. I was beginning to pine for him," Braedon muttered, rolling his eyes.

Nochdale joined Lord Hillingham, the Prime Minister. Lady Dianthe, Hillingham's daughter, glowing in all white, stood at his side fidgeting and twirling her parasol.

"Don't fret, Braedon. Your day has become brighter." She nodded in the direction of Dianthe.

He sighed heavily.

Dianthe closed her parasol, broke away from her father and, forgetting all propriety, *ran* toward them.

Ravenna chuckled. "And not a single soul at this party can be in any doubt of her affection for you. You must concede, she's an excellent runner." Walking backward, Ravenna smirked at him from under her black parasol. "I think I'll go speak with Lord Donovan since he isn't indisposed." She waved at Braedon as Dianthe passed her and leaped into Braedon's clearly unprepared and unwilling embrace.

Ravenna laughed at Braedon's baleful glare. As she turned away, she heard

Dianthe say, "What were you two discussing so seriously? You'd better not provoke my jealousy, you naughty man."

# Chapter Nineteen

L ord Donovan was still conversing with his friends when Ravenna passed, but he broke off and stepped out to walk beside her. "Good afternoon, Lady Birchfield. It's a pleasure to see you again."

His hair was brushed back off his face in thick waves, and his gray-green eyes glittered with good humor and gaiety. He smelled of sunshine with a hint of leather and his fresh citrus-noted cologne. It was a popular scent called Albany—a vigorous, refreshing scent that matched him well.

"Good afternoon."

He smiled, and the sun seemed to brighten. "I'm thankful to see you."

"Why is that?"

He leaned in, mirth in his eyes, and whispered, "I believe Catherine's attempting to form an attachment between me and that young lady over there."

Ravenna peeked around him to find Catherine in a far corner talking to a peach-skinned, dewy girl with blonde hair. She chuckled. "Yes, the only thing Catherine likes better than gossip is making matches. You could do worse. She's a pretty girl. Though I don't know her well, I've heard she's quite accomplished."

They turned toward the benches along an ivy-covered stone wall under an arbor decked in climbing pink roses in half-bloom.

"That's the problem. She's a *girl*, debuting this season."

"Isn't that the perfect time to snare a wife? *Before* she grows older and wiser." She smiled up at him, squinting against the sun.

He laughed. "I'm not particularly partial to fair-haired ladies. I prefer

131

dark hair and a seasoned mind. Heart, spirit, and mind are all infinitely more important."

Ravenna leaned in to sniff a rose on the trellis. "How radical and philosophical of you. What if a woman is as grotesque as a fairy tale hag, but has a brilliant mind?"

"You're teasing me."

"I am." She laughed, plucking a rose.

They shared the bench under the arbor.

After the usual pleasantries about the weather and their health, Ravenna, in hopes of ferreting out useful information, turned the conversation to politics.

"Wolfsham is dead, so soon after Hawkestone and my own husband. I imagine Parliament must be in a scramble to fill the post," Ravenna twirled the rose beneath her nose, its soft petals brushing her lips.

"Indeed we are. We need a strong man in the post as soon as possible, someone Napoleon can't intimidate."

"Who would you like to see in the position?" She plucked the thorns from the stem.

He thought for a moment. "Birchfield, certainly. He's a strong candidate. I wouldn't mind seeing Overton or Breeding. Even Massie would do, though he's not the best negotiator. He's like to give away Malta and other interests completely."

She studied the folds of the rose petals. "I notice you didn't mention Nochdale. Do you not like him? I've heard he's determined to have the post."

"Nochdale would be a good foreign secretary were he not so close to Fox."

"Do you reckon Nochdale is a dangerous man?"

"How do you mean?"

"Do you think he's vicious enough to destroy everyone in his path to get the office?"

He flinched and studied her. "What are you saying?" He whispered, "Do you mean you think he might've had something to do with the recent deaths?"

She stroked a soft pink petal. "Is it impossible?"

Pensive, he gazed across the lawn at Nochdale. Then he shook his head. "No. That's impossible. He may be ambitious, but he's not vicious. Ultimately, I believe he's a man of honor."

Lord Donovan could be right. Perhaps Nochdale wasn't a killer. "Is there anyone who wants the position who would do something like that?"

"No." He blinked at her. "To what do these questions tend?"

She took in the rose's perfume. "Oh, nothing. Only making conversation." She smiled from under her lashes at him.

Ravenna sat up straight and tucked the rose into the center buttonhole of her spencer. The way his eyes followed her movements and the way his cheeks flushed proved that she'd sufficiently distracted his thoughts. "Sounds like Nochdale may be your man." She pressed her knee against his.

She was flirting shamelessly to get at the information she desired, in the same way she'd once toyed with Hawkestone. A hot coal of guilt and shame burned in her throat. She wasn't happy about using her wiles to draw answers out of men. But he might know the killer. If she questioned him directly, she might unwittingly alert him to her suspicions and put herself in danger.

He glanced at their knees. "Were he not so sympathetic to Napoleon, Nochdale is certainly tough enough to contend with him. Napoleon has been stubborn. He doesn't seem inclined to accept or offer peace. He insists on pushing ridiculous demands."

"Such as?" Ravenna patted the rose, fluffing the petals.

He averted his gaze, wiping his palm on his thigh. "He doesn't like our newspapers publishing such vehement anti-French sentiment, and he wants us to remove the French expatriates from the kingdom."

She scoffed. "As if he has the right to tell us how to govern." She watched Braedon cross the lawn with Dianthe. Annoyance prickled her skin, but his apparent displeasure buoyed her spirits, bringing her to the edge of a smile. "Do you think Napoleon is using his demands as a ruse to divert attention from something bigger?"

"The central issue is Malta. Since Parliament loosened our blockades on

French ports, Napoleon has taken advantage of that freedom to expand into Haiti and America. So we want to keep British troops in Egypt and Malta, though it infuriates him and thwarts his plans of expansion. It's a little more complicated than that, but that's the crux of the matter."

"Yes," Ravenna said. Her voice sounded distant even to herself. "It's always more complicated than the surface would suggest." She feared the answer to her next question, knowing what the answer would be even as she asked it. "What will happen if we don't remove the troops?"

"We've already refused, and he's threatened war."

The breeze stopped. Her breath stopped. The birdsong floating in the air contracted into the sound of the blood rushing in her ears. War. Another war. She groaned inwardly. Once again, families would be ripped apart, men lying in bits on the battlefield, mothers and children starving in the streets because their only means of support was dead or his wounds rendered him incapable of working upon his return.

Food prices would shoot up to unfathomable heights. Honorable women would be forced to turn to prostitution or thievery (or both) to feed their children enough scraps to keep them alive. Perhaps she could be a voice of reason, make him reconsider war. Through him, as a friend, as so many other women before her had done, she might be able to influence political decisions.

"We discussed this all at Catherine's soirée, but I thought it was simply a philosophical or political conversation. The way you're talking now, this seems closer than we imagined and a very real threat." She glanced again at Braedon, who comversed with a mixed group, Dianthe hanging on his arm.

He looked down at his hands. "We're closer to war than anyone realizes."

Fear frosted the inside of her chest. "We can't possibly afford another war?"

Lord Donovan lowered his voice and leaned closer. The sun wove gold through his hair, and he smelled of moss and fresh springs. "We can't. Since the last one, we've made some financial recovery, but our coffers are bare. We aren't in a position for the enormous expenses a war entails. It could destroy us."

134

"What's to be done?" The frost traveled up her throat, pinching her voice. She shuddered, fighting to keep her calm.

"There's the rub. Napoleon met with the Russians last month to see if they would serve as a mediator. Instead, from what we have been able to discover, the Russians came away believing that Napoleon aims to seize Hamburg and Hanover."

"Is that true?"

He shrugged. "Who knows for certain? Napoleon is a master strategist and manipulator. No doubt he's playing some game of his own, and we're the pawns. That's why putting the right man in the foreign secretary position is so essential."

"Will the Russians go to war?"

He turned toward her, his knee pressing hers, his calm sea-green eyes almost blue in the light. "I'm certain the Russians want to avoid war, but I think Alexander feels pressured." He hesitated. He seemed to be struggling with something. "I probably shouldn't tell you this, but...." He leaned closer. She looked down at her folded fan as he spoke in a quiet voice. "I've had news that Russia has begun sending troops to the Baltic coast to protect interests in Hanover and Hamburg. I'm certain Alexander would support us if Napoleon's threats to invade England prove true."

Her stomach bottomed out. *How frightening!* In truth, while she understood Alexander's preemptive move, it wouldn't translate well. Napoleon would take it as an act of aggression. Fearing attack, he'd rally his troops. She sighed and pressed her fingers to the tightening spot between her eyes. Worse, the constant change in foreign secretaries left England's government and its ability to negotiate peace destabilized.

Lord Donovan leaned closer, claiming her free hand. His hand was strong, warm, but without the calluses that marked Braedon's hands. "Don't fear, Lady Birchfield. We will do everything in our power to stop Napoleon and avoid war."

Ravenna watched the guests mill about. The ashen and sweaty Nochdale crossed the yard to meet her stepson, Thomas, and his new wife, Lucy, as they entered the picnic. Her pulse quickened. She couldn't worry about

Napoleon. He was still far away on the Continent. She had more immediate concerns with a murderer circling among her own friends and family.

# Chapter Twenty

Removing her hand from Lord Donovan's, Ravenna nodded. "There's Thomas." She stood and waved. Perhaps she could get him alone for a few moments to warn him to be on his guard.

Thomas and Lucy waved and approached. Lord Thomas, third Marquess of Birchfield, shook hands with Lord Donovan and kissed Ravenna's cheek. "I hope we aren't interrupting, Amma," he said, using the pet name he and his brother, Harrison, had created as an alternative to mother.

Thomas was the very image of his late father. If there was a trace of his late birth mother, it could, in a certain light, be seen only in his oval face and thin lips. His once buoyant nature bore the weight of his father's recent death, managing his seat in Parliament and running the estate he'd inherited.

Thomas's wife, Lucy, had curly, cropped sandy hair and was dressed in a white gingham dress. She fidgeted and seemed vexed. "Good day, Lord Donovan, Dowager Birchfield."

The word "dowager" grated against Ravenna like sandstone. Lucy had said nothing wrong, but Ravenna hated the word. It seemed a word only for dusty old women who doddered in their parlors, taking naps with a pug on their knees.

"Lucy." Ravenna nodded, then turned to Thomas. "You're not interrupting at all. We were discussing Napoleon."

"Ah," his dark eyes danced. "The name on everyone's lips these days. And what have you two decided we should do about Old Boney?" He clasped his hands behind his back.

Lord Donovan said. "Lady Birchfield shares the views of most of the fairer sex. She'd rather have peace than war."

"You're right. I do prefer peace to having our young men blown to bits in a foreign land."

Lord Donovan lifted his brows. "And how else, madam, are we to ensure the freedom of our nation when other nations refuse to leave us to live in peace?"

He wasn't wrong, and her inability to think of a retort annoyed her. So, in a petty move, she ignored Lord Donovan's question and turned to Thomas. "Have you heard from your brother?"

"Not recently."

Lucy giggled. "He'll probably be writing soon to ask for more money, though."

Thomas offered a stilted chuckle. "Well, university is expensive."

Ravenna changed the subject. "How go the repairs to the old rector's cottage at Birchfield? Shall I move in before Michaelmas, do you think?"

"If that's your wish. The roof is nearly finished, and the cracks in the wall in the kitchen have been repaired. There is the matter of a new floor and fireplace for the drawing room, but I can't imagine it should take more than a month or two to complete. When that's done, I'll release the gardener to attack your shrubbery."

Lucy sighed and turned to look out across the yard. Thomas's jaw tightened, and his nostrils flared. There seemed to be some tension between the newlyweds.

Lord Donovan said, "Birchie, I've heard from some of the Pittites that they'd rather have you instead of Nochdale for foreign secretary."

"Must you men talk politics everywhere we go?" Lucy rolled her eyes and adjusted her bonnet.

Thomas stared at her pointedly. "Perhaps you'd like to visit with friends?"

Lucy cocked her head saucily at her husband. "Of course. Please, excuse me. I believe I'm not wanted here at any rate." She strode away to join Lady Braxton's circle.

Thomas sighed, clearly embarrassed. "My apologies."

"Think nothing of it." Ravenna waved her hand. "New marriages are difficult landscapes to traverse. Might I have a word with you in private? For only a moment?"

Donovan bowed. "Please excuse me." He followed Lady Lucy and joined her circle of friends.

Thomas said, "Is this about the calling cards you've left at my home?"

"Yes. Why haven't you responded?"

"I'm very sorry." He batted at a fly. "I've rarely been home. Every well-connected politician and his wife have clamored for my attention. What is so urgent?"

"I think you may be in danger. Your father, Hawkestone, and Wolfsham are all dead, and they all had one thing in common. They were foreign secretaries or being considered for the position."

"And you think someone is killing them?" His dark eyes filled with mirth, mingled with intelligence and wisdom. So much like his father, Philip. An ache opened in her chest.

"Doesn't it seem suspicious?"

He nodded and reached around her to pick a rose. He broke off the thorns. "It does put one on guard."

"Perhaps you should decline the appointment if it were offered?"

"So you would rather I be a coward? Shirk my duty and responsibility to serve and protect this nation? My days wouldn't be worth living if I lived so small."

"Of course, I don't want you to do that. You must do what you think is best. I only hope to warn you to be guarded and aware. Lady Violette and I were at an inquest this morning regarding Hawkestone's death." He frowned with concern. "The officials suspect poison is the cause. I implore you to be careful what you eat and drink and with *whom* you dine. That's all I can ask." She squeezed his arm. "I'd be shirking my duty to your father to try to protect you if I failed to warn you."

He smiled down at her, his eyes filled with warmth. "Thank you, Amma. I know you're following your conscience. I promise I will be careful." He bent down and kissed her cheek, then offered his arm. "I hear you've been spending time with Lord Braedon."

She took his arm and allowed him to guide her toward the party. "We travel in the same circles. That's all."

"Even in a curricle in Hyde Park? Where you two rode alone together?"

Embarrassment flushed her face. "I don't want you to think I'm dishonoring your father, or trying to replace him so soon after his death."

"Not at all. You're still young. I wouldn't deny you a future. I only ask that you use discretion. Especially where Braedon is concerned. He has a certain reputation."

"Do you not like him?"

"I like him a great deal. But that doesn't mean he's safe for ladies." He winked. "He's notorious for leaving broken hearts in his wake."

"I'm well aware of that. And there are no worries on that score. He and I are friends." She watched as Braedon and Dianthe separated from their circle, engaged in a serious conversation. "That's all. Besides, from everything I gather, he and Dianthe are entangled." Gradually, their conversation intensified until, at last, Braedon grabbed Dianthe's elbow and marched her like an errant child to her mother. He then spun on his heel to plant himself beside Catherine.

He laughed. "Entangled is the appropriate word, like a sheep gets entangled in a thorn bush. They seem to enjoy hating each other, yet some invisible thread linking them has yet to be broken. I only wanted you to realize what you might encounter in dealing with him."

She squeezed his arm. "It seems we both must be on guard."

He chuckled. "Indeed."

They fell in beside Lord Donovan and Lucy. Thomas handed Lucy the rose he'd picked and kissed her cheek. She linked her arm with his and smiled into the rose as Donovan drew Thomas into a political conversation. Yet, nothing they said indicated Nochdale's involvement in the deaths of the foreign secretaries and Lord Wolfsham.

Pretending to listen, Ravenna watched the crowd. Again her gaze fell on Braedon.

Always to him. He was searching the crowd, too. Their eyes locked, and a faint smile brushed his lips. Her cheeks heated, and she looked away first, trying to feign interest in Thomas and Donovan's conversation. In the corner of her eye movement caught her attention. She noticed the square-jawed maid who followed the path toward the house where she entered by a back door.

Ravenna studied the gathering in the yard. The placement of the tent and guests blocked a clear view of the rear of the house. She realized then what she needed to do.

# Chapter Twenty-One

A rector and a few clerics entered the garden. They made a direct path to Lady and Lord Nochdale, smiling and chatting. Ravenna was happy to see she wasn't the only person wearing all black at a picnic.

Lady Braxton called for everyone's attention, though she wasn't the hostess or the director of the charity. Guests drifted from all corners of the garden to assemble around her.

Now was Ravenna's opportunity. It was only a small window of time and space where she could be shielded by the crowd. She ducked into the closest garden exit and heading toward Nochdale's house.

Lady Braxton's powerful voice echoed over the hedges and stone walls as she spoke about the Penitent House, the need for it, the funds raised—all the usual things.

Given the amount of information that needed to be disseminated to the guests, Ravenna estimated she had at least a quarter of an hour—probably much longer, if Reverend Howarth spoke. He was one of those men of the cloth who enjoyed the sound of his own voice.

She slipped through the double glass doors and landed in a drawing room. Its worn, comfortable furniture and slightly cluttered space indicated a family drawing room. She ran across the room on her tiptoes, the fan hanging from her wrist, tapping against her leg. She cracked the door and peeked out to ensure she was alone.

With a deep breath to still her racing heart, she gathered up her skirts, tiptoed on phantom feet down the hall, and up the stairs to the first floor to find the study.

At the top of the stairs, she turned left to run down the shadowed hall. She pressed against the wall for a moment to catch her breath and be grateful for her bit of luck at slipping by unseen. She began opening doors and peeking in. The first was a billiard room, the next a gathering room, clearly intended for men only.

The next door she tried revealed the study. She stepped inside, closed, and locked the door. With the heavy, dark furniture and scent of cigar lingering in the air, she was certain this was Nochdale's study.

Ravenna ran to the desk and began pulling open drawers, searching for letters, documents, journals—anything that might hint at his plans for the foreign secretary position. Voices echoed in the hall. She paused to listen. The clipped rattle of the accents indicated that they were servants. Ravenna held her breath as they passed. She exhaled and gently replaced the documents in the order she'd found them. She quietly pushed the drawer shut and opened another drawer, rifling through the drawer, skimming the writing. Nothing. She craned her neck to look out the window. The crowd was still gathered around, listening to a speech.

Lady Augustina Hillingham was speaking. For once, Ravenna was thankful for Lady Hillingham's tangential tangents. She continued searching the desk, shifting papers, thumbing through books, careful to keep everything in its proper order. Nothing. She looked for secret drawers and couldn't find one. She was surprised a man like Nochdale wouldn't use such a device. Even her writing desks contained secret drawers and panels.

Dropping to her hands and knees, she searched under the desk, exploring along the sides and under the desktop, but found no hiding spot. She examined his bookshelf. Nothing. Moving quickly, she lifted the corners of his rug for loose boards. She even peered behind the tapestry for a secret panel and searched the fireplace mantle for a switch to a secret door, as if she were in one of Anne Radcliffe's gothic novels.

Standing in the center of the room, she sighed, opened her fan, and fanned herself, having worked up a sweat with her search activity. She planted a hand on her hip and looked around her. She'd exhausted all the obvious potential hiding places. Either Nochdale had hidden the information elsewhere, or he hadn't been foolish enough to write down anything incriminating.

She peeked out the window again. The rector was speaking, so the speech part of the event would soon end. She needed to return before she was missed.door. When she heard nothing, she eased open the door. Finding the hall empty, she stepped out and tiptoed toward the staircase. She glanced behind her. No one followed. She peeked over the balustrade. She was alone. She lifted her skirts and quickly descended. At the last step, she paused to look behind her as she stepped down.

When she turned back, Nochdale stood in front of her. She gasped loudly, throwing her hand to her throat, surprised by his sudden appearance.

He narrowed his hard eyes at her and ran his tongue over his teeth inside his closed mouth. "Now, now, my dear Lady Birchfield." He clasped his hands behind his back and rocked onto his heels. A large wet spot darkened the front of his waistcoat.

She lowered her hand, her finger brushing the medallion at the end of her fan guard. With a flick of her finger, she could extract the blade hidden there. She estimated the best spots to stick him—if it came to that. Though she hoped it didn't.

"What are you up to?" His gaze trailed up the staircase.

Her mind raced. "I was looking for Lady Nochdale. I thought I saw her come in here during Lady Braxton's speech. I wondered if she might have a needle and a bit of thread to mend the lace on my dress." She looked down and shifted her dress around, looking for the imaginary torn spot, hoping the mere mention of lace would bore him too deeply to care about her problem. "It's here somewhere. I can't seem to find it among all this black." She huffed and dropped her skirt.

His cold stare proved he didn't believe her.

"Well, don't I feel silly?" She chuckled. "I must have imagined it. I'll give it to my lady's maid. She'll find it." Ravenna attempted to edge around him angling for the door leading to the garden.

He blocked her path. The corners of his purplish mouth pulled back to reveal his yellowed, overlapped teeth. His mouth was much the same color as Hawkestone's had been. "I don't understand, Lady Birchfield, why you would think my wife is indoors when her hostess duties keep her in the garden with her guests." He pulled a handkerchief from his pocket and dabbed at the sweat along the edge of his wig and his upper lip.

She shifted to the other side to get around him. "I-I, well, clearly, I was mistaken. But I saw a woman walking up to the house, and I thought it was her, so I followed."

He blocked her and stepped forward.

She flicked the medallion on her fan and felt the blade release. Her body tensed with the anticipation of drawing her blade.

"Lady Birchfield. Why are you in my home, nosing about?" He stopped. His gaze swept slowly around the room. "Your stepson is behind this, isn't he? He sent you to look for secrets?"

She stepped back and to the side. "I don't know what you mean."

"I saw you two conversing together in the garden, thick as thieves. Birchfield sent you to spy." He grabbed her. "What's he looking for?"

"Unhand me," she hissed. "He did no such thing. That's an absurd accusation." She pulled and twisted to free herself, but his grasp was like iron. She hadn't expected such a doughy man to be so strong.

Female voices echoed in the hall, growing gradually louder. A couple of servants rounded the corner. They gasped, ducked their heads, and skittered away. Ravenna looked after them with dashed hopes.

Nochdale shook her once, his fingers digging deeper.

She could easily pull her blade and cut him before he'd realize it, but she didn't want to inflict violence on a nobleman in his own home unless absolutely necessary; it would create too much scandal. A scandal that her stepson's political career—or her reputation—could ill afford.

His face in hers, his sour breath mingled with the sage and lily scent of his cologne. "Listen to me, woman. You can tell Birchfield his plan has failed." Sweat beaded his upper lip. Veins bulged under his widened eyes. "I've found him out. You tell him I'll have the foreign secretary office."

Ravenna winced and pushed back on the anger that surged when his spittle specked her face. He released her, and she flew, wiping her face, as he shouted behind her, "I'll have the post or be damned. You tell him that."

She dashed from the house, glancing behind her repeatedly, slowing to a walk only when she neared the garden. It was clear that Thomas was in danger and that Nochdale would destroy him just as he'd likely destroyed Hawkestone, Wolfsham, and—her heart clenched into a tight fist in her chest—her own dear Philip. She had wanted so much to believe he'd died of natural causes, but now she could no longer hold on to that illusion.

She blew out a final ragged breath and entered the garden, searching for Thomas. She needed to warn him and try to dissuade him from pursuing the foreign secretary office. Her head throbbed from the strain of fighting against the rage and the grief. Her throat constricted. The speeches had finished, and people were again milling about. She didn't see Thomas or Lucy in the crowd, so she fell in between Catherine and Braedon.

"There you are." Braedon smiled at her. "I thought you'd run away again."

She ignored the remark and craned her neck. "Where's Thomas? I need to speak with him."

Catherine fanned herself. "Birchfield left. He looked for you but said he couldn't wait any longer."

Braedon frowned at her. "You seem unwell. Ravenna…." He touched her elbow. "Truly, you're quite flushed."

Ravenna stepped back. His touch was intended to soothe, but it grated against her skin like needles. "I'm sorry. I need to leave this instant. Catherine, may I borrow your carriage?"

Ravenna first visited Pelham House in search of Thomas, but he and Lucy hadn't returned yet, and she didn't know their plans or how long they would be away. She asked his butler for a pen and paper and left a note:

*After recent events, which I can explain to you later, I must insist that you do not pursue the position. I am now certain you are in danger. —Amma*

With no desire to return to the picnic, Ravenna returned home and sent Catherine's carriage back to Nochdale House. She then took up her fencing lesson—and immediately wished she had canceled. She was too unfocused, ruminating on getting caught in Nochdale's study and how much worse she'd likely made the situation for Thomas.

She received a painful poke to the leg from Mr. Norris's foil.

Then there was the matter of Hawkestone. He'd been poisoned, according to the coroner. Would the coroner make the same claim about Wolfsham? And if both of them had been poisoned, had her own husband suffered the same fate? If so, she had no way to prove it.

She resumed her stance and lunged forward, staging a fierce attack toward Mr. Norris, poking his padded stomach. They split and returned to their positions.

She whipped her foil through the air, making a low whistling sound.

Though it wasn't unheard of for men to murder with poison, it seemed an odd weapon for Nochdale since poison was a typically a woman's weapon After all, as a powerful politician, he could purchase an array of methods to dispatch an enemy. Yet, he wouldn't be the first politician to resort to the subtle and shadowy work of poison.

She resumed her stance.

Mr. Norris called *"Allez."*

She charged Mr. Norris, who parried her thrust. They locked foils. Mr. Norris pushed her back and thrust in a motion so quick she didn't see it soon enough to avoid, so she spun her back to the attack and received a hearty thwack to her shoulder. *Heaven's stars!* That stung. She grabbed her shoulder and rubbed it. That would definitely leave a mark. The larger question to consider, however, was how to best protect Thomas?

First, she needed to prove a political conspiracy to murder the foreign secretaries with poison was indeed afoot. If Wolfsham had died in the same manner as Hawkestone, then she knew with certainty that a murderer was lurking in her circle.

She lowered her foil. "Mr. Norris, I'm sorry to shorten our lesson, but I've remembered a prior engagement. I do apologize."

As soon as Mr. Norris left, she ordered the carriage to be brought around and ran upstairs to wipe the sweat from her skin and change into a muslin visiting dress.

When she'd descended the stairs, Braedon was standing in the foyer, staring up at a painting of a Birchfield relative.

"What are you doing here?"

"Inquiring after your health. When Catherine's carriage returned empty to Nochdale House, I wanted to know why you'd left in such a hurry."

"I'm well." She pulled on her gloves as she jogged down the steps.

"I'm unable to receive you. I'm on my way to Wolfsham House."

"Good, I'll go with you."

# Chapter Twenty-Two

Gray skies had moved in quickly to blot out the sun, and a light rain slicked the streets. Ravenna's carriage pulled up in front of the large gray structure in 26 Berkeley Square, known as Wolfsham House. The scent of wet dung, leather, moss, and fish competed with the nearby bakery and coffeehouse. Hatchments covered the windows, and a wreath with black ribbons fluttering in the wind indicated the state of mourning within.

Braedon jumped to the pavement and offered his hand to her.

Standing in the carriage, she glared at him, still annoyed. He had the gall to smile at her. Stubborn, beautiful, provoking man.

"Why don't you go home?" she asked, shaking her hand at the footman to get his assistance. "Or better yet, why don't you go to Dianthe's? I don't understand why you keep inserting yourself—"

Braedon stepped in front of the footman, grabbed her by the waist, and launched her to the pavement. "Because it's infinitely more diverting to vex you."

She looked around while correcting her clothes and scolded him. "I can't believe you did that, in public, no less...." She straightened her bonnet and cut her eyes at the footman to silently communicate he should keep his mouth shut.

They were shown into the drawing room. Family portraits lined the peach and white striped walls with large windows framed by sage curtains.

As they claimed their seat on the sofa, Braedon said, "Did you receive an invite to the Everleigh Ball tomorrow night?"

"I did."

"Good. Then I'd like to escort you. I'll come for you around nine."

"This is hardly the place for this conversation." A feather of joy brushed around her heart briefly that he'd wanted to escort her to a ball.

"You're so fond of running away, I have to catch you when I can."

She rolled her eyes at him, straightened the skirts of her weeds, and the joy dissipated. "It's quite presumptuous to expect me to arrive on your arm. It would be wildly inappropriate—"

She was primed to suggest he should instead escort Dianthe when Lady Wolfsham entered the room.

She was a woman in her late thirties, of average height, with fiery red hair. Her gaunt face hung with sorrow.

After greeting each other, Ravenna said, "I'm so sorry to impose upon you, but it's rather urgent, and I'll take as little of your time as possible."

Lady Wolfsham sat on the edge of a chair across from the sofa. "How can I help you?"

"First, please allow me to extend my sincerest condolences. I was so sorry to hear of your husband's passing."

"As was I. Please accept my condolences as well," Braedon said.

Lady Wolfsham nodded. "Yes, it was quite sudden and unexpected." She touched her handkerchief to her nose.

Ravenna continued, "If you'll permit me, I have some hard questions to ask concerning his death."

Lady Wolfsham straightened her back. "I can't imagine what they would be, but please, continue."

"Do you have any reason to believe that he might have been, forgive me, murdered?"

Braedon slowly turned his head to stare in shocked disbelief at Ravenna.

Lady Wolfsham's jaw hardened, but she didn't seem astonished or affronted.

"Actually, it wouldn't surprise me. In fact, I've been wondering that myself."

"Why do you say that?" Ravenna clutched her folded fan in her lap.

"The suddenness of his illness, for one. Also, Nochdale is a vicious man—the sort who will stop at nothing to ensure his ascension to power. My husband and Hawkestone, for that matter, were in his way."

Ravenna's breath caught. She hadn't alluded to Hawkestone, but it was most interesting Lady Wolfsham mentioned him. "What does Hawkestone have to do with it?"

"I overheard Nochdale speaking with another man, don't know who he was, about how he wanted the foreign secretary position and was determined to get it at all costs."

"I see." That didn't mean much. Nochdale may have been complaining to a friend. "Did Wolfsham have any reason to think he might be in danger? Did he say anything about it?"

"Not exactly. Only that Nochdale had, in his words, 'strongly encouraged' him to drop from consideration." She paused, cocking her head, her jet earbob dancing. "And to try to convince him that he didn't have enough experience to do the job adequately."

"Did he have any enemies?"

Lady Wolfsham chuckled. "Of course. He was a politician. Enemies come with the occupation, do they not?"

"Anyone other than Nochdale come to mind?"

She thought for a moment. "No one in particular."

"If you think of someone, can you let me know?"

"Of course." She cocked her head, perplexed. "Exactly what is your interest in this? Why are you asking these questions?"

Ravenna frowned and licked her lips. She didn't want to say too much. "I'm merely curious."

Lady Wolfsham tipped her head in disbelief.

"Very well. I have reason to believe none of the recent deaths, including my husband, are accidental."

Lady Wolfsham put a hand to her breast. "How dreadful. And you think Nochdale might be to blame for the deaths?"

"I don't want to say that without proof because I don't want to unfairly disparage him if he's innocent. I only want to get at the truth, so I beg you would remain discreet."

"Of course. You may rely upon my silence."

"You might be visited by an officer by the name of Mr. Chadwick. He's investigating Hawkestone's death."

Her brows lifted. "Do you think he's to be trusted? Most Bow Street Runners are little more than brigands and ruffians themselves."

"I can't be sure. He's quite sly and clever."

Braedon interjected, "I'd advise you to say only what is necessary. Do be careful in what you tell him."

Lady Wolfsham's jaw tightened, and she lifted her chin. "Understood. If, in the meantime, you discover my husband was murdered, I want to be informed. Because I will see the man hang."

# Chapter Twenty-Three

Ravenna strode out of Wolfsham House with Braedon on her heels. The weather had turned remarkably worse. A torrent of rain fell, the wind whipping it into her face and down the neck of her spencer. She ran toward the carriage as a footman approached with an umbrella.

She no longer held any doubt that Nochdale had something to do with the murders of Hawkestone and Wolfsham—and maybe even her own husband, though the thought turned her stomach. It was still possible that Julia Pence might've been involved. Perhaps she and Nochdale were colluding. Or perhaps Julia killed Hawkestone and unwittingly did Nochdale a favor by taking out one of his enemies. But possibilities weren't certainties. She needed to know something for certain—and her patience was nearing the end of its rope.

Braedon ran forward, grabbed the umbrella, and sent the footman away. Holding the umbrella over her head while he remained in the rain, he grabbed her arm and spun her around. "Am I to understand you're tracking Nochdale like some huntress to prove he's a murderer?" Rain dripped from the brim of his hat.

"I'm not at liberty to speak of it." She tried to ignore her wet slippers. "And it's rude to keep a lady in the rain."

His eyes flashed, and his grip tightened on her arm. "Don't toy with me, Ravenna."

She glared at his hand and jerked her arm away. "Do not presume to manhandle me. I not only owe you no explanations, I never asked you to

153

join me on this visit." She wanted to tell him everything, but she didn't want to risk exposing herself, who she'd once been. He wouldn't understand. He'd hate her. Maybe she shouldn't care if he hated her, but she did. Truth be told, it'd be a relief to share the burden. He probably knew people who had the answers she needed.

"Well, well, well," A man's voice called out.

*Mr. Chadwick.*

Braedon whispered, "We'll talk about this more later."

"No. We won't," she said.

Chadwick stepped through the gate. "How interesting that as big as London is, Lady Birchfield, you and I keep meeting at locations most central to my investigation."

"Pure coincidence, I assure you," Ravenna pulled her wet skirt away from her legs. "If I'd known you were going to be here, I would've postponed my visit." She clasped her hands in front of her.

Something between a smile and sneer tickled the edges of his mouth, then disappeared. The disdain in his eyes spoke clearly enough. Then he glanced between her and Braedon, "I do hope I'm not interrupting. Looked like an interesting scene unfolding, I daresay. Like something in a play." His steely eyes fell again on Ravenna. "Something I understand you're familiar with."

Her heart fluttered. He'd found out about her theater past. What else had he discovered? Words clogged her throat. She didn't know what to say.

Thankfully, Braedon stepped in. "Mr. Chadwick, it's rude to keep a lady talking in the street, especially in the rain. If you have any further questions, you know where Gordon House is. Good day." He pushed past Chadwick and opened the door.

Ravenna placed her hand in his, and she climbed into the carriage, thankful he'd intervened.

Mr. Chadwick's voice stopped her. "Lady Birchfield?"

She paused at the carriage door and looked over her shoulder.

"Your *cavalier servente* won't always be around to get between us. And I believe I'm closing in."

When they'd returned to Gordon House, Ravenna allowed Braedon to help her to the stones. The rain had eased to a drizzle, but she was wet, cold, tired, and longed for hot tea and a hot bath. "Thank you for coming with me today."

He lifted his brows, taking the umbrella from the footman, and holding it over her. "You didn't seem to feel that way earlier." They walked toward the house and stopped at the gate.

"I suppose I came around when you confronted Mr. Chadwick." She managed a fragile smile.

He squeezed her hand and lifted it to his chest. His intense gaze half-shadowed by the brim of his hat. "Ever your servant. " His blue eyes twinkled. "Especially if you need a *cavalier servente.*"

Conflicting feelings swirled inside her. Excitement that this handsome, sensual man was interested in her. Or the guilt that she was still a widow. Maybe shame that she still loved her husband and she wouldn't allow him to be supplanted so easily. Or the fevered, high-pitched trill of primal desire for this man that began to drown all the others. She withdrew her hand, shaking her head. "You forget yourself." Was she talking to him or herself?

"You'll find I'm a patient man. Where it matters." He touched a dark ringlet, coiled it around his finger. "Dark as a raven's wing." Her heart fluttered like a flock of pheasants flushed from a bush. Her gaze fell to his lips, full, velvety. "Good evening, my little raven."

She began to smile then it fell. Her skin prickled. She scanned the street.

Braedon frowned, and his gaze followed hers. "What are you looking for?"

"I feel as though we're being watched." Fear crept over her skin like a bunch of spiders.

He handed the umbrella to her. "Go inside. I'll wait here."

After dinner and an evening of reading, Ravenna dressed for bed in a white muslin nightgown, leaving her widow's weeds in a black, ink-like pool on the hearth to dry in front of the fire. She hadn't been able to stop thinking about her meeting with Mr. Chadwick at Wolfsham House. All evening she tossed back and forth in her mind if she should tell him her suspicions. If nothing else, it might deflect his pursuit of her and give him another focus.

She sat at her writing desk and took up her quill pen. With a deep breath, she began the note to Mr. Chadwick. She informed him of Lord Nochdale's deep lust for possessing the foreign secretary post at all costs. When Hart came in to collect her discarded clothes, Ravenna asked her to post the letter first thing in the morning. It was done. The chances of Chadwick learning anything from Nochdale were small, but it might delay his investigation and buy her some time.

She let down her hair and climbed into bed, the cotton sheets cool against her legs. She sank into her down mattress and snuggled deep under the covers. She tried to think of the investigation, to weigh the likelihood that Nochdale was a killer against the chances that he and Julia Pence were working together, and if there were anyone else possibly involved in the recent murders.

Thoughts of Braedon sneaked around the corners of her mind, chased by shadows of guilt for daring to think about a man other than Philip. She rolled to her side, fluffed her pillow under her neck, and squeezed her eyes shut in an attempt to force Braedon out of her head.

In the wee hours of the morning, her bedroom window shattered. She jolted up in time to witness a torch slice the air; it hit the glass-covered hardwood floor and rolled onto the carpet, catching it ablaze. Sparks shot off the crown and caught the curtains on fire.

She jumped from the bed and shoved her feet into her slippers. She half-hopped and half-ran across the floor, pulling on her shoes. She threw open the door and shrieked for help and water. Ravenna ran back to her bedchamber, grabbed the pitcher of water from the washstand, and poured it on the torch. Small flames hopped onto the rug, sparking independent flames. The curtains blazed with livid, greedy flames.

Mr. Banks ran in, his dressing robe flowing behind him and his cap askew. On his heels ran footmen and maids in their nightgowns and caps with pitchers of water, even chamber pots, from their own rooms. A cacophony of voices filled the room as the servants shouted at each other to hurry.

Above all the voices, Mr. Banks barked out commands as though he were leading his soldiers on the battlefield in the heat of war.

Mr. Banks and a few footmen remained behind to fight the fire while the other servants scurried away to gather more water from the kitchen and start a bucket line. Mr. Banks nudged Ravenna out of the way and took the head of the bucket line, throwing water on the curtains as the pitchers and pots were handed to him.

Hart ran in with a wet, heavy wool blanket and threw herself, blanket and all, on top of the fire. She rolled on top of the rug, attempting to extinguish the remnants of the fire. A flame caught the hem of her nightgown and ignited. She screamed and slapped at the growing flames.

Coughing, choking on smoke, Ravenna grabbed a pitcher of water and dumped it on Hart. They worked together to extinguish the rest of the fire on the carpet, then jumped into line to fight the fire licking at the casement.

Buckets upon bowls upon pitchers handed down the line of servants finally snuffed the fire. Ravenna slumped into a chair and took in the damage: the broken window, the black charred casement, the smoke stains on the ceiling, the burned rug and charred floor, the pools of water mixed with the urine from the chamber pots thrown by panicked servants. Ash fell like snow in the air. The rug was ruined. The curtains ruined. Windows had been thrown open to release the stench of smoke, but the cold, damp morning air did little to assist. The smoke stench clung to everything.

Hart stood at an undamaged window, looking down on the street. Her wet, fire-eaten nightgown, adhered to her red and blistered shins.

Shivering in the morning chill, Ravenna wrapped up in a shawl and toed her way through the water and broken glass. She picked up the extinguished torch and studied it.

Hart, frowning, left the window and limped toward Ravenna. "What shall we do, milady?"

"First, I'll put balm on your legs. Then we'll get everything cleaned up and make a list of the necessary repairs. The window must be covered up first thing, and I'll need to move rooms so repairs can be made." She looked again at the window, pensive.

Hart stepped closer and lowered her voice. "This was deliberate, wasn't it?"

Ravenna nodded. "I fear it was." This had to be the work of The Unity. Or...perhaps this was something Nochdale would do to threaten and silence her in hopes of making Thomas back off of the foreign secretary position.

"Who would do such a thing?"

"That's exactly what I aim to discover."

# Chapter Twenty-Four

It was a horrible time for Braedon to visit. The house had been upended all morning. She and the servants had just finished breakfast and were cleaning Ravenna's bedchamber when he was announced. As he removed his hat and stepped into the room, he looked around, astonished.

Ravenna swept broken glass into a fireplace shovel.

"I hope you don't mind the footman sent me up straight away." He scanned the floor, taking in the scene. "I came to see if you wanted to accompany me to the museum. I reserved a viewing for us, but it seems you may be too busy."

Ravenna pushed back a swathe of hair with a sigh and planted her fists on her hips. "I am. Though the museum sounds like a great deal more fun."

"What happened?"

She stood and handed the broom to a maid, gave a few directions, then turned to Braedon. She motioned toward the glassless window and the smoke-stained wall. "Someone threw a torch through my window."

"What?" He spun to face her and looked her over. "Were you hurt?"

"I wasn't hurt, but I am terribly...angry."

"Of course. Anyone would be. When did this happen?"

"Near dawn, perhaps. I'm not certain. I was asleep." She hugged herself. "All I know is I heard a crash and saw a torch flying through the air. Once it landed, the fire caught quickly."

"Dear God! You must have been terrified!"

"Absolutely. Houses burn in a flash. I'm eternally thankful for my staff. Without them...." She shuddered and hugged herself tighter.

He put a comforting arm around her shoulders and pulled her close. His sandalwood scent wrapped around her, warming her. She let him hold her for a brief moment, enjoying the small comfort. She broke away to sit on the sofa.

"I believe this was deliberate," he said. "No one throws torches through windows without a reason. But who? Why would someone want to attack your house?"

Could have been Nochdale, if he sensed she was closing in on him. Might also be The Unity. But it was best to not broach that subject. She kept her answer vague. "I think whoever did this is afraid to lose what they most desire."

"Yes." He looked down at her. "But you have your suspicions, I presume?"

She shrugged.

"If you have any ideas, please tell me. I may be able to help. What if you're attacked again?"

Nochdale had to be behind the attack, but she wasn't prepared to divulge her suspicions because it increased the risk of having to also give up her own secrets. She needed to confront him somehow, but going to his home or office was unthinkable. The location needed to be public, where he would be less likely to attack her.

Braedon touched her cheek. "Ravenna, what can I do?"

The idea fell into her mind like a raindrop on the pavement. Braedon had proven helpful and willing to protect her when necessary. Since Nochdale had proven himself violent, she was afraid to confront him alone. "You can escort me to the theater tonight."

# Chapter Twenty-Five

Braedon arrived that evening, on time, polished as a gem and smelling of an intoxicating blend of sandalwood and spices. He was dressed formally in his black suit with knee breeches and white silk stockings that revealed his chiseled calves. Ravenna should've been less happy to see him. Should've smiled a little less brightly. Should've taken the edge of delight out of her voice when she greeted him. But that was becoming increasingly difficult to do.

He seemed not quite vexed, but not quite his usual clever and charming self. He seemed preoccupied, if not a little tired.

"Have you had some difficulty since last we spoke?" She settled into the carriage seat.

"Somewhat." He sat across from her and looked out the window, though there was nothing to see in the surrounding darkness. The carriage lurched forward and carried them in quiet contemplation toward Drury Lane.

The plaza bustled with activity where society's highest and lowest classes—and everything in between—walked elbow to elbow. Salop vendors sold their warm, milky nectar, food vendors plied hot potatoes and mincemeat pies, and flower girls offered their violets. Carriages toted people to and from the theaters between gaming hells, gin houses, brothels, and homes.

Prostitutes, drunks, stray cats and dogs, and stray children littered the area under the feet of delicate, diamonded ladies in gossamer gowns who floated into the theater on the arms of their shiny gentlemen bound in their tight black suits and white stockings. The scent of urine and gin from the alley, and the smoke of nearby fireplaces, snaked through the air and mixed with the scent of wet earth, moss, and the colognes of passersby.

Ravenna pulled her purple pashmina tighter around her shoulders and linked her arm with Braedon's to keep from getting separated in the throng. Returning to the theater, especially as a patron, was always a bittersweet affair for her.

Braedon leaned close. "Do you miss being an actress, my little raven? Do you long to return to the night's adventures and mysteries?"

She stared at the woman peering from the shadows with deeply rouged cheeks and a skirt pulled up on one side to reveal her whole calf. She was probably in her mid-twenties. About the same age Ravenna had been when she met Philip. Ravenna shuddered, pulling her pashmina even tighter. "Not often."

"If you're cold, do allow me to hold you closer." Braedon drew her tighter against him.

She smiled up at him. His gaze lingered, searching her face. Heat bloomed in her chest, vining through her body.

Her beaded demi-train tugged at the carpeted stairs as she ascended to the family box. She searched the crowd for the Nochdales, uncertain if they would be in attendance since it was the opening night of a new play, when attendance was most unpredictable.

Braedon's agitation seemed to increase the longer they were inside the theater. His eyes darted. "Are you sure your attacker will be here?"

"No." She craned her neck to search the crowd. "I'm hoping a conversation with people close to my suspect will reveal the truth." When the Nochdales didn't appear, Ravenna resigned herself to taking a seat inside the box.

"I suppose you won't tell me whom you suspect?"

"I suspect Nochdale. Though I can't be certain." She ducked through the curtain. She wasn't going to say anything about The Unity.

"You think he threw a torch through your window? For what purpose?"

"Well, he probably paid someone else to do it. And the purpose is clear. He wants to intimidate Thomas and scare him away from the foreign secretary post by attacking me."

"You know that sounds mad."

"I don't care." Smoothing her skirt beneath her, Ravenna sat in the center seat. "I have my reasons, and I trust you to understand that."

She searched the pale blue theater with its gold lattice trim and domed ceiling. Four rows of boxes lined the walls from floor to ceiling. Candelabras in the boxes and on the stage lit the room. Only a few boxes remained empty.

*A Tale of Terror* had been a much-anticipated play. Behind the orchestra pit, commoners packed the benches, sitting elbow to elbow. Ravenna remembered from her orange-girl days how hot and uncomfortable it could be. In the warmer months, people fainted from the hot and stuffy conditions.

Ravenna leaned on the balustrade, searching for the Nochdales. In one box, a few rows down, she noticed a young-ish man with a long, narrow face, bumpy nose, and almost white hair pulled into a ponytail sitting alone. Ravenna had never seen the man before, but he reminded her of some of the theater managers she once worked with—clothing of quality pinned over a low-class man. She didn't like the look of him.

As if she'd never left, she could still feel the stage boards through her slippers, the trepidation and excitement of looking out on the sea of faces eager to be entertained.

Halfway through the second act, the Nochdales entered their box to catch the rest of the production, common enough behavior among the elites since the primary purpose was to see other people and gossip rather than indulge in a play.

When the play had ended, Ravenna said to Braedon, "The Nochdales are here. Let's go find them." They waded against the stream of people filing into the hall and down the stairs. On the first level, she nearly hit against Nochdale as he exited his box. He was pale, dabbing at his pain-twisted face and purpled lips with a handkerchief. He seemed on the verge of vomiting.

Mr. Fox walked alongside him, whispering. Both men halted and greeted her grudgingly. "Lady Birchfield." Nochdale made a stiff half-bow. He continued, "Been pilfering any studies lately?"

Fox lifted his thick black brows. "I believe this is a personal conversation.

Excuse me." He stepped away, too round to bow more than his neck to Ravenna.

Ravenna said to Nochdale, "And have you been breaking windows and setting fires lately?"

He scoffed. "You're a lunatic."

Braedon stepped up to Ravenna's side.

As Nochdale turned to leave, Ravenna said, "How goes your bid for foreign secretary?"

He stopped. "Better than expected." He coughed.

"Oh?" She stepped closer, gripping her folded fan, ready to extract her blade. "When a man in your position is desperate for power, to what lengths will he go to destroy his opponent?"

A storm brewed in his eyes. "What are you implying?" At his safe distance, he had the pluck to say to Braedon, "You need to take your new woman home. She's overreached."

Ravenna stood close enough to see the fine red veins in his rheumy eyes. "Does a man desperate for power turn to murder, you fiend?"

He stepped back. "What in the name of the heavens are you talking about?" He stared at her as though snakes wiggled out of her head.

She wavered. He seemed genuinely perplexed. Was it possible he was such a good actor? She was almost convinced. She screwed up her courage. "Play ignorant, if you so choose. Everything concealed will be brought to light." Her gut twisted in regards to the hypocrisy of hiding her own past yet calling him out on his secrets.

Then it happened all at once.

Nochdale pinched her at the underside of her elbow, right above where the joint knotted. It was a searing pain. He spat, "Listen, you addle-brained trollop…"

The pinch hurt like the devil but was cut short because no sooner than he touched her, Braedon slammed him against the wall. People nearby gasped and whispered. Braedon's other arm was already cocked to deliver a blow as Nochdale turned his head, throwing his hands in front of his face. "Wait, no…."

# CHAPTER TWENTY-FIVE

Onlookers gathered closer.

Ravenna rubbed the smarting area where Nochdale pinched her. "Brae-don, stop."

"Touch her again, and she won't be able to call me off. Understand?" He backed up, letting go of Nochdale.

Nochdale straightened his clothes, glaring at Braedon. "Threaten me and accost me all you wish, but I won't let Birchfield, you, nor anyone else prevent my rise to foreign secretary. I'm destined for the post."

Ravenna stepped closer and slapped him. "Is that what you told Wolfsham and Hawkestone just before you killed them? And what about my husband?" Rage coursed through her veins, sprouting tears in her eyes. "Since you didn't have the courage to face them with a blade, did you at least have the courage to deliver the poison yourself? Or did you hire some underling to do it for you?"

Fear feathered with anger brushed Nochdale's features. "You're mad."

Braedon wrapped his fingers around her wrist and whispered against her ear. "Let him go. This is getting out of hand."

Nochdale backed slowly away, sliding across the wall. Perspiration beading his forehead. "You, stay away from me. If you were a man, I'd demand satisfaction."

Braedon jumped in. "I'm pleased to give you all the satisfaction you require."

Nochdale walked away, dabbing the sweat with a handkerchief and glancing over his shoulder.

The scene at an end, the crowd dispersed, forming into little, whispering cells.

Braedon offered his arm. "Come along. I'm ordering the carriage."

Ravenna linked her arm with his. He left her by a window. She rubbed her arm, stood against the wall, racking her brain for an answer as to how she should proceed. Nochdale had seemed genuinely perplexed when she confronted him, but it was possible he was a skilled liar. He was a talented politician, after all, which required an equal measure of talent for acting when it served a purpose. No. She couldn't doubt herself. She was getting close to the truth. Why else would he turn so vicious and fearful? And he'd never actually denied her accusations. He'd only called her names.

Lady Braxton approached. "Good evening, Lady Birchfield." Her eyes lit with amusement. "That was quite the spectacle. Far better than the play, in my estimation."

Ravenna was still shaking with anger. "I'm not inclined to feed the rumor mill this evening, Lady Braxton."

Lady Braxton opened her fan and whispered behind it. "I wager it was about Birchie?"

Irritating woman. The presumption to refer to her stepson so casually. Only Thomas' closest friends called him Birchie. Ravenna shook her head.

She must have read something on Ravenna's face or demeanor because she gasped. "I knew it! I've heard Nochdale's upset that Birchie opposes him for the foreign secretary position."

"How quickly news travels."

Her violet eyes twinkled. "Indeed. But it doesn't signify because Birchie isn't interested in the position from what I understand."

"He's undecided at the moment, which isn't the same as lacking interest. Though, I'd prefer he refuse the position if it's offered."

"Why?"

Ravenna crossed her arms and shrugged. "With so many men in the office dying, it seems an unhealthy position to have these days."

"What do you mean?"

"Do you not see? Hawkestone and Wolfsham have both died in such a short time and not long after the death of my own husband. All in the space of nine months. The last two in quick succession."

She tilted her head. "I don't understand, dear."

Ravenna was saying too much in the heat of her anger and distress. "Never mind."

Lady Braxton studied her for a moment then her face brightened. "You don't mean...murder? Assassination?"

Her arms still crossed, Ravenna shrugged.

Lady Braxton's face tightened, locking a demeanor of pleasantness in place that gave her an air of discomfort. She seemed to be struggling with something. Then she burst into loud laughter. "Oh, my, Lady Birchfield, you almost had me fooled." She laughed heartily. "Perhaps you shouldn't watch any more plays like *A Tale of Terror*. It causes flights of fancy. Only comedies for you, I say. Excuse me, I see Lady Hillingham, and I need to speak with her before she leaves."

The strange man she'd seen in the theater stood across the room, staring at her. He was skinnier than he'd appeared earlier, and his pale skin and black eyes gave him a ghostly, almost other-worldly quality.

Ravenna shuddered and pulled her pashmina around her shoulders. She wanted to be home, in her dressing gown, in front of a fire with a glass of port and a book.

Braedon came to her rescue to announce their carriage was ready. "What's wrong? Are you still upset about Nochdale?"

"No. There's a strange man…." She nodded in the direction of the man, but he was gone. She craned her neck. "He was there. By that statue…"

Braedon glanced around with a hand on the small of her back. "Let's go, my little raven."

The temperature had dropped, and the air inside the carriage was chilled, but not uncomfortable. She settled against the soft kid-leather seat as the carriage pulled away from the theater, and the soft sway and clop-clop of the horses' hooves created a pleasant, steady rhythm.

"Do you believe me about the foreign secretaries?"

"I do agree it's strange for three men in the same position have died within such a short time. Murder is a grave consideration. That you think Nochdale may be involved…." He paused. "Though I don't like him, it seems an outrageous accusation."

"Why should it be so? You heard him this evening. He declared he'd stop at nothing to be foreign secretary."

"I suppose…" He trailed off.

"You were ready to cut him down on my behalf at the theater, yet you don't believe me?"

"That's different. That was because he laid hands on you." His voice was full of heat.

The rest of the ride to Gordon House was silent. When the carriage rolled to a stop, Braedon jumped from the carriage and lifted Ravenna to the stones. Fog snaked around her ankles and through the streets. Ravenna, empty and sad, stood and, for a moment, watched the fog curl around the buildings and trees in the half-moonlight before turning toward the house.

Braedon followed her to her doorstep.

She opened the door and stepped inside. "Thank you for taking me to the theater. Good night, Braedon." She started to shut the door.

Braedon stopped the door with his hand. "Ravenna, it's not that I don't believe you—"

"Never mind." She was too tired to engage in the conversation any further. She yearned for her port and book in front of the fire.

# Chapter Twenty-Six

She locked the door behind her and lit a tallow candle. Ravenna thumbed through her mail. There were a few letters from The Penitent House, one from Lady Braxton, one from Catherine, and a few invitations to dinners and balls.

Something banged against her door. It wasn't the knocker. She peeked through the window curtain near the door, but couldn't see anything. Maybe Braedon had returned? She set down her mail and picked up her fan. She cracked the door and peeked outside. She opened the door wider to get a better look. She heard something move in the bushes to the left, but still couldn't see anything. She stepped out on her doorstep, looking in the direction of the noise. "Who's there? Hello?"

It all happened in a blink. Before she'd quite realized the sound of shoes scuffing on the stones, a man's hand grabbed her around the mouth and pressed a knife against her throat. His breath was hot against her cheek, and it stunk of cigars and coffee. He jerked at her, pulling her out of her front gate. She struggled against him, attempting to wrench free of his grasp. She tried to bite his hand but grabbed a mouthful of leather instead.

He chuckled and spoke in a gruff voice, "You've got spirit. I like it."

He pulled her toward the alley by her house. She would not go easily into that alley. She dragged her feet to impede his progress. Her slippers scuffed and tapped on the stones in a wild dance. The metallic taste of fear coated her tongue and thrummed in black waves through her body, manifesting in a rapid pulse and shaking limbs. She fumbled with her fan, feeling for the medallion at the base of the fan guard. She needed to draw her dagger, but he was so strong, and her panic rendered her fingers dumb.

*Keep your wits.* She chided herself. *Stop flailing like a silly girl and think. What do you notice?*

He held her against his chest. Her head came under his chin, so he had to be at almost six feet tall. He seemed wiry, lean. Under his stinking breath was the sweet, flowery scent of his cologne. One she'd smelled before. Mayfair. It was a popular scent among gentlemen.

He had succeeded in getting her to the mouth of the alley. If he managed to pull her into the dark yawn, all was lost.

*No.* She let go of his arms, and the tip of his knife pressed deeper against her throat. She reached for her fan, swinging on her wrist. Her fingers searched for the medallion. It was her one chance. Fumbling over the disc, she couldn't quite get a hold of it. Her body was weakening, growing tired in the struggle; it was becoming more difficult to fight him. She tried again. Her fingers lit on the medallion, and flipped it. Springing the blade, she clutched it with desperation, and jerked it from its sheath.She whipped the dagger back and down as hard and fast as possible, right into the assailant's thigh. His knife clattered as he dropped it, and he loosed a high-pitched yelp and howl like an injured dog.

She shrieked, "Watch! Help! Gordon House!" The fog was too thick to see the watchmen's lanterns or anything at a distance. She spun around in hopes of seeing his face or any distinguishing feature, but saw only a lurching shadow retreating into the fog.

Before he could disappear into the fog, she ran and pounced on him, tackling him to the ground. She tried to straddle him as she sliced at him, but she managed only to cut his arms and coat as he attempted to fend off her attack.

A watchman called out for her. "Where are you?"

"Gordon House! Help!"

The attacker, cursing her, shoved her off of him as he scrambled away from her, then pushed himself to his feet.

Ravenna tried to stand, but her skirts tangled her legs. As she managed to perch on her knees, he struck her across the face. Pain splintered like lightning across her mouth, jaw, and nose. He'd hit her hard enough to unbalance her, and she toppled onto the stones. She tasted the coppery flavor of her own blood. She kicked at her skirts and tried to pull them over her knees as she struggled to get to her feet. She was too late.

He ran off in an irregular rhythm, his boots scuffling on the stones as he fled, limping as the boots of the watchmen closed in. She pulled herself to her feet. That mere act awakened the various spots on her body that stung and burned. She first saw the dim glow of the lantern, then a watchman emerged from the fog.

"Are you well, ma'am?" His buggy eyes searched her face. "What happened?"

"A man attacked me. He ran that way." She pointed. "The fog is too thick. There's no chance of you finding him now. But I stabbed him in the thigh, so he has a mighty limp now." She shivered as the damp chill settled around her.

"I'll see you to your house, ma'am, then I'll go in search of him. I might get lucky enough to find him."

"Thank you." She limped alongside him to her door, her face throbbing as she struggled to mask the state of near hysteria growing inside her. She shut herself inside her house and peeked out the window to watch the lanterns of the watchmen disappear into the fog in the direction of the attacker. She leaned against the casement, shivering, breathing heavily, and fighting against the reflexive crying.

After a few moments, she had rallied enough to drag her bruised and aching body to her bedchamber to survey and clean the wounds. The bastard had managed to nick her throat and arm before she'd stabbed him. Her throat and face were bruised, her lip cut and bleeding, her nose swollen, and her eye was growing dark and puffy. She applied a chamomile ointment to her injuries. Fortunately, nothing seemed to require stitching.

After taking a moment to think about her attacker, she couldn't imagine who it was. He'd come out of nowhere. Nothing about him was familiar. Perhaps he was one of hundreds of scoundrels roaming the streets of London at night, attacking innocent people. But that wasn't likely.

He wore Mayfair. Though it was a popular cologne, it was not one that a common thief, a street thug, could afford. Nochdale. He had to be behind the attack. He'd been angry after she'd confronted him at the theater, so he sent a lackey to silence her. Or it was The Unity. The attacker had spoken to her, but she couldn't discern any distinct accent or speech defect. In fact, it seemed as though he was attempting to mask his natural voice. She shuddered. Either way, she was incredibly lucky.

To dull her pain and calm her mind and nerves, she took a nip of laudanum, a bitter elixir, straight from the bottle and washed it down with a shot of brandy. Ravenna slipped into bed and floated to sleep.

A pounding sound jerked Ravenna from her sleep. She sat up in bed, listening, and was in such a fog that, at first, she couldn't discern where the pounding originated. When she realized someone was at her bedchamber door, she stumbled from her bed, wrapping her dressing gown around her, and opened the door.

Hart stood on the other side in the glow of a candle. She wore a nightgown wrapped in a shawl, and her brown hair trailed in a braid over one shoulder. Her limpid eyes shone with fright. "Lady Birchfield. What happened to your face?"

"Never mind that," Ravenna snapped, straining to open her eyes. Her head throbbed. "Why are you pounding on my door in the dead of night?" The attacker's grip had bruised her neck, and her mouth was swollen, making it difficult for her to speak.

"Lord Donovan is downstairs. He has an urgent message for you."

Ravenna threw on a dressing gown, strode down the hall, and descended the stairs, her gown billowing behind her. Hart ran alongside her, helping to light the way.

Lord Donovan paced in the foyer, his hair a halo, his cravat off, hanging from his coat pocket. He was the very image of a playful libertine. "Lady Birchfield—Dear God, what happened to you?"

"Doesn't matter. What's happened? Why are you here?"

"It's Birchie. He was at White's with us…"

"Us, who?"

"Braedon, Yarford, and myself. We were at White's playing billiards when Birchie fell violently ill." He ran his hands over his hair, panicked.

Ravenna couldn't help but think Braedon would handle a dire situation with a cooler head.

Donovan continued. "He vomited and collapsed. Yarford took him home, and Braedon went in search of a surgeon. Braedon insisted I should tell you."

"Yes. Thank you. I'm going to change and pack a few things. You'll take me to Pelham House?"

"Yes, of course."

She spun and ran upstairs with Hart.

Once in the bedchamber, Ravenna hrew off her clothing while Hart rummaged through the wardrobe for traveling clothes. Ravenna slipped into a black crepe dress. Not bothering to fix her hair, she chose to leave it in a long, messy braid. Donning a cloak, she grabbed her fan, reticule, and medicine chest. She asked Hart to stay behind and wait for word. Within a quarter of an hour, Ravenna was dressed and running down the stairs toward Lord Donovan, who paced the foyer, slapping his riding gloves against his thigh impatiently.

Ravenna and Donovan stepped into the night. The fog had lifted, and the light from the link-boy's lantern rippled in a nearby puddle. Lord Donovan opened the carriage door, assisted her inside, then climbed in beside her, the carriage rocking with his weight.

The carriage pulled into the street. Ravenna asked, "Did Thomas complain of feeling poorly before he became ill?"

"No, but he clearly wasn't comfortable. He was perspiring rather profusely, but I thought that was because the room was warm, stuffy. He was pale and seemed generally unwell. Then all of a sudden, he began vomiting. I didn't think he was going to stop."

*Blasted Nochdale. He must have a hand in this.*

Donovan continued, "We got him outside, hoping the fresh air might help him rally. But he fainted straight away, right into Braedon's arms."

"Poor Thomas." She rubbed her face, wincing. She'd forgotten about her own injuries. She seethed inwardly. *Nochdale will pay dearly for this.*

# Chapter Twenty-Seven

As soon as the carriage rolled to a halt, Ravenna and Donovan jumped to the pavement. She grabbed her medicine chest and charged through the iron gate Donovan held open for her. A thin scullery maid with a single candle opened the front door. Her mobcap sat askew. She yawned and fumbled to light another candle. Ravenna passed her medicine chest to Lord Donovan and accepted the candle from the girl who led them to Lord Birchfield's bed chamber.

The bedchamber was lit by a high fire in the fireplace, which had also rendered the room hot and stuffy. A faint scent of lilies hung in the air.

Chester, Thomas's valet, sat near the bed in his shirt sleeves, leaning his elbows on his knees, hands hanging between his legs. He looked up when Ravenna and Donovan entered and jumped to his feet to bow. "Lady Birchfield, I'm so glad you've come." His bottom lip quivered and his dark eyes pleaded from behind pockets of doughy skin. "I've been so worried...I-I..."

"There, there." Ravenna patted his shoulder. "All will be well, I'm sure of it."

Chester nodded and swiped at his puffy eyes. The aging valet was a lean, graying man with narrow, rounded shoulders. He'd been with Thomas for years.

Ravenna approached the bed. Thomas grimaced with pain, clutching his stomach. She touched his forehead. He was clammy and sweaty, but not feverish. She scanned the room. Someone was missing. "Where's Lady Birchfield?"

"She's in her bedchamber, milady. She's too distraught."

Ravenna frowned. She'd see to her later. "Has Lord Birchfield been ill like this before tonight?" She'd seen him at the picnic, but he hadn't seemed ill to her. He appeared tired and strained, but she'd put that down to his marriage—or, more particularly, his wife.

"Oh, yes, milady. He's not been himself for some time. But the illness comes and goes. He seems to get better for a short spell, then falls ill again. I believe he's sicker than he lets on, poor soul, but he never complains. In fact…" He paused and hemmed. Chester lowered his voice. "Perhaps I shouldn't say. It's not proper talk for ladies. It's too indelicate."

Ravenna crossed her arms. "Heaven's mercy, Chester, life is indelicate. You must tell me everything."

Chester licked his lips and rubbed his chin. "He came home a couple of nights ago extremely ill with his stomach. With all the particular symptoms of such a complaint." He gave her a pointed look. "If you understand me, milady?"

"Yes, I understand. Go on."

"He was also shaking and dizzy. Next morning, he'd rallied and joined the missus downstairs in the drawing room. But then the illness gripped him again."

"When was this?" Lord Donovan crossed his arms over his chest, his face marked with concern.

"Last night. I tried to persuade him to stay home, but he insisted on going to the club, saying he had important politicking to do. He was weak as a kitten when he finished dressing, though he did gain some strength by the time he'd left."

Ravenna slipped out of her cloak and untied her bonnet. "I'll need some vinegar, water, and a cloth. Let the fire die down. He doesn't have a fever, so we need not all suffocate." She dumped her things in a nearby chair, and Chester dashed from the room.

Donovan paced. "I wish the surgeon would hurry."

She studied Thomas, arms crossed, biting her lip. She wanted to believe he was suffering from natural causes, but given recent circumstances, she knew better. She lifted Thomas' hand and examined his nails. She squinted against the play of light and shadows, but she couldn't see any white crescent moons. She placed his hand on the bed and squeezed it, saying a silent prayer for his recovery. This had to be the work of Nochdale. She had hoped that her confrontation at the theater this evening would have given him pause, turned him away from his murderous behavior. Or maybe she pushed to quickly finish removing his opposition.

Donovan stood beside her. "I don't think I need to emphasize how important his recovery is."

"I'm aware of that." She bit down on her patience. "We'll do the best we can." How awful it would be for the Birchfield line, for England, if they lost him. He didn't even have an heir yet. So much hope rested in him.

She crossed the room and opened both casements. The cool air rushed in to break the heat in the room.

"Birchfield. Hawkestone. Wolfsham. All in the foreign office. Doesn't that seem strange to you?" Lord Donovan asked.

She moved to the fireplace. She couldn't tell him her thoughts. Yet, it was getting more difficult to remain silent, however, when she knew who the killer might be. She poked at the fire, spread the coals, and peppered the fire with ash from a nearby bucket. The fire receded, leaving a low flame and glowing embers. She wanted to explain, but without ample proof, she was afraid of accusing Nochdale or impugning his character based on supposition alone.

Chester returned with the supplies, and they set to work on Thomas. They removed his shirt and washed his back and torso to cool his skin. His eyes flickered as he attempted to wake. She pulled the counterpane up to his neck. "Don't worry. Just rest. Amma's here. The surgeon is on his way." Where was Braedon? And where was the blasted surgeon? They should've returned by now.

Lord Donovan poured two glasses of water. He and Ravenna watched over Thomas's bedside in stony silence like gargoyles.

The clock downstairs in the foyer struck twice. Shortly after, the door opened, and in strode Dr. Pullman. He still wore his nightshirt, half-tucked

177

into his pantaloons, and a great coat thrown over the haphazard ensemble. He removed his hat, sending his fawn hair in shocks around his head. He tossed his coat aside and immediately set about rolling up the sleeves of his shirt over his beefy forearms. Braedon swept in behind him, his cravat undone and his hat cocked slightly over his right eye. His riding coat billowed in his stride, revealing a pistol tucked into the band of his pantaloons.

Dr. Pullman offered a sharp nod by way of greeting and set to work.

Braedon stared at her, stepping closer. "What happened to you?" His hand hovered over her bruised cheek. "Tell me his name, and I swear, I'll hunt him down and make him sorry he ever touched you." The intensity of his gaze left her in no doubt of his sincerity. Like facing a wolf in the wild, he was all at once terrifying, thrilling, and beautiful.

She glanced at Donovan, who stood with the stiff indifference that signaled someone pretending not to eavesdrop.

Braedon lowered his voice further. "Was this the man from the theater? The one we spoke with?" He gave her a pointed look, silently communicating Nochdale's name.

"Please, not now," she said, her voice hoarse. She glanced at Donovan. "Certainly not here." She squeezed his arm, tense, through the superfine wool. "Thank you for bringing the surgeon. My family is grateful to you."

Dr. Pullman forced open Thomas's eyelids, looked in his mouth, felt his pulse, and studied his hands. "How long has he been this way?"

Ravenna related everything she knew. Donovan, Chester, and Braedon filled in the gaps.

"Hm. Mmm. How did this begin?" He tapped on Thomas's stomach.

"Milord complained of headaches at first," Chester said.

"Hm. Mmm." The surgeon scratched his beard as he stared at Thomas, nodding. "When did those begin?"

"About a month ago."

"That long ago?" Ravenna said. "It's the middle of May."

Dr. Pullman turned his scrutiny to the valet. "What else do you recall? Think way back. Any detail could be important."

Thomas groaned weakly from his bed.

Chester thought for a moment. "I've worked for Lord Birchfield for many years, and he's always been the very picture of health. But about a month ago, he began to have stomach complaints and breathing problems. Taking a flight of stairs knocked him up for several minutes. That's about when the headaches started."

"Hm. Mm-hm." The surgeon nodded, pressing a knuckle to his lips.

"What do you think is wrong with him, Dr. Pullman?" Donovan asked, his face pinched with worry.

Pullman stood and crossed his arms over his chest, and sighed. "It's difficult to say. It could be a bilious disease or the flux. I'll need to observe him longer to be certain."

"What if it's poison?" Ravenna asked.

Every man in the room stared at her.

Dr. Pullman frowned. "What poison? How would he have ingested it?"

"I don't know for certain he's been poisoned. I only have suspicions."

Dr. Pullman pulled on his chin. "I could try a couple of things. If he wakes up, I can give him a tartar emetic to purge him, followed by a brandy or a cordial. In the meantime, I'll let some of his blood to balance the bile as a precaution."

The surgeon opened his bag and pulled out a tiny knife. "I'll need something to catch the blood." Ravenna handed him a chamber pot. The surgeon sliced a couple of inches up Thomas's arm. Blood trickled slowly down the pale skin, dripping off the wrist into the chamber pot below.

After some blood pooled into the porcelain pot, the surgeon said, "There, there. That ought to suffice." He applied a tourniquet above the cut and cleaned up Thomas's arm. Dr. Pullman mixed a purgative and handed the jar to Ravenna. "When he wakes, give this to him. It will take about thirty minutes to work." He began packing up his instruments. "When he's purged give him warmed brandy or whisky. Repeat this a few times. Do you understand?"

"I do."

He nodded. "Very well. Good evening. I'll return tomorrow to see if he's improved."

# Chapter Twenty-Eight

Ravenna asked Chester to have the carriage brought around to take the men to their homes.

"Do keep me informed of his progress, if any." Dr. Pullman tapped his hat in place before leaving the room.

"Yes, do keep me apprised as well," Donovan said.

"Of course." Ravenna stood by the bed, unwilling to leave Thomas. "Will you do me the favor of contacting Thomas's brother Harrison to apprise him of the situation?"

"I'd be honored." Donovan kissed her hand and bowed.

"I'll join you directly," Braedon said to Donovan. He shut the door and turned to Ravenna, his hands on his hips.

She steeled herself for a scolding.

"Do you care to tell me what is happening? First, your house is set on fire, and now you've been attacked. I want to know who attacked you."

She leaned against the post of Thomas's bed. "I didn't see him. He came out of nowhere." If she talked about it, she would cry, and crying in front of him when she was trying to be strong was not an option. With some strain, she managed to say, "But, I can't think of any of that when my stepson is so gravely ill."

"I should've been there," Braedon rubbed the back of his neck.

She blinked. "How absurd. You can't blame yourself."

"Let me stay here tonight. I'll sleep on the sofa in the drawing room. You clearly need protection."

The idea gave her pause. His presence wasn't entirely unwelcome, but ultimately, it was a bad idea. "No. I thank you, but you should go home. We've been spending too much time together, I think. There will be rumors."

"Who cares about idle rumors?" He touched the side of her cheek. The tender gesture almost broke her resolve.

She averted her eyes and stepped away from his touch. "I do. Besides," she shrugged and searched for something to busy herself with. "I have Chester and the footmen, and the night watch is outside." She picked up discarded clothes and laid them in a nearby chair. "All will be well."

"If you need anything, no matter how small, please send for me. I'll be here in an instant." He stepped toward her and cupped her face in his hands. He placed a lingering kiss on her forehead, then turned and left, casting one hopeful glance back at her over his shoulder before closing the door.

She blew out a breath and hugged herself. The room had chilled considerably. She closed the casements, removed a blanket from a portmanteau in the corner, and curled up on the small sofa to keep watch over Thomas. Though exhaustion weighed like a stone between her shoulders, Ravenna knew she'd never be able to sleep. She stared at the glowing embers in the fireplace. She missed Philip, his quiet but strong and steady presence. If she tried hard enough, she could recall the scent of his balsam cologne and imagine herself riding with him through the sun-dappled park at Birchfield. Dear God, she missed Birchfield Manor, too.

She had never expected sleep to visit her, yet, at one point, in a state of half-consciousness, with her head resting in the corner of the sofa, she heard something like a dish being placed on a table and a light splash.

She opened her eyes enough to see a maid with a curvy figure and burnished-gold hair leave the room. Were there black flowers in her hair, or was it an illusion, a play of the light and shadows and her half-sleepy state? She wanted to sit up, but her body seemed to be tied to the sofa, her eyes too heavy to open. Or perhaps she dreamed it all. A brief spell of disquiet skittered through her body then settled like a mouse in the darkest recesses of her mind. Like an anchor tied around her, sleep dragged her under again into a world where she searched for her long-lost sister until a faceless man attacked her in a dark alley. When she broke free, he gave chase. She ran through labyrinthine streets and alleys in darkness and an impenetrable fog.

A housemaid made a noise, dropping the poker on the floor. Ravenna bolted up, blinking, heart-racing. Dawnlight tinted the room.

The maid jumped to her feet and curtsied, keeping her eyes lowered. "I'm so sorry, milady. It was an accident."

"It's nothing." Sore and stiff, Ravenna pushed herself from the sofa to finish her watch. Her face ached. She stretched her mouth open to release the stiffness in her face.

Within the hour, Chester entered the room to relieve her and show her to the guest room he'd had prepared for her. "Your portmanteau has arrived. Everything you need is here. I took the liberty of having a bath drawn for you. Breakfast is on the table."

She ate a breakfast of stout tea and buttery Bath cakes spiced with caraway. Her body and face ached terribly. She put a few drops of laudanum in her tea to ease her pain, then stripped and sank into the copper tub filled with hot water. Black and purple bruises bloomed all over her legs and arms. Fencing caused some of them, while the rest resulted from last night's attack. She drew the soap over her skin. Something niggled at her mind, a vague thing she was supposed to remember; it had happened while she slept. Now it lurked in the shadows of her memory, eluding her. It was difficult to think through the veil of laudanum. Each time she grabbed at a piece of a memory, it flitted away. Something about a woman washing Thomas? It must've been a dream.

After her bath, she dressed her wounds with chamomile ointment, then collapsed into bed for a nap. When she woke, she removed a dress from her portmanteau and pulled it down over her bruised and aching body, her arms moving stiffly. A splash of water on her face, followed by rose water, refreshed her for a meeting with Lucy. She wanted to find out why she hadn't been at her husband's bedside in his worst hour.

She found Lucy in her drawing room, dressed in pale blue muslin with a persimmon-colored bandeau in her hair. She sat at a table by the window, awash in sunlight, painting a still life of wilted peonies and lemons in watercolors.

"Good afternoon, Lucy."

Lucy didn't look up. "Good afternoon, dowager."

Ravenna's skin crawled. She shook it off and stood over Lucy, watching her paint. The girl had talent. Ravenna sat in the other chair at the table. "Have you checked on Thomas this morning?"

"Yes, not long ago. I sent my ladies' maid, Milby to ask about him, and then I went myself soon after."

That must've happened while Chester watched Thomas.

"I'm surprised you weren't there last night when he was ill. Were you also ill?"

"I sat with him in the beginning before you arrived. I grew so faint from watching his distress, I needed to lie down. It was unbearable to watch him suffer."

Ravenna crossed her leg, resting her hands in her lap. "Oh? I hadn't realized you were so...delicate."

Lucy cut a side glance at her. "What could I do? I'm not a surgeon or a healer." She sat up, cleaned her brush in water, and wiped it on a cloth. She dipped the brush in the yellow pigment, leaned close, and swept it over the lemon shape.

"I see." Ravenna paused, weighing her words. She didn't want to lecture the girl since she wasn't Lucy's mother. Lucy's mother. "You might've come to the room and I could've taught you some things about caring for illness, as my mother did for me. So you'll know it for the future. For instance, Thomas didn't have a fever, so the high fire wasn't required. If he'd had a fever then—"

"Thank you." Lucy cut her off.

Ravenna tensed and bit back sharp words. With a great deal of composure she added, "You have a duty, however, as his wife to be at his bedside."

"My husband and I appreciate your concern, dowager." She locked eyes with Ravenna. "*I know *my* place.*"

Ravenna didn't miss the intended message.

Lucy resumed her painting and said, "I will visit him again this afternoon or this evening before I go out."

"Go out?"

"Yes. Lady Jersey invited me to dinner."

"Surely you aren't serious about going out while your husband is ill?"

Lucy lowered her brush and looked at Ravenna, puzzled. "Of course I am. Why wouldn't I?" She put the brush down, wiped her hands, and sat back. "For instance, Thomas has his politics and never misses a chance to advance himself and our reputations. I want to be a grand hostess, like Lady Jersey. I want to host fine parties with the most powerful, creative, and intelligent people in society. Therefore, I must cultivate those connections and work them in much the same way my husband works his."

"How shrewd of you. But you must accept there is more to being a good hostess than fine connections."

"Of course, one must be pretty, a graceful dancer, and accomplished." She motioned toward her painting.

"Yes, that's true. Yet, have you considered that to have conversations with such people, you must be equally educated and knowledgeable? You must know politics, geography, art, French, Latin, astronomy. All manner of things. You must improve your mind with constant study and reading."

Lucy pursed her lips in disbelief, sighed, and resumed painting.

Ravenna added, "I could help you get into Lady Braxton's exclusive women's club, *Les Roses Noires*."

"I've never heard of it."

"It's a club dedicated to getting educational and suffrage rights for women."

Lucy wrinkled her nose, studying her painting. "Sounds awfully dull."

"Not at all. We do charity work and arrange to have experts visit to lecture on a wide variety of subjects from biology, to geology, to…"

Lucy looked as though she had stepped in a pile of horse dung in new slippers.

"Biology and geology? How horrid. Why would I want to listen to lectures about any of that?" Lucy laughed. "I'd rather die than become a stuffy old bluestocking."

"Refinement and intelligence are important for the best society hostesses, especially for those married to a man of distinction. If Thomas becomes foreign secretary—"

Lucy shoved her chair back with a loud scrape and jumped to her feet. "Thank you for your concern, Lady Ravenna, but I'd thank you to mind your own affairs and leave me to mine." She started to walk away.

Ravenna said to her back. "I'm happy to leave you to your own devices when you prove yourself a decent wife to my stepson."

Lucy slammed the door.

Ravenna had tried for months to like Lucy, to get along with her, but she couldn't seem to penetrate Lucy's determined ignorance, immaturity, and spoiled nature. Ravenna muttered under her breath, "Insufferable brat."

# Chapter Twenty-Nine

Returning to Thomas' room, Ravenna sent Chester off to work on his chores. She bathed Thomas in water and vinegar again, held his hand, and talked to him. As she watched peace and pain ebb and flow over his features, she sang and read to him. When she'd grown tired, she sat in the window and stared out across the city, a book open on her lap. Instead of reading, she listened to his raspy breath interspersed with moans of pain.

In the evening, she had given over the watch of Thomas to Chester while she retired to her bedchamber to write some letters for the Penitent House and take supper. A knock sounded at her door. Ravenna continued writing as the maids entered and placed dinner on the table near the fireplace. The scent of food filled the room and coaxed Ravenna's stomach to grumble.

A familiar mellow baritone rose from the doorway. "Good evening, my little raven."

She turned in her seat. His navy-colored coat and gray pantaloons perfectly traced the lines of his athletic physique. Relief, and something like happiness, washed over her. "I wasn't expecting you."

The maid blushed and smiled conspiratorially at him.

"Thank you, Smith. Have a place brought up for Lord Braedon, too." A maid trailed with a second setting. "I see you've anticipated me."

The two maids curtsied and lowered their heads to hide their smiles as they dashed from the room.

When the door closed, Braedon said, "I think we'll be the subject of much discussion in the kitchen."

"I imagine so." Ravenna set aside her pen and stood, wiping the ink from her fingers with a handkerchief. "They're young, full of romantic fancies."

"I hope you don't mind the company?"

"No, not at all."

"I came to see Thomas, and Chester insisted I stay. He ordered my plate."

Braedon removed his great coat and tossed it, along with his hat and gloves, in a nearby chair. The moment recalled something deeply intimate, like a quiet evening at home between spouses, one she'd experienced often with Philip. Her heart both warmed and shrunk as she poured two glasses of Madeira from the occasional table in the corner.

She limped toward him and handed him the glass of wine.

"I see you have a limp to go with your black eye and swollen lip. You've donned quite the accoutrement of battle. You still can't recall who attacked you?"

They sat at the table.

"I remember almost nothing about him." She stirred her beef stew. "He stood about your height, strong, but a wiry sort of fellow." She grabbed a chunk of buttered bread, tore off a piece, and popped it into her mouth. It was hard to chew with her swollen jaw. The taste of food ignited a ravenous hunger. She hadn't realized she was so hungry.

"That's all?"

"He smelled of Mayfair cologne."

He narrowed his eyes and cocked his head. "That's an odd thing to recall."

She shrugged, taking a spoonful of stew. "I remember it only because I once knew someone who wore it."

He frowned with thought. "That means he's a gentleman?" Then with a skeptical grimace, he added, "A gentleman attacker?"

"It's not impossible." She arched her brow. "I've known some vicious gentlemen."

"True enough." He conceded with a nod as he sipped his stew.

"Besides, I don't think he's necessarily a gentleman. I think he's most likely a pretender. Someone who has all the trappings of wealth without the breeding."

"Why do you think that?"

She shrugged one shoulder and took a drink. "Nothing specific. Only intuition."

He swirled his wine in his glass, then sipped it. "Is that all you can recall about this man?"

"There is one other thing. He also has a limp." Ravenna took a spoonful of stew, full of tender meaty bits and carrots.

"How do you know that?"

"Because I stabbed him in the leg when he tried to drag me into the alley." She relaxed into her chair and dabbed her mouth with her napkin.

He lowered his spoon and stared at her in astonishment. "You *stabbed* him?" He shook his head and tore off a chunk of bread. After a moment, he shook his head and chuckled. "I can't decide if I should be charmed or afraid."

"I had to defend myself."

He swallowed a bite of bread. "I'm glad you had the strength and wherewithal to do so. Things might have ended very differently."

"I'm all too aware." The ghost of her attacker's touch sent a chill up her spine. She shook it off. "He tried to drag me into an alley, where I would've surely died. I did what I could to prevent it."

"Something puzzles me, however. Why would a well-to-do man, or even a pretender, want to attack you?" In deep thought, he gazed at her over his soup bowl. "It's Nochdale, isn't it? He attacked you on Nochdale's orders." He sat back in his chair, one hand touching the stem of his wine glass. His eyes blazed with anger.

"I suspect him, but until I can prove he's to blame, there's nothing I can say or do."

He tapped a finger on the stem of his wine glass. "That means you must know something he wants to keep silent. What do you know, my little raven?"

She stared at the thick brown broth in her bowl and the bits of beef and vegetables rising through the surface like little stones. She stuffed her mouth with food and chewed slowly. If her mouth were full, she wouldn't be expected to talk.

"You'd be wise to tell me. I'm certain I could help you out of whatever trouble you may be in. I've many useful connections."

She shook her head. Part of her wanted to tell him everything. About the spying, the betrayal of both Hawkestone and England. About The Unity. However, the larger part of her was convinced he'd hate her. An awkward silence gaped between them. She finished off her wine and crossed the room to get more.

Braedon followed her. "You're clearly in serious trouble. If something were to happen to you, I couldn't forgive myself."

"I appreciate the sentiment…" She poured her wine. "However, I'm not your wife, Braedon. You've no cause to worry about me or protect me."

He touched her elbow, guiding her to face him. "Someone attacked you in the streets and threw a torch through your bedroom window." His voice was strained. "How can you pretend you're not in danger?"

"I'm not the target." She pulled away from him and stumbled a little, spilling wine. "Devil take it," she whispered.

She sank to her knees, pulling a handkerchief from inside her sleeve, and blotted at the spot. "I believe Thomas is the target." She sighed and sat back on her heels, frustrated. She stared at the purple stain on the ivory Turkish rug. Lucy had made a poor choice in rug color, at any rate. Ivory too quickly showed dirt in spite of dutiful cleaning. Placing both hands on the floor, she pushed herself to her feet. "Please believe me when I say I wish I could confide in you, but there are extenuating circumstances."

"Such as?"

Shame, embarrassment, and anger wrestled each other. She wanted to talk to him, to share the burden of her secrets. But she'd been a spy for the Franco-Irish rebels. She'd done it to save her family, but she didn't anticipate that her co-conspirators would kill her family anyway. She looked down at the crumpled cloth in her hands, swallowing the hard lump of emotion clogging her throat.

"Even if I wanted to tell you…" She shook her head. "I…can't. There are some things too difficult to talk about." She downed what remained of her wine and lifted her hand for him to help her stand.

"I only want to help. Anything at all you can tell me?" He cupped her face with his hand and gently stroked her cheek with his thumb.

The touch of his calloused thumb ignited her like dry kindle. If she were being honest with herself, she wanted him. Wanted his attention, his protection, his company. In spite of her mourning. In spite of her guilt. In spite of his reputation and entanglements. It was like eating a second dessert on top of a painfully full stomach: it would bring her immediate pleasure, and she'd probably regret it later, but the temptation was nearly too much to resist.

And what about Dianthe? It wasn't fair to her. Even if Ravenna didn't like her. She wasn't the sort of person who came between lovers or fiancées or whatever Braedon and Dianthe were to each other. The wine wove its vines through her mind and body, loosening her resolve. It was hard to understand why she should avoid Braedon. Her eyes locked with his.

Like preparing to swim in the cold sea, she drew a deep breath and plunged in, pressing her lips to his. She kissed him. She should've felt guilty for kissing a man while she wore widow's weeds, kissing a man who was rumored to be entangled with another woman. But she didn't. His strong mouth, full, soft lips, the current of their passion pulled her deeper. He drew her closer, his hands in her hair, on her hips. She was drowning in him. She didn't care that her face still hurt from last night's attack. She unbuttoned his waistcoat and ran her hands inside, over his chest. His muscles tensed under his soft cotton shirt. She wanted to forget all about Nochdale, and Thomas, and responsibility, and propriety, and grief. She wanted, for one night, to lose herself, completely, in him.

He broke the kiss but held her forehead against his with an iron grip. He struggled to speak and finally released his voice. "If I don't stop now, there'll be no saving you."

"I don't need to be saved."

He closed his eyes and pressed his forehead against hers. "I believe the wine is speaking for you." He placed a lingering kiss on her forehead. He pulled away and gathered up his coat and hat. "I should go." Lust and resolve warred in his features. "I'm sorry. I'll probably hate myself for the rest of the night and many nights hence, but it's the right thing to do." He kissed the palm of her hand.

She followed him into the hall. "Braedon, wait—" She was on the verge of asking him to stay when she glimpsed a movement from the corner of her eye. "What's that?" she whispered.

A shadowy figure entered Thomas's room.

# Chapter Thirty

Ravenna pushed past Braedon and strode down the hall, with Braedon trailing. She eased the door open to Thomas's bedchamber. Where was Chester? "Pardon me." Ravenna stepped into the room.

The curvy woman with burnished-gold hair jumped. Something about her tugged at Ravenna's memory.

"Who are you? And why are you in this room?" Ravenna demanded.

The woman rallied enough to pop a curtsey. "Begging your pardon, milady. I'm Milby, Lady Birchfield's lady's maid."

"I thought her lady's maid was Becker?"

"Yes, ma'am. Becker is in the country helping her sister through her lying-in. I'm working in her stead until she returns. We expect her in a few weeks."

"Pray tell," Ravenna came around to Thomas's bedside. Braedon leaned a shoulder on the bedpost behind her. Ravenna continued, "Does Lord Birchfield require his hair in the French ladies' fashion?" The scent of lily with a hint of sage and bergamot tickled her nose. She glanced down at Thomas. He seemed at peace.

Milby smirked, far too insolent for a servant, glancing between Ravenna and Braedon. "No, ma'am, milady asked me to look in on Lord Birchfield and report back to her."

"When does she plan on coming to see him for herself?"

"I can't say, ma'am. She didn't mention it, but I expect she'll come in after her dinner at Lady Jersey's tonight."

"Very well." Ravenna studied the woman, her rodent eyes, square jaw, and rough skin. "Do you always keep your hands in your pockets in the presence of your employer?"

"Begging your pardon, ma'am." Milby narrowed her eyes and removed her hands from her pockets. "It's a habit of mine. Though I do hope you're not accusing a faithful servant of stealing."

*Insolent wench.* "Thank you, Milby. You're dismissed."

"Thank you, ma'am." She dipped a curtsey. "Goodnight." She cast a final glance over her shoulder at Braedon and Ravenna.

"Goodnight." Ravenna watched the round hips sway toward the door. "Milby?"

"Yes, ma'am." She turned.

"Have you and I ever met?"

"I can't say as we have, milady."

"You seem very familiar to me."

A half-smile crept over the thin lips under her sharply upturned nose. "Oh, you know we servants are so plain we all look alike."

"Were you at a ball recently?"

"I work many balls."

"I mean as an attendant."

Milby snorted, and her eyes glittered with contempt. "Servants don't attend balls but to work, ma'am."

Ravenna frowned. "You're dismissed."

Milby nodded and left the room.

Braedon said, "Why were you interrogating her like a common thief?"

"I don't like her. There's something off-putting about her."

# Chapter Thirty-One

The next morning Ravenna read a letter from Harrison, regretting he couldn't attend his brother's bedside immediately. He assured her he would try to visit soon. She stood at the drawing room window, wrapped in a shawl against the unseasonably chilled wind. Dark clouds hung over Grosvenor Square. She bit her lip and watched the bustle of pedestrians and carriages. Harrison didn't give a substantial reason, only stated that upcoming exams and "current engagements" kept him away. She wasn't stupid. She knew "current engagements" was code for liquor, women, and gambling away whatever money Thomas last sent to him. He ended the letter assuring her of Thomas's strong constitution. Harrison was certain his brother would pull through famously, but insisted she should keep him apprised of his brother's condition. In a postscript, he made it plain he would appreciate a bit of money sent to him if she could afford it.

The difference between the two brothers was astounding. The elder exhibited all responsibility and filial duty, whereas the younger lived as a spoiled and idle spendthrift. If their places were reversed, Thomas would've dropped everything to come look after his young brother. But as it stood, Thomas would have to be content with distant well-wishes from his younger brother written with one hand while the other lay open for money. No doubt Harrison actually loved and cared for his brother, but his letter indicated his doubts that Thomas's illness was so serious. He didn't state it directly, but Harrison insinuated that he thought Ravenna had fallen vulnerable to "female hysterics."

She crossed the room to write another letter to Harrison, imploring him to come visit his brother and reiterating the seriousness of Thomas' illness, careful that her emotions and language didn't descend into panic. And she'd send him money for travel since he likely didn't have a single shilling to travel on.

After posting the letter, she rubbed her face and dragged herself down to the library to select a book, coming away with *Lyrical Ballads*. On her way upstairs, she met Milby coming down, dressed to go out. She needed to secure some time with Milby to see if she could find out more information about this mysterious woman. She'd been in Thomas's room last night, and Ravenna didn't believe for one moment that she'd been instructed to look in on him.

Ravenna paused. "Good Morning, Milby. Lady Birchfield speaks so highly of your hair-styling skills that I was wondering if you might fix mine for a dining engagement I have this evening at Adair House?"

Milby hemmed, her mouth opening and closing silently like a landed fish.

Ravenna pushed further. "I don't require anything too fancy, and since I don't have my own lady's maid with me, I would certainly appreciate your expertise." She forced a bright smile.

"Very well, ma'am." She bobbed a curtsey and continued on her way.

Later that evening, Milby ran a brush through Ravenna's hair.

"Thank you for styling my hair tonight, Milby. It's a terrible thing to be without a lady's maid."

"Yes, milady, I imagine it is."

"How long have you been in service?"

"Going on these twenty years."

"That's a long history. Were you a lady's maid that whole time?"

"No, ma'am. I'm not a lady's maid. I'm only helping with the duties until Milady Lucy's maid returns." She divided the hair into separate strands.

Milby certainly wasn't going to offer any additional information. Ravenna toyed with the handle of her hand mirror as she decided on another tack.

"But you must have had prior experience?"

"I had done some hair. The rest of the job is little different than an upstairs chambermaid, aside from knowing how to behave in a manner as reflects well on milady."

"What houses have you worked for?"

"Oh, here and there and all over, it seems." Milby chuckled.

"Did you ever work for Lady Hawkestone?"

"No, can't say as I did." She began plaiting Ravenna's dark tresses.

"What about Lady Nochdale or Lady Wolfsham?"

"No, ma'am." She tied a ribbon at the end of the braid and began on another strand.

"That's odd because you bear a striking resemblance to a maid I saw at the Nochdale garden party recently. The same color hair, the same face shape." She studied Milby's reflection in the vanity mirror.

Milby didn't look up. "That one? Yes. I was hired for that day only and wasn't needed any longer. So I went to the registry and found this position."

Blood rushed into Ravenna's limbs. She bit her lip and glared at Milby in the mirror as the woman worked on her hair. What part had she played in Nochdale's schemes? Worse, was she still working for him and trying to get close to Thomas?

Milby twisted the central strand into a chignon, garlanding the braids around. She inserted a few pins, then stepped back to admire her work. "There, milady. How do you like it?" She planted her hands on her hips and smiled at Ravenna in the mirror.

Ravenna turned in her seat with the hand mirror to look at the back of her hair. Very plain. Quite simple. And very English. If this was the latest in French hair fashions, then Ravenna would sprout wings and fly.

She smiled up at Milby. "Wonderful. I think you've really proven yourself here."

# Chapter Thirty-Two

Uneasy about Milby, Ravenna decided to send her excuses to Catherine to bow out of the dinner party and came up with a feasible lie for staying home should she run into Milby. She took her hair down, twisted it into a single braid, put on a plain black muslin dress, and planted herself in Thomas's bedchamber with a book.

She relieved Chester and curled up under a blanket with her book and a glass of port. She couldn't think of a better way to spend an evening. The wind howled outside, causing tree branches to scratch at the window. Dogs barked and howled in the distance. Church bells rang. The last chime she heard from the clock downstairs rang ten.

The next thing she realized, it was morning. Stiff and her head as heavy as if it was loaded with rocks, she didn't want to get up yet. Ravenna snuggled deeper into the blanket, then heard the soft rustling of someone trying too hard to be quiet. She sat up on the sofa, her body grousing, and stared at a young maid.

When the maid noticed Ravenna staring at her, she jumped to attention. Her round green eyes wide, she pushed a tendril of brunette hair behind her ear. "Begging your pardon, milady. I'll leave. Give you privacy." Freckles sprayed over her nose and rounded cheeks.

"No. Please continue. This room needs attention." Ravenna pushed herself to stand, aching. She stretched and, pulling the blanket around her shoulders, she checked on Thomas, who slept soundly. Then she sat on the window seat to look out at the morning sky, gray and dull as slate. The stones were slick with the overnight rains. She opened the casement and inhaled the welcoming scent of wet moss, earth, horse, herbs, and flowers. The sun grappled with the clouds, yet the fresh air beckoned her outdoors for some much-needed exercise.

From her perch, she turned her attention to the young maid who knelt at the fireplace to scoop the cold ashes into a bucket. Then she set about the task of oiling, scouring, and blacking the iron grate.

Ravenna said, "Such dirty work, cleaning a fireplace, isn't it?"

"Indeed it is, milady. But necessary. Houses'll burn down if the chimneys aren't managed properly."

"That's true." The memory of her own fire a few days ago sprang to her mind. Thinking of the fire dredged up flashing thoughts about all the strange and mysterious events of late—and the strange and mysterious people. She thought of last night and Milby. She, too, was strange and mysterious. She wondered if this girl knew anything about Milby.

"What's your name?"

The girl stopped and sat back on her heels, surprise marking her features. She wiped her forehead with the back of her arm, which marked her face with soot. "Keene, milady."

"How long have you worked here, Keene?"

"Not long, milady. Near six months."

"Do you like being a housemaid?" Ravenna tugged at the long sleeves on her dress, smoothing the ruffled lace into place over her wrist.

She laughed. Then cut the laughter short. "Sorry, milady. I don't mean to laugh. But I think anyone who enjoyed being a housemaid would be mad." She looked down at her black rag with a shy smile. "To be honest, I'd much rather be a lady's maid someday, but there's so much to learn. Some days I think I'll never learn everything."

"That depends on who you'd want to work for. If you worked for a royal house, you'd need to be far more educated than working for a baron's lady."

Keene blushed. She was a fresh, pretty sort of girl with the dewy, supple skin of a lass blooming with youth. "Oh, I'm not proud enough to think I could ever work in a royal house."

"Your modesty becomes you, but you're still young. A great many things can happen in even a year's time if you work hard. Are you currently working on your education?"

"Yes, ma'am. Milby promised she'd teach me how to do hair before she leaves when Becker returns."

"I met her last night." There was the opening she needed. "What do you know of Milby?"

"Not much, ma'am. She's not been here even a month."

"Has she said anything about where she came from, her family, her former employment?"

"Milby isn't given to chattering away about her past, but I think she's from Bristol. I don't know nothing about her former employers or family, ma'am."

"What's your opinion of her?"

Keene rubbed black polish on the iron grating with force. "She ain't given me any reason not to like her."

"You should understand that part of being a lady's maid is being observant. Have you ever paid attention to Milby's schedule?"

"Sometimes."

Ravenna rose from the window and approached the fireplace. She eased herself onto a footstool near Keene, leaning her elbows on her knees. "What have you observed about her comings and goings?"

Keene averted her gaze, staring into the empty fireplace.

"You can speak freely."

She rubbed her forehead with the back of her blackened hand. "I don't want to cause trouble, ma'am."

"You won't. This conversation is strictly between us."

Keene glanced up through her short lashes. "To be honest, ma'am, I like Becker much better. This one's a bit spoilt, if you ask me."

"What do you mean?"

"She acts as though she ain't really a servant. Superior-like."

"Well, she is a lady's maid…"

She scooted around on her knees to face Ravenna and wiped her blackened hands on a rag. "I mean, even for a lady's maid. I've met a

200

few lady's maids in my time, ma'am. They do put on airs because they're at a higher station, but they still know they're servants and don't balk and grumble when their ladies tell them to do their job."

"Perhaps she doesn't like her job? That's not so uncommon, is it?"

"There's more to it than that. She talks as if she's too good for her work." She lowered her voice and leaned forward, supporting herself with her hands on her knees. "She even argues with Lady Birchfield sometimes. In front of the staff."

Ravenna cocked her head. "Is that so?"

Keene nodded, wide-eyed.

"Give me an example."

She hemmed.

"Are you afraid of her?"

"A little."

"Why is that?"

"I saw her flog one of the upstairs maids with a closed parasol because the girl accidentally broke a bottle of her perfume when dusting her room. The girl gave her all the money she'd saved up to pay for it, but Milby wouldn't be satisfied. She kept saying it was special and couldn't be so easily replaced. I've never heard such oaths as what Milby used on that girl. Of course, the girl cried like a babe. She left the house the next day and never returned."

Ravenna inspected her cuticles. "So Milby has a violent temper?"

"Oh, yes, ma'am. She's not to be crossed." Keene glanced over her shoulder at the door.

Ravenna smiled. "Yet, I'm not a fellow servant, so whatever you tell me will stay between us. After all, why would I tell Milby anything? I'm simply curious how she spoke to her mistress and what Lady Birchfield did about it."

She tipped her mouth to one side and seemed to be thinking it through. "Well, this morning, for instance, Lady Birchfield was in a high dudgeon about one thing or another. Her eggs were too soft, her bread too burnt, her tea too cold. Though all of it was cooked as she always liked it before. Then she had a headache and wanted Milby to rub the pain with mint and

anise oil. Milby crossed her arms and looked down her nose at milady..."
Keene acted out the part. "'You act like you're some sort of sultana sitting
on a throne' and 'I'm not rubbing oil on your addled head when what it
likely needs is a sound rapping. You're not as ill as you claim.'"

Ravenna suppressed her laughter at watching Keene imitate Milby
imitating Lucy.

"Is that true? Does Lady Birchfield have many illnesses?"

Keene rubbed her nose, leaving a smudge of blacking polish behind.
"No'm. Not so bad to take to her bed as she does. I sometimes think she
rather likes being sick."

Keene seemed sincere. And Lucy often irritated Ravenna. No doubt,
Thomas might've secured a better wife, but for a servant to speak to her
mistress in such a manner was inexcusable. "Milby said that to her ladyship?
You're sure of it?"

"Yes, ma'am. I witnessed the whole thing as I was cleaning her fireplace
at the time."

"Do you know of any other improprieties Milby has committed?"

"Yes. She has a fancy beau. She sneaks out with him."

Ravenna perked. "Oh?"

Keene's hesitancy had vanished. She scooted forward on her knees. "A
few times I seen her with a gent in a red carriage. It was a nice one, too.
Almost as nice as his lordship's."

"Was there a crest on his carriage? Or did he have a tiger or a footman in
livery?"

"No, ma'am. I didn't see any. I think he's new money. I talked to Sally, the
scullery, who told me his name is Larson. She helps to pass letters between
him and Milby sometimes."

"What does Mr. Larson look like?"

Keene's eyes rolled upward as if the answer was written on the ceiling.
"He's at least average height, thin. His hair is almost white, though he's not
an old man."

"Would you recognize him if you saw him again?"

"Absolutely, milady."

A footman announced Dr. Pullman was downstairs. Ravenna thanked him and waited for the door to close before she spoke again. "How long has Sally been sneaking letters in and out of this house for Milby?"

"For as long as Milby's been here."

"If you hear of anything, or if you see him again, would you tell me? I'll pay you well."

Keene's green eyes brightened, and her freckled cheeks rounded as she smiled. "Absolutely, ma'am. I'll keep a watch for ye."

"That's a good girl." Ravenna forced a bright smile. "And I give you my word that this conversation will remain between us."

"Thank you, ma'am. I'd hate to be crossways of Martha Milby."

# Chapter Thirty-Three

After Dr. Pullman had completed his examination of Thomas and bled him again, Ravenna tiptoed down the hall to Milby's room. She knocked. There was no sound from within. She looked over her shoulder and put her hand to the cold brass knob, opened the door, and stepped inside, leaving the door open wide, so it wouldn't appear as though she were snooping.

She hadn't intended to investigate the room, but her natural curiosity compelled her forward. There was something interesting about the room. It had the stuff of life in a way that aristocratic rooms often wanted. It reminded her of her mama's room in Ireland or her aunt's room in Whitechapel.

Along one wall was a clutter of laundry and sewing implements, including a long sewing table. At one end of the long table were starching tools, clothes brushes, flat iron, sewing box, scissors, slips of fabric, and a dress shell pinned to its pattern stretched out on the long table. In the window sat a bonnet sitting askew, a bit of lace pinned around the brim, and the trimmings of satin flowers, ribbon, and feathers lay scattered on the windowpane. A pile of linens, waiting to be pressed, sat in the chair by the window.

Otherwise, the room was neat and spare. A small bed ran parallel to the sewing table and was so neatly made up as to seem as though it had never been slept in. The washstand and small vanity in the corner was tidy, everything in its proper place. A wooden rocking chair and footstool occupied the round braided rug in front of the fireplace. The rocker had worn trench marks in the wool. She moved to search the wardrobe by the bed when she noticed a small writing desk tucked in the corner beside it. Everything was put in its proper place.

A book rested on the table. No surprise since lady's maids often had large swaths of time between attending their mistress' whims. She was reading *Independence* by Elizabeth Meeke. An interesting selection revealing much about the reader since the hero, Egbert, lived as a commoner, running through a series of low-paying jobs, only to discover he was actually born into nobility.

As she turned from the book, a gap in the pages caught her eye. She opened the book, and the pages fell open to expose a letter tucked within. The seal was black. The image on it had been marred. Was it a wreath? A flower? Intriguing. She held it closer to inspect it, but the light in the room was too dim. She closed the book and moved to stand near the window for better light. As she angled the letter in the sunlight, attempting to make out the shape on the seal, she heard a rustling noise and sensed the undeniable presence of another person. She spun around, instinctively holding the letter behind her. Milby.

Her back rigid, Milby's eyes darted over the room. She looked askance at Ravenna. "Pardon me, milady, but is there something I can help with?"

Ravenna hesitated in order to bide enough time to roll the letter and secret it up her sleeve. "Oh, uh, well, actually, I was looking for you. And then my curiosity got the better of me. I'm fascinated by the work you're doing on this bonnet." She successfully tucked the letter and motioned to the bonnet in the window.

Milby stepped into the room, narrowing her eyes into dark slits. "And why were you looking for me?"

"I'd heard Lady Birchfield was ill. So I wanted to see if the surgeon was required since he's in Lord Birchfield's room."

"I hadn't heard about any illness, and I'm certain I'd be the first to hear of it." Milby folded her hands in front of her and tipped her head. "But it occurs to me, madam, that you might've asked her that yourself."

"Yes. I thought she might be sleeping, and I didn't want to wake her, so I came to ask you." It was a flimsy explanation. She regretted having left her fan in her bedchamber.

"Yet," Milby said menacingly. "That doesn't quite explain why you're in my room while I'm absent, ma'am." Milby moved further inside to stand in the center of the room.

*Impudent little....* Ravenna glared at her. She would have to stand her ground with this woman. "You forget yourself, Milby. I'm not required to explain anything to a servant. Your privacy is at the discretion of this family." She crossed the room and paused at the door. "Oh, one more thing. You would do well to remember I'm nothing like your mistress. And I'll see you turned out of this house, without reference, if you dare overstep your station with me."

Malevolence flashed in Milby's hard little eyes. She said through gritted teeth, "Begging your pardon, ma'am. If you like, I can go check on milady this instant and give you the information you seek." Her mouth twisted into a dark smile.

Ravenna straightened her back and looked down her nose. "That won't be necessary. I suppose I'll do it myself after all." She walked quickly back to her bedchamber, resisting the urge to look over her shoulder.

Once inside, she closed and locked the door. She sat in the window and pulled the letter from the inside of her sleeve. She looked closer at the black wax seal. It was a wreath of some sort. No. A trio of roses over a harp. Uneasiness settled over her. She'd seen that image before. When she worked for the rebellion. Her fingertips turned cold, almost numb, as she unfolded the paper.

The single page read only: *H. will find you at the opera this evening. You will know her by her Black Roses. She will have what is required. The lady is a slight woman with short curls. Secure yourself with her.*

She flipped the page around. No direction, so it must have been hand-delivered. What a curious letter. Whatever the meaning, the description of the lady sounded a great deal like Lucy. If so, why would this mysterious person want to connect with Lucy? Could this have been sent by Nochdale or one of his minions? Was this connected to Thomas's illness somehow?

Perhaps Milby acted as an intermediary and was supposed to deliver this letter to someone else. Or, perhaps this letter was intended for Milby. But to what end?

# Chapter Thirty-Four

Ravenna tucked the letter into her bodice. She needed to speak with Lucy. She wanted to discover more about this Milby woman and why she was in this house. She strode down the hall and knocked on Lucy's door.

"Come in," called a drowsy voice.

Ravenna opened the door to find Lucy stretched out on a *chaise longue*, her white silk and lace dressing gown trailing down the side, her ankles crossed, and a green paisley pashmina shawl draped over her lap. She didn't even bother to lift her head.

"Good morning." She spoke in slow, drawn-out speech, as though it almost hurt to speak.

"Lucy…." Ravenna stepped inside and shut the door behind her. "What's the matter with you?"

A smile spread slowly over Lucy's lips. "Nothing. Nothing at all."

Ravenna looked at the sofa table covered with newspapers, books, wads of handkerchiefs, bowls, and cups. Beside one of the cups was a small glass vial full of a dark liquid. It was almost empty. Ravenna lifted it up to the sunlight. It was red-brown. "This is laudanum. Where did you get it?"

"From Milby. She says it's the best curative for what ails me."

"Oh? And is Milby a healer?"

Lucy shrugged and flopped her head up. She shifted and sat on her side, propping her head in her hand. She looked at Ravenna through heavy-lidded eyes.

"When did Milby give you this bottle?"

"A few days ago, when I had a headache."

"A few days ago? This bottle is nearly gone. How much was in it when you received it?"

Lucy rolled her eyes upward to think. "Less than half."

"Lucy, you're only supposed to take one or two drops at a time and only when you truly need it."

"I did need it." Lucy reached forward and snatched the bottle from Ravenna's grip. "You're not my mother. I'm a married woman now, and I'll do as I please."

"You're right. I'm not your mother, but we are part of the same family. While you are a married woman with a little more freedom, you can't behave entirely without consequences. behave entirely without consequences. You still have responsibilities..."

She made a rude noise and put her hands over her ears. "I don't want to hear your lectures. Milby says I need to be more forward in being a true mistress of this household."

"Is that so?"

"Yes. She says I've been weak for too long and I need to assert my superior station in this house—especially since I'm about to be married to a foreign secretary."

Ravenna held up the bottle. "And is this how one takes charge of a household?"

Lucy looked down and stuck out her lower lip.

"Milby gives you a great deal of advice. Did she advise you in humility or grace while she was at it? Why on earth are you taking comportment lessons from the likes of Milby?"

"She speaks the truth. The truth can come from any station in life."

"I suppose she told you that as well?"

"Yes," she said with an insolent air.

Ravenna locked her fingers together in front of her as a measure to keep from delivering the hard slap this stupid girl so well deserved.

"Did you think Milby might have an ulterior motive for infecting your mind with her brand of truth?"

Lucy blinked slowly. Then she shrugged and toyed with her curls.

"You are not as ill as you think, Lucy. You need to be at your husband's bedside, taking care of him. That is how a proper wife of a foreign secretary responds. That is how a woman in charge of her household sets an example."

She had the nerve to simper. "Thomas is a strong, strapping man. He'll pull through better without me. I know nothing of healing the ill, and since he finds me…what were the words he used…oh, yes…" She held up a finger for each one. "… 'Frivolous.' 'Wayward.' 'Silly.' I'm certain I'd only hinder his progress."

"So instead, you send some strange woman, Milby, to check on him in the middle of the night last night?"

Lucy seemed confused. "Did I?" Then she chuckled and rubbed her nose until it turned red. "I must have if she was there." She waved her hand. "It doesn't signify. She's my lady's maid, for a time. It's as good as having me there."

"She's temporary. She's a stranger. Think, Lucy, did you actually ask her to look in on him? It's important."

Lucy screwed up her face as if in thought as she played with her short curls. Then she sighed. "I don't recall, but I must have. Why else would she be in his room? I'm sure she wouldn't take it upon herself. That would be out of line."

"Where did she come from?" Ravenna cleared a spot on the table to sit beside Lucy. "You'd better recall quickly or I have a good mind to whip it out of you."

"I am the lady of this house." She seemed to struggle to keep her eyes open. "I don't have to justify anything to you."

"Yes, but clearly you have only half the sense of a goose, which is evidenced by your gross neglect of your ailing husband in favor of tipping the laudanum bottle. So, you'll forgive me if I don't trust your choices." Ravenna's voice darkened into a warning. "Where did that woman come from?"

"I don't know," Lucy shouted. She pulled her shawl up to her chin and pouted like a petulant child. "Leave me alone."

# CHAPTER THIRTY-FOUR

"Where, Lucy?"

She rubbed her forehead with rough, frustrated strokes. "She was recommended to me by Lady…uh, uh." She closed her eyes and shook her head. "Becker left to help her sister, and I needed a woman. I was talking about my plight for a good hairdresser, and Lady Braxton offered a suggestion. That's all. Frankly, Milby is the best woman I've had, and I have half a mind to let Becker go and keep Milby." She ran her fingers through her curls.

"You need a hairdresser for that? Goats have longer hair."

Lucy scoffed with exasperation. "It wasn't always short. It was her idea to cut my hair *à la Napoléon*. She sets the curls. Otherwise, my hair is straight as pins. I could never set all these curls myself. She's a master of the hot irons. Hasn't singed my hair even once."

Ravenna inhaled some patience. "She lied about her experience with French fashions, Lucy. She did my hair last night and it was an English style after I specifically asked for French."

"Tell me one servant who hasn't misrepresented their skills to get a job. Perhaps she forgot you wanted French hair."

"It wasn't even a good English style."

"I like her." Her head lolled against the *chaise longue.*

"That may be, but you need to let her go. She has overstepped to attend your husband's bedside. Even if you asked her to, it was your place to be there, not your woman's."

Lucy jumped up and snatched the near-empty laudanum bottle from Ravenna's hand. She tossed one end of her shawl around her shoulder. "I don't have to answer all these questions. Leave me alone."

"I'm not finished with you." Ravenna jumped up.

"Well, *I'm* finished." She half-staggered out of the bedchamber.

"Where are you going?" Ravenna went after her.

Lucy kept walking. "I don't have to tell you anything. I'm lady of this house—"

"I've often observed that one who needs to remind everyone of her power has none at all."

Lucy stopped and turned. "I could cast you out of this house this instant if I wanted."

"I dare you to try. You'll find it more difficult than you imagine. You can't be mistress of a house that has no respect for you."

Lucy worked her jaw and glared at Ravenna. She jerked her body around. She stumbled, tripping down the stairs and out the front door, giving it a hearty slam.

Ravenna strode to her room, muttering to herself, "Spiteful Jezebel. I'd like to jerk every curl from her stupid opium-addled head." She sat at her desk and took out her writing implements. "There's more than one way to get the information I want." She dashed off a letter to Hart to have her learn everything possible, if anything, about the Mr. Larson that Keene had told her about and to see if she could discover anything about Martha Milby.

She rang for Keene and handed the letter and two farthings to her. "Take this to Gordon House and put it only into the hands of a woman named Charlotte Hart. No one else. Understand?"

Keene beamed, bobbed a curtsey, and ran to fulfill her errand.

Ravenna needed to return to Thomas's bedside, but wanted another book to entertain her. She jogged down the stairs and crossed the foyer to the library. It was a dim room with dark blue and gold velvet drapes at each window and a round table and gold jacquard chairs in the corner by the window. A sofa sat across the room between a bookshelf lined with books and a table with a glass dome housing a stuffed bird on a pine branch. She selected a book of astronomy, thumbing through the pages, attempting to forget about her daughter-in-law.

There was a knock at the front door, and she heard a man's voice ask for the Dowager Lady Birchfield. The word "dowager" stuck like a barb in her bodice. It sounded so old and musty.

The guest's voice sounded familiar. Her curiosity pulled her toward the library door. She stepped into the foyer to receive her guest. "Lord Donovan. What a pleasant surprise."

He bowed. "Lady Birchfield. I hope I don't interrupt you." In his olive coat, tan pantaloons, crisp, white linens, and immaculately polished Hessian boots, he was utterly 'shiny.' The seas in his eyes were calm, almost placid, and reminded her of still waters sparkling in the sun. "I saw Lady Lucy a moment ago. She seemed to be upset. I hope she's well?"

"I apologize for her. She's overtired. Come, join me in the library. I was about to select a different book. Would you like some refreshment?"

"No, thank you. I won't stay long."

After the usual pleasantries about the weather and the gossip from the newspapers, she sat in a chair by the dark fireplace. "I'm sure you didn't come to discuss the impoverished Lord Manderley escaping to the continent to avoid his debtors."

"You're right. I came to inquire after Birchie's health. We are all very eager for his recovery, especially Hillingham's camp. It's the perfect time for him to swipe the post from Nochdale, since he's also ill."

She perked, scooting to the edge of her seat. "Are you sure? Nochdale is ill too?"

He nodded, frowning. "It's true. He took to his bed last evening."

She stared at him, letting the news sink in. If he was now ill, then it was possible he had nothing to do with Thomas's illness or the deaths of Hawkestone and Wolfsham. That would certainly complicate things. Perhaps no one was murdered, after all. Perhaps it was all coincidence, and the men were all unfortunate enough to fall victim to the same contagion. Her hopes sank. No. That wasn't true, because the men's families and friends weren't falling ill. Further, Nochdale might've still been involved in the other deaths and became ill himself coincidentally.

She snapped her mouth shut and composed herself. "That's unfortunate, but I confess, though I'm sorry to see anyone suffer, he is a hateful, disagreeable man, and I hope this will keep him from becoming foreign secretary. You must acknowledge his illness isn't entirely unwelcome."

Lord Donovan's eyes lit with humor. "True enough. With Nochdale's ties to Fox and his French sympathies, his condition can be seen as a boon."

"Have you heard what's wrong with him?"

"I haven't. But he's expected to recover."

"As was Wolfsham, I believe." And Thomas. A cold, heavy stone settled in her stomach. He must recover. Too much was at stake. But what if he didn't?

Lord Donovan wavered. "I suppose Birchie hasn't woken yet?"

"I'm sorry to say he hasn't. I assume your urgency to speak with him means negotiations with Napoleon are faltering?"

He nodded. "We've lost so many valuable negotiators in such a short time that all is chaos. As soon as we get a new secretary prepared, he dies, and we have to begin again. If we cannot make this Amiens Treaty stand, then I fear we'll be thrown into another war. Some of my colleagues are already bidding to declare war against France."

"That is terrible news. Who calls for war?"

"Charles Yorke and William Pitt, among others."

She inched to the edge of her seat. "That's madness. We've had our troops spread over the earth, fighting for years. We can't even send adequate provisions to the troops currently at war. We can't possibly fund another war."

"Exactly. If we can intervene and calm the storm brewing over Malta, then we may yet prevent war, though sometimes I fear we may be too late. I've had reports that Napoleon is already amassing troops in Boulogne to prepare for another invasion."

Ravenna frowned and wrung her hands.

He reached over and placed his hand over hers. "Don't fear, Lady Birchfield. It's only talk at the moment. When Birchfield's health is restored, I'm certain he will settle a peace and prevent another unwanted war."

Lord Donovan's hands were warm and soft. His thumb traced the back of her hand. The silence between them grew awkward.

She cleared her throat. "Yes, thank you for the reminder." She eased her hands from under his. "I'll try to keep that in mind. I'm sure all will be well."

He flushed and averted his gaze. "I think I've taken enough of your time." He stood and tugged the bottom of his coat, looking around, distracted. "I won't importune you further. Please give Lord and Lady Birchfield my regards."

"Is there a message you would like me to give him when he wakes?"

"No, thank you. Though, perhaps you won't mind writing to inform me when he wakes? I'm at 35 Piccadilly."

"Certainly. I'd be happy to." She offered her hand.

He bowed and kissed her hand. "Good day, Lady Birchfield."

She watched his broad shoulders disappear through the library door as her mind fell back onto Nochdale. She needed to confirm the seriousness of his condition. After all, if he died, it'd mean her investigation thus far was lost. She couldn't go on her own, as much as she wanted to. She had to look after Thomas. If Nochdale had said something to his wife about catching Ravenna in his study, she might not be welcome at Nochdale House at any rate. That would have to wait.

# Chapter Thirty-Five

Ravenna returned to Thomas's bedchamber. She and Chester bathed Thomas and applied the poultice to him, drawing a bit of color back into his grayish skin. He was sleeping fitfully, so she hoped he might be close to waking. She read her astronomy book until the sunlight had faded, straining her ability to read, and forcing her to light a few candles.

The clock downstairs rang seven. Keene had been gone for far too long. The errand should've taken no more than an hour. She'd been gone well over two. Ravenna needed to know her letter had been delivered to Hart safely. She stood at the window, biting at her lip, watching London slip into the shadows.

Something wasn't right. She opened her door and stepped out to see a couple of maids leaning over the gallery balustrade. "What's the matter?" She stepped down the hall toward them.

The maids jolted upright. The chubby one fidgeted with her cap. "Begging your pardon, milady, but we was watching them carry in Keene."

The other one said, "The footman, Wilson, is carrying her through. Looks like she took a tumble."

Ravenna lifted her skirts and ran down the stairs, craning her neck to look over the balustrade to catch a glimpse of the footman. As she rounded the corner, she caught sight of him and shouted, "Wilson, hold there."

The man turned and faced her. His red brows shot up when he witnessed Ravenna jump from the last few stairs to the marble floor and sprint across to him.

"Wait, please." She peered at the ragged girl in his arms. Her face was swollen and bloody, her charcoal gray dress torn, her dark hair fell, half-knotted in a loose hanging chignon. "Oh, Heaven's mercy, Keene. What happened to you?"

Keene lolled her head to the side, her green eyes no more than little slits in the puffy, bloody mess around them. Her lip and jaw were equally swollen. When she spoke, she sounded as if cotton was stuffed in her cheeks. "He beat me, milady."

"Yes, I see that. I'm so sorry, Keene. Please, Wilson, take her to the library and put her on the sofa." Ravenna ran to open the door for him. "Come along, do make haste."

He shuffled, bent-kneed, to the sofa and lay down his bundle with a soft grunt.

Keene whimpered, wrapping an arm around her ribs and favoring her left arm, which appeared bruised and swollen near her wrist.

Wilson stood, stiffly, and with a heavy sigh, he dabbed his forehead with his coat sleeve. "She's a sturdy girl, that one. Solid as an anvil, though you wouldn't know it to look at her."

"Yes, that'll do. Thank you, Wilson." She set about issuing orders for supplies.

Once all the supplies were delivered, Ravenna dipped the rag in the cool vinegar-water. "This might sting a bit, but we need to clean you up and see how deep these cuts are." She touched the dampened cloth to the cut above the eye, and Keene sucked in her breath. "Try to relax. When we are done, you shall have something to eat and a good rest. Then we'll discuss what happened to you."

It was a tiresome task, wiping clean all the cuts and bruises over the girl's face.

She inspected Keene's face. "I don't think you'll need sewing up. So that's a blessing." She stood. "Let's have a look at the rest of you." She closed the curtains over the windows and helped Keene ease out of the tattered dress, and lifted her chemise. Purple and blue bruises covered the maid's rib, arms, and legs. "Can you take a deep breath?"

Keene took a deep breath, wincing.

Ravenna sighed and sat back. "Doesn't seem like your ribs are broken. But they're definitely bruised. They'll hurt for some time. I'll wrap them. Let's see your arm."

Keene held out her arm, her hand balled in a fist.

"There are some cuts and scratches. Can you open and close your fist?"

Keene opened her hand. She spoke with a swollen lip. "I've been holding this. Ripped it off him, I did." In her palm was a small brass button. "After I scratched him up good." A feline light shone in her green eyes.

"Good for you." Ravenna took the button and held it close to the candlelight. Troubling. The button looked very much like what decorates a family's livery, and the design in the center looked very much like a family crest. "Thank you, Keene. You are incredibly good. I'm so sorry this happened to you." Ravenna washed the remaining cuts and bruises and applied a chamomile ointment to Keene's wounds. She wrapped the poor girl's ribs and wrist and poured her a glass of claret. "I think after today, you deserve a bit of this. Drink it slowly."

"Thank you, milady." As she sipped it, some dribbled out of the swollen side of her mouth. She dabbed it with her sleeve.

Ravenna sat on the footstool by the sofa, looking up at Keene. "Can you recall what happened?"

Keene thought for a moment. "After I dropped off the letter, I walked by some shops. I shouldn't have done it, but I saw a pretty bonnet in the window with fine lace and a gingham ribbon and thought how nice I would look in that bonnet at church on my half day. And I thought since I had the money you gave me...well...." She looked down at her lap, where she held her claret with both hands.

"Never mind that. It's your money. You can do what you wish with it."

She nodded and seemed relieved. "When I came out of the shop, I headed home. Before I knew it, I was grabbed into an alley. He smashed my face into the wall first thing, knocking me half out of my senses. I tried to take hold of him. But he was faster and stronger than me, milady. I fell on the ground, fighting on my way down, and I guess that's when I grabbed this button. He kept punching me all about the head and face. I tried to scream, but when he kicked me in the ribs, it took the wind out of me, and I couldn't make a peep."

"Do you remember anything about him at all?"

"He weren't a burly man, and he were dressed like a gent with the hat and all." She worked her swollen mouth. "Seems he had brown hair."

A chill passed through Ravenna. He sounded similar in build to her own attacker. Perhaps the beating wasn't meant for Keene at all. "What made him stop?"

"I can't say, because there were no reason for him to. None of the people passing by seemed to notice or care. Only when he was ready to knock me again, he turned me around, looked in my face. He had his fist pulled back to hit me, then he swore and ran off. I never got a good look at him."

Ravenna instructed the maids to help Keene to bed, then she took the girl a bit of sherry with a few drops of laudanum to help Keene sleep and to cut the pain.

Sitting by the fire, sipping her favorite port, Ravenna studied the button Keene had ripped from her attacker's coat. It was brass with a white stag on a green background, topped with a black falcon with arrows in one claw and a branch of ivy in the other claw. She didn't have to memorize *Debrett's* to know which family this crest belonged to. She closed her fist over the button and ordered the carriage to be brought around. She was going to handle this immediately.

# Chapter Thirty-Six

Ravenna jumped out of the carriage and stormed through the gate at Hillingham House, a neatly kempt, yellow Italianate with white cornices and a sturdy oak door. She clutched her fan tightly in one hand and pounded the knocker with her right, forgoing all propriety.

A stuffy butler in blue and gold velvet livery opened the door.

"Good evening, milady."

Ravenna stepped inside. "Let me see your buttons."

He harrumphed. "I beg your pardon, milady." His thick black brows dove against the bridge of his large, hooked nose.

She dug in her reticule. "Please, humor me. I have this button, and I want to be certain." She found the button and held it up for his inspection.

"Very well." He held out his arm, and she studied the button on his cuff. It was an exact match.

"Just as I thought." She closed her fist around the button. She seethed. "I insist on seeing Lady Dianthe, this instant. Please."

"I'll see if she's home. May I tell her who's calling?"

"I don't think you understand. This is of the utmost importance, or else I wouldn't have come at this hour. She will be home, or I will leave here and return with a Bow Street Runner."

He bowed, frowning with thinly veiled chagrin. "Very well, please follow me." He led her upstairs to the drawing room and opened the door. "Lady—"

"I don't need to be announced, thank you." Ravenna swept around him into the room. Lady Dianthe leaned over Braedon, who sat on the sofa with his legs stretched out and crossed at the ankles. They were dressed to go out.

Shock stretched Dianthe's mouth, and her eyes widened.

Braedon jumped to his feet and bowed. "Rav—uh—Lady Birchfield. What are you doing here?"

"Yes." Dianthe stood. "Why are you here?" Her gossamer white silk flowed to the ground, diamonds and sapphires sparked in the candlelight around her neck and hair. Considering the thinness of the silk and the minuscule bodice, it was clear modesty was not her priority.

Ravenna clutched the button in her fist. She wore a black crepe dress and a black velvet spencer, the top ruffle buttoned up to her chin. She felt every bit the dowager matron in comparison, but she didn't let that sway her purpose. She removed one glove as she marched over to Dianthe. And, without a word, Ravenna soundly slapped her across the face.

Dianthe gasped and cupped her cheek.

"Whoa there!" Braedon stepped between them.

Dianthe seethed. "How dare you. You common gutter wench, you...." She visibly quaked with rage.

Braedon grabbed Ravenna and attempted to shuttle her toward the door. "Have you gone mad?" he muttered. "If this is provoked by jealousy..."

Ravenna dug in her heels and turned on him. "You flatter yourself. This isn't about jealousy. It's about self-defense."

"You attacked her."

"Yes, because she sent someone to attack me."

"Wait." He paused, blinked. "Pardon?" He glanced between them.

She slapped the button into his hand. "That's her family's crest, is it not? One of the Pelham House maids, Keene, was attacked in the street tonight by shops near Gordon House. She managed to tear this off the attacker's coat. Further, I believe that beating was intended for me because when the attacker got a look at the girl's face, he ran away."

Braedon faced Dianthe. Disappointment diluted his voice. "Dianthe? What's the meaning of this?"

Ravenna stepped around him and pointed her finger at Dianthe. "Did you arrange to have a man accost me in the street?"

Dianthe shook her head, deep lines of confusion puckering her brow. "No. Absolutely not."

Braedon stepped toward her, his hands balled in fists. He growled, "Dianthe. Is this true?"

She backed up, glancing between Ravenna and Braedon. "How dare you ask that of me? How could you take her word over mine?"

"Because she's never given me reason to doubt her veracity, whereas you have rarely given me reason to believe in yours."

She gasped, offended, one cheek turning bright red to match the slapped cheek.

He gritted his teeth. "You will tell me the truth."

Her bottom lip quivered, then she ran and pressed herself against the wall, hiding her face against it. "You're always so cruel to me."

"Dianthe, right now. The truth."

Petulant, still half-pressed against the wall, she rubbed her cheek and heaved a sigh. "It wasn't supposed to be her maid. It was meant to be Lady Birchfield, but my idiot footman got them confused." She rolled her eyes.

"Why would you do such a thing?" he said.

She sobbed, her head dipping deeper between her shoulders. She whispered, shaking with emotion, "She was stealing you from me."

"I can't believe you did this. I'm so disappointed in you, Dianthe." He sighed and rubbed his eyes and forehead. "Moreover, I don't belong to you. Haven't for some time. I've tried to be kind to you. I've tried to help you. But you...." He stared at her, baffled. "You destroy everything you touch."

Quiet tears rolled down her cheeks. She sniffled.

A realization dawned on Ravenna. Perhaps Dianthe had a hand in other attacks. She stepped toward Dianthe, her fists balled at her sides. "Did you also have a torch thrown through my bedroom window?"

Dianthe seemed confused. "No. I didn't have a hand in that."

"What about the man who attacked me a couple nights ago?" Ravenna glared at her, seething. "You'd better not lie to me."

Dianthe shook her head. "No. I swear it."

Ravenna gathered her skirts and moved to leave, pausing at the door.

"Dianthe, you'll stay away from me this night forward, or I'll make you regret ever laying eyes on me." She glowered at Braedon and left the room.

# Chapter Thirty-Seven

Ravenna returned to Pelham House. She would take over watching Thomas and send Chester to bed as she was too angry to rest or sleep. When she entered the room, she found Lucy at Thomas's bedside, talking to him sweetly and washing his bare arms. Chester wasn't in the room.

"Good evening, Lucy. Where's Chester?" She stood by the door, removing her bonnet, gloves, and spencer.

Lucy jumped. "You frightened me. I sent Chester away to do his work or rest." She ran the water over Thomas's bare chest, matting the thin patch of black hair. "I've been thinking about what you said to me earlier. You were correct. I should take better care of my husband."

"I'm glad you've come around." She dropped her discarded items in the chair and moved to a table in the corner to pour a glass of port.

Lucy nodded, looking down. "Things haven't been perfect between Thomas and me, it's true. I feel as though I disappoint him often."

"I'm sure that's not true. But things are never perfect in marriage. The best we can hope for is mutual respect and contentment." She sat on the window seat, holding her port glass in her lap, taking in the scents of the cool London air as it tickled the sweaty curls on the back of her neck.

"I'm ashamed to say it, but I didn't really want to marry him." She tipped her head, her face masked with a dreamy quality, as she rubbed the wet cloth over his shoulders and arms.

Lucy's candor shocked Ravenna into silence.

"My father strongly encouraged the match because of Thomas's influence and connections. I think he hopes Thomas might work on his behalf for a powerful position." She sighed. "But here we are, and so I, we, must find a way to be happy or at least, as you say, content." She combed her fingers through his hair with a wistful smile. "It helps that he's handsome and kind. I think I could find my way to love in time."

"Contentment is far superior to happiness. Happiness is an emotion too easily blown about and led astray. Contentment is a solid foundation, based on a firm decision, therefore less capricious." She looked out at the street below and listened to the splashing of water. The scent of lilies tickled her nose. She snapped her head around to look at Lucy. She eased off the window seat and moved toward Lucy, sniffing the air. "Do you smell that? It smells like lilies."

"Yes. It's probably the tonic Milby gave me. It smells like the new cologne Thomas has been wearing of late. I wonder if she mixed them together."

Ravenna dashed to the bed. "What tonic? Was it prescribed by Dr. Pullman?"

"No, I don't think so. Milby said it's an old curative passed down in her family for generations."

Ravenna smelled the water bowl: lily, supported by a cushion of sage, underscored by bergamot. "You shouldn't use this. I don't trust Milby. Besides, it might conflict with Dr. Pullman's medicines and make the matter worse."

"Surely this once won't hurt."

Ravenna grabbed the bowl. "You could be poisoning him." She wrenched the cloth from Lucy's grip.

Shock marked Lucy's features. "Do you understand how lunatic you sound? I'm his wife." Lucy's face flushed, and her lips pinched together, growing white around the edges. "I'll take care of him." She grabbed for the cloth.

Ravenna pulled back. "You don't know what you're doing. You weren't here for Dr. Pullman's instruction, and there's something off-putting about Milby. You shouldn't trust her."

Lucy reached around Ravenna and picked up the bowl of water. "I'm doing it." Lucy pulled on the bowl.

Ravenna held fast.

"You can't bear it, can you? That you're only the stepmother and now a *dowager*. You're no longer wanted or needed. And you can't abide not being in control."

Ravenna tugged at the bowl. The water sloshed, dribbling over the side, the cloying scent of lilies turning her stomach. "I've had the care of him while you've been holding court in your chamber to be fussed over by all the maids or flitting about at social functions. You're unable to make sound decisions with all your laudanum use, so I'll decide what's best for him."

Lucy shouted, "You'll give me this bowl and get out of this room this instant, you gutter-born actress, or I'll..."

A fiendish spirit rose up in Ravenna and she twisted the bowl, causing the tonic to dump onto the carpet.

"Look what you've done," Lucy huffed. She threw the bowl to the ground and crossed the room to tug the bellpull. "You've never liked me. I displaced you as mistress of Birchfield Manor. I promise you now, you'll never have a place at Birchfield Manor. You will not be welcome under our roof, and I'll see to it you'll never live in the rector's cottage. I'll throw you back into the very gutter out of which you crawled."

How dare Lucy try to chase her from the place she'd shared with her husband, a place she'd grown to love as much as her family and homeland. She would die before she let go of the Birchfield Manor estate. White-hot fury flooded Ravenna's veins, blinding her ability to think clearly. She delivered a hard slap across Lucy's cheek. Slapping saucy women seemed to be her new habit these days. But it all happened reflexively, as thoughtless as breathing. She panted with rage. "You sniveling, wretched brat."

Lucy stared wide-eyed, holding her cheek.

The door creaked, and both women glanced at the entry, where Braedon stood, leaning against the door jamb, his arms crossed. Mirth and questioning lit his features. "Please, continue. I'm interested to see how this unfolds."

Hazel eyes flashing and her cheek turning red, Lucy stomped her silk-slippered foot. Rage quivered in the curls at her temples. "I want you out of this house. Immediately." She spun and retreated from the room as Braedon stepped aside to allow her exit.

Ravenna ran after her, screaming at Lucy's back as she stormed down the hall. "I won't leave until I'm certain Thomas is safe. Until then, if you want me out, you'll have to burn the house down around my ears."

A maid inched from the staircase and froze, wide-eyed and shrunken. "You rang?" She squeaked.

Ravenna reined in her anger. "Lady Lucy rang for you to clean up a spill. Please bring cloths to mop the rug."

The maid popped a curtsey and vanished.

She spun back into the room and slammed the door. She flashed a heated glance Braedon's way as she made her way to a glass of port.

Braedon held his hat in his hands. "I can't speak to your fencing prowess, but I wonder if you should take up pugilism instead. You seem to enjoy striking people. I once recall watching a fight between two women in St. Giles. I lost three guineas on the bet. You might do well enough to win my money back, if you should be so inclined."

She blew out a breath and turned on him. "Why are you here?"

"Dianthe and I had a falling out. Our last."

Ravenna shook her head. "I don't—"

A gagging, gurgling sound rose from the bed. Thomas's body lurched. He gagged and lurched. Vomit bubbled and frothed from his mouth. He was choking on it. "Oh, my God. Thomas!" she shouted. She set down her glass, and ran to his side. "Help me roll him to his side!" She shouted at Braedon.

They worked together to place Thomas on his side. She positioned his head to allow the froth to spill onto the rug. As he hadn't eaten anything, he fell into dry heaves and spasms.

Her own throat seized at the sound of his sickness. She closed her eyes and turned her face as she continued to hold him in place. When his hacking had stopped, she released him, and he fell back on the bed, wheezing

A maid entered the room with cloths. "Oh, dear."

Braedon shouted. "Lord Birchfield has become violently ill. Send a footman for Dr. Pullman this instant. He lives in Russell Square, number 34. Go! Make haste!"

"And send someone to clean this mess," Ravenna added.

The maid dropped her cloths and ran off, shouting through the house.

Within minutes, the entire house staff surrounded the room and took up the task of gathering supplies, watching for the surgeon, or gaping silently from the corners and shadows.

Thomas was once again frothing at the mouth. His eyes rolled back in his head, and fell into seizures.

Ravenna directed Chester to watch Thomas while she ran to her own room for her medicine chest. She ran to Lucy's room to tell her about Thomas, but Lucy wasn't there. She couldn't worry about Lucy right now.

When she returned, Braedon had stripped out of his coats and waistcoat. His shirt sleeves were rolled up over his elbows, and he was washing Thomas in plain water while Chester held Thomas on his side.

Ravenna placed the medicine chest on the bed, searching frantically through all the bottles and vials. With a shaking voice, she tried to talk to Thomas, to calm him, unsure if he heard her or understood her. She found her camphor ointment and set it aside.

She climbed into the bed behind him and touched his forehead to gauge his temperature. He was clammy and sweaty. Veins protruded all over his face as he strained and writhed. If he'd had a sore throat or a wound, she could fix those things. But this? She wasn't sure what to do with this. All of her mother's instruction had never prepared her for something this dire and elusive. She could only go on instinct and whatever previous treatments she'd administered to ill family and friends.

A maid appeared with the requested supplies, and another maid stood nearby, ready to clean the mess.

Ravenna jumped from the bed. "When he stops heaving, lay him on his back." She poured vinegar and water into the bowl and waited.

Soon, Thomas calmed and Braedon and Chester eased him onto his back. Ravenna dipped a cloth in the vinegar-water and rubbed his chest, arms, and abdomen vigorously. After two rounds of the wash, she handed the camphor to Braedon. "Rub this on his arms while I wash his front a third time."

Braedon worked the camphor into Thomas's arms. He locked his frosted blue eyes on Ravenna's face. His features were weighed with worry, fear, and determination. "Will this work?"

Ravenna pushed a dark tendril of hair out of her face with the back of her hand. "I don't know. Hand me the camphor. Please lift him again."

Chester and Braedon pulled Thomas to sit up. Thomas heaved, wheezed, and groaned.

"Hold him. Don't let him fall." Ravenna washed his back and slathered the skin with camphor. She whispered to him that all would be well. When she was finished, she asked the men to lay him down. Within minutes, Thomas had sunk into a fitful sleep as the camphor settled in.

Chester patted Thomas's shoulder. "There, there, milord. We'll have you right as rain soon."

Ravenna cleaned his face and around his discolored lips.

Ravenna then rubbed the camphor on his chest, feeling the ridges of his bones through his skin. She pulled the covers up to his chin, and his breathing became slow and even.

Ravenna turned to the waiting maids. "Please clean up the floor. Be careful to dry the spot first. But..." She handed them a pair of tongs from the fireplace. "Don't touch the rag. It could contain poison. Use these to drop the rag in a dry bucket. Then bury the rag in the yard. Scrub the spot with lye twice to ensure the poison is sufficiently diluted."

The maids gaped at her in fear. "Yes, ma'am," one said, taking the tongs.

Ravenna continued. "Then take the rug away and bring fresh water and vinegar." She poured two glasses of wine and handed one to Braedon. "Chester, go rest. Thank you."

Chester left the room, and Ravenna and Braedon occupied the window seat, their bodies depleted as they sipped their wine. Footmen filled the room and lifted the bed corners as the maids rolled up the rug. The night air, laced with noise from the street below, poured from the window around Ravenna and Braedon. It had chilled considerably, and a rising wind spoke to pending rain. The footmen carried out the rug as the maids knelt to scrub the floor. When they had finished, Ravenna dismissed them with a request to send up Dr. Pullman the moment he arrived.

She swallowed the hard, burning knot of emotion in her throat and willed her eyes to soak up the tears that had begun pooling at the rim of her lids. She would not cry, especially in front of the staff, who all looked at her with a blend of admiration and fear. Nor would she cry in front of Braedon. She had to be strong. *Don't panic.* She had to be clear, steady, and ready to act at a moment's notice.

Ravenna returned to her seat beside Braedon. Silence yawned between them. Once again, Braedon's annoying presence had turned into an unexpected blessing. And his cool, collected behavior in an emergency was a boon.

Braedon spoke first. "I thought he was recovering."

"He was. Lucy..." She shook her head and looked down at her feet.

"Ah. Now I begin to understand the earlier scene witnessed. What happened?"

"I'm not certain. She put a curative on him that her lady's maid, Milby, had suggested. I don't like Milby, and I don't trust her."

"Do you think Milby would've hurt him intentionally?"

She drank her wine. "I don't know for certain, but I certainly aim to discover more about her. It could be coincidence that she recommended a curative that unintentionally conflicted with Dr. Pullman's medicines and caused Thomas's regression."

Thunder rumbled in the distance. She rubbed her eyes to relieve the pressure of tears.

He laid a hand on her knee, a bold move. "Ravenna, I can help if only you'll tell me how."

She glared at him. "You cannot call me a friend while you give attention to a woman who tried to have me attacked." She pushed his hand from her knee. "Do you truly believe her when she says she's not responsible for the fire and the attack on me? Better yet, what's to prevent her from doing it again?"

He sighed and scratched his jaw. "She's not thinking clearly. Her jealousy and the laudanum...." Ravenna lifted a brow. "She is ensnared by the laudanum. It has her in a perilous grip. She hasn't been herself for some time. I've explained to her repeatedly she and I will never be engaged, we are finished."

Ravenna rolled her eyes and moved away from him, flopping down in a nearby chair. "And you think her opium-addled brain understands and accepts that? She clearly still loves you, whatever you may or may not feel for her. That's all she sees and understands. The more time you spend with her, the more you prove, in her mind, you still love her. I suppose I can't fault her logic. I have no recourse but to believe that myself."

"There's a difference in caring for someone's welfare and being in love with them."

She shook her head. It was her own fault. She knew his situation, knew his reputation, yet she'd allowed herself to get sucked in. Sucked into those beautiful eyes, that handsome face, his perfect form, his sensual lips. She propped her chin in her hand and averted her gaze, refusing to look at him lest she be sucked in again. Then the guilt gripped her, pulled her under. She closed her eyes. A throbbing headache bloomed in the center of her forehead. Thunder grumbled.

Braedon glanced outside and closed the window. "I apologize, Ravenna. I never meant to hurt anyone." He stood and unrolled his shirt sleeves and grabbed up his coats, waistcoat, and hat. "I know what my reputation is, and it's not unfounded, so I understand your apprehension. I also understand your situation." He crossed the room and stood over her. "People do change. Sometimes, I allow people to think the wrong things about me because it gives me an advantage. Should I need it. But I won't allow you to think wrongly of me."

"Brae—"

He held up a hand to still her voice. "I do still care what happens to Dianthe. But I don't love her. I believe if I can help release her from the laudanum and restore her to her previous character, then I can extricate myself from her forever. She can find another and be happy. And perhaps so can I." He locked his pale blue eyes on her face, his demeanor full of weariness and sincerity. "She needs a friend right now. I can't turn my back on her simply because it would be convenient for me to do so." He crossed the room. "That might be a quality of my character you'll find favorable someday." He opened the door and bowed. "Good evening, Ravenna." He closed the door.

Ravenna sank, unsure what to feel. A flood of competing emotions—compassion, tenderness, sorrow, guilt, irritation, and anger—jockeyed for her attention. She put her head in her hands, opting to allow a lid of numbness to close over them. She didn't have the energy to address any of this right now. She rubbed her face, downed her wine, and stared into the fire.

The sound of boots thumped in the hallway, and the door opened to give entrance to Chester, followed by Dr. Pullman. The surgeon stripped out of his coat, dumping it into Ravenna's hands, as he headed straight for Thomas. He was still dressed in his evening clothes, his hair slicked off his forehead with pomade. "How is the patient?" He removed his evening coat, too.

"He seems to have calmed for now."

"What happened?" He rolled up his shirt sleeves.

"I'm not sure. He had been calm since your last visit. I followed all your directions. We've not yet been able to apply your remedy because he hasn't been awake to be purged. This evening, I came into the room to find Lady Birchfield, his wife, washing him in a tincture that her lady's maid had given her."

"What was in the tincture?"

"I don't know."

"I'd like to speak to both women, please." Dr. Pullman felt for a pulse.

Ravenna rang for the maid to have her fetch Lucy and Milby. After ten minutes, the maid returned. "Neither one is home, ma'am. Both are out for the evening."

The surgeon shook his head, his lips pinched tight. "Very well. And what happened after that?"

Ravenna explained Thomas's violent reaction and her, Chester, and

Braedon's efforts to help him. She wrung her hands, looking down at Thomas's wincing face. "I didn't know what else to do."

"You did well, milady. I applaud you." A fatherly kindness infused his eyes. "I'm going to wet cup him and leech him. It could be that the tincture has interfered with the treatment I issued, and now his blood is severely infected. This is all internal, and we need to bring it out of his system." He gazed at her. "I trust you have the constitution to assist me?"

She nodded, glancing at Chester. "Yes, sir." Chester hovered nearby, ready to assist.

"Then let us begin." He opened his case of medical secrets and withdrew a jar of leeches and a few glass cups.

Dr. Pullman talked more to himself than anyone else as he announced his procedure. "We'll cup the ribs here to stimulate the lungs. And we'll place one here to stimulate the liver. One here to stimulate the stomach. Each side of the chest to stimulate the heart and blood flow." He held up a finger. "Very important."

Ravenna watched, soaking in his instruction as if she were one of his medical students.

When the glasses had all been placed. He crossed his arms over his chest. "Now we wait." After a few minutes, he removed a cup, made a small incision to draw blood, and followed the same course for the remaining cups. Soon Thomas was covered in small cuts oozing with blood. The surgeon then drew two gray, slimy leeches from the jar with his fingers and attached them to Thomas's temples. One by one, he drew the leeches from the jar and attached them to the insides of his arms and over the multiple cuts. As they worked, he mixed a liniment of almond oil, witch hazel, and camphor.

"You were wise to use the camphor ointment, Lady Birchfield. Once we have balanced his humors, you should bathe him in vinegar water three times a day, then rub this liniment vigorously over his chest and leave it on. When he wakes, I can provide additional treatments for him to ingest. Let's cup him again on the back." He removed the leeches, dropping them into a glass jar. He said to Chester, "Help me flip him to his stomach."

On the count of three, Chester and Dr. Pullman rolled Thomas over.

The cups, incisions, and leeches were again utilized. Once finished, they returned the patient to his back.

They all stood around the bed, expectant, observing Birchfield, measuring each breath.

After some time, the surgeon, satisfied with Thomas's progress, packed his instruments into his case. "I've done all I can for now. He's resting well." He wiped his broad brow with his handkerchief and smoothed his hair back with his hand. "I'll trust him to your capable hands, Lady Birchfield, and will check on him when I next make my rounds."

When Dr. Pullman left, Chester said, "Forgive my familiarity, milady, but you seem quite tired. If I may be so bold, perhaps you should go rest, and I'll stay with him."

"He cannot be left alone for an instant."

"I promise I won't take my eyes off him."

She started for the door, then paused. "Chester? What do you know of Milby?"

"Not much, milady. She keeps to herself. When I attempt to converse with her, she provides short answers with little information."

"Do you not find that suspicious behavior?"

"Not particularly. There are many who prefer to keep to themselves."

That was true. A quiet, reserved person didn't immediately equate to a wicked one. "Granted. I won't go into particulars because I don't have proof, and I'm not interested in hurting someone's character without a basis. However, I would prefer that Milby is not allowed anywhere near this room. Further, no one except myself or Dr. Pullman should administer any treatment to Lord Birchfield. Even Lady Birchfield should not administer any treatment. Am I understood?"

"Of course, milady." Chester frowned. "But Lady Birchfield is my employer."

"I understand your concern, Chester. I promise you will be protected. Even if you're forced out of this house, I will ensure your employment elsewhere. You won't go without work."

"Thank you, milady." He frowned. "Do you suspect Milby of objectionable behavior?"

"Possibly, but I can't say more without proof. I'm working on that."

"I understand, ma'am."

"If you find or hear something suspicious about Milby, I need you to tell me immediately, please."

"Of course, ma'am. If it helps Milord Birchfield, I'm yours to command."

# Chapter Thirty-Eight

The next morning, Ravenna looked in on Keene, who was sleeping off her injuries, then she and Chester worked together to bathe Thomas in vinegar and apply the liniment Dr. Pullman gave her. Afterward, Chester left the room to retire for rest. Ravenna ate her breakfast of currant scones and ham while watching over Thomas and reading the newspapers. She had just settled by Thomas's side with a book when a knock sounded at the door.

A maid entered and bobbed a curtsey. "Pardon, milady. Lady Wolfsham is downstairs to see you."

That was odd. As a new widow, she shouldn't be out of the house paying visits. She couldn't go down to see her because there was no one to watch over Thomas and poor Chester needed his rest. "Bring her here, please."

Ravenna opened the windows to air the room and drew the curtains on the bed. She stood in front of the sofa by the fireplace, ready to receive.

Lady Wolfsham entered the room, dressed in black from her feathered bonnet to kid slippers, to the lace veil covering her face and fiery curls. She lifted her veil and looked around the room.

"Lady Wolfsham, what a surprise. I'm very sorry to receive you in Thomas's sick room, but it's become necessary to watch him every minute. May I offer you a drink? I don't have tea at the ready, but I have sherry or cordial."

"No, thank you. I won't trouble you."

"Please, have a seat." Ravenna motioned toward the sofa and waited for her guest to sit before taking her own seat.

Lady Wolfsham perched on the edge of the sofa and folded her hands in her lap. "First, I wanted to say how terribly sorry I am Lord Birchfield is ill. I heard the news this morning and wanted to come immediately. I pray it's not what afflicted my husband and that he soon recovers. Is he very ill?"

"Thank you. He is quite feverish and has suffered severe stomach distress. He's not yet woken from his stupor."

"Do you suspect it's natural? Or that something has been done to him?"

"I can't tell. He's been asleep the whole time I've been here, but we maintain hope."

Lady Wolfsham twisted the strings of her reticule around her gloved finger. She seemed troubled. "I've been thinking about the questions you asked when you visited about whether or not I suspected anyone of harming Wolfsham, and it occurred to me that there may be someone working with Nochdale. A man, Mr. Larson. He's new money and has a lot of it. I've never seen him or met him before, but he's been buying a certain amount of influence with some of our less scrupulous politicians. I've heard he's been trying to get near the crown through men like Fox and Nochdale."

Shock rattled Ravenna's senses. She'd heard of Mr. Larson from Keene. He was apparently Milby's beau. Perhaps they were working together, and Ravenna's instincts about Milby were right. She tried to keep calm so she could think straight. "How do you mean?"

"I can't say because I wasn't there. It was something Wolfsham complained about at dinner one night. You understand how it is when you're a politician's wife. You listen for a few minutes, then think about something else. Especially Wolfsham. He'd go on all night if I entertained him for more than ten minutes."

"Thank you for telling me. I've heard of Mr. Larson recently for the first time."

"Oh?" Her red brows arched.

"Indeed. I have it from one of my servants that the substitute lady's maid might have an entanglement with him."

"How fortuitous." Lady Wolfsham touched her arm. "You might be in a good position to find out more about him."

237

"My thoughts precisely.

Lady Wolfsham stood, tugging at her gloves. "I won't keep you. I need to return home before I'm missed." She paused, frowning, heavy bags under her eyes. "I hardly slept last night. I wonder if I shall ever sleep again."

"You will. Eventually. Though it may be in fits and starts at first. I still sometimes wake in the middle of the night, expecting my husband to walk in from a night at his club or to be lying next to me, his clothes scattered all over the room." The memory tugged painfully at the space between her breasts. She walked Lady Wolfsham to the top of the stairs. "You'll forgive me for not seeing you to the door? I'm afraid of leaving Thomas for even a minute."

"Of course. Good luck." She squeezed Ravenna's hand. "If you hear of anything new about Mr. Larson, you'll let me know? If my husband did not die of natural causes, I'll see the killer is punished."

"Of course."

Milby ascended the staircase.

Lady Wolfsham said, "Good day. How do you do? I wondered what happened to you."

Milby's eyes darted, and she froze on the steps. "Pardon me. I didn't mean to interrupt." She turned to descend.

Lady Wolfsham said, "Smith? Are you unwell?"

Milby continued down a couple of stairs, and Ravenna said sternly. "Milby. Lady Wolfsham is addressing you."

Lady Wolfsham glanced at Ravenna with puzzlement. "Milby?"

Milby paused and turned, her face pale. "I am sorry. I didn't realize."

"You are Hannah Smith, are you not?" Lady Wolfsham chuckled.

"I beg your pardon, but my name is Milby. I think you must be mistaken." She clasped her hands in front of her until her knuckles turned white.

Examining her for a moment, Lady Wolfsham blinked and shook her head. "You look the very spit of a maid I had in my house not long ago. Her name was Hannah Smith. She was my chambermaid. Kept my room beautifully. Lady Braxton recommended her to me."

"I see." Ravenna looked between them. "Are you certain you've never worked for Lady Wolfsham?"

Milby laughed. "Begging your pardon, milady, I think I'd remember. But as her maid was Smith, a chambermaid, and I'm Milby, a lady's maid, I reckon the mistake isn't mine." She shifted. "If I may go, I need to finish my sewing."

Ravenna dismissed Milby, who changed her path to run up the stairs past them. When she had disappeared with a glance over her shoulder, Ravenna turned to Lady Wolfsham. "How long was Hannah Smith in your employ?"

"Only a few weeks."

"What happened?"

"She simply disappeared one day. She didn't leave a note or say anything to the rest of the staff. Your woman looks remarkably like her." She put her hand to her head. "But I suppose I could be confused. The grief and lack of sleep has addled my brain."

"Did your maid leave before or after Lord Wolfsham died?"

She frowned, thinking. "I believe she left a day or two before." She put her hand to her temple. "I can't recall for certain. Everything has been in a fog." She blinked.

When Lady Wolfsham left, Ravenna returned to her watch over Thomas and paced near his bed, pulling at her bottom lip. Someone who looked a lot like Milby had worked at both Wolfsham and Pelham Houses. She wondered if this was true of Hawkestone or Nochdale's Houses?

She rang for a footman. "Please rouse Chester with my apologies and ask him to come sit with Lord Birchfield and have someone prepare the carriage. I need to leave the house for a brief time."

Within a quarter of an hour, Chester came into the room, looking refreshed but for his bloodshot eyes.

"I'm so sorry to wake you, Chester. Please sit with Lord Birchfield until I return. I have to attend to some urgent business. I won't be long."

Chester agreed and took the seat at Thomas's bedside.

She ran to her bedchamber, threw on a spencer and bonnet, hooked her fan on her wrist, and rushed down the stairs. She exited the home.

"Lady Birchfield."

She turned to see Braedon. He jogged up to her. "You look panicked. Has Thomas worsened? I came to ask after him and to see if the surgeon came to inspect him."

Thick gray clouds filled the sky, and the wind whipped their coats. The horses whinnied and tossed their heads.

"Thomas is well. For now. Dr. Pullman did come after you left and returned Thomas to a restful state. I'm just on my way to Nochdale and Hawkestone Houses. I must make haste."

"I'm coming with you. With everything that's been happening, you're not going alone." She opened her mouth, and he cut her off. "I'll brook no disagreement on the subject." For once, she didn't argue.

# Chapter Thirty-Nine

Braedon assisted her into the carriage, and they settled against the soft leather seats. Ravenna was both relieved and agitated to be in Braedon's presence. She was glad for his protection should she need it, but was still uncomfortable since their conversation last night.

Braedon seemed on edge, glancing out the window. "Why are you in such a rush to visit Nochdale and Hawkestone Houses?"

"The strangest thing has happened." She explained the conversation with Lady Wolfsham regarding Milby. "I'm wondering if Milby is whom she claims to be."

"So then you're no longer pursuing Nochdale?"

She ran a finger under her bonnet strings. She'd tied the bow too tight. "I didn't say that. I don't yet have a reason to stop pursuing him. I'm still looking for explanations."

"But you think Hawkestone and Wolfsham were, in fact, murdered? And that Birchfield's illness is no accident, but a murder attempt?"

"It's very likely." She watched the shops and homes roll slowly by and watched the rain spangle the glass. "I believe Lucy's new maid may be somehow working with Nochdale. Or she may be working with a man named Mr. Larson. Or all three are working together."

"Mr. Larson?"

She told him what she'd learned about Mr. Larson. "Do you know anything about this newcomer?"

He frowned, shaking his head. "Can't say I do. But I will certainly try to find out something about him."

241

"Discreetly." She lifted a brow.

He smiled. "Is there any other way?" He crossed his arms over his chest and relaxed into the corner. "You're quite the Bow Street Runner, going about asking questions and investigating."

"My stepson is currently on his deathbed. I'll do whatever it takes. I have to prove Milby is behind this so I can have her removed from the house, and have her thrown in prison where she belongs."

He glanced out the window. "It occurs to me, as I think back over the past week or so, you've been involved in this before Birchfield fell ill and that there might be more to this than Thomas."

She averted her eyes to stare out the window. "I don't know what you mean."

Thankfully, the carriage pulled up in front of Nochdale House in Park Lane. As she reached to open the door, Braedon put his hand on top of hers. "Won't you let me help you? I have a great many connections—"

She held up a hand to cut him off. "While I appreciate your sentiment, Braedon, did it ever occur to you I have reasons for keeping my secrets? Did you ever consider not every woman needs to be rescued?"

Mirth sparkled in his frosted blue eyes. "It's been my experience the women who need help the most are the very ones too proud to accept it."

Lady Nochdale met them in the drawing room. She was a dumpy woman with white-streaked gray hair under a lace mob cap and a fine lace fichu pinned over a mauve and pink striped muslin dress. "Nochdale is quite ill and isn't receiving." She pulled her needle and thread through the large frame in front of her. "I'm working on embellishing this counterpane for my bed."

"I do understand, but it's a matter of state. I would speak with him on Lord Birchfield's behalf."

"I'm sorry. I can't allow him to be disturbed."

Ravenna couldn't blame her, so she resigned herself to another tack. She selected a dry piece of cake and settled in for something resembling a social call. Perhaps she could still discover something.

"What do you think of this pattern?" Lady Nochdale tipped her head, studying her work.

Ravenna inspected the sage green vines and white daisies with yellow centers and small lavender butterflies around the edge of the fabric. "I like it very much. I think it will be lovely."

"Yes, quite." Lady Nochdale smiled up at her. She wasn't a particularly handsome woman. She had a boxy face and nose and dull gray eyes that displayed neither spirit nor intelligence.

Ravenna brought the conversation back around. "Has Lord Nochdale shown any improvement at all?"

Her short, knotty fingers worked the needle through again. "Not really. I'd say he's gotten worse."

"How long has he been ill?" Braedon asked.

She looked down her nose at the stitch she'd made, picked at it, and started another stitch. "In truth, his health has been in a steady decline for some time. But it's been coming on so slowly. I suppose I didn't take notice until recently."

Ravenna clutched her folded fan in her lap. "My stepson has been terribly ill, too. Spasms, shaking, digestive distress, fever, delirium. He hasn't even been awake for a few days."

Lady Nochdale looked up. "I'm sorry to hear it. Poor dear. Nochdale's illness has been quite the same, except he's been awake. And has been trying to work, if you can believe it."

"Astonishing."

She leaned forward a little. "I finally had to say..." She held up her finger, re-enacting the exchange. "'Dear, you shouldn't be working while you're sick. You'll destroy your health, and then you'll never get better.'" She sighed. "But he insists on working, working, working. He writes his letters and meets with his clerk. He's incredibly determined to be the next foreign secretary. It's a wonder he's not sicker."

"Yes, I've heard he's so desperate for the post that he's resorted to threatening those who dare oppose him."

Lady Nochdale perked. "Threatened? Nonsense." She snorted a laugh. "I wouldn't believe everything you hear, Lady Birchfield. He wants the post, to be sure, but he's not foolish enough to go around threatening the men from whom he'd need cooperation later." She pulled the thread through, inspected her spot, and began another stitch. "He's determined and bold, and in his zeal, he often says things that might be misconstrued as threats or viciousness, but he doesn't mean any real harm." She stopped sewing to take a sip of tea. Then she laughed, her round body jiggling, "La! If I had a guinea for every time he made empty threats or spoke forcefully to me, I'd be rich as Croesus."

Ravenna sipped her tea and nibbled at her dry cake to give herself space to think. It was possible that Lady Nochdale misunderstood her husband. It could be that she was such a cork-brain she couldn't see him for what he truly was. She put aside the remains of the cake and tea.

"Lady Nochdale, have you had any new staff here recently? Or did you hire temporary help for the garden party?"

"Oh, yes, I did hire a few temporary maids to help with the garden party. You know how it is. The usual staff can't do everything. There was also an upstairs chambermaid I hired when I let go of the one who stole from me."

"When did you hire her?"

"Oh, back in March."

"Is that around the time Lord Nochdale's health began its decline?"

She paused and stared at her needle. "I can't say for certain." She chuckled. "My memory isn't what it once was. But I suppose it's not impossible."

Ravenna exchanged a glance with Braedon.

Braedon said, "What was the name of the girl you hired?"

Ravenna frowned at his bold insertion into her investigation.

"Jefferson was her name."

"What did Jefferson look like? Do you recall?" Ravenna asked.

"Fair hair, but not blonde exactly, a masculine jaw. I haven't seen her since the day of the party, though."

"Why?"

"I'd hired her for the house, but on the day of the picnic when one of the temporary maids didn't come to work, I'd asked Jefferson to help. I think she felt it was beneath her, so after that day I never saw her again. Went off in a miff. Or so the other maids say. The help these days are far too high and mighty, thinking themselves so superior to do this work or that work. They won't hardly do anything at all." She shook her head and resumed her sewing. "A saucy-tongued girl with a most petulant air. I assure you it's the last time I'll take one of Lady Braxton's references." She paused her sewing and looked up. "I think Lady Braxton owes me an apology."

# Chapter Forty

Ravenna nearly ran to the carriage in her struggle to contain her excitement. She called out to the driver to take them to Hawkestone House. The woman Lady Nochdale had called "Jefferson," seemed similar in looks to Milby and Lady Wolfsham's "Smith." She couldn't be certain yet, but it seemed the same woman was connected to all three houses. She was certain she remembered seeing a servant at Hawkestone House who resembled Milby, but she wanted to get confirmation from Lady Violette—and a name; though the name was likely fake.

Interestingly, this woman "Jefferson" had also been referred by Lady Braxton. Women in her circle often referred servants to each other. But was Milby or Smith or whatever she called herself an actor in someone else's political game? Was the servant an agent working with Nochdale and his illness was mere coincidence? Was Lady Braxton tied in with Nochdale? Or was that also pure coincidence? Perhaps Nochdale, cunning as he was, planted his agent with the unwitting Lady Braxton. In which case, Lady Braxton would unknowingly recommend Nochdale's agent to every house he hoped to target. If only she'd had an opportunity to speak with him.

"How disappointing that you didn't get to see Nochdale," Braedon said. "Though I don't think it was a complete loss since you discovered he likely isn't the killer you seek."

"I don't see how you come to that conclusion." A steady rain pelted the window. "As Lady Nochdale said, he has a volatile temper. She doesn't have the sense of a goose. She may perceive his threats as innocuous, but I

246

daresay he's more cunning than that."

"She should understand her husband better than anyone for all the years they've been married."

"She wouldn't be the first wife to be fooled."

They pulled into the heavy traffic of Piccadilly. Passing the budding trees dotting Green Park, they inched along in silence while Ravenna stared out the window, ruminating. The carriage turned right onto St. James Street.

Braedon checked his pocket watch. "Interestingly is both Lady Wolfsham and Lady Nochdale mentioned hiring a new upstairs maid on Lady Braxton's recommendation." He clicked the lid closed over the watch face and returned it to his pocket.

"Yes. And, oddly, the description is quite similar. Light hair, strong jaw."

"Which means there are several women who greatly resemble each other, or—"

"Or, more likely one woman is changing her name whenever she moves to a new house." Ravenna completed his thought.

"More importantly, the men seem to be getting sick around the time she appears in the houses."

"Yes. Lord Birchfield began getting sick about the same time Milby arrived at Pelham House to replace Lucy's lady's maid. I'm almost certain it's the same woman. Which, if true, means Thomas is in great danger."

"But why would a maid want to poison these men, especially foreign secretaries? What would she have to gain from it?"

"A simple maid would have nothing to gain. But, what if she's a political pawn and working in league with Nochdale to poison his enemies and keep the foreign secretary position open for himself? Isn't that possible?"

"But Lady Braxton referred her. Could she be involved?"

Ravenna shook her head, playing with the fingers of her black gloves. "I don't know. I'd considered that myself. Briefly. But I can't imagine it. She has been such a pinnacle of charity and generosity. Granted, she can be brazen, but she's been responsible for educating women, furthering our rights and place in the world, redeeming prostitutes and helping them to have a better life. I'd much sooner believe Nochdale is using her for his wicked ends, without her knowledge. After all, what would Lady Braxton possibly have to gain from the deaths of foreign secretaries?"

The carriage slowed to a stop in front of Hawkestone House as Ravenna slid to the edge of her seat.

He frowned and nodded. "You could be right. But to make such an accusation against Nochdale..." He winced and tsked. "He's a powerful man, Ravenna, a peer, potentially the next foreign secretary. It's dangerous. If you accuse him and you're wrong, he'll destroy you."

"Yes. But what if I'm right?"

"Is that a risk you're willing to take?"

"I don't have a choice if it means saving my stepson." And herself.

At Hawkestone House, Ravenna and Braedon were shown into the music room where Lady Violette played a bittersweet Haydn sonata on the pianoforte. Somber and pale in her widow's weeds, she stopped and stood to greet them.

"Your playing is lovely, Lady Violette," Ravenna said.

"Please, you must call me Violette. I think all we're going through has quickly united us in friendship."

Ravenna smiled warmly. "Thank you, I shall. And you'll call me Ravenna." She motioned at the pianoforte. "I'm deeply envious of anyone who plays. I never learned."

"There are women far more accomplished than myself, but Charles insisted I play for him every evening after dinner. When he was here for dinner, of course." Her face was gaunt and pale, dark circles under her eyes. A wan smile played on her lips. "Hello, Lord Braedon. A pleasure seeing you again." She extended her hand.

Braedon bowed over her hand and kissed it. "The pleasure is all mine. I wish the circumstances were better."

She placed her other hand over his. "You're very good. You've always been a great friend to us."

His voice grew watery. "The friendship I've received from you and Charles has always been a boon to me."

Ravenna watched Braedon. His jaw knotted and his eyes watered. He cleared his throat and stepped away to stare out of the window. He was getting emotional. She hadn't realized he was close friends with the Hawkestones. It dawned on her how little she knew of Braedon, and what she did know was informed by erroneous rumor and supposition.

Violette glided across the floor toward the sofa and chairs. "Please, be seated. Would you like refreshment?"

"No, thank you," Ravenna said, taking a seat in front of the dark fireplace. Braedon sat beside her on the sofa, and Violette sat on the edge of a chair across from them.

Ravenna folded her hands in her lap. "Thank you for receiving us. We won't intrude long. I'm curious about something. Have you recently hired a new maid?"

She frowned with confusion. "If you need a recommendation—"

"No, it's not that. I'm looking for someone. The woman in question would have had red-gold hair, a stern jaw."

Violette frowned. "In fact, I did have a woman by that description—"

Ravenna scooted to the edge of her seat. "How long ago? When?"

"A-a-about a month ago, maybe a little longer. Why?"

"What was her name? Her position?"

"She was an upstairs maid. Her name was uh-uh Jones. Jane Jones."

Scoffing, Ravenna shook her head. "Another common name."

"Ravenna, you're frightening me." She glanced between her visitors. "What's the meaning of these questions?"

"I'm sorry. I don't mean to frighten you. I'm suspicious of a woman living in Pelham House, but I can't quite pin her down. What do you know of this Jane Jones? Anything at all you can tell me would be helpful."

"Not much, really. She said she was twenty-seven, unmarried. No family to speak of. She seemed to be a very private person, so I didn't press her beyond her references. Which were impeccable."

"Do you remember any of her references?"

"I'll get the letter. I'm sure I still have it." She left the room. She soon returned and handed the paper to Ravenna.

Ravenna ran her finger along the paper and read aloud. "Mrs. Hurst in Maple Lane." That meant nothing. The name could have been made up. "Lady Braxton." Not much of a surprise since she'd referred the maid to Lady Wolfsham. "And a Mrs...." She looked at Braedon. "Milby." He arched his scarred eyebrow. She handed the page back to Violette. "The woman at Pelham House is using the name Milby."

Braedon said, "That can't be a mere coincidence."

"No, it can't."

"Oh, dear," Violette said.

Ravenna stood, clutching her folded fan. "I need to return to Pelham House directly. Thank you for your time, Violette." Ravenna turned to go. Braedon followed.

Violette stood, hugging herself. "Ravenna..."

Ravenna paused and faced her.

"You should know, Mr. Chadwick has come back asking questions, and he seems particularly focused on you. I expect he will visit you again soon."

Ravenna's breath caught, and she flushed. The snare seemed to be closing tighter around her. She needed more time. She nodded. "Thank you. I understand."

Ravenna and Braedon returned to Pelham House. The wind whipped their coats as they pushed through the gale into the house.

The butler greeted her. "A Mr. Chadwick stopped in to see you not twenty minutes ago." He handed her a card.

Ravenna accepted the card and crushed it in her hand. "Thank you. Any time he calls. I am not home. Understand?"

"Yes, ma'am."

"Is Milby or Lady Birchfield here?"

"No, ma'am. Both are out."

"Where?"

"Lady Birchfield is dining with Lady Jersey this evening. She told me not to expect her return until very late. Milby did not say where she was going or how long she would be gone."

"Thank you. Please have Milby sent to my room, if you happen to see her. And have a tea sent to Lord Birchfield's room."

"Yes, ma'am."

She and Braedon ran upstairs to Thomas's room to check on him. His valet, Chester, was at his bedside, reading to him. He looked up from his book, his face drawn and haggard from exhaustion.

Ravenna removed her bonnet and spencer, dropping them in a nearby chair, and fluffed her hair into place. "Has anyone else been in here?"

"No, milady."

"I'll take over from here." Relief washed through her. "Please, go rest now. You'll need your strength. I'll do my best to not bother you again."

He bowed and left the room.

Ravenna stood in front of the fire, as Braedon removed his great coat and hat, dropping them on the sofa. She pulled at her bottom lip, staring into the fire, thinking.

Braedon stood beside her. "Tell me how I can help."

"I don't know. I'm inclined to say you can leave me be. I don't mean to be rude, but I'm certain a dozen other women would trip over themselves for your attention, and I need to think."

"I understand, I suppose." An undercurrent of hurt was in his voice. The wind whistled in the chimney, fluttering the fire. The rain started up again, pecking softly at the windows.

Her rudeness pricking her conscience, she forced a smile. "Of course, you can have some refreshment before you leave. I won't send you away hungry."

Humor lit his eyes. "I know one way I can be of help." He crossed to the occasional table and poured a glass of wine for each of them. He handed her a glass. "And you should know, I don't like those dozen other women."

She accepted the wine. "Thank you." She drank deeply. "You should know, I'm all wrong for you, Braedon."

A maid knocked and entered with a tray, placing it on the table by the window.

Ravenna sat at the table and cut a slice of bread and cheese for each of them.

"What makes you so sure?"

"Because I'm a widow. I'm Irish, a commoner, and a former actress. Everyone believed my husband was mad to marry me, but through his grace and extensive efforts, I have become somewhat accepted by society, though the tiniest scandal could rip all that from under me."

"Do you really care what society thinks?" He sat across from her and accepted the plate of food she offered.

"For myself, no. I've been invisible before, and in some ways, it would be a relief to be so again. But for my stepsons and their futures, it would bother me very much to have them dragged through the muck with me."

"Fair enough."

"Besides, you're clearly still entangled with Dianthe."

"Therefore, I can't be entangled with you." His eyes shone with mirth.

"Precisely." She bit into the cheese. "And if you cared for me one wit, you wouldn't try to seduce me into harming my reputation."

He sniffed a chuckle and cut a slice of cheese and bit into it. "In that case, until I can fully extract myself from Dianthe's grip, let me be your friend and confidante."

She chewed her food, shaking her head. She couldn't possibly tell him about her past, about her share in the Irish rebellion, her treason. The truth was too ugly. With The Unity possibly following her, she didn't want to put him in danger as well. "It's best if you don't know everything."

"I understand, but I won't leave you alone until I'm assured you're truly safe. Whatever else I am to you, above all, I'm your friend, and I think you need a friend who will protect you, stand for you, support you."

She washed her food down with wine. "Why? Why me? Why are you so adamant about being my friend?"

He sat back, studying her with his frosted blue eyes, his wolfish gaze. "I don't know. There's something about you I like, something that intrigues me. A mystery I want to unwind." He tipped his head to the side. "And something adventurous in you. Maybe a little dangerous. You're certainly no ballroom wallflower who is barely out of the nursery." He sipped his wine, gazing at her over the rim of his glass. "More than anything, I believe you and I are more alike than we are different."

She flushed and stared at the dark red pool in her glass. "We are very different. I'm not proud of my missteps and transgressions as you are."

He sniffed. "You severely misread me, madam. It's not pride you see in me. It's a façade. As I told you before, sometimes I allow people to believe the worst in me so I can see who *they* really are. That façade is a protective device. It also allows me to get information, develop alliances with important and useful people."

"How can I trust you and develop a friendship with you if everything I see is a mask?"

"Darling, we are all in our masks. Whose bare face have you truly ever seen?"

She stared at him. What a bleak thought that everyone she'd ever encountered had been presenting one version of themselves to her and another version to someone else. But wasn't that how humans behaved? She turned the mirror on herself. Even she showed one version of herself to Braedon, another version to Catherine, another version to servants or acquaintances. She looked at her reflection in the rain-specked window. Everyone she encountered carried the risk of hurt and betrayal. She couldn't go her whole life keeping people at arm's length. She needed people, connections, and a support network she could rely on in hard times. But she also needed loyalty.

Ravenna looked at him, gauging the sincerity in his eyes. Lady Hawke-stone had been grateful for his friendship and she seemed a good judge of character. Maybe he was worth the risk. She sighed, leaned on the table, and rubbed the tension between her eyes. "I don't tell you everything because...." A band of tightness pulled across her chest. "Because I'm ashamed." A knot formed in her throat. She chased it down with wine. Then poured another glass and bit off a chunk of bread.

"There's no shame among friends, my little raven."

Her cheeks warmed. She didn't need to tell him everything. Maybe she could test the waters to judge his response and his willingness to accept her. "Suppose you knew someone who was a traitor to self, king, country, friends, and family. Could you be friends with such a person?"

He chuckled. "Yes. In fact, I'm friends with a few such people."

She picked at her cheese, her heart beat thrumming in her ears. "I don't know." She wiped her sweaty palms on her napkin. It would be nice to share the secret, to relieve her conscience, to let more than only Catherine and Hawkestone know who she really was. Even Philip hadn't known everything. She'd told him that The Unity was after her because of her brother. Which was only partly true. It was a desperately lonely life to not be fully known.

Wavering, she traced the lace pattern of the tablecloth with her fingertip. "I assure you, I can stomach anything you tell me."

"You're aware I'm from Ireland?" Very well, she would test the waters. The moment she sensed disapproval in his looks or voice, she'd stop talking.

"I am."

Her stomach fluttered as she pushed forward. "My family were Protestant. Loyalists. Except for my youngest brother, Niall, who sided with rebels because of his friends. You know how it is with young men trying to grow into their manhood by being different from their fathers."

Braedon grinned. "All too well."

"I don't think Niall understood what he was getting into, and he fell in with a bad sort. In ninety-six, these rebels, The Unity, began to collude with the French. For two years, he assisted them in their plans to invade England from Ireland, which was unknown to me until the Battle of Wexford broke. We lived in County Wexford in Enniscorthy." Her whole body grew rigid as she fought to suppress the memories and force them back into the hell that occupied the recesses of her mind.

His features sank into a deep frown. "I've heard about the atrocities in Wexford from friends who were sent to quash the rebellion in ninety-eight. Those men came back shadows of themselves."

"At least they came back."

"I'm not sure that was a blessing. I wouldn't wish what happened in Wexford on my worst enemy."

"A great many innocents and loyalists died, too."

"I'm grievously sorry." Sadness softened his voice.

"My father, mother, most of my siblings, and my brother-in-law died there that day. Burned alive in a church."

Her breath caught. Her mind pulled her back to that day, to the chilling sounds of people screaming, the smell of fire, the sting of smoke in her eyes and lungs, the naked terror she'd never experienced before or since.

She downed her wine and continued. "A few of my family escaped. Me, my brother Niall, my eldest sister, and her daughter. It was late May. The story is far too long to tell. It could be a book. The short of it is that Niall put my sister, her child, and me in a boat, and he stayed behind to help with The Cause, promising to find us in London. We came to London to seek out my paternal aunt, Brendae. That's when I met Catherine, started selling oranges in the theater, and, within a month, I was acting to make more money. I wanted to afford a small place for my sister and me so we could get away from our Aunt's house. She was ghastly."

"I remember those early days. You weren't a particularly good actress in the beginning, were you?" His eyes sparked with humor.

She chuckled, wiped her eyes. "No. I wasn't. My sister was soon lost to the streets as she tried to support her daughter. I haven't seen her since. I've been searching for her."

"Thus, your particular interest in the Penitent House charity, I presume?"

She nodded. "I'm hoping she'll show up there, though I'm not certain she's still alive." A chill traveled down her spine, and she moved from the table to stand by the fire. "It was during this time Catherine introduced me to both Philip and Hawkestone. Hawkestone and I became fast friends, though, in time, he wanted more. I admired him, and we had much in common, but it was Philip who won my heart and affections. I remember they were both new to their positions at the time, Philip as foreign secretary and Hawkestone as the British ambassador to Spain."

Braedon followed her, relaxing into a wingback chair. "That seems a lifetime ago."

"It does." She watched the fire dance in her crystal glass. "Around that time, my brother had finally found us. I'd been happy to see him at the time. I was amazed he'd actually survived. I guess it was early September. The rebels had lost a battle." She glanced at Braedon and didn't detect any aversion, so she continued, inching her way toward the truth in the cold, dark depths. "When Niall saw I had some powerful connections, he wanted to save his neck by taking some government secrets back to his camp. Apparently, he'd crossed one of the rebel leaders, and they were hunting him. They found out he'd been paid a high price by an English agent to report on The Unity. He was going to keep the Englishman's money, which he desperately needed, and try to get back in The Unity's good graces by providing them English secrets. He first tried to convince me to spy on Hawkestone. When I refused, he brought in one of The Unity leaders who made it plain he would torture my brother to death, then come for me, my aunt, and her children." She drank her wine. "So, I did it."

"You stole secrets from Hawkestone?"

She stared into the fire, nodding, shame branding her skin. She couldn't bear to look at him for fear she might detect disgust or hatred. "He was so eager to impress me and prove his power. So I encouraged his attention and affections, made him think I was interested in him and no longer interested in Philip." Tears filled her eyes, and her voice quaked. "He was Philip's colleague and knew a great many secrets regarding the Irish and French and English intentions for military campaigns."

"Why didn't you go directly to Philip since he was the foreign secretary?"

Her eyes swimming in tears, she looked at him. "I loved him. I didn't want to use him and abuse his trust in that way. I didn't really want to do that to Hawkestone either, but—"

"But it was easier because you didn't love him in the same way."

She nodded. "Right." Tears slid down her cheeks. She swiped them away. "But I'd only gathered a little information about the English watch of the coast between here and Ireland. I discovered it was lax, that it'd be an easy entry point between the two countries.

"Then Hawkestone caught me. He was livid, of course. I confess, I was a little relieved at being caught, because I thought it could all be over at last. But then Hawkestone wanted me to fix the situation by feeding false information to the rebels and made me extract information from my brother to discover the details of the French invasion planned for October of that year. I had no choice but to comply. He said if I cooperated, he wouldn't report me. His silence would save me from being tried and executed for treason."

"That's a difficult position."

"But when the rebels found out what my brother and I had done, they threatened to come for both of us. My brother ran away to America. I married Philip and kept my mouth shut."

"Did Phillip know about your spying?"

"I didn't tell him everything. I was too scared. I only told him that the rebels were angry with my brother and me and wanted to have us killed. He ensured that troops were sent to that particular encampment and the rebels were destroyed."

"All of them died?"

"I thought so, but…" She shuddered. "I have reason to believe some survived and are very much seeking revenge. I think at least a couple of the attacks I blamed on Dianthe might actually have been The Unity."

His eyes widened, filled with concern. "Is your brother still alive?"

"I hope so. I haven't heard from him in nearly a year, and I've heard America is a brutal place to survive."

Braedon stared at the dark fireplace, his gaze distant. He was clearly ruminating on something. He finished off his wine and put the glass on the occasional table between them. "That is quite a story. Thank you for sharing. I hadn't realized things were that…dire."

Apprehensive, she studied his profile. "I'm sure I disgust you, and you want nothing more to do with me. But now you know everything Catherine knows about me and why I wanted to keep my secrets."

He looked at her as though she had three heads. "Not at all." The clock in the hall chimed six. He stood. "I do hate to rush away, but I have a prior engagement. I must go. Though, I do thank you for a most diverting adventure today. I find you, my little raven, always full of the most charming surprises."

And now he was running from her. She had disgusted him. She revealed her secrets, and he couldn't bear to be in the same room with her. He'd never want her friendship now, never trust her. Wobbly from the wine, she rushed forward and grabbed his hand with desperation. "I can count on your discretion, I hope?"

Much to her surprise, he cupped her face, stroking her cheek with his thumb. He brushed her lips with his, pulling her close, drawing her into a tender, lingering kiss. "In all things. Always."

# Chapter Forty-One

The next morning, Ravenna checked on Keene who, stiff and weak, sat up in bed eating broth, bread, and tea. Then she returned to her own bedchamber to dress and nibble at breakfast while writing letters. A loud knock rattled her door. Chester shouted from the other side, "He's awake. Lord Birchfield is awake."

Ravenna grabbed Thomas's thin hand and squeezed it. "My God, we're ecstatic that you're awake." She kissed his hand, wiping her tears from his knuckles.

He managed a weak smile and whispered, "Amma. I'm so glad you're here." He smacked his dry lips.

Ravenna lifted his head and gave him a drink of water. "Drink easy."

"Where's Lucy?" he croaked.

"I'm sure she's coming." Ravenna eased his head onto the pillow. She stroked his hair off his face and kissed his forehead. "I've been so worried about you. Don't bother with trying to speak. Think only about getting stronger. It'll take some time. You've been incredibly ill."

He nodded. His gaze rolled toward the door, where Lucy appeared in her white dressing robe, her hands over her mouth. He wiggled his hand free of Ravenna's grasp and reached for his wife. "Lucy," he wheezed.

Lucy beamed and scurried forward to take his hand. "We're so glad you're awake." She smiled down at him. "You rest. I'll have some broth sent up." She kissed his forehead and stroked his cheek. Then she stood and faced Ravenna, her hazel eyes hard. "Now you can have no compunction about returning to Gordon House." She knocked shoulders with Ravenna as she passed. "As soon as possible."

Ravenna wasn't going anywhere until she knew Thomas had fully recovered. She spent the day reading and checking in on Keene and Thomas, ensuring they had all they needed. After dinner, Ravenna looked in on Thomas again. Chester, all rosy-cheeked smiles, bowed out to get his own supper. Thomas was propped up with a tray of broth, dry toast, and tea. He already appeared a bit stronger, with more color in his face. His voice had also gained some vigor, though it was still weak.

He stirred his broth. "Chester told me you went to great lengths to take care of me, Amma. I'm grateful to you. It would've gone hard on Lucy were I to die."

"I was happy to do it." She recalled her promise to Lord Donovan. "I know you still need time to mend. I'm deeply sorry for broaching this matter, but it's necessary."

"What is it?"

"I've made a promise to Lord Donovan to speak with you about the foreign secretary position. He came here to beg you to push for the nomination and to accept the offer if it's made to you. With Wolfsham dead and Nochdale taken ill, he's certain you're the only one who can successfully secure peace with Napoleon."

"Nochdale is also ill?" He lowered his head to meet his spoon. "That's unfortunate."

"Lord Donovan is certain peace negotiations will fail, and we'll be thrown into war with France if you don't intervene. In fact, he seems to think we're on the cusp of declaring war. Apparently, Napoleon has begun amassing troops in Boulogne in preparation to invade."

His eyes darted up, filled with trepidation. "What? Have things gone so far during my illness?"

"Yes, unfortunately."

"The demmed Bourbons have failed us at every turn." He tore a chunk from his toast and dipped it in his broth.

"What do you mean?"

He swallowed his food. "Without divulging the particulars, we've been attempting to rid ourselves of our troubles using a more…covert method via the Bourbons."

Ravenna turned his words over in her mind a few times. "You mean…" She lowered her voice to a whisper. "Assassination? I can't believe you would be a party to such an endeavor."

He nodded, wiping his fingers on the cloth napkin at his side. "You're right. It's ungentlemanly behavior, but the wretch would destroy us all to build his empire. Which is another reason why I wasn't so interested in peace treaties that could, and would, be broken. I was working with the Bourbon family to gain a more lasting peace."

"What would your father think?"

He scoffed. "It was his idea." He spooned more broth into his mouth. "He set the whole thing in motion right before he fell ill."

She stared at him, aghast. She mulled that over in her mind. "Then I'm disappointed in you both."

"Would you have us at war then?" His eyes glittered, hard as garnets.

"Of course not."

"It was the least bloody and inconvenient solution." He dipped another chunk of bread in his broth. "Think of it, Amma. One dead man or thousands. One dead man or many nations at war." He shoved the bread in his mouth and washed it down with a gulp of tea.

He was right, but assassination was such dastardly behavior. "What will you do?"

"What any politician worth his salt would do. I'll play the hypocrite and smile at my enemy's face while I scheme against him behind his back." He scratched the short beard that had formed on his face during his illness. "I think you know the cost of indiscretion?" His gaze was direct, cold.

She blinked at him, hardly recognizing him. "Of course." The politician was so different from the stepson she knew. "I wouldn't dream of interfering. So, you will accept the position if Lord Donovan offers?"

He shrugged. "I have no choice, do I?" He drank the broth from the side of the bowl.

Ravenna picked at her nail. "There is another matter I would discuss with you."

"What's that?"

"There's a woman in Lucy's service. She calls herself Milby, and she's standing in for Becker. I believe she's dangerous."

"Oh? How?" He relaxed into his pillows with a satisfied air.

"I think she's working with Nochdale to murder men being nominated for the foreign secretary post."

He squinted with disbelief. "That sounds—"

"Mad. I know. Maybe it is. I've tried talking to Lucy about it, but she won't listen. You need to have that woman removed from the house. I think she's the reason you've been ill."

"What proof do you have?"

"None. Yet. But I think poison is involved."

"How is she meant to have poisoned me?"

"I don't know. I think the tincture she gave Lucy might've been poisoned because you became ill again immediately after."

A dimple formed in one cheek. He looked so much like Philip.

"I'm serious, Thomas. Please be careful. If you don't believe me, then look into it yourself. But you need to cast her out of this house. I think she's dangerous."

He frowned. "I will see to the matter."

# Chapter Forty-Two

Now that Thomas was awake and recovering, Ravenna prepared to leave Pelham House as Lucy had demanded. He was a grown, married man, and she'd exhausted her attempts to warn him and protect him. All she could do now was continue her investigation and worry about outcomes.

Ravenna was leaving, but she wasn't going alone.

She called Keene to her room. The girl came in, her face still bruised and swollen. "Keene, you've proven invaluable to me. If you'd like, you can come with me to Gordon House for a new position. You'll start as an upstairs maid while you assist my lady's maid to learn the trade."

Keene's demeanor grew gradually more excited as Ravenna spoke until her eyes were as large as goose eggs.

"The work will be difficult and tedious, and there will be a great deal of it. I don't know what you're being paid, but I assume nine pounds per annum will suffice?"

Keene nodded enthusiastically. "La, milady. That's a whole pound more than I'm making here. I'm most grateful to you." She curtsied clumsily. "I'll pack my things now."

"When you're finished, make arrangements for a hackney to pick us up."

Ravenna closed the lid on her trunk and donned her spencer. She had only to say goodbye to Thomas before she left Pelham House. She found him in his bedchamber standing by the fireplace, reading a newspaper. He was clean-shaven, washed, and wearing a gold and black banyan. He looked identical to his father.

263

"Good afternoon, Amma." He closed the newspaper over his finger.

"I came to say goodbye."

"So soon?" He laid the newspaper in the chair seat.

"It's for the best, I think. Lucy is ready to be the sole lady of the house again." She chuckled. "I won't provoke her more than necessary. More for your sake than mine. Please give her my regards. I would've bid my own farewell, but she's already away from home this morning." She clasped her hands in front of her. "Besides, I've neglected my own household for too long."

He shuffled toward her, his arms outstretched. "I can't thank you enough." He embraced her. "You saved my life. I owe you everything."

Her fingers felt the edges of his bones through his banyan. Her throat tightened. "I'm so glad you're safe. Should you be on your feet, though?"

"Yes. It's the only way to get my strength back faster. Besides…" He motioned toward the bed, stripped of its linens. "I've insisted the maids clean up the bed and air the room."

"Promise you won't push yourself too hard." She put a hand to his cheek. "And that you'll rid this house of Milby immediately."

"As soon as we can locate her. It's my understanding she has been away. I'm having the maids and footmen gather and pack her things now, though Lucy won't be happy to be forced to find another lady's maid."

"Good. It's for the best."

Ravenna left Thomas and passed down the dimly lit hall. She encountered Chester. "I'm leaving now, Chester."

"You will be missed, milady."

"I am deeply grateful for your loyalty to my stepson. If you should ever find yourself in need of a position, you will always have one at Gordon House." She offered her hand, and he shook it.

"You're very kind, milady."

After leaving Pelham House, Ravenna stopped first at Catherine's for a visit and to tell her of everything that had transpired. As expected, Catherine lapped up the gossip, especially loving the bits about Braedon.

By the time Ravenna left Catherine's, the wind had picked up considerably and fluttered her skirts as she stepped toward the carriage. She held her bonnet, ducked her head, and pushed toward her carriage through the people. She glanced from under the brim of her bonnet and was certain that she glimpsed a pair of men's shoes near her rear wheel. Then like a pheasant flushed from a bush, a pale man in a black hat and great coat spun from the carriage and headed down the street.

In that instant, someone called her name. Reverend Howarth. She turned to address him while keeping her eyes on the street. The man darted between people and carriages, his coat filled with wind like black sails.

Reverend Howarth wanted to talk about the next Penitent House gala, as Ravenna's attention focused on trying to remember what the strange man looked like and the direction he ran.

But Reverend Howarth was always eager for a chat. He entirely disregarded the rules of propriety about keeping a woman standing in the streets and talked *at* her until the thunder clapped and a light rain began to fall. She finally broke off the conversation and climbed into her carriage. She'd never been so thankful for the rain in her life, though it did prevent her from trailing the strange man. She wanted to know who he was and why he was hanging around her carriage.

The storm broke in earnest only moments after Ravenna arrived home. Thunder grumbled and roared, the winds whistled, and lightning ripped through the blackening skies. The ominous black clouds sank around the buildings, causing all the white stones to glow in contrast.

Content to have an evening in front of the fire in her bedchamber, Ravenna wrapped herself in her lavender satin dressing gown with ivory lace. She settled in a chair with the newspaper and tea. She tried to read, but the thought of the strange man continued to niggle in her mind.

Hart entered the room with a ball gown. "Good evening, Lady Birchfield. I'm glad you are returned. I have your gown for the Everleigh ball this evening."

Ravenna was apprehensive about the ball. Braedon had said he would like to escort her, but after their recent conversation and his abrupt departure, she wasn't certain he would wish to be seen with her. He'd assured her of his dedication, but he might've had second thoughts. "Thank you, Hart. How is Keene getting on?"

"She is settled upstairs."

"I'm glad to hear it. I think she'll be a good assistant for you."

"I hardly need it, though. You're so easy to attend." She opened the wardrobe and packed the folded dresses inside.

"Granted, but she's eager. I think her comportment lessons and education will keep you both quite busy." She laughed.

Hart chuckled. "Indeed. I also wanted to inform you of my discoveries regarding the Mr. Larson you'd inquired about."

Ravenna folded and set her newspaper aside. Pulling her shawl tighter around her shoulders, she motioned to the other chair by the fire. "Sit, please. Tell me what you've learned."

The wind howled outside. Tree branches scratched the windows, and the rain lashed furiously.

Hart sat primly in the other chair, her hands folded in her lap. The firelight and shadows danced on her features, rendering her brown eyes mysterious, warm, and sharp all at once.

"Mr. Larson rose up out of the gutters of Spitalfields. His father was a butcher, and his mother was a tavern wench until gin had its way. I've heard different reports as to his heritage. Some have said American. The one that sounds most plausible is that he's at least part Irish and felt some allegiance to the struggles in that country. Some say his father had connections to the Irish Unity."

Fear, heavy and metallic as a pile of coins, slid down Ravenna's throat and rolled into her stomach. The Unity. "Go on," Ravenna urged.

"Apparently, his mother abandoned him and his father, never to be heard from again. Mr. Larson is new money, but the means of his wealth is suspect. Probably smuggling and piracy, though he tells people he's a merchant. He's rich enough to make loans to Prince George."

"At an exorbitant interest, no doubt."

"No doubt." Hart lifted a brow. "Whatever he is, Mr. Larson is a procurer of goods, including exotic women, for the Prince to enjoy. So the Prince is in no great hurry to be rid of him."

"Where does this Mr. Larson spend his time?"

"He tends to frequent the Blue Rooster in Albemarle Street."

That was a problem. The Blue Rooster was renowned for its radical patrons. It had been a haunt for Jacobins, traitors, and radicals of every stripe since King Charles II. It was raided often in the fall of ninety-eight when the English learned of the Franco-Irish collusion.

Hart continued. "One woman, a shopkeeper, says Larson especially enjoys putting on airs and spending time with high society. She said that he recently visited her shop to purchase new silk stockings to wear to Lady Corliss's salon Thursday night."

Lady Corliss's party would be little more than a zoo of the most exotic philosophers, artists, and libertines. Her gatherings were usually a favorite of Prinny and his inner circle because they often descended into a saturnalia of every sort of overindulgence and vice. If Mr. Larson was indeed invited to that salon, then he'd gained not only considerable wealth and power, but Prinny's friendship—which made him especially dangerous to England and The Crown.

Ravenna bit the inside of her lip and nodded. She stared into the fire, thinking. "Did you get a description of this man? What does he look like?"

"Average height, thin, a crooked nose, and very blond hair that many described as almost white."

Ravenna froze. Her mind reached back to recall where she had seen such a man. She turned to Hart. "That sounds identical to the man I saw at the theater a few days ago." The clock struck seven. She'd have to think about Mr. Larson later. It was time to prepare for the Everleigh ball.

# Chapter Forty-Three

By nine o'clock, the storm had subsided and gave way to a cool spring evening. Ravenna was dressed for the Everleigh Ball in a black silk underdress covered with a sheer black beaded overlay. Braedon would arrive soon to escort her to the most elegant of the Penitent House fundraiser events. She paced, watching the clock on the fireplace mantle, thinking about the investigation, the dead and sick lords, the white-blond man at the theater, and all the strange events of late, trying to make sense of it all.

Fifteen minutes drifted by, and Braedon hadn't yet arrived. Ravenna considered worrying but thought better of it. Fifteen minutes wasn't so late. When the clock struck half after the hour, she began to fret in earnest. When the clock struck ten, and Braedon had still not arrived, anger flared.

"Damn his eyes," she muttered to herself. She called for her carriage. She shouldn't be surprised. She'd expected this when she'd revealed her past to him. Yet, she allowed herself to believe otherwise, because he'd kissed her. She swept her black cloak around her shoulders. Never mind him. She'd go anyway. Ravenna was a grown woman and a widow. As such, she had many of the same freedoms as a man. She certainly didn't need anyone's permission to do anything. She clutched her fan, threw the hood of her cloak over her head, and trotted down the stairs to her carriage.

Ravenna was not going to let Braedon determine her happiness on this night or any other. She was a fool to trust him at any rate. Girls half her age made such mistakes. This was not the sort of mistake a woman of her age and experience should fall prey to.

Everleigh House rested on the other side of Hyde Park, in a less populated area on the fringes of London. It was the pinnacle of understated elegance: a rectangular edifice, three stories high of buff stone, with a row of windows across the front. Neatly shaped hedges lined the front and along the edge of the roundabout where the long drive ended in front of the house. She'd been here once before in the daylight and had admired the long rectangular pool stretched in front of the house, giving the illusion from a distance that the house sat on water. Tonight, torches lined the perimeter of the pool, stretching an orange glow through the dark waters.

A crowd of bodies packed the ballroom, making it difficult to move and breathe. She wound through the people chatting and laughing in the ballroom awash in candlelight. Dancers skipped down the line to lively music, holding hands and smiling at each other.

Ravenna happened upon Thomas talking with some friends.

"Good evening, Amma." He kissed her cheek, and they turned together to press through the room.

"You're mad to be at a ball. You can't possibly be recovered enough."

"I'm still weak, but I thought it best to begin politicking as soon as possible, given the information you related earlier. I may still sway the nominations."

"But you're going to destroy your health."

He smiled weakly. "I promise I won't stay long. Another hour, maybe two, and I'll return home."

"Do you swear it?"

"I do."

"But as long as there's a chance Nochdale might recover, and as long as he has a strong backing, I must remain vigilant. I guarantee he and his cronies have had many closed-door meetings with the Prime Minister to influence his decision."

Lady Braxton passed by, offering a smug smile to Ravenna. Then she paused, her fan halting in its stroke. "Lady Birchfield. So good to see you again."

"Good evening, Lady Braxton."

A hint of the lunatic lingered in Lady Braxton's eyes when she looked at

Thomas, but her voice lilted with unsuppressed joy. "Lord Birchfield. This is a pleasant surprise. I'd quite thought we'd lost you forever. What a happy day to see you completely recovered."

"Thank you, Lady Braxton. I'm glad to be in good health again." He bowed. "Pardon me. I see Lord Hillingham there. I must speak with him." He bowed and walked away.

After exchanging some pleasantries, Lady Braxton looked at the fan in Ravenna's hand. "What a lovely fan."

"Thank you. It's a gift from my late husband."

"I've never seen one with its guard decorated like that." She leaned closer and squinted at the gold medallion. "Is that an X?"

"In its essence. It's a saltire."

"What's that around it?"

"Clover."

"Oh?" She tilted her head, a spark of fascination jumped in her eye.

"And what's that on the other side?"

"A falcon."

A sly smile crossed her lips. "Interesting symbols. Falcons do not rest until they achieve their goals. Is that you, Lady Birchfield? Are you a falcon?" She sneered.

"It's the animal on my husband's family crest. However, I like to think it was a trait we shared."

"A providential match then." She chuckled drily. "And the saltire I find most interesting of all. That's the symbol of a Loyalist. Is it not?"

Ravenna looked askance. "It is."

The corners of her lips tugged faintly in the corners. "Fascinating." A tense silence lingered between them for a moment, Lady Braxton's stare unwavering. She seemed to be attempting to view the inner workings of Ravenna's mind and heart.

Lord Donovan approached. He bowed and greeted them. Ravenna was thankful for his presence.

Lady Braxton offered her hand and spoke with brightness. "Lord Donovan, so good to see you here this evening. I hope you've spared a dance for me."

Caught off guard, he dithered. "In truth, I'm not much of a dancer. I think I would embarrass you on the floor, Lady Braxton." He didn't leave space for any witty repartee she might throw at him. He turned to Ravenna. "I beg your pardon for the interruption. I wanted to spare a moment to thank you for convincing Birchie to pursue the foreign secretary nomination in earnest."

"There's no need to thank me. I believe he'd decided quite on his own. I think his recent illness has instilled in him a greater sense of purpose and renewed determination."

Lady Braxton blanched, the smile faltering on her lips. "Is that so? He's pursuing the appointment, after all?" The lunatic gleam reappeared in her eye. She gushed at Ravenna. "Well, what happy news. I hope he's successful in his endeavor. England needs him."

Lord Donovan nodded. "Indeed. With Birchie in office, I think we can once again hope for peace."

Lady Braxton beamed, though her mouth pulled tight at the corners. "Yes. That's fantastic news. Please, do pardon me." She rushed away in a sweep of dark green silk.

The conversation turned to theater and books, and Ravenna found Lord Donovan well-versed in the best dramas and poetry. To her surprise, and his slight embarrassment, she found they liked many of the same novels. As she was about to tease him for also liking Regina Maria Roche's *Claremont, a Tale*, she noticed Braedon and Dianthe walk in together. That cad. She snapped her fan shut.

Lord Donovan grew concerned. "Lady Birchfield?" He touched her elbow.

With a sharp inhale, she drew down a mask of cool composure. She blinked, then squeezed his hand. "I do beg your pardon, Lord Donovan, but I, uh…so sorry. I need to step away for a moment."

"Please, wait…."

She pushed her way through the crowd. She would not stay here and endure this humiliation. She clearly couldn't trust Braedon. Shame and rage twisted and knotted around each other such that she could hardly discern one from the other. They were two halves of the same animal. Her face burned with this monstrous emotion as it snaked into her throat and chest. Her eyes burned and tingled with the pressure of unshed tears.

The door stood only a few feet away. Almost free. She paused, alert, like a deer sensing a hunter it couldn't see.

Dianthe and Braedon stopped inside the doorway to speak with Lady Everleigh. Braedon smiled warmly and carried on a concentrated conversation with her while Dianthe hung coolly at his side, shoulders hunched with fashionable ennui, her gaze wandering distractedly over the room.

Once Ravenna passed through the door into the foyer, she could dash for the main entrance and outside to the sweet darkness and her carriage. If she could make it to the privacy and safety of her carriage....

"Yoo-hoo, Lady Birchfield," A singsong voice rang out. Lady Catherine, standing only a few feet from Braedon and Dianthe, waved her hand and began pushing toward her. Both Dianthe and Braedon perked and turned to look at Ravenna, who looked away too late.

A stony mask fell over Braedon's face, rendering it unreadable. However, Dianthe pulled a faint smirk. She stepped into Ravenna's path. "Good evening," she purred.

Ravenna stopped short as Catherine stepped into place beside her.

Dianthe closed the space between them. She was too close.

Braedon put a hand on Dianthe's elbow and warned her. "Not here."

She wasn't listening. "I recall a time when you thought you had won the prize. Yet, look..." Her icy eyes glinted darkly as she slipped her arm into Braedon's.

Ravenna's hand itched to slap the hussy. Again. Instead, she did something more satisfying to herself, something that would drive Dianthe to the edge of madness. She smiled. "Yes, Dianthe, I can see how you might believe that, since he's here with you tonight."

Her smirk faded, replaced by puzzled suspicion.

Ravenna continued, "Yet, I think you should know he spent much of yesterday, well into the evening, with *me*."

People nearby giggled behind their fans and whispered.

Braedon's face drew downward like a melting candle, and he closed his eyes. Clearly, he was not looking forward to the aftermath of this farce.

"You're lying," Dianthe said, uncertain, glancing between Ravenna and Braedon.

"Oh, but I'm not. Surely you mustn't blame him. After all, it's to be expected. We actresses are so accomplished in the art of seduction. I'm sure he couldn't help himself. And, I assure you, the rumors about his prowess are not exaggerated."

Dianthe turned pain-filled eyes at Braedon, who shook his head in disappointment at Ravenna.

Ravenna lifted a brow at him and delivered her final blow to Dianthe. "Do enjoy your prize. While you have him." She shot a rueful glance at Braedon. She had no illusions about Braedon's preferences. But Dianthe's jealousy would eat her alive. That was Ravenna's prize.

Ravenna brushed past them out of the ballroom, with Catherine following close behind, shouting her name.

In the foyer, a cooling breeze swept through the open space. She asked for her carriage to be brought around. The butler assisted her with her cloak, then, in an eccentric whim, decided to wait outside. The fresh air improved her spirits immediately.

Once on the pavement, Catherine caught up to her and grabbed her arm. "Please, stop. For only a moment. I'd like to talk to you." Her frosted blonde hair wound in intricate curls at the crown of her head, and her dress of pale pink and gold silk draped her petite form. Her diamonds glimmered in the torchlight. She looked like a delicate spring dawn over dewy meadows. "I've heard about Nochdale and came directly to tell you. He has died."

Ravenna flinched as though slapped and fixed her gaze on Catherine. It took her a moment to fully comprehend what Catherine had said.

"Didn't you hear me? Nochdale is dead!" Catherine did little to mask her glee. In the play of shadow and light from the torchlight, she looked like a madwoman. "This means Birchfield no longer has to worry."

"When did he die?"

"This morning." The breeze toyed with her frosted curls. "I had it from

Lady Harrow, who had it from Lady Nochdale herself."

Stunned, Ravenna's mind struggled to hold onto complete thoughts like a drowning man grasps at driftwood. She put her hand over her mouth.

Catherine touched her arm, drawing her back to the moment. "But darling, I thought you would be relieved. Do you not see what this means?"

Ravenna blinked at her.

"We've won the day."

Why did it not feel like a triumph?

"Don't you see? Birchfield will likely have the foreign secretary post unhindered. Fox will fail. England is safe."

Braedon's voice fell on them from the top of the stairs. "There you are, my little raven."

Ravenna glared at him for a long moment.

"That was a dirty trick you played on me in there." A blend of playfulness and annoyance passed over his demeanor.

Catherine turned. "I should let you two speak privately. I wanted only to give you the news."

"You don't have to leave Catherine. I'm leaving. I've had enough of this evening, and I'm going home."

"You should speak with Braedon." Catherine squeezed her arm, then turned and darted up the stairs.

Braedon crossed his arms. "Thank you for creating that little spectacle in the ballroom."

She pointed her fan at him. "Of your own design when you chose to not keep your word about escorting me tonight."

"She provoked you. Perhaps she deserved it. But you realize your little speech has also speared your own reputation? There were people nearby who heard the entire exchange. By morning, everyone will think you and I are lovers. Which, as you know—"

"Spare me your lecture and your concern. I know exactly what I did and what it means, and I don't care." A throbbing sensation formed behind her eyes. She did care, but in her current dudgeon, she'd be hanged before she admitted as much to him. She pushed her fingers into the center of the blooming pain. "I'm in desperate need of a glass of port." She stared daggers at him. "And solitude."

"If you put only a thimbleful of trust in me, I might be able to help you."

"I did trust you. And you failed me."

"I'm sincerely sorry." He touched her cheek. "Look at me."

Refusing to look at him, she looked away into the darkness and heard the distant clip-clop of the horses as they approached.

He pressed his lips against her ear, whispering, "I can explain if you give me a moment."

His warm breath sent a light thrill through her. She pushed away and slapped his upper arm with her fan with a loud pop. "You're an insufferable cad." She slapped his arm again. "Who thinks you can bed one woman and play the gallant with another, making false promises to each." She burned all over with enraged humiliation. "I've had enough of you."

The horses emerged from the darkness, pulling her carriage. They eased to a halt in front of her. Thank the stars.

She tried to step around Braedon, but he cut her off. She glared up at him and grabbed the hilt of her fan. "If you don't step aside, I'll use the deadlier bit of my fan."

"Please, Ravenna, listen to me. I can explain."

"The only thing you can do for me at this moment is get out of my way."

He held her shoulders and spoke quickly. "Yesterday, when I left your house, when I arrived home, Dianthe was in my bedroom. I don't know how she got into my house. She was under the influence of a great deal of laudanum and alcohol. She flew into hysterics. For her protection, I allowed her to stay until I could bring her around to her senses. She's troubled."

Arms crossed, she shrugged. She couldn't believe she was actually listening to him. However, there was sincerity in all his looks.

"She has made my life a hell. The laudanum is a demon that has grabbed hold of her and turned her into a poppet. On more than one occasion, she has attempted self-harm. The last time she threatened to harm herself, she drank a large amount of laudanum. Had we not called the surgeon to purge her, I'm certain she would have died."

"So, you're meant to be responsible for her for the rest of your lives?"

"She made other threats as well, threats I deemed more serious."

"Like what?" Ravenna sneered. "What sort of threats could that slip of a woman make to frighten a worldly man like you?"

Knots formed in his jaw, and his nostrils flared. "She threatened you."

Ravenna blinked at him.

He shook his head and averted his gaze, staring at the carriage to collect himself. He turned back to Ravenna. "When she's intoxicated, she's capable of absolutely anything. Unpredictable. Violent. The chances are high she'd act on her threats and I'd have no way of knowing when or how. Her beauty makes her all the more dangerous, because it blinds everyone to her cunning mind and treacherous behavior. So…" He sighed, "I gave in. Escorting her to the ball tonight was the only way I could hope to protect you."

Ravenna nodded. "I see." It seemed when one problem went away, another jumped into its place. This was all too much. When she'd returned to London, she'd wanted only a quiet, peaceful return to society. A few dinners. A few balls. Charity work. A continued search for her sister. Instead, she'd somehow become entangled in a murder investigation, espionage, jealous love triangles, and attacks on herself, her staff, her family, and her house. This was all so outrageous. She didn't want to fight, and it was silly to fight with a man who didn't belong to her. And since she'd foolishly divulged her secret to Braedon, she couldn't make an enemy of him. She sighed, shaking her head, looking down at the toe of her black slippers peeking from under her dress. There was a hope. The repairs on the rector's cottage at Birchfield Manor were nearly complete. She needed only to weather this season. Then she could leave London forever and never have to deal with any of this again.

"Ravenna?"

She stood on her tiptoes and kissed his cheek. He smelled of sweet and spicy sandalwood and shaving soap. "I'm going home." She moved toward her carriage and gave her hand to a footman who handed her up into the carriage. Braedon hovered close behind. As the footman stepped away, Braedon stepped into his place. Dark circles under his eyes betrayed his frayed, exhausted condition.

An unexpected tenderness for him swept through her.

He said, "So, is all forgiven?"

One corner of her mouth ticked upward. "Goodnight, Braedon." She pulled the door shut.

# Chapter Forty-Four

Over the next day and a half, the Everleigh ball slipped from Ravenna's thoughts as she turned her efforts to the Penitent House. The committee still needed a few thousand pounds to meet their goal, and she found work kept thoughts of Braedon out of her mind.

She sat in the study writing fundraising letters for the Penitent House campaign as the fresh scent of damp earth, blended with herbal and floral notes, swirled in from the gardens. A footman delivered a stack of mail to her. Ravenna shuffled eagerly through several letters and invitations. With Catherine's assistance, she hoped to get invited to Lady Corliss's party in an attempt to meet the elusive Mr. Larson. Unfortunately, as she discovered upon opening the invitation, the Corliss party was the same evening as Lady Braxton's gala for the Penitent House. Lady Braxton had obligated all of the committee members as co-hostesses, so participation was mandatory. Ravenna sighed and cast the Corliss invitation aside. Mr. Larson would have to wait. Her work with the Penitent House was far too important.

On the evening of the gala, Ravenna arrived at Braxton House in a black silk ball gown with embroidered bodice and hemline, a demi-train, short puff sleeves, and long black opera gloves.

The house was a Grecian-style monument in Jermyn Street. Attendees of the gala entered under the portico supported by great marble Corinthian columns. The dark green marble entrance hall was awash in candlelight and accented with gold statuary and gold-lined wainscot. The ceiling was painted with cherubim and clouds.

The anteroom to the left was filled with music and would later host dancing while the room to the right, as well as the crimson drawing room, were filled with gaming tables. Beyond the drawing room was the long dining room, papered with a palm-tree design and filled with all manner of rich food and drink. Laughter, music, and chatter spilled out into the entrance hall. The party was well underway on the ground floor. Above, people lingered in the gallery, chatting and looking down on late arrivals. No doubt, the upstairs rooms were full of dancing and cards as well.

Ravenna spent the first part of the evening welcoming guests and speaking with potential donors, attempting to convince them of the necessity of the Penitent House. Once the dancing began, she slipped out of the ballroom into the refreshment room for some champagne punch.

The portraits lining the walls captured her interest. She sipped her punch staring at the portrait of the late Lord Braxton hanging over the green marble fireplace. The painter had masterfully captured the kindness in his eyes, reminding her a great deal of her father. A pain and nostalgia yawned inside her.

A familiar male voice rose behind her. "I knew him."

Ravenna jumped, splashing her punch on her gown. She had been concentrating so hard on the portrait she hadn't heard Braedon's approach.

Laughter glinted in his eyes as he handed her a handkerchief from his inner pocket.

She dabbed at the spot on her dress. "Must I see you everywhere I go?"

"It is unfortunate that we run in the same circles, isn't it? But I think you forget I'm a contributor to the Penitent House."

She attempted to shove the damp handkerchief back in his hand.

He rejected it. "Perhaps you should keep it. You might need it again before the evening is over."

She held it out. "I have no place for this."

His eyes dropped to the spot on her dress. "Shall I recommend you tuck it close to your heart?"

Narrowing her eyes, she stiffened her spine and threw the handkerchief at him. "I will gladly refund your money if you will find another circle of friends."

He laughed aloud, catching the cloth and returning it to his inner pocket. His laughter drew the attention of the other couple in the room. "I'm sorry I must disappoint you, my little raven. I'm rather attached to this circle of friends. So I fear you must bear the inconvenience of my company."

She was both annoyed and glad that he stayed.

He motioned at the portrait of Lord Braxton over the mantle. "I saw you were admiring this portrait of the late lord."

They turned to look at the portrait, he with his hands clasped behind his back, she clutching her punch glass with both hands.

Ravenna said, "Admiration isn't quite the word. I was attempting to remember something I might've heard about him since I'd never met him. You said you knew him?"

"A little. He was a friend of my father's."

"He seems much older than Lady Braxton."

"He was. At least thirty years her senior and, in the last years of the marriage, a paralytic confined to a wheelchair."

"When did they marry?"

He squinted, thinking. "Seems it was late ninety-seven or thereabouts. I remember she'd come from Ireland."

"She's from Ireland?" Her mouth dropped open again.

"As I understand it. I can't say for certain. Her background is a little obscure, but that's what I heard from the gossips."

"But her accent is English."

"As is yours. Mostly." He lifted his brows. His eyes twinkled. "Except when you're angry. At any rate, I imagine she practiced the Irish out of her voice as much as you did. So she'd be accepted."

"Of course."

"I was still in university and had happened to meet her at one of Lady Melbourne's salons when she was at the height of her popularity. Not long after, she was married to Lord Braxton."

"Did he have a position in parliament?"

"Actually, he was foreign secretary for a short time until he was thrown from his horse and paralyzed."

"When was that?"

"A few months later. Then apparently, an influenza set in, and he died shortly after—only a few months before you arrived in London."

"Not long before my husband became foreign secretary."

"Yes. I think the late Lord Birchfield had held that post approximately a year, maybe two, before you came along."

Ravenna looked up at the portrait again. Something was very troubling, something she couldn't quite put into a coherent thought.

She sipped her punch and turned. A thin man with white-blond hair pulled back into a short ponytail stood in a corner sipping punch and staring up at the portraits. This was the same man she'd seen in the theater, and he also matched the descriptions she'd heard of Mr. Larson. But why was he here? He was supposed to be at Lady Corliss's party tonight.

She had no idea he was in any way affiliated with the Penitent House or philanthropy. She hadn't seen him at any of the other functions. He must be acquainted with one of the committee members if he was invited to this gala.

This man was meant to be Milby's lover? Though he was common-born, she found it hard to believe that a self-made man would entangle himself with a lady's maid. Keene might have been wrong about this man, though he could well afford expensive cologne. Of course, wealthy men had affairs with women of lower stations while courting and marrying women of a higher station all the time. Perhaps Milby was nothing more than a lover.

The man must have sensed her watching him because he turned his dark reptilian eyes, glittering in the candlelight, on her. At seeing his long face with a pointy chin and broad forehead, Ravenna knew this as the same man she'd seen at the theater. He glanced at Braedon, and the corner of his mouth twitched. He lowered his head in polite obeisance and then he resumed his portrait study.

"Pardon me, Braedon, but I need to speak with that man."

"Why?"

"I've seen him before, and I recently learned he might be connected to the lady's maid at Gordon House. I want to see what he knows about her."

"I'll come with you, then."

"No, truly. I fear with another man around, he might be less than forthcoming."

"If you insist."

"I do. I feel I'm awfully close to some answers. Please wait for me in the ballroom. I'll be out directly."

He nodded and left the room. After a moment, she approached the man, stopping to stand at a slight distance from him. She summoned every bit of her former acting skills to smile at him coquettishly, as if he were just the man she'd waited for her whole life.

Leering at her, he smiled and nodded.

She spoke first. "I know it's shameless to speak to you without a proper introduction, but I'm certain we've met before."

He bowed. "Mr. Franklin Larson at your service, milady." She was certain she detected a hint of Irish on his tongue. "Where do you think you've seen me?"

She gave her best effort at being the addle-brained coquette, though she knew this was the same man from the theater. "I simply can't recall at this moment. Perhaps if we talk longer, I'll remember." She moved around him to sit in a nearby chair "Do you often ride in Hyde Park?"

"Not particularly. I spend my days working for my money." He put his hands behind his back and cocked a smug smile. "I suppose you find that repulsive?"

"Not at all." She smiled vapidly. He clearly didn't think well of the elite classes.

"Why would a genteel lady such as yourself not be put off by someone in trade?"

She shrugged and fluttered her eyes at him. "Well, because I wasn't born genteel. I married into it."

"You're married?"

"I was. I'm a widow these nine months." She performed a pout.

# CHAPTER FORTY-FOUR

"So, you're on the hunt for another rich husband?"

She pretended to be affronted and playfully tapped his arm with her folded fan. "Shame on you, making such accusations." She giggled.

He crossed his arms. "I don't blame you, dear. Money empowers kings and princes and commands nations and armies. Why wouldn't a pretty, lonely widow not want some of that for herself?"

He possessed an off-putting, lusty, piratical quality, but she giggled again. "Your wife must enjoy a husband with such power to command."

"I'm not married, pet."

"No? A handsome man like you?" She pinched the inside of her wrist to keep from balking. He wasn't handsome at all. With his bony frame, pock-scarred skin, and hard demeanor, only his roguish air and money could recommend him to any woman—which rendered his affair with Milby less mysterious.

"But then, you never know when that might change." He reached over to run a tendril between his thumb and finger. "I do like a dark-haired, black-eyed beauty like yourself. You're the sort to turn my head." The Irish accent was more pronounced now. Panic fluttered in her chest. Was this the same man who had been hovering around her house? The one who attacked her? She wanted to see if he had a limp.

"Do you know a woman named Martha Milby?"

His dark eyes narrowed. "Might be I do." He smiled, almost sneering. "Are you the jealous type?"

She smiled. "Perhaps." She chuckled. "Truly. Do you know her? She worked for me at one time, and I'd heard she courted a gent who matched your description."

"Oh. Did she steal your spoons?" He joked.

"No. I-I-I rather liked her and was hoping she might find a nice gent like yourself."

His dark eyes glittered coldly. "Well, pet, I'm not one to kiss and tell." He ran a bony finger under her chin.

His touch unnerved and repulsed her. "I'd love some champagne." She linked her arm with his, pressing her bosom against his arm—a move that did not escape his notice—but made her skin crawl.

He stood about Braedon's height and had a small but hard, wiry frame. This close to him, she caught a whiff of his cologne, a sweet flowery scent. Mayfair cologne. Alarm bells sounded in her head. She was almost certain this man had attacked her. Her eyes locked with his, her mask dropping. "It's you. You're the one who attacked me." She glanced around the room. They were alone.

"That's right." He pulled a knife from the waist of his pantaloons and jammed it painfully against her rib. "Come with me, pet. If you scream or fight me, I'm in a position to kill you in an instant. Best cooperate." He gripped her upper arm and guided her toward a door in the corner of the room. She walked, but he limped. And she recalled the horrific night in the street outside her home where she'd fought for her life.

He guided her toward the double doors that led toward the promenade that ran parallel to the gardens.

She tripped along beside him. "No, wait. I—"

He opened the French doors and shoved her through them while grabbing her stole.

She stumbled against the balustrade.

He wound her stole around the doorknobs to prevent their opening. "Do you truly think I don't know who you are?"

Ravenna slipped her blade from her fan and hid it in the folds of her skirt as she turned to face him. "You're with The Unity, aren't you?"

"Did you think you'd get away with crossing us? Did you think we'd forget what you did to us? Because of you, we lost our greatest opportunity to separate ourselves from English tyranny."

"I guess you were behind helping Milby to kill the foreign secretaries?"

"I've been spending time with Milby, but I haven't had any part in what you're talking about. I've been looking for you. And your brother. I want to know where he is." She tried to step back, but he held her hip. "You're a juicy bit of flesh, aren't you? I wasn't paid for this. It's an extra treat."

She struggled against him, while trying to maintain the grip on her knife. "I don't know where my brother is."

"Oh," he chuckled, disbelieving, and tsked. "I think you do know where he is and…" He put the knife against her throat. "I'll slice the truth out of you inch by inch if necessary. Now, where's your brother?"

"I swear, I don't know. I haven't heard from him in over a year, when he last wrote to me."

"Don't toy with me, wench." The tip of the knife dug into her throat. "Where did the letter come from?"

This man would likely kill her if she told the truth or not. She'd burn before she told him anything about her brother. She inched her blade from the folds of her skirt, edging it closer to her mark. She lied. "I don't know. He said he was living in a small town in Brussels and was considering running to Greece. That's all I know."

"I don't believe you."

Malice lit his eyes briefly then quickly drained as she forced her knife into his gut. She spun away from him and felt the sting of a cut on her arm, where he slashed out, nicking her. "You bitch," he growled, holding his wound. He doubled over, thrusting his knife at her with his other hand as she stumbled away from him.

She lunged one way, faked, and quickly lunged to the other side to aim for his knife hand. She slashed the back of his hand.

He shouted and dropped the knife, then charged at her.

She stepped back and around him, in a grappling stance, trying to recall how Mr. Norris would direct her. She glanced down at his knife lying only ten or fifteen feet away. She ran to grab it, but he launched himself between her and the knife, backhanding her. She spun and dropped her own blade. It clattered to the stone as she lost her balance and fell to her knees. Pain shot into her knees as the taste of copper flooded her mouth. She spit out the blood. Her injured mouth throbbed with her heightened pulse. Unsure where her own knife had landed, she spotted his a few feet away and crawled for it. The beads on her dress dug like sharp rocks into her knees, but she ignored the pain in her pursuit. She couldn't, however, ignore the way her skirts snarled her legs. Infernal dresses. She kicked wildly to free her legs as she pulled herself toward the blade.

Larson looked around frantically. He spotted his weapon, and stumbled toward her.

Her fingers touched the hilt as Larson snatched it up. He fell to his knees, panting and holding his wound as he grabbed it. His energy waned.

He closed his fist over the hilt, blade tucked against his forearm, and swung, punching her in the face, knocking her back. She fell back, her head thumping against the stone. The impact and the pain rippled over her skull and rang in her ears. Her eyes fluttered.

He was a blurry mass above her, dimly outlined in the light from the nearby door.

She needed to sit up, but she was so weak and tired. She reached out, grabbing the stone ground for support, to push herself up. She rolled onto her side. The pale gold candlelight from the door reflected on a thin piece of metal out of her reach. Her knife. She pulled herself toward it, her elbows and hands scraping against the cold stones.

He rose up on his knees, both hands gripping his blade.

Her hand fluttered on the ground, searching blindly for her knife. When her fingers brushed the cold metal, she clutched it with desperation.

He lifted his blade over his head. Seeing her last chance, in one move, she rolled and stabbed him in the side with her dagger.

He cried out and doubled over.

She scrambled to sit up and back away from him.

He lunged toward her, swiping with his knife, slicing her across the right cheek. *Bastard.* She grabbed her cheek as if it could stop the searing pain.

He fell onto his stomach, then rolled to his back as she shuffled backward, pushing herself away from him. She took a moment to catch her breath. Her cheek stung. She swiped at it. Blood. In an odd moment of detachment, she wondered what critiques her fencing instructor, Mr. Norris, might have made about her performance tonight. She vowed to increase the number and length of her fencing lessons—if she survived this.

She pushed herself to her feet. Standing in the shadows, she looked down on him. He lay very still in the growing pool of blood. He was dying or dead. She hadn't intended to kill him, only to get away from him.

She reached over, keeping her eye on him, and unwound her stole from the doorknobs. In the dim light from the door, she noticed her dress was ripped, and her chest and arms were splattered with blood. It was impossible to return to the house in this condition. And she needed to get away in case Mr. Larson roused.

She edged around Mr. Larson's sprawled form and climbed over the balustrade, landing between the rose bushes. She jerked herself free of the thorns, further ripping her dress and skin, and ducked into the shadows near the house. Light spilled out of the house as the doors to the promenade opened. Ravenna darted away from the promenade and tiptoed around the corner toward the front of the house.

A scream rang out.

# Chapter Forty-Five

Here on the far end of Jermyn Street near Haymarket, Ravenna was only about a mile from home. She'd considered walking home or hiring a hackney, but at this hour, there would likely be a dozen thieves and rapists between here and Gordon House in Curzon Street.

She covered herself the best she could with her stole. Aching, stiff, and tired, she picked her way along, glancing over her shoulder, fearful someone might have followed. The trickle of blood tickled her cheek where she'd been cut. She pressed her stole against the wound. Her mouth was swollen.

It occurred to her that Braedon's house was on Bennet Street, which was much closer than her own. She'd have a better chance of getting to his house unscathed. Perhaps she could talk her way in and have one of his servants get a message to him at Braxton House. Dagger in hand, she said a silent prayer that she wouldn't need it again as she ran all the way to Bennet Street.

In the light of the half moon, she found Braedon's red brick townhome among a row of neatly kept homes with bay windows and black doors surrounded by keystones. She opened the black wrought-iron gate, stepped up to the front door, and employed the heavy brass knocker.

A stocky footman in a dark green coat and a paisley waistcoat answered the door. He held up a lantern. He wasn't a footman nor a butler, but it wasn't unusual for bachelors to have a starkly reduced servant staff where a man might serve as valet, footman, and butler to a gentleman. His dark hair was a thick mat of tight curls. He was barrel-chested and double-chinned with thick angular brows.

"I'm sorry to trouble you."

His dark, round eyes widened almost comically when he examined her face.

She continued, "I'm Lady Birchfield. I attended a party with Lord Braedon tonight." It was getting harder to talk through her swollen lip, and her cheek hurt like the devil. "I had a mishap and was forced to leave. He's still there. I'd rather not travel the streets alone at night. Might I briefly impose myself on your hospitality? Would you allow me to stay here while someone goes to retrieve Lord Braedon?" She wrapped her arms around herself as an instinctively protective measure rather than in response to cold.

The man looked around her. He held the candle closer to her face and squinted, seemingly measuring her truthfulness. Then his gaze trailed downward to the dagger in her hand. He raised a questioning brow.

She looked down where he had been looking. "Oh, uh, that's my dagger. I use it for protection."

"The marks on your face say your little dagger doesn't work too well." A language unfamiliar to her accented his English.

"You should see the man who attacked me."

He grunted, his eyes lighting with mirth. Then he burst into laughter. "Yes. You must come in." He shut the door behind her. "Please, this way, milady." He crossed the foyer and went to the last door at the end of the short, dark hall.

"This is Lord Braedon's study. He likes to come here in the evening. It is the most comfortable place for you. Fire is already built. There on desk is tray of wine, bread, and cheese. You eat. Please do make this your home, too. I'll go find milord. Where is he, you say, milady?"

"He's at Braxton House. Discretion is utterly essential tonight and hereafter, if you understand my meaning?"

His dark eyes glinted, and a faint smile teased his lips. He winked and laid a finger aside his bulbous nose. "Aye. I understand."

Braedon's study smelled of cigars, leather, old books, and earth. It was decorated simply, but tastefully, in a manner befitting a bachelor fascinated with a time of chivalry long lost. Swords and crests hung alongside family portraits on the wood-paneled walls. Stag horns hung over the fireplace and a large tapestry of a medieval battle scene covered the wall behind his desk.

But for all his fascination with the history of his own land, he was clearly intrigued with foreign lands as well. Two of the swords were strange, exotic weapons formed of curved lines with tassels hanging from their hilts. On the wall nearest his desk hung a small rectangular mosaic of sorts, with an image very much like a flower in the abstract. On a shelf behind the desk sat various japanned boxes and an eye made of blue glass hung on a tassel dotted with various beads.

Another shelf held vials of sand and dirt and a few seashells, some rocks, and stones. A few elaborate glass bottles, like perfume bottles from Arabia, lined the shelf. Books crammed other shelves. A colorful silk fabric full of jagged happy colors draped a tabletop beside the desk.

Braedon was clearly a well-traveled and well-read man. He'd been to lands she'd only read about and dreamed of. She suddenly felt like livestock hemmed into a pasture she'd never been allowed to leave. She spent all her days eating and sleeping and wandering in that pasture, never realizing a whole world thrived beyond her stone walls. Maybe instead of retiring to her cottage at Birchfield Manor, she'd spend her days traveling.

Ravenna laid her dagger on the desk. Her hands sticky with blood, she poured herself a glass of wine and downed it to still both her nerves as well as the envy and admiration fingering her ribcage. She poured another drink. She would need several glasses to equal the force of her usual port. But the claret was good: light, cool, fruity.

With her second glass in hand, staring at a sketch of some ancient structure that appeared to be Grecian or Roman, she concluded one thing, she needed to make some changes in her life. She looked closer at the sketch. Braedon had signed and dated it. Clearly, he was also a talented artist. One more thing to envy and admire.

Ravenna stared up at a tapestry, awash in candlelight, wondering how many hours, how many days went into its creation. It was clearly a battle scene of some sort, evident by the horses and swords, the men in armor, the prostrate bodies with spears jutting from their middles.

Men had killed other men for centuries. They killed men and earned honors, fame, glory, estates, riches, and the trust and friendship of kings. Why should it be any different for her? And she'd killed for something more important than titles and glory. She'd killed to protect herself and her family.

Mr. Larson had not been a good man. He was trying to kill her. He was a member of The Unity, who wanted to destroy England. He wanted to kill her brother. Of course, their cause wasn't without foundation. Many men she'd grown up with had joined the rebellion against the English and the horrors they'd inflicted on her people. They'd also died brutally for their trouble. Yet, her husband, her friends, her stepsons were all English. She would always walk in this bleak limbo, her heart torn between lands and loves.

She flopped down in a nearby chair, dropped her head into her hands, and whispered, "Heaven help me." A tickle ran down her cheek, and she scratched at it. More blood. She ripped off a patch of tattered cloth and held it to her face.

The door opened behind her. She jumped up, lowering her hand, rushing to meet him as he strode toward her, tossing aside his greatcoat and hat.

"Ravenna…." Fear and worry etched deep lines between his brows and around his mouth. "Darling, are you hurt? I'm so sorry I wasn't there. I wish I had been. I would've…" He snarled while tenderly supporting her jaw with his fingers, inspecting her face. "Your face," he breathed. His jaw clenched, and his nostrils flared. "That son of a demon. I'll kill him." He kissed her cheek right above the cut. He pressed his handkerchief to the cut and kissed her forehead. He pulled the handkerchief away. "The cut looks deep. I think you may need stitching."

"Are you sure?"

He nodded. "I'm afraid so. I'll get Dymas." He stepped into the hall and returned a few moments later with the man who'd answered the door earlier. "He's done nearly all my stitches. Trained on the battlefield. He's exceptionally good." Her face must have betrayed her doubt because he added, "I wouldn't trust you to anyone else. I swear it."

Dymas set a black medicine box on the desk and rolled up his shirt sleeves, revealing beefy forearms covered in a pelt of black hair. He pulled a footstool near the fire. "Please do sit, milady."

Ravenna sat, as skittish as a trapped rabbit, watching Dymas' every move. He opened his box, poured several drops of red-brown liquid into a glass, and said something in a foreign language to Braedon, who crossed the room to grab a bottle of whiskey from a cabinet.

"What language is he speaking?" Ravenna said.

"Greek," Braedon poured a splash of whiskey atop the red-brown liquid. "I met Dymas on my travels after university. He's been a devoted valet and friend." He handed her the glass. "Drink."

"What is it?"

"Laudanum and whisky. You're going to need it."

She took the glass with shaking hands and downed the drink in one fiery gulp. Right then, Dymas touched her face with a rag soaked in whiskey. She sucked in a sharp breath.

"So sorry, milady." Dymas worked at threading his needle.

Within minutes, a veil dropped. Dymas seemed to move slowly as if through a pool of mud, and Ravenna's mind floated, as if captured in the net of a dream. She smiled up at Braedon. Warmth and contentment oozed through her body, as golden and cheerful as honey. She wanted to stretch out on the plush carpet beneath her shoes and luxuriate like a cat in the sun. Her body went loose and limp, and her eyes grew heavy.

Dymas's dark eyes darted between her and his needle. He chuckled. "I believe she is ready."

Braedon removed his coat and jacket and rolled up his shirt sleeves. "Be as quick and gentle as possible. And neat." He knelt beside her, held her hand, and kissed it. "Be brave, my little raven."

Dymas tsked. "Is a shame. Such a pretty face." He stuck her with the needle.

She clutched Braedon's hand as she suppressed her scream.

# Chapter Forty-Six

Ravenna woke on a sofa, feeling as though her head and mouth were stuffed with wads of muslin, like she'd drunk too much wine. She hadn't felt this numb since her acting days, when the cast closed a play by getting deep in their cups.

Her right cheek ached and pulled tight when she moved her face. She touched the wound. Tender and raw, it was a relatively straight line right along her cheekbone, about two, maybe three inches long, and ridged where the stitches held the skin together. Her entire body ached from the tussle and was covered in bruises and little surface cuts, but someone had cleaned the blood off of her. Spots of recollection lifted out of her haze like the lights at Covent Gardens on a foggy night. Would there be a time when her body wasn't beaten?

Soon she pieced together enough of the events of the night before to create a memory. She looked around. What time was it? The drawn curtains blocked any indication of day or night.

Ravenna pushed herself up from the sofa, lightheaded and nauseous, and wobbled to the curtains. It was still the wee hours of the morning. She listened for a few moments, but bells didn't ring, and she didn't hear the night watchman call out the time.

She looked around. Enough of the fire light remained to see Braedon. He slept in a wingback chair, his head resting in the wing and one leg thrown over the arm. He couldn't possibly be comfortable. He had removed his waistcoat and ascot and the neck of his shirt lay open against his chest.

Thirst gripped her throat. In the dim light, she could make out the crystal decanters across the room. Ravenna crept over to the liquor stand, quietly poured a glass of water.

Braedon sat up, looking around. "What are you doing?"

"Sorry to wake you. I was thirsty."

"What time is it?" His head was laid back against the chair, eyes shut.

"I don't know."

"How do you feel?"

"Sleepy, hurting, addled."

"Good, that means you're alive."

"For now."

"What do you mean?"

"Once the magistrate finds out I murdered a man at Braxton House, they'll arrest me, throw me in prison, and likely execute me."

"Not likely. In fact, you probably did the Prince a great favor. You killed a man to whom he owed thousands of pounds. His councilors will consider the debt relieved, will count their lucky stars, cover up the murder, and try once again to rein in the Prince so he doesn't get into any deeper debt."

"Do you truly think it'll go over so quietly?"

"I do. Everyone in Prinny's circle knows Mr. Larson was a scoundrel and a criminal. He won't be missed."

She broke into tears and sat on the edge of the sofa. Her face hurt when she cried, and the tears stung her fresh scar. "I never meant for any of this to happen. But he forced me outside." She might have to rededicate herself to prayers, church, and Bible study again. How would she ever erase this stain from her soul? "I simply wanted to find out more about Mr. Larson. I thought maybe he and Milby and Nochdale were somehow working together to help Nochdale attain the foreign secretary post."

He handed her a handkerchief, and she blew her nose. He said, "You did what you had to do. No one will blame you. If they even know you were involved."

"Further, Mr. Larson was the man who had attacked me on the street outside my home." Her sobs took her breath. "He was with The Unity. He was looking for my brother. But I lied about Niall's whereabouts. So I stabbed him to get away, but he continued to come after me so I was forced to defend myself. We grappled—and—and…"

"He lost."

She nodded. With a fresh wave of guilt, she put her hands over her face and doubled over in her lap, sobbing still. She heard a rustle of cloth, and his hand rested on her back.

He stood beside her chair. "Don't worry, my little raven. You can't be so hard on yourself. He attacked you, and you defended yourself. It was justified." He kissed the back of her neck. "Come now, be still."

She gripped the handkerchief in a tight fist. "How can I be still? He was with The Unity. I'm now certain they're after me and know where I live!" She jumped up and paced in wild circles, her mind flailing like a landed fish. "They've found me. I thought after I married Philip, I was safe. I thought his titles and power would protect me. I thought they'd let it go because they'd been arrested or killed. I didn't think any of them were still free or alive. What am I going to do?"

He put his arm around her and pulled her against him. There was great comfort in laying her head against his chest, listening to his heartbeat, feeling his warmth. "Try not to worry about that, my little raven. All will be well. You'll see."

"How can you possibly know that?" She stared into the dying fire, wishing this moment of security would last forever. His soft musky scent soothed her.

He pulled back and brushed his fingers over her face to tuck a lock of hair behind her ear, careful to avoid her scar. "Look at me."

She looked up at him.

"I'll do everything in my power to protect you."

"That's sweet of you to say, Braedon, but that's impossible. You can't be with me every moment—"

"You have my word."

She wasn't going to argue with him. She'd let him have his chivalric illusion if it helped him to worry less. Men so often liked to believe themselves in control, but then, she too liked to feel that she held the reins on her life—even though lately she felt as if the reins had slipped her grip and she was riding bareback on a wild horse. "Will you take me home to Gordon House?"

# Chapter Forty-Seven

Ravenna arrived at Gordon House, and Braedon assisted her inside. "If you need anything at all, don't hesitate to let me know." He kissed her forehead. "I'll let you rest and will check on you soon. I'll see what I can learn about what happened to Mr. Larson and if anything will be done about it."

"Thank you, Braedon. For everything." He squeezed her hand and left the house. Aching, she dragged herself up the stairs. She opened the window to clear the stuffy room and decided to let the fire burn down. She desperately wanted a bath, but would wait until the morning. She collapsed into bed on top of the covers and pulled the edge of the counterpane over herself like a cocoon.

Ravenna woke with a headache, a stuffy nose, and congested chest—the curse of falling asleep with a low fire and windows open to a cool, damp night. Her stitched cheek ached and burned. She squinted, feeling the tug of the thread in her skin.

She ran her fingertips over the stitch bumps. Her face was thick and tender around her eyes, and breathing through her nose was impossible. She inhaled through her mouth. Her breath rattled in her chest, causing her to cough. She groaned and fell back against her pillow. Some broth and tea would set her up nicely. A hot bath. A hot brandy. And some tonic. She could make an elixir and a camphor liniment to progress her healing.

Grunting, she rolled out of bed to ring for servants to set her healing in motion.

In an hour's time, her belly was full of broth and tea, and she was sunk in a bath near the fireplace with a high fire, sipping a hot brandy. She sat in her bathwater studying the many scratches and bruises peppering her skin.

When she was as pink and wrinkled as a newborn, and the water had grown cool, she stepped out of the tub, mixed the elixir and liniment she'd promised herself, and dabbed chamomile ointment on her scar. Exhausted from her healing enterprise, she returned to bed.

She woke around three in the afternoon, drank hot ginger lemon water made from fresh ginger and greenhouse lemons, drank more broth and tea, and began dressing.

Hart entered with a small package and a letter. "Lord Braedon visited while you slept. He left this."

Ravenna accepted the package and letter and waited until she was alone. She untied the twine from the cloth around the item. The wrapping consisted of his handkerchief with his initials embroidered in the corner. It smelled of him. Inside was her Spanish fan with the dagger inside. She gasped and held it clutched to her chest. "Thank God."

She opened the letter. It read:

*Good Morning, my little raven. I thought you might be missing this. I found it last night lying on the promenade. I nicked it before anyone else noticed it, and you left the dagger on my desk. I'd forgotten about it until this morning. I will visit you at my first opportunity.*

*Ever yours,*

*B*

She smiled to herself as she folded the letter and stashed it in her vanity drawer. She quickly finished her toilette. She had things to do.

First on her list was to visit Lucy and Thomas.

She dressed quickly, stopping to catch her breath, cough, or blow her nose. She reeked of camphor and looked a fright from the tussle the night before, but she didn't care. She launched herself into the sunny day, into the carriage, and toward Pelham House.

Lucy sauntered into the room in a thinly concealed dudgeon, looking tired. She was dressed to go out on her rounds and was focused on tugging on her gloves as she entered the parlor to greet Ravenna. "Good morning,

Dowager." When she glanced up, she froze. Lucy's eyes and mouth popped open wide. "Dear heavens, what happened to you?"

"I was hoping to see you and Thomas." Her nose was stuffy and caused her words to come out stunted.

"I'm sorry. He's upstairs finishing his toilette and I'm on my way out to make my calls and do a bit of shopping. What happened to your face?"

"I was attacked last night by a man named Mr. Larson. Do you know him?"

Lucy perched on the edge of a nearby chair. "No. I've never heard of him. Why did he attack you?"

"The primary issue is that I believe he and Milby are working together to destroy Thomas, and I think they attacked me to hurt him." It was as close to the truth as she could comfortably get with Lucy.

She frowned. "That doesn't make any sense. Why?"

Ravenna shook her head. "The only thing I can think of is it's somehow politically motivated." Ravenna coughed. She searched through her reticule to find a peppermint comfit to soothe her sore throat. Her voice came out crackled. "So, I've come to ask you to reconsider having Milby in your house. I believe she's a danger."

"I suppose you're the one who put that nonsense in Thomas's head then?"

She found the comfit and popped one in her mouth. The peppermint soothed her scratchy throat. "What do you mean?"

"He went on and on about how Milby was trying to poison him. I think his recent fever turned him half-mad. So, Thomas called her into the drawing room and told her she was no longer needed. She was allowed to collect whatever she could carry with permission to return with a cart to remove the rest of her belongings once she found new lodgings."

"I assure you it's for the best. Do you know when she will return?"

"I don't, but I hope it will be soon."

"Have you started looking for a new lady's maid?"

"No. I've written to Becker, and she'll return next week. I'll make do with a chambermaid until then."

On their way toward the front door, Ravenna said, "Who are you going to visit with?"

"Lady Braxton. I have a *Les Roses Noires* meeting there, actually."

"Oh? I hadn't realized you'd joined the club. I thought you weren't interested."

She lifted a shoulder. "Lady Braxton convinced me. It's my first meeting. I thought I may as well join since I'm expected to make important connections with the other society hostesses to begin my own career." She smiled with a touch of sarcasm. "Because the wife of a politician is also a politician, isn't she? Or at least that's what Thomas says."

"That's true. I remember having to play the part of society doyenne at one time."

"I'm glad I joined *Les Roses Noires*. So many of the women have been quite helpful. Especially Lady Braxton. She's been so kind, involved, and attentive."

# Chapter Forty-Eight

Ravenna bid farewell to Lucy and waved as her carriage pulled away. As she turned toward her own carriage, she noticed Milby emerge from the alley beside the house, look up and down the street from the house on Berkeley Square, and walk briskly toward Burton Street.

Ravenna told the footman to hold the carriage, and she would return directly. She followed close behind as Milby's coppery cloak bobbed and wound through the crowd.

Milby walked fast, and Ravenna had difficulty maintaining the pace with her stuffed nose and congested chest. She was forced to breathe through her mouth, which only dried and irritated her throat, making her cough. She dug up another comfit.

After some ten minutes of walking, dodging people, carriages, horses, mud, and dung, they arrived at the Blue Rooster. Ravenna stood across from the white stone tavern with a large blue rooster hanging over the blue door. Once Milby crossed the street and disappeared inside, Ravenna crossed to peer in the window.

The place was dimly lit, and the greasy windows made it difficult to clearly see the face of the man Milby was meeting with. But it didn't signify because Milby was inside only a few minutes. Then Milby exited and stood outside of the tavern, as if waiting for something or someone. Ravenna ducked her head to hide her face and moved to the shop next door, pretending to look in the window, while watching Milby.

After some minutes passed, a thin woman with hunched shoulders, darting eyes, and tendrils of fawn straight hair hanging from under her

301

mob cap approached. The stranger passed two small bottles to Milby, who then tucked them into her basket.

The woman left Milby and walked toward Ravenna, who spun away to buy a mincemeat pie from a nearby vendor. She gave him a penny and lingered, playing with the greasy brown paper wrap. Ravenna followed the stranger, trailing her out of the nicer neighborhood into a less reputable area. She needed her hands free to unsheathe her blade in the event of trouble, so she handed the pie off to a street urchin.

She continued her pursuit, her fingers tickling the gold medallion at the end of her fan, ready to draw her weapon if necessary. Though the area wasn't as dilapidated as a rookery, it was certainly no Mayfair. They passed a series of shops, milliners, and such until they came to a shop called Sylvan's Luxuries. A bowed window flanked each side of the bottle-green door. The paint around the windows peeled and flaked to reveal rotting wood beneath.

It was a sundries shop with a wide variety of goods on display. The woman disappeared inside Sylvan's Luxuries and walked into the shadows at the back of the building. She didn't re-emerge, so Ravenna assumed the woman might live above the store as so many shopkeepers did.

Ravenna stepped inside and a small bell jingled above her head. She looked around at the dark wood shelves lined with rows and rows of bottles of different hues and shapes, gleaming like jewels in the sunlight. A tapestry of scents, like a garden filled with herbs, wood, and flowers all topped with light citrus notes filled the air. Throughout the shop were several tables loaded with sundry goods, like brushes, mirrors, gloves, stockings, fans, and other such accessories as compliments a lady's toilette.

A rotund woman with bright pink cheeks and jolly blue eyes came from the back room. "Good day, milady. How can I help you?" She was clearly trying not to stare at the scar on Ravenna's face.

Ravenna hadn't thought this far and wasn't sure how to proceed. Her hand fluttered around her scar self-consciously. She wanted to hide it but also realized that would only draw more attention to it. "Oh, I, uh—uh, am looking for a perfume."

"I've got many to choose from." She motioned to the shelves.

"Yes. I'm wondering what may be the most popular among the ladies and gentlemen of Mayfair these days? Is there one, in particular, you've sold a great deal of in the past few months?"

She thought for a moment. "There is one." She limped toward the shelves and selected a bottle, and opened the gilt-edged cap.

Ravenna took up the bottle, a black enameled bottle, slightly pear-shaped, with gold trim. Around the bottle were a few panels of scantily-clad women lounging or dancing against a pink background. She inhaled the scent. Lily, sage, bergamot. It turned her stomach. She'd smelled this before. "Hm. That is rather pleasant," she lied, trying not to gag on the lily odor. "What do you call it?" The perfume triggered a cough.

"Well, for the ladies, I call it Lily Dew, but that won't do for the gents. They rather like a bolder sounding name, so for them, I call it Widow's Blush."

"Widow's Blush? That's an unusual name."

"I tell them it's seductive enough to make a widow blush." She winked. "They snap it up fast enough, then." Her ample frame shook with laughter. "For what man doesn't want to make a woman blush now and then, eh? And it's extra powerful for a gent to make a somber widow blush, ain't it?" She laughed again.

The woman's mirth and high spirits were contagious, and Ravenna couldn't help but chuckle through her coughing.

The woman added with happy mischief, "Shall I wrap up a bottle or two for your ladyship?"

She didn't want the perfume, but if she bought something, it might loosen the woman's tongue. "Yes, please, and a pair of those blue kid gloves." She watched the woman gather the items. "Who buys this most often?"

"Oh, I can't say as I remember all the names. Lord Palmerstone enjoys the scent, as does Lady Braxton."

"Lady Braxton?" That was most interesting. "And would you ever deliver to my home if I needed you to?"

"But rarely, ma'am. And those times, only when the price is right, if you get my meaning?"

"I see."

The shop woman brought the gloves and bottle to the counter to mark her ledger. She dipped her pen and bent low over the book. "I wish it weren't so, ma'am, but it's only me and Betsy in the shop, and sometimes it gets busier than the two of us can manage."

"Betsy? Is that the girl I saw come in not long ago?"

"Yes, that's her."

"Is she your daughter?"

The woman demurred with something like a bashful mirth. "Oh, no. I never married nor had children."

"I'm sorry. How long has Betsy worked with you?"

"Only a few months, but I wish I could keep her forever. Betsy Moore is the best worker I've ever had here."

The shopkeep looked at her like she was daft. "Yes'm." Then she turned to yell through the curtain behind her. "Betsy, come wrap up these things for the lady."

The thin woman came from behind the curtain, her dark eyes darting. She took the items in her hands. She wasn't near as old as Ravenna had first thought her. She was little more than a girl—maybe no more than sixteen or seventeen.

Ravenna searched her face for a resemblance to Lucy's maid, Milby. She asked, "You're Betsy Moore?"

The girl nodded shyly. "Yes, ma'am." She stared at the scar on Ravenna's face. The scar tickled and itched.

The shopkeep nudged her with a chubby elbow and whispered, "Milady."

The girl muttered, "Milady."

"You know, you're about the age of my niece. Can you help me select a gift for her?" She pointed to the table of knickknacks.

The girl glanced at the shopkeeper, who nodded her approval and nudged her. Betsy followed Ravenna.

Ravenna said, "What would a young girl like you enjoy?"

Betsy picked out a silver brush and mirror set. "I think any girl would like this, milady."

"Thank you. I'll take that. Please wrap it." As the girl turned, Ravenna touched her arm and whispered. "I saw you earlier with a woman I know. How do you know her?"

"She's my sister, ma'am."

"Your sister?"

She nodded. "Yes'm. She were my elder sister, milady."

"Have either of you been married?"

The girl frowned. "No'm."

Ravenna wasn't sure what she might be uncovering, but it seemed Milby was another false name. She also didn't want to say what she had witnessed. If it was an innocent exchange, she didn't want to potentially get this girl in trouble with her employer. "What's your sister's name?"

The girl tipped her head, her face marked with suspicion. "I thought you said you knew her."

The shopkeep watched the exchange with intense interest. Ravenna opened her mouth to make an excuse, but was interrupted by the shopkeep who said, "Betsy, don't keep milady waiting. Go wrap up those things now."

The girl nodded and returned to the back room. The chignon peeking from under her mobcap was ringed with a trio of black roses.

# Chapter Forty-Nine

Ravenna collected her package from the shopkeeper, thanked her, and stopped by the confectioner's for peppermint comfits to soothe her throat. She returned to Pelham House with the hope Thomas would be home so she could check on him and to see how he was recovering. Lucy had not yet returned home, so she waited in the drawing room for Thomas to come downstairs. She sat on the sofa, looked around at the paintings, and listened to the muffled chatter of the gardeners outside the window.

A bone-cutting shriek echoed through the house.

Ravenna jumped up and ran into the foyer. A maid appeared at the top of the stairs, red-faced, and tears streaming down her cheeks. She shouted, her voice cracking, "Please, help! It's Lord Birchfield!"

Ravenna pulled up her skirts, dashed up the stairs, and ran down the dark hall with servants behind her. They all ran into Thomas's room. The air was filled with the scent of lily and sage.

"No!" Ravenna screamed, rushing to his side.

Thomas sat in his bathtub, slumped to one side.

She bent over him, lifted his eyelids, felt his neck. He was already cool to the touch, and no heart pulsed against her fingertips. She stood, limp as a rag. "He's dead. Lord Birchfield is dead." Her throat constricted into a tight knot. She had failed to protect her husband's legacy. Failed to protect her stepson. She doubled over, sobbing.

Chester, the valet, rushed in. "What's happened?" He paused and whimpered. "Oh, Lord Thomas." He rushed to Ravenna's side and helped her to stand. Fear and worry carved deep ravines in his brow and around his mouth. She drooped in his arms. "Come now, milady." He helped her to sit in a nearby chair, then left her side to tend to Thomas.

Chester cried out and fell beside Thomas' body, holding him and crying over him like a father. Something in Chester's grief plucked a chord of strength deep in Ravenna. She stood, wiped her face with the handkerchief she pulled from her reticule, and knelt by Chester to comfort him. She whispered her condolences to him and said, "Come now, Chester, we need to cover him."

His sobs waned into gasping sniffles, and he stood, wiping his nose on a handkerchief, staring down at Thomas' lifeless form. "Rest easy, lad." He and a footman carefully covered the body in a towel.

Ravenna turned to the servants huddled by the door, crying. "I'm very sorry for our loss, but we have work to do before we can mourn Lord Birchfield." She instructed a couple of footmen to open the window to air out the stench of lilies.

She sent another footman to call for the coroner and sent Lucy's chambermaid to find Lady Birchfield at Braxton House and bring her home. She ordered the rest of the staff to prepare the drawing room downstairs. "Chester, I'll need you and the butler to contact the upholsterer and undertaker. Miller & Hatchett are the best. They'll see to the preparations. I will write to his brother, Harrison, and have him brought home." She rubbed her face and continued. "A couple of men should lift Lord Birchfield from the tub to the bed until he can be moved downstairs. Be very careful of the water. You should wear gloves. I believe it's poisoned. Dump the water in the farthest corner of the garden."

The maid, who had screamed and alerted the house to Thomas's death, hovered in the corner, red-faced and crying. Ravenna turned to her. "Please tell me everything you know."

The girl spoke through tear-stained gasps, wiping the tears with the hem of her apron. "I made the fire this morning for milord like always when he was still a-bed. Then he said he wished to take a bath, so I brought up his water. He asked me to put more coal on the fire because he was cold. Only there weren't no more coal up here, so I had to get more. Before I got up here, Milby stopped me. She were needing crates to pack her things. I told her I would get them after setting milord's fire, but she threatened to flog me, saying she needed the crates to finish packing so she could leave. I told her I weren't scared. She said she'd get me tossed out of my job if I didn't go right away. So, I searched out in the alley and the kitchen and took them to her room, but she wasn't there. Then I brought my coal and…and…" Her bottom lip quivered, and her voice cracked. "And I found milord like this." She dabbed her eyes with her apron, then held it over her mouth to catch her halting sobs.

"You didn't hear anything or see anything else?"

"No'm, milady. Only there was a scent of lilies that wasn't there before. But I didn't think anything of it because milord sometimes liked to put a splash of cologne in his bath."

"Is the name of his cologne Widow's Blush?"

The maid shrugged. "I don't know the name of it, ma'am."

"Thank you. You're dismissed. Help the others gather supplies for the preparation of his body." The maid curtsied and ran from the room.

Ravenna approached the tub to look for a cologne bottle. Nothing. The scent of lilies, sage, and bergamot was overpowering near the tub. She held her breath. Her fingers went cold, and blood pooled into her feet. This was the same scent that Nochdale had worn at the garden party and the theater. She'd smelled this odor the night she'd caught Lucy washing Thomas. She smelled it earlier in the perfumery. Then she recalled when she'd seen Milby exchanging a bottle with her sister. It wasn't Nochdale. She'd thought Nochdale had been responsible for attacking Thomas, but Nochdale was dead. The sisters, if they were working with him, would have no reason to kill Thomas if Nochdale was dead. That meant the sisters were doing this for their own reasons. But why? What would compel two common women to target foreign secretaries? There had to be someone directing them. Someone with a greater purpose. She searched the rest of his room, looking for a cologne bottle, and found nothing.

Ravenna balled her hands into tight fists. She marched from the room, her pelisse billowing behind her, prepared to drag Milby from her room by her hair, if necessary.

Not bothering to knock, she threw open the door. The bed was empty and made up. The room, too, was empty. The fireplace was dead and cold. She opened the drawers of the simple vanity. Empty. She opened the wardrobe. Empty. Milby had already moved her belongings. She might never find her now.

Panic fluttered in her chest like a caged bird. She ran from the room. She looked up and down the hall, her mind racing to grasp a notion of what she should do, how she should proceed. She noticed a shadowy figure at the end of the dim hall going toward the servants' stairs. "Milby," she shouted. "Come here." The figure paused, then quickly disappeared through the door, carrying a long, thin box about the size of a pistol case.

# Chapter Fifty

"Damn her eyes," Ravenna hissed. She pulled up her skirts and ran down the hall. She jogged down the staircase, her fan tapping against her thigh. She flew out the door and into the courtyard. She drew the blade from her fan and ran through the courtyard toward the alley. As she passed through the gate, Milby exited the alley onto the street.

Ravenna let the gate door slam shut and ran down a narrow alley stinking of rotten cabbage and urine. Rubbish lined the buildings. She jumped over puddles and a dead rat. Live rats scurried along the walls and ducked into dark holes. The alley grew narrower causing her to turn to the side and skip through the crevice. "Stop," she shouted. "Milby, stop."

The woman looked back, but had a veil pulled down over her face. They continued to push through the alley until stumbling out on the other side.

Ravenna was hard on Milby's heels. Ravenna's thin leather slippers offered little protection against the hard stones. They were for riding in carriages and paying house calls, maybe walking through a garden. They were not meant for running through streets of rough cobblestone, broken glass, mud, puddles, and rubbish. They pushed through the crowd of servants, gentlemen, gentlewomen, and vendors.

Milby ran across the street to the other side, jumping a dung pile, nearly toppling a street sweeper, then turned right onto the narrower Clarges Street, with its neat row houses.

Ravenna stepped in a puddle, a mélange of mud and dung-water beading her dress. The fetid water soaked through her shoes and stockings. There was no shortage of onlookers stopping to stare and hoot at the spectacle of a supposedly well-bred, but bruised and scarred woman chasing a servant through the streets. Likely, it was as fascinating to the crowd as the female boxing matches that sometimes sprung up in the poorer neighborhoods.

They continued down the uneven pavement until Milby reached the corner and rounded left onto Piccadilly.

Ravenna groaned inwardly. Not Piccadilly. She kept her eye on the top of Milby's head as it bobbed and weaved through the crowd. She hoped the chase would end soon; she was getting a stitch in her side, and her throat was dry and scratchy as wool. Her breath came short and raspy in her chest as she hadn't recovered completely from her cold. She wasn't sure how much longer she could run.

Apparently, Milby was in the same condition. Her pace slowed until she stopped altogether. She slouched, panting, grabbing at her side. She glanced over her shoulder at Ravenna. Then she looked out across the wide and tumultuous Piccadilly, as if she were considering crossing the street. Piccadilly was nothing short of mayhem, a hive of activity.

Hot-blooded, inebriated Corinthians raced their sporty phaetons between hackneys driven by rough, foul-mouthed drivers who were intent on getting to their destination. Farmer's carts lumbered down the street, succeeding only in hindering everyone's passage. Urchins and stray dogs darted in and out of pedestrians and traffic. Vendors of all varieties hooted and shouted, hawking their wares. Pedestrians of every rank and status flooded the streets.

Milby hopped and shuffled sideways along the edge of the pavement, looking for an opening.

Surely, Milby wasn't that stupid.

Ravenna was wrong.

Milby found an opening and darted into the street.

Ravenna growled and followed, cutting around an old farmer driving a cart pulled by a pair of even older mules. He shouted oaths at Ravenna.

They zig-zagged through the traffic and somehow arrived safely on the other side. Milby ran toward St. James Street.

Fueled by the relief of having survived the perils of crossing Piccadilly,

Ravenna picked up her pace, closing in on her prey.

Milby paused at the corner. Looking up and down the streets, she was clearly trying to decide. She glanced back at Ravenna. In a panic, she inadvertently stepped directly into the path of a young gentleman on horseback who had sought to circumvent the slower-moving carriages. The horse screamed in fright and rose on its hind legs, his front hooves pawing the air. The rider attempted to gain control by grabbing a fistful of mane and shouting at the startled creature, but the horse's front hooves came down hard on Milby's head.

Screams and gasps of onlookers went up as Milby rolled and tumbled under the horse's hooves. The rider shouted at the horse and jerked at the right rein to direct the horse away from Milby, but terror had gripped the poor animal. Snorting and squealing, it reared up again and crashed down onto Milby's body.

A man shouted, "Good God! Get that woman out from there!"

A few men ran to assist. Two men presented themselves as human shields, whipping the air in front of them with riding crops as they pressed forward to direct the horse to turn away. Another man dragged Milby from the street onto the pavement. Her dress was torn, her body broken, the veil tangled around her head. She moaned.

The rider jumped down and ran toward them. A crowd had already gathered around the mangled woman.

Ravenna pushed her way to the center of the crowd. "Move, please," she shouted. "I know her." The crowd parted to allow her through.

The rider's pock-marked cheeks reddened. He couldn't have been more than eighteen or nineteen. "I'm sorry. She ran right out in front of me. I couldn't stop."

Panting, Ravenna dropped to her knees. She spoke through gasps for air, "I know." She coughed, struggling to catch her breath. "It's not your fault."

People behind her whispered, "Who is she?"

Ravenna gingerly, but quickly, unwrapped the veil.

The people behind her gasped and commented, "The poor dear" and "How dreadful."

Blood trickled from Milby's brow and caked in her hairline where her skull had been crushed by the hooves. Her mouth was full of blood, her teeth and gums outlined in dark red. She dragged sharp gasps of air into her lungs. Opening her purpled eyes, her lips moved in an attempt to talk.

"What's your real name? I know it's not Martha Milby."

Milby's eyes fluttered, and she winced, her head lolling from side to side.

"Who asked you to kill them?" Ravenna said, shaking her. "Why did you do it? Tell me."

Through her gasps, she managed her final word. "… freedom." Milby wheezed deeply. She hacked, choking on the blood. Milby's eyes rolled back into her head and fluttered.

That didn't make any sense. Ravenna shook her and screamed through the pressure of tears on her throat. "Tell me. Why did you do it?"

Milby's head lolled to the side, eyes open, and her breath gurgled out of existence.

Ravenna screamed, "Tell me. Why did you kill my stepson?"

A unified gasp went up among the crowd that had formed around her. A wave of low whispers rose up.

Tears formed in her eyes, but she refused to cry here in the street for the crowd to gape at her. She looked up at the gray sky, the ruffle of clouds. She wasn't sure how to proceed. She picked up the scuffed box Milby had dropped.

Someone slipped a hand under her arm, and a familiar voice whispered near her ear, "Ravenna."

She looked up into Braedon's pale blue eyes. A swell of emotion surged upward, crashing against the back of her throat. Her bottom lip quivered. The dam was weakening.

"Come, my little raven." He helped her to stand, removed his great coat, and draped it around her.

"Can you walk?"

She nodded. He took the box from her as she leaned on his arm, certain her own legs would give out as he led her further down St. James Street. She watched the stones under her feet as she walked. To her right was an empty alley, dim and dark, and she pulled him within. She grabbed his coat and broke against his chest into unpretty, heaving, uncontrollable sobs.

When she had composed herself, Braedon guided Ravenna to his home, and now she stood in his study near the window, staring at the street below, grasping her glass in both hands. His great coat rested heavy, but comfortingly, on her shoulders like an embrace. A dull ache throbbed in her feet and ankles. Grief, heavy and numb, filled her mind with a dense fog.

"Thomas is dead," she whispered, closing her eyes. Her body was surely filled up with sand, heavy and gritty. She drank deep of the claret, emptying her glass and setting it on the table. She needed to say it again to ensure she could believe it. "He's dead." The hope of his father. The hope of England. Gone.

"I'm so sorry, my little raven."

She sank her aching body into the nearby chair and stared out at the gray sky. "First, my husband, now his first son."

Braedon knelt at her feet and held her hand.

Her voice strained against the mounting pressure of another round of tears. "His younger brother, Harrison, is all that's left to me. He's now Lord Birchfield." She sighed, remembering she still needed to write to him to tell him. "To be honest, he's ill-prepared for the role."

He ran his thumb over the back of her hand. "What happened? I thought Birchfield had recovered."

"He was. I don't understand what happened." Her voice broke, and she covered her eyes to cry. "Milby was involved, but she died before I could get the truth." She told him everything Lucy had told her, what she'd discovered about Milby and the perfume shop, and what the Pelham House maid had told her.

Braedon squeezed her hand and gave her a handkerchief. "Perhaps he was more ill than he let on. Sometimes these things are mysterious. Relapse is common enough. It's possible, isn't it?"

She wiped her tears and blew her nose. "Not this time." In spite of the gray clouds, the day was waning. It'd be dark soon. She glanced at the clock on the mantle. The hands were nearing six of the clock. "I-I really should go." She stood. "Lucy will need help with preparing Thomas. And I'll need to contact his solicitor to manage the final details."

He stood with her, still holding her hand. "Ravenna." His voice was a warning. "If you're right, and I suspect you are, you chased a woman down in the street. She killed herself to get away from you. There's a reason for that. It means that whomever is behind this is still out there among our peers." He looked past her at the wall behind her, deep in thought.

"I've considered that. But who could it be?" She rubbed her forehead. "I thought I knew, but...." She sighed. "I thought she was working with Nochdale, but he died. Then I thought it was Mr. Larson, but...."

"Do you know how Thomas was killed?"

She coughed. "Poison. I have no doubt. There were no marks on his body. No violence done to him."

"Do you have any evidence?"

"Not exactly. Not yet." She ran her hand over her hair and brought it to rest on the back of her neck. "We will see what the coroner's autopsy reveals."

"What was in that box you collected from the street?"

She'd nearly forgotten about it. "Where is it?"

He collected it from the sofa table and set it in her lap. It was a black leather case about one foot by two feet long, scuffed. She lifted the latch and opened the lid. Inside were several letters addressed to Milby. Ravenna opened them and skimmed the writing, unable to discern who the writer was. Nor did she recognize the writing. But they all referred to Milby picking up bottles and supplies or going to this or that house for employment.

Behind the letters rested glass bottles—some full of powders, some full of liquids. There were a few small white cologne bottles just like the one she'd seen in the shop earlier: a black enameled bottle, slightly pear-shaped, with gold trim and the pink panels of scantily-clad women lounging or dancing. Widow's Blush.

315

# Chapter Fifty-One

Ravenna and Braedon returned to Pelham House. The house was in disorder. Servants dashed up and down the stairs and from room to room carrying supplies, trays, flowers, and blocks of ice.

Ravenna spoke to Paulson, the butler. "Has the coroner arrived yet?"

"No, milady, though we expect him any moment."

She handed him her gloves and bonnet. "Very well. Has Lady Lucy returned?"

"She has, ma'am. She's grief-stricken and has taken to her bed." He paused and licked his thin lips. "If I may speak plainly, ma'am?"

"Please, do."

"I worry that in her grief, she doesn't have the constitution to make the necessary preparations for Lord Birchfield's body. I can have one of the maids—"

She lifted her hand. "No. I'll do it, but I have some urgent business to attend to first. Besides, it's probably best for the coroner to see him before he's prepared. Has he been moved?"

"Yes, ma'am. We have him in the formal parlor resting on ice and covered with a sheet."

"Very good. First, I need to inspect Milby's room. I believe she is connected to Lord Birchfield's death. Do you mind if we go upstairs for a moment?"

Fear rounded his eyes. "Ma'am, after recent incidents, you belong as much to this house as your own."

"Thank you, Paulson." Ravenna and Braedon swept up the stairs and down the hall to Milby's former room.

The space brimmed with the clutter and trappings of a lady's maid busy with her day's work, but it had been emptied of her personal effects.

Ravenna flopped down on the end of the bed. How could anyone manage to sleep in such a lumpy bed? She hoped the beds at the Penitent House would be better than this one. Not if Lady Braxton had anything to do with it. "I don't see anything. Do you?"

Braedon squatted, looking in the fireplace. "What about this?" He lifted a fragment of paper from the ashes in the grate. The paper was burnt at the edges. He stood and carried it to the window.

"What does it say?" She slid from the bed, joining him at the window where he tilted the paper toward the sun filtering through the fog.

He said, "The smoke has made it difficult to read, but I can make out o-o-s-t, a partial letter, and t-o-n and -en." He held the paper for her to see and pointed at a charred letter. "What's that letter there?"

"An 'r,' I think."

"What words have this system of letters o-o-s-t? Boost, roost…"

"Rooster!" She exclaimed. She remembered seeing Milby near the Blue Rooster Tavern before. "The Blue Rooster Tavern. It has to be that."

He pointed at the paper. "Do you think the -en here indicates a time?"

"Possibly. It would have to be seven, ten, or eleven in that case."

"Is there a day mentioned?" She pressed closer to look at the paper. "Or a date?"

He looked at the paper, flipped it. "Here, it's dated today."

"She must have received the letter this morning."

"More importantly, who was she meant to meet?" He flipped the paper again. "There's no indication of who wrote the letter."

"You won't go there alone."

Ravenna wasn't going to argue. In fact, comfort and relief enveloped her to know he would be with her.

Ravenna and Braedon came out of the room, and as they neared the top of the stairs, Ravenna noticed Mr. Chadwick, the coroner, and a magistrate standing in the foyer. She stopped short and ducked back into the shadows, pulling Braedon with her.

"What's the matter?" Braedon asked.

"It's Mr. Chadwick."

"Are you afraid of him?"

"Yes. I've also been avoiding him. He aims to find me and Violette guilty of Hawkestone's death. If he sees me here with Thomas dead, I'm sure he'll accuse me. I need to get out of here and solve this matter before he comes to all the wrong conclusions." She glanced over her shoulder. She tugged his sleeve. "This way. We'll take the servants' stairs."

# Chapter Fifty-Two

Ravenna and Braedon jumped in the carriage and headed to Gordon House. Braedon dropped her off. Finally, with some free time, Ravenna wrote to Catherine to tell her of Thomas's death, knowing she would take up the business of spreading the news among their friends. She also wrote to Violette to share the news with her, but assuring her she had discovered at least one of the killer's agents. She explained about Milby and the case full of letters, powders, and liquids. She promised to visit soon, with answers, God willing.

She posted the letters and had a brief fencing lesson with Mr. Norris. Her stiff and aching body cried out against the activity. After a quick afternoon tea of ham, cheese, bread, small ginger cakes, and tea, she prepared to go to the Blue Rooster Tavern.

The sun sank low and somber gold into the horizon, and the clock in the foyer struck six. Hart loaned her a castoff dress and a deep-green wool cloak to render Ravenna less conspicuous. Thankfully, Braedon had hired a hackney coach for further anonymity, though he remained in his gentleman's clothes. He was sure to attract attention. Too anxious to talk, few words passed between them as the hackney carried them through the streets.

By the time they arrived at the Blue Rooster, only a sliver of the sun remained to cast a faint purple light that stretched shadows over the alleys, streets, and buildings, though it had little effect on the steady energy of the city dwellers. They passed bowed windows, painted doors, window boxes bursting with various flora and fauna.

The hackney pulled up in front of the Blue Rooster.

Braedon helped Ravenna out of the carriage. She pulled the cloak hood over her head. A cool tendril of air snaked through the atmosphere, bringing the ever-present fog rolling in on the streets. City smells permeated the burgeoning night.

They sat at a corner table at the back of the tavern, where the shadows hung darker along the walls. Braedon relaxed in his chair, his legs crossed, running a finger along the handle of his beer tankard. They watched each person entering and leaving the establishment.

Ravenna sincerely hoped, given the loud, smoky atmosphere, that she wouldn't have to be here until ten or eleven. After only fifteen minutes of sitting in the wooden chair, a dull ache settled in her lower back. Three or four hours in this chair would nearly cripple her.

They passed the time in anxious silence, peppered with an occasional remark on the weather or a book. For her part, Ravenna was too nervous and too distracted to direct much energy toward conversation. She didn't want to miss the person they were searching for.

Within a half hour of their arrival, Betsy Moore, the girl from the perfumery, came through the door. Her clothes were worn but neat. Her eyes darted, searching the tavern.

"That's her," Ravenna whispered, tapping his arm. "The one with the black roses in her bonnet. She works at the shop I visited yesterday."

He craned his neck to look.

"The black roses are a symbol of *Les Roses Noires*, the club I belong to. But the Moore sisters wouldn't be members. So the black roses mean something else. I'm sure of it. Her sister also wore black roses."

"That can't be coincidental." He took a swig of his beer. "We should surround her so she can't run. Then we'll extract the truth from her."

Braedon sauntered across the room, taking his post at the door in front of Betsy's table. He stood with his back to her and looked around as though he were meeting someone.

Ravenna eased along the back wall to come up behind the woman. Once in close range of the girl, she said, "Hello. Betsy, isn't it?"

Betsy turned around. Her eyes widened. "Uh, good evening, milady."

"I need to speak with you." Ravenna sat at her table.

Betsy looked around nervously.

"I'm sorry to tell you that your sister died today."

Betsy's face went slack, and tears sprang to her eyes. "How did she die?"

"She ran out in front of a horse, and it crushed her in the street." She didn't care to be gentle with a woman who might be involved in the death of her husband and stepson, among others.

"How did that happen?"

"I was chasing her, because I believe she murdered my stepson."

She shook her head. "No, that—"

"Your sister was up to some evil deeds. What do you know about that?"

Betsy jumped up to dash away but ran smack into the wall of Braedon's torso. He clutched her arms. "It's time you spoke with us," he said.

Betsy snapped, "Let me go, or I'll scream."

A smile hinted at his lips. "You may attempt it. I'll simply tell everyone you tried to steal my watch. Whom do you think they'll believe?"

Ravenna closed in, and the woman looked between her captors. "What do you want from me?"

"Only the truth," Ravenna said.

Braedon pulled out the chair and pushed Betsy into it. She looked up at him, both doleful and fearful.

"Do you know Lady Lucy Birchfield? Lady Wolfsham? Lady Nochdale? Lady Hawkestone?" With each name, she watched Betsy's features for signals of recognition or knowledge.

She shrugged, her eyes darting. "I don't know those people."

Ravenna grabbed the back of her neck, digging her nails into the flesh, and whispered in her ear, "Don't make the mistake of assuming I'm a proper lady. I'd just as soon wring your neck as look at you." Fear flooded in Betsy's eyes. "I'll ask you one more time. Do any of those names sound familiar to you?" She released Betsy's neck and asked the names again.

Betsy looked at the table. "A wet whistle sure helps a bird sing, milady."

*Insolent wretch.*

Braedon signaled the tavern wench for an ale. The wench delivered the ale with a rakish glance over Braedon.

Betsy drank deep from the tankard. She wiped the foam from her lips with the back of her hand. "I never knew any names. Besides, you ladies are all the same to me. One of you looks much like the other."

"I saw you deliver something to Milby yesterday. What was it?"

"Cologne."

"Cologne?" Braedon's brows furrowed.

Ravenna pulled a bottle from Milby's case out of her reticule and set it on the table. "Was it this?"

Betsy turned the bottle in her hand. "Might be." She popped the top and smelled it. "That's it."

"How do you get this?"

She shrugged and looked down at the table.

"You steal it, don't you?"

"Maybe."

"This is the Widow's Blush cologne, isn't it?" Ravenna asked.

"Yep."

"Does your employer know anything about any of this? Is she involved?"

"No, ma'am. It were me and my sister."

"Why?"

"Because we was hired to do it and were paid a great deal of money for our troubles. We needed the money desperate like. My papa was killed in war, and my mum was left with a passel of children's mouths to feed."

"After you gave it to Milby, what happened to it?"

She shrugged. "That was her business."

Ravenna frowned. "I'll tell you what she did. She mixed poison in it and used it to kill my stepson, my husband, and three other lords."

Betsy's eyes bugged, her mouth dropped open, and she shook her head, looking between Ravenna and Braedon. "I didn't give her no poison. And she wouldn't do that. My sister is...was...no poisoner."

"How do you know she wasn't adding poison to the bottles?"

She crossed her arms. Her skirt sunk between her spread legs. "We may be poor, but we go to heaven or hell the same as any, and we knows right from wrong."

Braedon crossed his arms over his chest. "Why do you wear the black roses?"

"I wear them for Irish freedom from English tyranny and to remember the men who were massacred by English invaders. That's what Milby told me they was for when she gave them to me." She glowered at him.

Braedon and Ravenna exchanged a glance.

"You're Irish?"

She nodded proudly. "Yes."

"Those massacres were several years ago," Braedon said.

"Tell that to those whose wives and daughters were raped and sons and husbands murdered. They still mourn. And tell that to the Irish who are kept under the tyranny of King George and have to bow to his every mad whim."

"I'm not here to discuss politics with you," Ravenna said. "I want the truth. Was your sister murdering people or working with someone to murder people?"

"I done told you." She seemed affronted. "My sister would do no such thing."

"When did she begin to ask you for the perfume?"

"Seems it was about nine or ten months ago." About the time Philip died.

"Don't you find it coincidental those ladies I mentioned are all now widows? Their husbands all died of a mysterious illness. These men all had in common their position in government and this cologne." Ravenna held up the bottle. "The very cologne your sister got from you and had in her room. It so happens this is the same scent that was in my stepson's bath when he died today."

Betsy leaned forward, her coffee-brown eyes glinting. "You're a mad bird. Elsewise, I'd box your ears for insulting my dead sister. And you shouldn't speak ill of the dead, or they come back to haunt you. You might look to your own to find the poison." She sat back with a huff and drank down the rest of her ale.

323

Ravenna scoffed and fought the urge to slap the saucy wench.

Braedon said, "What do you mean we should look to our own?"

"Lady Braxton is the bird who hired us."

The breath flew completely from Ravenna. She had only briefly suspected Lady Braxton because she had been the one recommending Milby to the houses now in mourning. She'd believed Lady Braxton had been used by Nochdale to filter his agents through her without her knowledge. "Lady Braxton? Are you sure?"

She shrugged. "It were her who had me deliver the perfume."

"I-I don't understand…"

Betsy frowned and sat back in her chair, and crossed her arms. "I do. I understand that poor folks is always getting blamed for things rich folks is doing. The way I see it, the rich folks make all the troubles for the poor folks." She bounced her leg, agitated.

"Are you sure Lord Nochdale wasn't involved somehow? Maybe he told her where to send you?"

"I don't know nothing about any of that."

"How did Lady Braxton find you and the perfume?" Braedon asked.

"I guess my sister told her. She worked at Lady Braxton's."

"What did she do there?" Ravenna and Braedon exchanged a glance.

"She started as an upstairs maid, then became an assistant to the lady's maid. All I knows is Lady Braxton came in the store one day when my employer was out. She asked for a new perfume, and I showed her the Widow's Blush. She offered to pay me a whole pound to bring her the perfume whenever she needed it."

"She must've ordered a great deal of it for you to agree to deliver it."

"Oh, yes." She gulped her beer. "She ordered four bottles right away and insisted I bring more as soon as Mrs. Sylvan could make it."

"Did Lady Braxton tell you what she wanted with all that perfume?"

"She didn't tell, and I daren't ask. It weren't my place."

"Did Milby ever mention if Lady Braxton told her anything about why she wanted all that perfume?" Braedon asked.

"Nope."

"What about Mr. Larson? Ever heard of him?" Ravenna asked. "I'd heard your sister was courting him."

She downed her beer and slammed the tankard on the table, shaking her head. "Nope. Never heard of him." She wiped her arm across her mouth. "If she was courtin' a man, she never told me about it. I need to go…." She pushed her chair back with a loud scrape on the wood floor. "There are young ones at home I have to help my mother with."

"I have one last question. What was your sister's real name?"

"Sarah Moore."

Ravenna grabbed her arm and stood. "Not yet. You're coming with us for a moment."

"Get your bloody paws off me. You may be a lady, but that don't mean you can…"

"Hush. All I want is for you to repeat your story to a constable, then you may go."

Betsy began to balk until Braedon pulled a pouch of money from inside his great coat.

He plucked out four shillings, and she stared at the coins lustily. "You get two now." He placed the coins in her hand. "I'll give you the other two after you tell the constable what you told us here tonight."

# Chapter Fifty-Three

Ravenna found Mr. Chadwick at Pelham House, where he was still with the coroner examining Thomas's body.

He joined them in the foyer. "Lady Birchfield," he cooed. "I've been searching for you, and you've been avoiding me, haven't you?" His hard blue eyes bored into her.

"Yes, as a matter of fact. I've been searching for the killer of our foreign secretaries."

He sniffed a laugh. "Indeed."

"I have someone you should speak with. Will you join us in the library?" She motioned to the door across the hall while Braedon nudged Betsy Moore into the room.

After Betsy Moore had relayed the same information to Mr. Chadwick that she'd told Ravenna and Braedon, Ravenna held out the case she'd taken from Sarah Moore.

He took it. "What is this?"

"I took this from the body of Sarah Moore, once known as Martha Milby after she was killed by a horse in the street. Open it."

He opened the case, studied the contents, and looked up at Ravenna and Braedon. "Is this what I think it is?"

"Yes. A few of the letters. Though I suspect not all. And I think if you test those bottles, you'll find a variety of powerful poisons."

He closed the lid gently and looked at Betsy. "Child, you're making a very serious accusation. Are you certain Lady Braxton is connected to this?"

She crossed her arms and pursed her lips. "As sure as the sun rises and

326

sets."

Ravenna, Braedon, and Mr. Chadwick were shown into Lady Braxton's drawing room, where she stood with her housemistress, looking over a paper.

She seemed confused. "Lady Birchfield. This is quite unexpected. It's a little late for a social call, isn't it?" Lady Braxton nodded a dismissal at the housemistress.

"This isn't a social call."

Braedon said, "This is Mr. Chadwick. He's a constable who has been investigating the death of Lord Hawkestone."

"A Bow Street Runner in my drawing room!" Her brows shot up. "How theatrical. Please, do be seated. Shall I offer you all some tea?"

No one sat.

Ravenna said, "I've had an interesting conversation this evening with Miss Betsy Moore. She claims you bought perfume from her and her sister."

"Is it a crime to buy perfume?" She chuckled.

"No, but it is a crime to poison the perfume and use it to murder people," Chadwick said.

Lady Braxton's laughter jostled her ample bosom. "Whose fanciful imagination dreamed up such a scandalous accusation?"

"It was simple enough to deduce based on the poisoner's box we uncovered and what Betsy explained to us. According to her, you asked her to procure the perfume, and you had her sister, Sarah, your lady's maid assistant, to transport it to you. My question is: are you the one who poisoned it? Or did you have someone else do it for you?" asked Chadwick.

She snorted. "You're going to believe that chit over me?"

"So far, yes. I have no reason not to. Unless you can convince us otherwise."

Lady Braxton waved her hand. "Nonsense. How can you prove the perfume was poisoned?"

Ravenna stepped forward. "Because my stepson died in a tub with the stuff in the water, and the air reeked of lily, bergamot, and sage. The same

327

scent of the Widow's Blush cologne, which is made and sold only at Sylvan's. The same place from which you purchased the perfume."

"This is madness. Such profane accusations!" Lady Braxton pressed her lips into a thin line. A tightness seemed to encircle her eyes, which blazed with an intensity. She worked her jaw. "And why, pray tell, would I want to poison perfume and kill people with it?"

Chadwick crossed his arms over his chest and planted a wide stance. "I was hoping you would tell us that."

"I have my ladies club to help educate women and work for our opportunities. I work diligently for charity. I give freely of my money and time. Are those things a murderess would do?"

"Then why would this poor shop woman accuse you, of all people?" Ravenna asked.

Lady Braxton blanched and toyed with a black teardrop pendant around her neck. She stammered. "Well, I—not per se—I, well…."

Braedon said, "You're from Ireland, from common stock, married up in a *mariage de convenance…*"

She scoffed. "You've described your own *affaire du coeur.*" She motioned toward Ravenna.

Ravenna said, "We are not having an affair, and while I'm from Irish stock and a commoner, my marriage was real enough. I loved my husband."

Lady Braxton turned from them, crossed the room to stand at the window, and stare out of it. The darkness outside caused her reflection to shine in the glass like a ghost. Three black roses dotted the back of her head. "Love is a terrible thing, isn't it, Lady Birchfield?"

She exchanged a confused glance with Braedon. "I don't see…."

"I was married before I came to England. I loved him. Desperately. My heart actually leapt for joy when he walked into the room. And he loved me in equal measure. We would've died for each other." She looked over her shoulder at Ravenna, her eyes rimmed with tears, and her voice choked with emotion. "Have you ever known that sort of love? A love where no one else exists or matters except that one person? Where life has no meaning if they aren't in it?"

Ravenna shrugged one shoulder. Her cheeks burned, and her scar ached. And Lady Braxton's uncharacteristic display of emotion unsettled her.

"I wouldn't wish that sort of love on anyone." She swiped at her eyes.

For the first time, Ravenna considered this once vulgar, fast woman in a vastly different light. She was a broken, sad thing.

"And yet…." Lady Braxton sighed. "For all of that, nothing is more terrible than hope. Because hope holds on like a devil, forcing you to do things you otherwise wouldn't do. And as much as I loved, I hoped."

"Lady Braxton, we do not have time for this." Chadwick crossed his arms and rocked back on his heels. "Did you kill those men? Lords Hawkestone, Birchfield, Wolfsham, Nochdale?"

She ignored the question. "My husband, the first one, the real one, Lucas O'Fannon, was a fine man. Kind, generous, strong, and like many of the other men in our village, he had a temper where matters concerned their families and lands. We resented the English, but we resented the Loyalists even more because they betrayed us to the English."

Ravenna's face grew hot, and her insides twisted and coiled on itself like a python. Her family had been Loyalists. Except her brother Niall and her cousin, Marcus.

"The loyalists gave their devotion to the English Crown for a few more pennies, a wee bit more land." She turned to Ravenna, her violet eyes flashing. "I ask you, what's more important, your fellow countrymen and the land of your birth? Or foreigners' money and promises for land and high titles, only to live a life under the tyranny of foreign kings who would rather gut you than shake your hand?"

Ravenna's throat tightened, and she blinked. The heat in her face spread down through her body. She felt as though her skin had grown two sizes too small. "My family were Loyalists to the Crown because it was a better life for us and because we were allowed to practice our Protestant religion freely without interference. Your lot killed my family, not the English."

Not all Loyalists were bad or wrong. Her own family had been butchered by the Irish Unity. Catholics and Protestants killed each other. Loyalists and Rebels killed each other. There was such a confusion of political and religious leanings that it was impossible to tell where loyalties lay. Catholic Rebels, Catholic Loyalists. Protestant Rebels, Protestant Loyalists. It was a swarm of confusion and mixed ideals and beliefs.

Lady Braxton continued. "That's what you Loyalists never understood. The Englishmen you colluded with would have betrayed you in a blink if it suited them to do so." She touched the pendant at her throat again, her eyes growing distant. Her mind had gone elsewhere, to a time, a place that lived only in the mists of memory. "Nevertheless, the long and the short of it is my husband and the others worked to get the French to come to Ireland in ninety-six, and we paid dearly for it. By ninety-seven, the English came and issued their own brand of justice."

Ravenna's shoulders tightened. She knew all too well the English justice against her countrymen.

Lady Braxton's lip quivered and her eyes flooded with tears. She drew in a sharp breath, and her emotions slid beneath her cold mask. Her eyes once again went distant and empty. "My husband and the other men were captured by the troops. The women and girls raped. Little boys cut down. Babes torn from their mothers' arms and crushed under boot heels." She lowered her eyes and glided across the room to the sideboard, where she poured a cup of tea. "Villagers were burned alive in their houses."

Ravenna lowered her head. Her memory recalled smoke, fire, and screams from those years long ago, when her family's village had been pillaged by the United Irishmen who clashed with the Orangemen in her village.

"Sometimes at night, in my sleep, I still hear their screams." Lady Braxton said in a low, distant voice. Then she snapped from her reverie. "That is, when my own screams don't wake me. I still have nightmares about the gang of men who abused me on the ground beside another woman bleeding to death, all while our husbands watched, tied up, and powerless to help us. I still smell them, too." She grimaced, a hand pressed to her stomach. "Their sweat and cologne, the alcohol and tobacco on their breath, the damp leather and wool of their uniforms."

Lady Braxton braced herself against the sideboard for a moment and grew quiet. Her head hung between her shoulders. "Those of us who lived were forced to watch the rebels, our loved ones, hang one by one to save the English bullets. Then the general gave the order from his saddle that it was forbidden to cut the bodies down. If anyone dared, they would come back and finish their work. As the summer came on, the stench from the rotting bodies became unbearable."

She sighed and raised her head, the petals of the black roses brushing the rigid line of her broad shoulders. She stirred her tea, the spoon clinking softly against the china cup. "I was never again the same woman." She eased into a chair by the fire, sat very primly and dolefully, with her cup resting in its saucer in her lap.

Braedon's brows furrowed. "But then you married the enemy. An English lord."

A sweet smile inched over her lips. "Oh, yes. How better to position myself to exact my revenge? Every day when I passed by the rotting body of my husband hanging from the tree, I swore I'd avenge his death and the destruction of my village." She sipped her tea.

Ravenna said, "And your plan was to kill these innocent lords?"

"Innocent?" Lady Braxton snorted. "They were foreign secretaries. They were behind the decisions to invade Ireland, kill our people, destroy our villages. They were responsible, in large part, for sending husbands and sons off to wars." Lady Braxton sipped her tea and gently set her cup in her saucer with a self-satisfied air. "I targeted the foreign secretary's office because it would unsettle the office and thus our parliament's plans for peace with Napoleon."

"My enemy's enemies are my friends," Braedon said.

She lifted her brows with an air of appreciation. "Precisely. I find the ancients' wisdom is still apropos."

"How did you manage it?" Chadwick asked.

A mysterious smile brushed her lips. She pulled a handkerchief out of her bodice and dabbed at her hairline and upper lip. "I'd hear at various parties or balls when a particular man was being considered for foreign secretary. Then I'd simply become the very closest friend of that man's wife by bringing them into my little club."

331

Chadwick said, "Did you have other helpers involved?"

"Oh yes, many. That's why we had the roses. It was our way of helping them pick each other out in a crowd, which was necessary to transport the poison. Meanwhile, I'd place my little birds in a lady's nest to create a downfall for the lady's maid. After all, who is closer to a lady than her lady's maid?" She shrugged and sipped her tea. "Once inside, it was so extremely easy for my little birds to plant bottles of the precious cologne in the toilette kit of the master of the house." She asked no one in particular, "Have you ever heard of *La Légion Noire*?"

Chadwick said, "Yes. They were a Franco-Irish faction formed to help Napoleon invade England via Ireland back in ninety-seven or ninety-eight."

"Quite right," Lady Braxton said. "But they were all men. We female rebels wanted a way we might help our men, so we formed our own little group and called it *Les Roses Noires*. The Black Roses." She winked at Ravenna. "Clever, no? To create a club as a disguise for our rebellion." She sipped her tea again and coughed. Her hand shook, rattling the cup against the saucer.

Ravenna pulled the bottle out of her reticule. "Was this the cologne?"

She passed the bottle over to Lady Braxton, who took the bottle into her hand. She examined it, opened it, and sniffed the perfume. "Ah, yes, the Widow's Blush." She smiled nostalgically. "A delightful scent."

"And deadly."

She closed the bottle and handed it back to Ravenna. "Quite."

"Didn't the men or their valets see something was amiss? Didn't the wives realize when their husbands wore a different cologne?"

"Oh, that was easy enough to preempt. I simply had it delivered. Then my little birds would explain to the valet that the lord ordered it from the parfumier, or that it was a gift from another lord, or a gift from his mistress. Who cares what they were told? Any number of explanations might have worked, and my little birds were experts at explaining it away."

"What was the poison?" Chadwick said.

Lady Braxton blanched. She closed her eyes and pressed her fist to her lips, fighting something internal. "Oh, this and that." She swallowed hard and seemed to have difficulty focusing her eyes. "I'd rather keep my little receipt a secret." She smiled weakly.

"What of Mr. Larson?" Ravenna asked.

"Who?"

Ravenna said, "He was thin, with fair, almost white hair. A self-made man."

Lady Braxton's eyebrows puckered, and the lines around her mouth deepened. "Never met him. Don't know him." She dabbed at the sweat along her hairline.

Chadwick narrowed his eyes. "I rarely find criminals as forthcoming as you have been, Lady Braxton. I wonder at your openness when you'll go to prison and then the scaffold."

Her violet eyes glittered. "Why hide? My revenge is complete." Her breath came in short and raspy. "There is more to come, I assure you. The Irish Unity has not forgotten."

"What?" Ravenna said. "What are they doing? What plans do they have?"

She smiled faintly, her eyes again growing distant. She downed the rest of her tea and set it aside. "I fear you're too late to thwart the plans that have been laid. Shortly..." She seemed to be struggling to breathe. It may have been a trick of the light, but Ravenna was certain that Lady Braxton's lips were beginning to purple. "I will join my Lucus and be truly happy and at peace again." She began to wheeze as she spoke, and her eyes bugged. "I wonder at Lady Birchfield's apparent ignorance about her own husband." She tried to laugh, and it descended into a fit of coughing.

Chadwick said, "Are you unwell, Lady Braxton?"

She waved her hand and shook her head. "No time.... Lord Philip Birchfield convinced parliament ...sent English troops to Irish soil." She chuckled and coughed between phrases. Her violet eyes bore into Ravenna. "What irony. Your husband... responsible...in deaths..." She pointed a shaking finger at Ravenna. "*Your* family, friends, and countrymen."

The floor fell away, and the air thickened and stilled. Ravenna swayed. Braedon's hand cupped her elbow to steady her.

Lady Braxton leaned over, fell out of her chair onto her knees, and shook her head with a maniacal smile stretched across her lips.

Mr. Chadwick rushed to her aid.

Drool dripped from her bottom lip. She attempted to laugh and vomited. They all grimaced, though they watched with curiosity. She continued, hovering on all fours over the pool of vomit on the floor. "I p-poison..." She labored to breathe and speak. "H-his food at a dinner. But food was too difficult...to access...devised the cologne instead...." Veins bulged in her neck and forehead. Her pulse drummed visibly in her neck veins. "Perfume. Subtle. Perfect."

Ravenna's mind spun, and she reeled. Panic, grief, rage, and confusion strangled her and choked her ability to breathe, to think, to speak. Philip? The man she loved was, in essence, her enemy. The pressure of tears filled her head and throat. She clutched Braedon's arm, her nails digging into his sleeve.

Lady Braxton fell forward to the floor and convulsed, foaming at the mouth, her eyes rolling back in her head.

The men rushed forward to assist. Ravenna stood, rigid, her world crumbling around her. Everything she had believed and known about her husband's death turned her upside down. Before she had only suspected he'd been murdered. Now it was confirmed. But she'd never known about his part in the massacre of her countrymen. She floatid, suspended, disconnected from her body and the floor. She approached the dying woman and stood above her, fists clenched.

Even as she spasmed in death, Lady Braxton's eyes met Ravenna's and glittered in malice. Then she fell into another fit of spasms, sweating, and frothy blood spewing from her mouth. She cried out in pain and clutched her stomach until the light flew from her eyes, and she exhaled her last breath.

In her last act of rebellion, Lady Braxton had robbed them all of justice. Cold numbness oozed through Ravenna's body. She turned, dazed, and drifted out of the house and into the darkness.

# Chapter Fifty-Four

Ravenna, Lucy, and Harrison, Thomas's younger brother, gathered in the parlor at Pelham House to receive guests for a private viewing of Thomas's corpse wrapped in white silk, resting in a coffin upholstered in purple velvet surrounded by lilies. The awful lilies. Black crepe draped over the windows and mirrors, the clocks were stilled, and hatchments hung over the windows' exteriors.

The faintest scent of decay rode the undercurrent of the overpowering scent of lilies. Again, Ravenna had to endure the assault of the lilies. Soon, Thomas would be interred in the family tombs after a public viewing in St. James Street, leaving Harrison to carry the burden of the Birchfield line and legacy alone, though he was ill-prepared to do so. As the youngest son, he never expected to take on the responsibility so soon. His coppery hair was cut a la Napoleon, and his pale face was puffy with grief. He was shorter and more powerfully built than his brother had been.

Catherine entered the parlor, flanked by her co-habitant lover Yarford. Her black silk floated around her as she passed through the room. How different she looked. Ravenna couldn't recall ever seeing her in dark colors.

She reached out to Ravenna, taking up her hands. "I wear this dreadful color for your sake." A weak smile faltered on her face.

Ravenna couldn't help but smile. "Your sacrifice is not lost on me."

She squeezed Ravenna's hands. "Sincerely, I am so deeply sorry for you. Poor, dear Birchie." Tears filled her eyes. "Such a tragic loss and so soon after his father. How much sorrow sits with you this year, my beloved friend." She kissed Ravenna's cheek. "I need not tell you I'm at your service.

Always."

Catherine didn't yet know the half of Ravenna's sorrows. Preparations for the funeral preoccupied her and prevented Ravenna from telling her closest friend the grief she would forever carry: she'd loved and married the man who had arranged the massacre of her people. "I know. Thank you."

Yarford offered his sincere sympathy and moved to condole with Harrison.

Catherine said, "Where's Braedon? I haven't seen him in days."

"Nor have I."

Lord Donovan entered the parlor. He radiated strength and light, even in his black clothes, as though he sauntered through sun-kissed fields. He wanted only a bird dog at his side, a gun tucked under his arm, and game slung over his shoulder. Sorrow and pity weighed on his mouth, tugging the corners downward into a deep frown, so out of place with his usual natural radiance. He headed straight to Ravenna and bowed.

He kissed Ravenna's outstretched hand, then clapped his other hand over it. The stormy gray seas in his eyes pulled her in. "I'm terribly sorry about Birchfield. He was the best of men, and so many of our hopes rested in him." His nostrils flared, and tears formed in his eyes. "He was a dear friend, so if there's anything I can do to assist you or your family, please don't hesitate to call on me. No matter how big or small the service, you may rely on me. I'm your devoted servant."

She nodded. "Thank you."

Later in the gathering, after visitors had scattered into their circles of conversation, a footman passed through the room and handed Lord Donovan a note. He opened it, read it, and then wadded it up in his fist. He returned to Ravenna's circle. "I apologize for the timing, but I've received word." He lowered his voice. "Our Navy has moved in at the ports to board and capture French and Dutch ships that have docked or are sailing nearby. I was afraid of this."

Yarford shook his head with disappointment. "Dear God."

"Why are they capturing the ships?" Catherine said.

"To seize commodities, anything we can use. Food, weapons, clothing, money, anything."

"So, we're at war?" Ravenna asked.

"It hasn't been officially declared, but I wager it won't be long before it is. Please, I do beg your pardon, but I am needed on government business." He rushed away.

*Dear God, not another war.*

After the wake, and when the guests had all dispersed, Ravenna dragged herself to Gordon House and up to her bedchamber. She sat on the sofa with a glass of port and stared into the fire, letting her mind wander over the past couple of days. So much grief. So much death.

That special pain that came with grief, that burning in the center of her body, consumed her. She curled on the sofa and let loose her grief. It was as if Philip had died afresh, and she was losing him all over again. He hadn't died of an influenza. He'd been murdered. Even when she'd suspected he'd been killed, she'd held onto a quiet hope it had been an influenza, after all.

Then she recalled what Lady Braxton had told her about Philip's part in the Irish massacres. Bile rose in her throat. She had been in love with a man who played a part in the destruction of her family, friends, and village. He had been good to her, but to know he had played a part in those things—she couldn't reconcile it with the man she knew. She wanted to believe Lady Braxton had lied, just to toy with Ravenna's mind, to create a mental terror in an enemy. But Ravenna knew, she could see it in the woman's eyes. She told the truth. Ravenna pulled herself into a tighter ball and sobbed harder, the fury and the sorrow splitting her in two. She would need to find a way to forgive Philip, even if to save her own sanity, but she didn't know how she possibly could. Maybe someday, but not now. The best she could do in the moment was fight against the hate threatening to consume her heart.

And now his son had been murdered, too. By her countrymen, in retaliation for atrocities his father had sanctioned. She had loved Thomas too, but in the moment, it felt like a stroke of justice. She cried harder. Justice was a cold blade. She disliked these feelings of rage, vengeance, and hatred glittering darkly, creeping through her veins, filling up her body; it disgusted her, but in a perverse and baleful way, it buoyed her, electrified her. It was a sinister feeling she had to fight. She couldn't let the evil of others make her evil in turn.

She cried until she felt like a wrung rag. Ravenna sat up, her body limp and drained and her head throbbing. She felt as though her face and nose were stuffed full of cotton. She crossed the room, washed her face at the washstand. After rubbing lavender water on her face to reduce the puffiness, she took a dose of lavender spirits to quell her melancholy. She ordered a tea service to be brought up and set about writing letters to Reverend Howarth about The Penitent House. It would be opening soon, and she wanted to ensure everything was prepared. She needed to occupy her mind to distract from her current misery.

Lady Hawkestone was announced. Ravenna had her shown into the drawing room and descended the stairs to meet her. Lady Hawkestone wore a black crepe dress beneath a black pelisse buttoned up with frog buttons to her neck. She carried a small parcel wrapped in brown paper, tied with string.

"Hello, Violette." They clasped hands as they kissed each other's cheek before sitting on the sofa. The tea service was delivered, and Ravenna poured them a cup of tea and served a slice of moist ginger-orange cake.

Violette looked at Ravenna with pity. "How are you, my dear?"

She handed a cup and saucer to Violette, then poured her own cup. "I confess, I'm awful. I've learned Lady Braxton's wicked involvement with the rebellion murdered my husband and stepson. Though I'd suspected it, I continued to hope it wasn't true. I didn't want it to be true. I was too blind to see." She choked back tears, washing them down with tea. She wanted to tell her the rest, that her husband had arranged the destruction of her village and people, but she couldn't bear to say the words aloud. She tucked it away in her mind's shadows.

Violette took her hand. "No, darling, you shouldn't do that to yourself. You couldn't have known. None of us knew. I, at least, am very thankful to you. You discovered who killed my husband, too. I'm glad I'll never wonder or be left in the dark. I'm eternally grateful to you."

Ravenna's bottom lip quivered. She looked down at her lap, dabbing her eyes with her handkerchief. "Thank you, but I truly feel as though I deserve no such praise."

Violette smiled warmly, tenderly, as though Ravenna was a lost child. "You deserve all that and more. And as you comforted me in my grief, I've come to comfort you. First, should you need anything, I insist on being the first person to know. Day or night. Second, I have a gift for you." She grabbed the bundle beside her and placed it between them. "These are Hawkestone's personal diaries." She whispered conspiratorially, "I kept them hidden from Mr. Chadwick."

Shocked, Ravenna shook her head. "I can't possibly accept these."

"You must." She stared at her in a manner that would brook no disagreement. "I've read them. I know what's in them." She cocked a brow. "So, these must rest with *you* now where they will be safest. It's the only way I could think to repay you."

Ravenna blushed. "I—"

Violette raised her hand. "You and I are friends now, bound by our common tragedy." She stood. "You can be assured of my discretion. I will carry your secrets, and his, to my grave."

When Violette left, Hart delivered a letter.

Hart said, "I fear this came for you."

Ravenna frowned. "Fear?" It couldn't be a good letter. She looked at the seal: black, no crest or symbol to indicate where it came from. She didn't recognize the writing, either. She broke the seal on the letter to read the simple message scrawled across the page in jagged writing:

*We have not forgotten.*

Mr. Larson had said something similar to her when he had attacked her. Lady Braxton had also said that before she died. The Irish Unity had not forgotten. She knew she should be afraid, but she couldn't muster the spirit for it. She sighed and folded the letter.

After a supper she barely touched, Ravenna retired to the window seat in her bedchamber to watch the sun set over the city. The newspaper lay on the floor beside her, folded open to reveal the main headline of the day: *England Declares War Against the French.*

She hadn't the heart to read the article. She knew what it meant. More death. More destruction. At home and far away. More sorrow and suffering for people who wanted nothing more than to live their lives and care for their families in peace.

Braedon was announced. It was later than appropriate for visitation, but she decided to see him anyway. Let the whole *ton* talk. At this moment, she couldn't summon the energy to care. She carried her heavy body downstairs to the drawing room.

She entered the room. "Good evening, Braedon."

He stood and bowed.

Ravenna hadn't seen him in days. A sort of relief washed over her at the sight of him. She stopped in front of him, frozen inside and out, like Daphne transforming into a tree to escape Apollo. Mechanically, she offered her hand.

He took her hand. His hand was warm, strong, comforting. He kissed her knuckle. "I wanted to see to your health, to see if you needed anything."

"Thank you. I'm well." That was a bit of a lie. Something sorrowful and pained in his demeanor disturbed her.

He guided her to the sofa to sit. He sat beside her, his knee touching hers. Though he sat so close, holding her hands, his thumb stroking her fingers, he seemed a thousand miles away. "How have you been?"

"I'll rally soon enough. I always do." Something she'd been thinking about since reading the letter sent from the Irish Unity occurred to her. She said, "Do you remember the night I was attacked at Braxton House?" Her scar tingled and itched. She fought the urge to scratch it.

"Yes, of course."

"When you found my fan, did you see the man who attacked me? Was he dead?"

"There wasn't a man. Only his blood. And your fan. Why do you ask?"

A sliver of fear haloed her grief. She considered telling him, but thought

340

the better of it. She shook her head and looked down at her black slippers peeking out from under the black muslin hem. "No reason. I was only wondering."

"Do you think he'll return for you?"

"Possibly."

Something was working in him, evidenced by the clenching and unclenching of his jaws and the frown line between his brows. "I've owed you better," he said, his voice strained.

"You've owed me nothing. We're not married or promised to each other or related."

He sighed and rubbed his brow. "I have...bad news." He squeezed her hand and stared across the room. "I came to tell you that I'm escorting Dianthe and her mother to Italy to help Dianthe recover from her laudanum addiction."

The pressure of tears pushed against her throat and forehead. "Why you?"

"Her father can't go. His business with the parliament demands his presence. Especially now that we're at war again. Since Dianthe has no uncles or brothers...." He shrugged. "Lady Hillingham asked me. She said she trusted me to protect them. I couldn't say no."

Ravenna stared into the empty fireplace and nodded, numb.

"But there's more. I wanted to apologize for not being here in your hour of grief. Dianthe has been demanding my attention with threats of self-murder. And...." He linked his fingers with hers, an intimate manner of hand-holding that gave her pause. "She's still threatening you. I felt I'd best serve you by keeping her far from you." His voice broke, "However much it pains me to do so."

Yet another man leaving her. For once, she wanted to be in control of the leaving, to be the first to say goodbye. Unable to control the rising emotion in her voice, she said, "Please, leave now." She pulled her fingers from his and turned her head from him, unable to look at him. "Goodbye, Braedon."

"I understand." He pushed himself to his feet, and cool air swept in to embrace her with the absence of his warmth. He knelt in front of her. She averted her gaze. He removed his signet ring. Taking her hand, he slipped the ring onto her index finger. "This is my faithful pledge to you. A pledge of love, friendship, and fidelity, always, with the hope that someday you'll forgive me. I will work all of my days for that forgiveness and for your love." He kissed her cheek, right below the scar. "I'll write to you, if you'll accept my letters."

He waited for her answer, but she couldn't speak. He took her hand and, turning it, kissed her palm. "Adieu, for now, my little raven. We will meet again. And you and I together shall put to shame all the happily-ever-afters boasted of in fairy tales." He squeezed her hand and pressed it to his cheek. "I would ask for a lock of your raven hair, but I daren't hope for such a favor just now. Perhaps someday, you'll see fit to send it to me in a letter scented with your perfume." His pale blue eyes gleamed with pain, hope, and admiration.

He leaned in, taking her face in his hands. After a long, lingering kiss that seemed to sparkle in her blood like champagne punch, he was gone. Like a ghost. Yet another ghost to haunt her days, invade her dreams.

Ravenna spent the rest of the evening sipping port and reading through Hawkestone's journals. Near the end of the last journal, a year after she'd betrayed him, he'd written:

*I hate her. I love her. I forgive her. Almost from the moment I discovered she was stealing from me, I forgave her. I loved her too much to harbor condemnation and vitriol. My pride has kept me from telling her the words stamped forever on my heart: I forgive.*

A sob escaped her mouth, and she broke down, releasing the guilt, the shame, the tears that she'd been holding captive since the moment she'd betrayed him, since his death. The forgiveness for which she'd hoped had finally been delivered like a gift from the beyond.

When she'd recovered, she tore the page from the journal, folded it, and tucked it into her bodice, close to her heart. Then she gathered up the journals and dropped them into the fire, watching her past burn. The flames licked the pages as she recalled the last time she'd seen her friend Hawkestone, sprawled lifeless on her floor. She'd believed his forgiveness had been cut off from her forever. Solving his murder had been her way of reclaiming that forgiveness.

As the fire consumed the journals, the flame shot higher and brighter. The ghosts of Philip and Lady Braxton hovered over her shoulder, whispering their desire for forgiveness. Ravenna shrunk into herself, her spirit coiling like a venomous serpent. She wasn't sure she could forgive them. Ravenna had stolen government secrets, but she hadn't murdered innocent, albeit rebellious, people as her husband had sanctioned. The worst of it was that Philip hadn't even had the courage to look her people in the eye as he ordered their deaths. He did it from a distance, in a comfortable chair, full of good food, and warmed by a hearty fire while their bones were wracked with hunger. She never imagined he could be so cruel. How does a man make such a decision? Her eyes filled with tears. Forgiving him seemed so far out of reach. She couldn't possibly forgive such barbarous behavior. In her mind, his offense had been far greater than that of Lady Braxton's.

Lady Braxton. She'd had her merits. A worker for charity and the rights and education of women. She'd been in love and had hopes and dreams for her family and their future. Philip's troops had ripped that from her. Ravenna understood Lady Braxton's rage, understood her desire for vengeance. Yet, Lady Braxton had been responsible for the deaths of innocent men. However, those men were politicians who played God and decided the fates of common people—for better or worse. Ravenna rubbed her face, careful to avoid the scar. How could she forgive Lady Braxton for the part she played in destroying Ravenna's family and the families of her friends? Somehow she thought it would be easier to find her way to forgiving Lady Braxton first.

The pages of the journals shriveled and blackened, disappearing in the greedy mouth of the consuming fire. Then there was Braedon. Braedon, handsome, aggravating, charming, protective, bold, and loyal. His loyalty was a gift rarely bestowed, so she valued his loyalty to her. But for now, she would have to share that loyalty with Dianthe. It was both endearing and irritating. He was so loyal and protective that he would escort the woman and her mother to Italy to help Dianthe heal in order to protect Ravenna from Dianthe's laudanum-fueled jealousy. It was outlandish; it was absurd; it was beautiful. But because he had once loved Dianthe and she needed a friend, he couldn't abandon her in her time of distress. Ravenna couldn't fault him for that, but she also wouldn't readily give her heart to a man so divided. Her friendship would have to be enough. But, he'd left her with no notion of when or if he might return. He'd left her in the hour of her grief to take another woman to Italy. The fire leapt and burned brighter as the pages turned to ashes.

She wondered when or if she'd see Braedon again.

# A Note from the Author

Though *Widow's Blush* is not historical fiction, many things in the story are inspired by real history.

The poisonous Widow's Blush perfume is loosely based on an occurrence in 17th-century Italy when a strong poison called Aqua Tofana circulated among a network of professional poisoners. These poisoners sold Aqua Tofana to men and women who wanted to rid themselves of inconvenient or abusive spouses.

The creation of Aqua Tofana has been linked to three different women: Giulia Tofana, Francesca la Sarda, and Teofania di Adamo. So it's a little confusing who may have actually created the toxic formula consisting of arsenic, lead, and possibly belladonna. Since it lacked color or flavor, it could be easily slipped into a victim's drink or food. According to legend, over 600 people fell victim to the deadly Aqua Tofana.

Most interesting of all, it was sold openly in Italy as a cosmetic and also as a devotionary object with pictures of St. Nicholas of Bari on the vials. This use of poison in cosmetics inspired the cologne in *Widow's Blush*. In another interesting note, from what I could find, cologne in this era seems to have been unisex, with men and women sharing many of the same scents, which is why Mrs. Sylvan, in the story, discusses selling the Widow's Blush cologne to both men and women.

Additionally, many of our notions about historical mourning are based on the Victorian Era, so readers might be surprised to see Ravenna attending balls and parties, which would've been unthinkable in the Victorian Era for a woman concerned about her reputation. However, in the early 1800s, the customs for mourning weren't as strict or formalized. Sometimes, a widow might wear black, sometimes not. Sometimes, a widow might mourn for a year; sometimes, it could be a couple of months. It wasn't until the Industrial Revolution and the reign of Queen Victoria that mourning became more formal, laden with etiquette rules, and commercialized. When the Queen lost her beloved Albert, she set the trends for what constituted "proper" mourning, and her subjects followed suit.

Further, I used the term "widow's weeds" in reference to the clothing worn during mourning. Though "widow's weeds" has long been thought to be a term affiliated with the Victorian Era, I've found evidence that the term "widow's weeds" was in use in the Georgian Era. Since etymologically, "weeds," meaning "garments," comes from Old English *wæd, wæde* "robe, dress, apparel, garment, clothing," it would not surprise me to discover the term has likely been around much longer.

Lastly, the exclusive ladies' club in *Widow's Blush* is inspired by a real French militia called *La Légion Noire* (The Black Legion), which was a military unit of the French Revolutionary Army. They colluded with the Irish rebels to invade England in 1797. They landed at Bantry Bay on the west coast of Ireland and then planned to invade Liverpool or Bristol. Ultimately, their mission failed completely. When conducting research for this story, I found this bit of information so fascinating that I wanted to create a parallel network of female political rebels who operated under the name of *Les Roses Noires*.

If you would like to learn more about these and other historical topics, I write about them on my blog, *Michelle's Musings*, at michellebennington.com.

# Acknowledgements

*God, you are my rock and my refuge. All glory goes to You.* (James 1:17)

No book is written in a vacuum. I'd like to thank the team at Level Best Books for their excellent work and support. Shawn, you're the best!

Thank you to my awesome agent, Dawn Dowdle, for always being there.

To Grace Au, Shannon Powers, and Brack Benningfield for beta reading and providing feedback. This book was a long time in the making, I'm so sorry if I've neglected a beta reader or critique partner.

To Brack Benningfield for being the best husband a girl could hope for. I'm so thankful for you every day.

To Carmen Erickson for being the absolute best critique partner. I'd also like to thank Carmen and Hallie Lee for your unique friendship and for holding my hand on this wild writing ride (say that three times fast).

I'm ever grateful to my family and friends—you all know who you are. Your encouragement and support have been my anchor in the storms and a soft place to fall in joyful moments.

To anyone who has bought a book, shared my books with others, left a review, followed my social media, or even asked me how my work is going—Thank you! You keep me going.

# About the Author

Michelle Bennington was born and raised among the rolling hills and lush bluegrass of Kentucky. Her early and avid love of books inspired her desire to write and has developed into a mild book-hoarding situation and an ever-expanding To Be Read pile. She currently resides in central Kentucky, where she spins tales of mystery and intrigue in contemporary and historical settings. Aside from reading and writing, she enjoys a wide range of arts and crafts, touring old homes, attending ghost tours, baking with various degrees of success, and spending time with her family and friends.

SOCIAL MEDIA HANDLES:
  Facebook: https://www.facebook.com/michellebenningtonauthor
  Instagram: https://www.instagram.com/michelle.bennington.author/
  Pinterest: https://www.pinterest.com/michellebenningtonauthor/_saved/
  Goodreads: https://www.goodreads.com/user/show/4055592-michelle-bennington

AUTHOR WEBSITE:
  https://www.michellebennington.com/

# Also by Michelle Bennington

Small Batch Mystery Series
  *Devil's Kiss*, Level Best Books
  *Mermaid Cove*, Level Best Books

Hazardous Hoarding Mystery Series
  *Dumpster Dying*, Charade Media

"Killer Thanksgiving"
  Short story in the *Sampling of Sleuths Anthology*, Thalia Press

Printed in the USA
CPSIA information can be obtained
at www.ICGtesting.com
JSHW082159281123
52701JS00001B/13

9 781685 124571